S.P.
Suto

*

AA

M. Swaga.
.I. Grey.
.A. Crean.
∧

LITTLE NIGHT

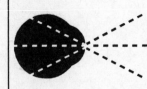

This Large Print Book carries the
Seal of Approval of N.A.V.H.

LITTLE NIGHT

LUANNE RICE

WHEELER PUBLISHING
A part of Gale, Cengage Learning

GALE
CENGAGE Learning·

Detroit • New York • San Francisco • New Haven, Conn • Waterville, Maine • London

GALE
CENGAGE Learning®

LIBRARY OF CONGRESS CATALOGING-IN-PUBLICATION DATA

Rice, Luanne.
    Little night / by Luanne Rice. — Large print ed.
      p. cm. — (Wheeler Publishing large print hardcover)
    ISBN 978-1-4104-4886-6 (hardcover) — ISBN 1-4104-4886-X (hardcover)
    1. Large type books. 2. Sisters—Fiction. 3. Nieces—Fiction. I. Title.
PS3568.I289L58 2012b
813'.54—dc23   2012008180

Published in 2012 by arrangement with Pamela Dorman Books, an imprint of Viking, a member of Penguin Group (USA) Inc.

Printed in the United States of America
1 2 3 4 5 6 7 16 15 14 13 12

For Joe Monninger, true north

ACKNOWLEDGMENTS

I am thankful to everyone at Pamela Dorman Books/Viking and Penguin, especially Pamela Dorman, Kristen O'Toole, Julie Miesionczek, Clare Ferraro, Kathryn Court, Dick Heffernan, Norman Lidofsky, and their sales teams; Lindsay Prevette, Carolyn Coleburn, Nancy Sheppard, Andrew Duncan, Stephen Morrison, John Fagan, Maureen Donnelly, Hal Fessenden, Leigh Butler, Roseanne Serra, and Amy Hill.

Deep gratitude to Andrea Cirillo and everyone at the Jane Rotrosen Agency: Jane Berkey, Meg Ruley, Donald Cleary, Mike McCormack, Peggy Gordijn, Annelise Robey, Christina Hogrebe, Brooke Fox, Ellen Tischler, Eleanor Cicconi, Donald W. Cleary, Carlie Webber, and Liz Van Buren.

Thank you to Ted O'Gorman for his constant support coast to coast.

I'm grateful to Tamara Edwards for the

myriad ways she has contributed to this project.

My deep thanks to Rubie Andersson, Maesa Pullman, Rosa Pullman, James Gallagher, Amelia Onorato, and Cynder Niemela.

As Mim would say (in a Providence accent), "The family should be together": Maureen and Oliver Onorata; Mia Onorato; Molly, Alex, and William Feinstein; Audrey and Robert Loggia, and William Twigg Crawford.

I'm thankful to Jim Weikart, Tim Donnelly, Lyn Gammill Walker, Paul Gordon Hoffman, and Adrian Kinloch.

Bruce Springsteen, always a source of strength and inspiration.

Much gratitude to Armondo Aguilar.

PROLOGUE

February 14, 1993

My hands are bandaged, but I'm not supposed to care that they hurt. When I was treated at the scene, the husky EMT said flatly, "He's a lot worse off than you." The police officer had to remove my handcuffs; he snapped on latex gloves to avoid having to touch my burned palms and wrists.

They drove me in a squad car to the East Hampton station house for booking, and finally into the sheriff's van for the ride here to the county jail, fifteen miles away in Mashomuck.

I'll tell you one detail because it's frozen in my mind. The phrase "two to the head." That's what I've been hearing since the police arrived. "She gave him two to the head." Then they laugh at me. It's supposed to be a big joke about how inept I was.

This enormous, shaved-head bodybuilding sheriff acted it out for me in the van on

9

the way here. "One," he said, pretending to clobber the other sheriff over the head. "Two." He imitated the second blow. Then, "Ouch," he said as he waggled his fingers at me and winked nastily at my bandaged hands. "You burned yourself as bad as you hurt him, but he's going to the hospital and you're going to jail."

I'd like to block his words out. They make this seem like any other crime, one of the salacious stories you see on CNN Headline News. To the outside I suppose all crimes are the same — someone attacks, another is injured. It's only in a person's mind and heart, only within the soul of any given family that the entire tender, brutal, surreal story makes any sense.

I say "family," but it might only be me. I have three blood relatives in this world: Anne, my older and only sister, and her children, a niece and nephew I barely know because her husband has cut us off so thoroughly. Blood is one thing, but to be family, you need so much more.

This morning I'd reached my breaking point on that and taken the LIRR out east, unannounced, to show up with roses for Anne and books and Valentines for the kids. I chose late morning, when Frederik would be at his gallery. The day was bright blue

10

but frigid, no humidity, a sharp wind whirling around Montauk Point.

I caught a cab from the station to their house on Old Montauk Highway. I was a wreck, thinking she'd slam the door in my face. But she didn't — she let me in. Right now I can hardly stand the memory of seeing the shock and joy in her eyes, feeling our strong embrace, as if our lives in that instant had been reset, back to the time before him.

The children didn't know who I was. They're only three and five, and I last saw them all at my mother's funeral a year ago, when Frederik had dragged the family away from the gravesite before Anne and I had a chance to console each other, or even speak.

For twenty minutes today we had a good time. The house was freezing; obviously the heat was turned way down. Anne, Gillis ("Gilly"), and Margarita ("Grit") wore warm shirts and fleece pullovers. I kept my jacket on. We huddled around the hearth where two logs sparked with a dull glow; a third had barely caught, flames just licking the top edge.

The brass screen had been set aside, as if to keep the wire mesh from holding back the fading warmth. I glanced around for a poker, but saw nothing to stoke the fire.

There didn't seem to be any more wood either.

I was afraid to ask about the heat, or lack of it. Anything can trigger Anne, especially when it comes to Frederik. She might have taken my question as implied criticism of his ability or willingness to provide basic needs for his family. She's very defensive about him. But the truth is, she's always had a strange, secret side when it came to men. She puts them on pedestals, and then subverts them in ways they'd never guess.

I'll confess something else: Anne and I had probably been the closest sisters on earth, but we have never been completely, one-hundred-percent easy with each other. I don't believe Anne can be that way with anyone.

While we sat and talked today, she was old Anne, and it felt as if she'd spent the last five years waiting for my visit.

The children seemed numb at first. They smelled the pearl-white roses I'd brought, and touched the Valentine cards and books, and looked up at me as if they weren't sure whether they should smile or not. I'd brought my camera, and I took a picture. Their hesitant smiles killed me.

"Who is she?" Gilly whispered to Anne.

"She's your aunt," Anne said.

12

He stared, as if he'd never heard the word before.

"I'm your mother's sister," I said.

"Mommy doesn't have a sister," Gilly said.

"I do," Anne said. "Just like you do."

She squeezed my hand so they would see. Grit broke into a smile.

I asked if they drew pictures, and they both ran to get their drawings. Soon we were coloring together, and Anne seemed happy and almost relaxed, and except for the cold, everything was all right.

I hadn't been to the house in five years, since right after Anne married Frederik. They'd invited my mother, Paul, and me to their *Jul* party. That night of the party is stamped in my mind. Climbing out of the car, I had my first look at their formidable glass house on the lighthouse road, surrounded by acres of scrub pines and thick brambles, an incredible habitat for birds. We rang the doorbell, and Frederik answered.

He kissed my mother and me, once on each cheek, and shook my fiancé, Paul Traynor's, hand. He took our coats, gestured around the majestic, cathedral-ceilinged room. "I'm king of all I survey," Frederik said in his elegant Danish accent. "And now Anne is queen."

13

"King Frederik and Queen Anne!" I said.

Frederik didn't smile, and he backed away. "Please enjoy my glasswork and help yourself to glogg and the buffet. I must find Anne and tell her you are here."

"That was weird," I said to my mother and Paul. "Did I do something wrong?"

"No," Mom said. "Maybe the humor got lost in translation."

"Maybe it's not a joke and he really thinks he's king. He's definitely an over-shaker," Paul said, flexing his hand.

We laughed because Paul was six-three, a rock climber, park ranger, and long-distance runner, and Frederik was five-eight tops, bald, with a slim, even fragile build, dressed head to toe in black. He gave the impression of either a retired cat burglar or a ballet dancer.

Sarah Cole, Anne's and my childhood friend, and her boyfriend, Max Hughes, came over, hugs all around.

"Have you seen her yet?" Sarah asked.

"No, have you?"

"It's totally mysterious. We've been here half an hour, and no sign yet."

Loud voices echoed under the cathedral ceiling. Simple, pale wood furniture filled the room and rya rugs — contemporary, coarsely woven wool patterned with striking

14

red and orange squares — covered the bleached pine floor.

Within a few minutes, Anne entered the room with Frederik. Her pale skin and dark hair looked striking against her long green velvet dress. He held her arm, led her to a group of Danes. They entered into earnest conversation, and I could tell my sister was resolutely keeping her focus on his friends to avoid making eye contact with us. Sarah walked over, stood by Anne's elbow, but Anne pretended not to see her.

"Wow," I said when Sarah came back without speaking to her.

"Bitchy the Great rides again," Sarah said. We'd adopted the name from Hemingway's *Islands in the Stream*. It was the nickname of a character's mean girlfriend, and Sarah and I used it when Anne's dark side took over.

I looked at my mother, who knew exactly what Sarah and I were talking about. She put her arms around our shoulders; she had become more confident and motherly since my father's death. "She's the hostess, and this is new to her. She'll come over as soon as she can."

"You're right," I said. "Can I get you something from the buffet, Mom?"

"We'll all go," she said.

15

Frederik's delicate, eccentric glasswork filled an entire wall of thick, rough-hewn shelves; the contrast between gossamer glass and heavy planks made an austere statement. I saw small white dots on each glass piece and moved closer to see them marked with prices in both U.S. dollars and Danish kroner.

"It's not very kingly," Sarah said. "Pricing out the treasures."

"It's odd," my mother agreed.

A large red-and-white Danish flag stretched across the wall above a sideboard laden with food and spirits: aebleskiver — ovals of fried dough topped with raspberry jam; boiled potatoes; roast pork; a basket of bread and plates of cookies.

The glogg — red wine mulled with nutmeg, cinnamon sticks, and slices of pear — bubbled in a large Crock-Pot. Several brown ceramic bottles of Bols Genever gin clustered behind a pyramid of clear glass mugs. Sarah and I ladled hot wine into mugs and passed them around.

A fire roared in the stone fireplace, throwing off so much heat the sliding porch door had to be opened. In the room's center, a twelve-foot white spruce, decorated with iridescent ornaments, towered over the guests. Our group stood together, still waiting for Anne and Frederik to come over. We took plates of food, hung out with Sarah and Max, made conversation with a few people we'd met at the wedding, and waited some more.

The scent of spiced wine and gin filled the air, along with pine and smoke, and people milled about, many of the men smoking pipes and speaking Danish. One of their wives told us the party was intended to display and sell Frederik's glass pieces: strange, abstract tubes of orange, scarlet, cerulean, and turquoise glass.

We read his artist statement posted by the shelves: *From crashing spheres and the existential abyss I employ techniques born in the last century B.C. to merge the elements — air, water, earth, fire — refine them in my furnace, and blow the molten gob to create thinner and thinner layers, spun into "tunnels," swirled with jewel tones, left open on either end, through which may pass spirits on their way to Himmel.*

"Okay, I'm going to crack up," I said. " 'Molten gob.' "

"You are an immature brat," Sarah said. "Remind me again, what's *Himmel?*"

"Danish heaven, weren't you listening at their wedding?" I asked.

"Please, girls," my mother said. "Be kind.

17

Frederik is an extremely talented and *accomplished* glassblower."

Why did that make us laugh? No good reason, relief of tension probably, plus the oddness of being in my sister's home for the first time, seeing how she'd become instantly Danish, hurt because Frederik kept her talking to his friends instead of us. It stung when I glanced over, smiled at my brother-in-law as he accepted a check from a tweedy-looking man, and he did not smile back.

The food was delicious. Eventually Anne walked over with a tray of cheese, made a beeline for me. I was sure she'd say something sister-crazy about the madness of the party and how busy she was with the other guests and how she couldn't wait to get to me, but instead she said, "Try the flatbread; it's homemade."

"By little elves?" I asked, joking along.

"No, by me," she said, seeming honest-and-truly taken aback.

"Come on." The Burke sisters had many talents; baking wasn't one of them. I tried to laugh, but her expression was cold steel.

"Are you trying to ruin the party?" she asked.

"Hello, I'm your sister," I said. "Balducci's? Catering? I assumed —"

"That's the trouble, Clare. You assume everything stays the same. My life has changed, and you'll never get it."

Huge metaphorical slap across the face — so sharp, my eyes stung. When we'd shared an apartment during college, we'd loved throwing parties but hated cooking, so we'd make secret runs to Balducci's, miraculously located just a few blocks away. We'd arranged the prepared food on family china, thrown out the foil containers, and taken credit as if we'd cooked it all ourselves.

"I'm sorry," I said. "I know things are changing. You're married, and —"

"Thank you. On that note, are you going to buy something?" she asked.

"Really?" I asked.

"Don't you think his work is amazing?"

"Of course."

"Frederik thinks you don't like it."

"I'm so sorry!" I said. "Why would he think that?"

"Because he suggested you look at it, and you haven't said a word to him since."

"Are you kidding? He's ignoring us."

"He has a lot of clients. Some came from Denmark just for this party."

"Okay, that's impressive," I said. "But we're you're family, we love you, and —"

"And you know something else?" she

19

interrupted. "He told me you made fun of his lineage."

"*Lineage?* What are you talking about?"

"He has royal blood," she said. "He said you were jealous and he's right."

"Of you being royal? Wow, let's start over. We are not getting anything right tonight. Could you, like, snap out of it, and be my sister? I realize you're in love, and Frederik is your husband, but I know you, all right? And you're acting like an idiot."

"How dare you speak to me that way in my home!" she said, backing away. Even before she could speak to our mother, who stood there waiting, Frederik called her over, whispered in her ear, and ushered her out of the room. She didn't return for the rest of the night, and when we asked for her as we were leaving, Frederik said she had a headache.

I felt stunned, iced out by my big sister, alarmed by how not just mean — I could have handled that — but Stepford it all felt. She was under a spell. Was it possible Anne had met her male match? He was in complete control as he helped my mother into her coat and essentially pushed us out the door.

When Frederik called late that night, catching me just as Paul and I walked into our Chelsea apartment, he told me I had insulted his wife by claiming their party was catered and I would never again be welcome in their home.

He continued, saying I had demeaned his art and his family background, and that Anne wished to sever ties with me and wanted me to know that our relationship was *over.*

For a second I thought it had to be a joke. Ha, ha, I tried. But his voice was glacial as he repeated what he'd just said, and I turned livid. Here was a man I'd met a handful of times telling me how it was between Anne and me. Did he have any idea who we were, what we'd been through together, what we meant to each other? I was drunk on the mulled wine and my blood shot to the boiling point.

"Fuck you, asshole!" I told him to put Anne on the phone.

He hung up on me.

It took me years to understand that Frederik had laid down the law, and, even more horrifying, Anne had signed on to obey it. When I called her the next day, she yelled at me and hung up. That became a pattern. She declined every invitation, even from our mother, for dinner, holidays, mother-daughter days at the Met or MoMA, a walk across the Brooklyn Bridge.

After a while, the tide changed. We stopped pursuing her, and my mother and I began getting hang-ups. Sarah did, too. We'd answer and hear Anne breathing, but she wouldn't say anything. "I know it's you," I'd say. Sometimes the silence would stretch on for a minute or two before she broke the connection.

Finally, after weeks of this, she called and we spoke.

"I'm pregnant," she said.

"Oh, my God. Anne! I'm so happy for you. A baby!"

"I know. It's blissful. We are over the moon."

I wanted to ask why she'd been calling and hanging up, but forced myself not to. Our connection felt so tenuous, and the fragility in her voice scared me.

"A new baby in the family — oh, Anne. Nothing could be more wonderful. How are you feeling? What's it like?"

"I throw up constantly, but I've never been happier."

"When are you due?"

A long silence. "We're not giving out any details yet," she said, her voice suddenly tight and stressed.

"Oh. Okay," I said. I felt Frederik enter

the conversation as surely as if he'd picked up the extension phone. "Whenever you're ready, I want to hear everything. I can't wait to be an aunt."

"Aunty Clare," she said.

I loved that. Her words warmed me, and I wished she were there in the room with me, so we could hug, celebrate, and plan, and she could tell me her dreams, like the color she hoped to paint the nursery.

"I have an idea," I said. "Let's have tea — the way we used to, with Mom and Sarah. We'll go to the Met and look at Renoir's paintings of mothers and children, to celebrate you and the baby —"

"You don't even mention Frederik," she said.

"Well, of course, Frederik, too. But I thought of tea as more of a girls' thing. You know — mothers and sisters and aunts."

"I don't think getting together is a good idea. After the way you've treated him."

"I'd treat him fine if I ever got the chance to see you."

"He says you're obsessed with our lives instead of your own."

That stopped me cold. "Because I care about you? That's so warped, Anne — why can't you see it?"

"He said you'd deny it and turn it back

on him. You so clearly have it in for him."

Her voice caught on a sob, and she hung up on me. All I wanted was to call her back, start from scratch, figure out a way to keep her on the line. My hands were shaking, I couldn't dial the number, but worst of all, I couldn't figure out anything to say that would fix the icy distance between us. Because the issue, it had become clear, was Frederik.

I thought back to the very beginning of their time together. One week before their wedding, Paul and I had dinner with them in the back garden of Chelsea Commons, our favorite neighborhood haunt. We'd been so excited about meeting this guy Anne loved so much.

"How did you get into glassblowing?" Paul asked.

He chuckled. "That's such a funny way to put it. I'm not sure one gets 'into' glassblowing."

"Well, I meant, what sparked your initial interest?"

Frederik sipped wine and leaned into Anne, shoulders touching.

"It's good of you to be so interested," Frederik said. "I just don't want to bore you."

"Come on, I really want to know," Paul said. "It's art, but I'm also interested in the science. The way you work with sand and fire."

"It's very strange," Frederik said. "A type of, how do I put it, spiritual madness? I literally have to do it."

"I can understand that," Paul said. "The way work becomes an obsession, when you really love the work to begin with."

"Tell him, Frederik," Anne said. "It's so fascinating, the way —"

"There's nothing fascinating," Frederik said. "It's hard to explain art."

"Well, how about from the scientific perspective?" Paul asked. "The method you use, and the materials; what temperature do you have to reach in order to make glass?"

"I use a high heat, 1040 degrees Celsius," Frederik said. He smiled and dropped the subject. Paul seemed not to notice, but my stomach flipped, feeling Frederik's condescension, as if he thought speaking to an Urban Park Ranger was just an amusing waste of time.

I wanted to tell Frederik if he desired art, obsession, or spiritual madness, he should try Central Park. Paul is one of the great sky watchers. By night he guided star walks, taking people into the darkness of the park and watching the Perseid and Leonid meteor showers, the transits of Mars and Venus, phases of the moon, constellations bright enough to be seen through the city's ambient light.

Some days Paul incorporated bird walks with "skying" — a term he'd picked up from a note by John Constable, the nineteenth-century British artist and possibly the greatest cloud painter ever to live. Paul could identify every cloud in the sky — cirrus, stratus, nimbus, cumulonimbus, nimbostratus, cumulus — feel the wind speed and direction, and predict the weather.

Paul knew every tree by its bark and leaves, every flower in the Shakespeare Garden and the plays and lines in which they were referenced. We were in love, but we were also partners in nature and the city. How could Frederik think that was anything less than passionate obsession, gazing at the sky but with our feet on the earth we loved?

Anne had quit her job as a researcher in the NYU Biology Lab when she'd married him — giving her scientist boss three days' notice.

"How can you just give up your work and screw your chances of any kind of recommendation?"

"Frederik wants to take care of me."

"That's a weird way to put it."

"Why? I've always wanted that."

"Love is one thing, but why do you need him to take care of you?"

"Because no one ever has."

The words stung. Hadn't we looked after each other our entire lives?

"Be happy for me," she continued. "Frederik says we're *fremstillet i himlen*. Made in heaven."

"I am happy for you," I said, and I meant it, but I already felt worried. Turns out, I had reason to be. Frederik's heaven meant separating Anne from our family. He'd controlled her the best he could, and I'd never returned to their house until I showed up today.

Gilly, five, colored pictures for me as I held three-year-old Grit and read her *Owl Moon,* one of the books I'd brought. I wanted Anne to remember our own owl story, to remind her of how close we'd been. Grit clutched my hand, excited to find the hidden creatures in each illustration. I stroked my niece's dark curly hair, thinking of how much it was like Anne's when we were little.

We drew pictures. Trees, owls, clouds. I sketched the three cats, telling Grit and Gilly about each of them, how they liked to sleep on the bed just as if they were people, but how they stalked at night, chasing

27

shadows and moonlight.

Through it all I kept watch on Anne. I saw bruises on her wrists and cheek.

"Did he do that?" I asked.

The kids were listening. She hesitated.

"Daddy hurts her," Gilly piped up, throwing his arms around her neck.

"Come with me," I said. "Pack some things, and let's go."

"Where would we stay? The three of us —"

"In the apartment, in your old room! Come on," I said, driven by Gilly's words and the fact that she hadn't denied them. "Anne, we can figure out everything later. Let's just leave."

"Where are we going?" Gilly asked.

"To New York," his mother said. "To your aunt's house."

She rose, stood looking around the room as if saying good-bye, or deciding what to take, or perfectly stunned by what she had just decided to do. Or maybe she had heard the front door lock click. Frederik stepped inside, a mild smile on his face.

"If I hadn't come home for lunch, would you have left me?" he asked, shining that frightening half-smile on Anne.

"Daddy," Gilly said.

"You're not going anywhere," Frederik

said, knocking Gilly aside to grab Anne by the throat.

I slapped and scratched Frederik, tried to pry his hands from Anne's neck. The kids screamed, and so did I. I reached into the fire and grabbed the charred end of the burning log. I swung it like a baseball bat, straight into his face. It smashed his cheekbone with a loud crack, and he let go of my sister. That's all I cared about.

The cops don't believe my version of what happened.

After being booked I called Paul and asked him to have my lawyer meet me. She never made it to the station house and hasn't yet arrived here at the jail.

Now I'm in a cell. No window, no natural light, but there are brash greenish-white overhead fluorescent tubes over which I have no control. There's a half sink/half toilet, stainless steel with no seat. Just the bare frame like the kind you see at arenas.

The cell is cinder block with a drain in the middle of the concrete floor, and a narrow bed attached to the wall. I'm alone. They're not granting me privacy out of kindness; they consider me dangerous to others and myself. It's a fact, and I'm not denying it, that I bashed my sister's husband in the face with that burning log.

I hear my sister choking, the children shrieking, and see myself dive at the fireplace and come out swinging. The smell of my burned flesh makes me throw up. Or maybe it's the sensation in my wrists, bones reverberating with the violence, the impact of the log breaking Frederik's nose.

I'm on suicide watch. When the sheriffs turned me over to the prison staff, a female guard strip-searched me. I looked at her nametag: Officer Fincher. She is tall, stocky, and muscular. She's built like marble. I had expected depersonalization, but her eyes met mine. I saw a woman-to-woman flicker, almost as if she was sorry for me.

She told me to strip, and I did. Everything off — underwear included. My gauze-wrapped hands are like paddles, so she helped me unclasp my bra. Clothes went into a pile. Then she slipped on a pair of latex gloves and had me stand tall, spread my arms and legs.

"Open your mouth," she said, and looked inside with a flashlight. She checked my ears, up my nose. She examined my armpits, navel, and the hair on my pubic bone.

"Hands on the wall, bend over," she said, shining her light at my buttocks.

She gave me cotton underwear and an orange jumpsuit, a pair of sneakers with Velcro closures. No belt, no laces.

"Your lawyer coming?" Officer Fincher asked.

"My boyfriend called her," I said.

"What's her name?"

"Mary McLaughlin," I said.

"I know her," Officer Fincher said. "I know most of the defense attorneys." I waited for her to make a comment about Mary McLaughlin being smart, or good, one of the best, but by then our eye-to-eye, woman-to-woman moment had passed.

Finally Officer Fincher left, and I was alone.

I lay down on the bed and closed my eyes. I couldn't stand looking at those scrubbed mint green walls terrorizing me with the idea I might be here forever. I kept hearing the panic and disbelief in Paul's voice when I called him at our apartment. I wondered if I'd ever get to return to Chelsea, to Paul, our cats, our friends, and my work at the Institute for Avian Studies.

I thought of Anne. She must have gone to the hospital with Frederik. I wondered how badly I had injured him — not because I care about him, but because I'm worried about my sister and what he'll do to her and the children if he recovers. He doesn't deserve her lying for him.

31

On my way into jail, I passed through two sets of locked metal doors. The sound of them clanging shut has lodged deep in my brain. Guards were stationed at desks behind bulletproof glass, with just a slit at the bottom, through which one sheriff's deputy handed my papers. A radio was playing, and between the first set of doors I heard the sung phrase *"We stole some clothes, but I wanted love; I know that my sister did too . . ."* And by the time the sheriff's deputies, one on each side of me and my heart skittering up my throat, rushed me through the second set of steel doors, my mind called up the next part of the song: *". . . Lilly Pulitzer gave up her ghosts; we wore pink, but inside we were blue . . ."* I can't be sure whether I actually heard that second phrase or only imagined it. But it didn't matter because suddenly I was not only hearing "Crime Spree" — a song from long ago — but singing along with Anne, years before she'd met Frederik, one summer day in Central Park, lying on our blanket in the Sheep Meadow, tanning in bikinis and listening to WABC. We were fifteen and sixteen. Blue sky, sun, the park, being together.

The Sheep Meadow was packed with sunbathers, but we found a clear spot without too many little kids around, within easy sight of three Collegiate School boys we knew from the Gold and Silvers, the Christmas dance at the Plaza, who were playing Frisbee.

We sprayed Sun-in on strategic face-framing strands of our black-brown hair — blond was one dream that would never come true. My hair was long and straight, Anne's short and wavy; I wanted hers, and she wanted mine.

Scorching heat filled the city like milk in a bowl — it rose up from the sidewalks, the pavement, and the park's walkways, benches, dry grass, and lumpy boulders of New York gneiss and Manhattan schist.

"Crime Spree" came on, and we liked the song's cockiness, the attitude: two sisters against the hard world, behaving badly in ways we would only sing about. They'd lost each other somehow, an idea unthinkable to us.

> She kissed the lawyers on Folly Beach
> I scammed on Azalea Square
> Northern good girls on a southern crime
>   spree
> On the road with nothing to wear.
> Sometimes the world is a crazy place,
> It gives and it takes right away,

If I could trade everything just for a space
In her life, well I'd do that today.
We had to leave home but we didn't know
 why
We each had a stone in our shoe
We spoke the same language no one
 else could hear
Big sister, you know I miss you.

Kids came around with black garbage
bags full of ice and Heinekens, and Anne
bought six beers for us.

We were underage, but she was my older
sister, and no one cared anyway. We both
liked to get numb. We lay on our stomachs,
bikini tops untied to drive a group of
Frisbee-playing Trinity School boys crazy,
and she told me the tallest was named Park,
and she kind of liked him.

Sitting in jail, I wished for "Crime Spree"
to be a sign. I felt the spirits of our young
selves fly down from the heaven where wisps
of brave, radiant teenage girls go once their
dull, inducted middle-aged replacements
take over.

I had to believe that the ghosts of the
young, wild Burke sisters had taken over
the guards' favorite radio station just long
enough to blast twelve seconds of that song
to give me strength and remind me of my

sister: not the Anne now, but the Anne then. To remind me of why I'd done this for her.

I want the song and memory to drive away the knowledge that I'd completed Frederik's job for him, convinced Anne to cut me from her and the children's lives for good. The spider silk of today's reconnection would break. We would become reestranged, only in a much worse way. The song is in my head, but so is a map of the future.

I tried to kill her husband. My lawyer will say I was defending my sister, but Frederik will convince Anne at least to pretend to see it his way. He will get her to deny my story and show the court my letters and e-mails, proof of my feelings about him. I will serve time in jail, no matter how good Mary McLaughlin — a friend of Sarah's — might be. Anne will never visit or write to me. Her kids will grow up and I'll never know them.

A man who fears and despises me will write my future.

PART ONE

CHAPTER ONE

November 8, 2011

The letter arrived the second Tuesday in November. Standing in the narrow vestibule of her West Chelsea brownstone, Clare Burke unlocked the creaky brass door to her mailbox and reached inside. There, among a pile of bills and flyers, was a single ivory envelope.

She stepped into her parlor floor apartment, slung her messenger bag off her shoulder. Still holding the mail, she removed her notebook and camera and placed them on the kitchen table. Three cats — Blackburn, Olive, and Chat, all named for passerines they would most certainly kill if they had the chance — darted around her feet as she opened the refrigerator door and filled their bowls.

Setting the bills aside, Clare turned to the envelope. In a world of e-mail it stood out for being personal, an actual letter — people didn't write each other anymore, and she felt instantly curious. She saw the name in the return address, and her breath caught.

Rasmussen was written in a tiny, sharp hand, above the address: P.O. Box 1041, Millinocket, ME. The handwriting was not her sister's. Clare turned over the envelope and saw the Burke crest stamped in blue sealing wax. Their parents had given the sisters family crest rings on their twentieth birthdays, and the seal had been imprinted with Anne's.

Clare walked into the living room; trying to keep her hands steady, she opened the letter and started to read:

Dear Aunt Clare,
We don't know each other really, but I'm planning a trip to New York and wondered if we could meet. I'll be doing research for a project. I read your Institute for Avian Studies blog and look at your photos — I especially love the one of the snowy owl. I didn't know they wintered on city beaches.

This letter must seem really out of the blue. It is for me, too. I didn't plan on writing it, but then this opportunity came up, and I thought who do I know in the city? This is not a trick to get

40

revenge for my father or something. Please do not be worried about that.

Just so you know I'm a serious person, I'm in my senior year at Emerson College in the Documentary Production program. I am inspired by nature, and am working on a project that combines sculpture and film. I have something under way, and I want to visit New York to film a certain habitat.

I know you spend a lot of time in the parks and at the beach, and are very busy. From your blog, it seems you watch birds all over the city. I'm sure you know the place I'm interested in, and I'd love to tell you about it when I see you.

It's funny, I haven't been to New York City since I was in third grade. My father had an exhibit and we drove in and stayed for a few days. While he was setting up the show, my mother took Gilly and me to the Met. She showed us lots of her favorite paintings, but there was one in particular she said you and she used to love. It was by Winslow Homer, and there was moonlight. I remember she looked happy and sad, staring at it, both at the same time.

This might seem presumptuous, but I

was wondering if I could stay with you a few days while I work on my project. I know the address, of course, from family history. Your number is unlisted, so I can't call; I plan to show up at 495 West 22nd St. and hope for the best.

Love,
Grit

The letter felt real in her hands, but nothing else did. The day's last light spilled through French doors, burnishing the oak floor and washing the books that filled the tall bookcases with gold. In the small park across Twenty-second Street, bright yellow ginkgo leaves glinted on dark branches. She hadn't had contact with anyone in her family for nearly two decades. Clare felt as though she were dreaming.

Bowls rattled in the kitchen, the cats finishing their dinner. Old radiators clinked and hissed as Clare turned on a lamp and sat on the couch. "Love, Grit." Clare had assumed Gillis and Grit had been raised to hate her. The part about not wanting revenge: did that mean forgiveness? "Love": what a peculiar way to sign a first letter, or maybe it was not strange at all. Clare seemed to have lost all perspective.

Somewhere in the apartment, probably in

a box at the back of her closet, Clare had the picture she'd taken the day she'd attacked Frederik. Anne, Gillis, and Grit huddled together by the dying fire, all looking shell-shocked. Clare's lawyer had offered the photo at trial — an exhibit to show Clare's state of mind (immediate concern for her sister's life) and Anne's affect (beaten down, fearful), hoping to convince the jury that Anne was being abused, and that Clare had attacked Frederik to defend her.

Eighteen years had passed, two of them in prison. Now Grit was twenty-one, a college senior. Any moment the doorbell would ring, and a young woman would be standing there. She would be just five years younger than Anne when she'd married Frederik and estranged herself from her family.

Clare had a sudden, crazy desire to talk to Anne. In spite of everything, even in prison, the need for her sister had never gone away. She remembered their old pre-Frederik ease, the way they'd check in constantly no matter where they were, just to talk, remind each other to watch for the full moon, tell each other what they were having for dinner. In spite of not being cooks they loved food. They fought, but they always laughed.

Before and during the trial, Clare had been barred contact with Anne. After the verdict Frederik sold the Montauk house and moved the family away. Clare couldn't stop herself from hoping Anne would write, or even visit. But it never happened.

Sarah had heard from Anne during the first couple of years after Clare's conviction, and told her they were living in Newburyport, Massachusetts. But then the family moved to Denmark, and Sarah never heard from Anne again.

After closing arguments, the jury had been instructed to consider charges of attempted murder as well as the lesser charges of various degrees of felony assault.

Six hours later they returned with a verdict for assault.

Although the first police officer on the scene hadn't insisted Anne take off the scarf she wore to hide Frederik's handprints on her neck, one forensic technician had taken a picture of Anne with the scarf on, and Mary McLaughlin had presented it at trial.

When the trial was over, the foreman told reporters the jury had seen redness and swelling in the photo. They had debated finding Clare not guilty, but couldn't completely discount Anne's and Frederik's testimony. Still, they found that Clare had truly believed she was protecting her sister, and they considered her state of mind to be a mitigating circumstance.

Instead of fifteen to twenty-five for attempted murder, Judge Berman sentenced Clare to two to four years for a Class E assault. She was driven straight from court to Bedford Hills Correctional Facility, New York State's only maximum-security prison for women.

Stuck in her cell, Clare had felt tortured by memories of being at the Montauk house that morning, knowing Anne had been ready to pack up the kids and leave — in contrast with how she'd been on the witness stand, stiff and wooden, never meeting Clare's eyes, saying she couldn't imagine what threat Clare had perceived, that she had gone after Frederik for no reason. But the worst part for Clare came afterward, when she never once heard from her sister. It felt like hell.

After Clare's release, early days on the Internet, she found Frederik's Web site; his bio said he lived and worked in Ebeltoft, a coastal town on the Danish peninsula of Jutland, known for its glass museum. It mentioned a wife and children, but gave no details.

Now the cats wandered into the living

room and settled in their favorite spots, cleaning their whiskers after dinner. Clare ran her thumb over the envelope's raised wax seal. Perhaps Anne had given the ring to Grit on her twentieth birthday.

The letter had been postmarked two days ago, Scarborough, Maine. She tried to imagine why Grit might be up there instead of in Boston at Emerson College, heading toward the end of the fall semester.

Clare couldn't sit still; she needed to move, get some air. It was nearly dusk, a perfect time to head back to the park and pursue what had become her owl-stalking, night-exploring obsession; besides, she could probably make it in time to watch four long-eared owls, residents of Central Park's Cedar Hill, fly out for the night. But instead she texted Sarah: Meet at Clement's?

Five seconds later, Sarah's reply: Hell yeah!

Clare pulled on her jacket, stuck the letter in her pocket, and locked the door behind her.

Stepping outside into the cold, she stood on the brownstone's top step, saw people hurrying by, and found herself studying their faces. Would she recognize Grit? She scribbled a note for her, saying she'd be home by eight, and stuck it in the brass frame above the buzzers.

As she headed down Tenth Avenue to Clement's, her local pub, the scars on her hand began to ache and she realized a long-buried thought had come to the surface, the question, after all these years of silence. When Grit arrived, Clare could ask if her sister was still alive.

Sean Kilroy stood behind the long mahogany bar, pouring Guinness right: He filled the glass halfway, let the dark magic settle, and then resumed his pour, ending with a half inch of creamy head.

Clement's wasn't even an Irish bar, not like Paddy Reilly's or Connolly's — it was named after Clement Clarke Moore, the rich Anglo-Saxon landowner who'd once farmed the plot on which it stood — but it served Guinness and therefore was lucky to have Sean as head bartender.

And who should come through the door but the resurrected angel Clare Burke. She had powder-white skin, long dark hair with a silver streak, blue eyes with the depth and treachery of Clew Bay. The ugly burn on her right hand looked as if she'd reached straight into hell and stayed there awhile.

"How's it going, Clare?" he asked, fixing her a generous Talisker single malt, neat.

"Good, Sean. You?"

"Not so bad. You meeting Sarah?"

"Yes, she'll be here soon."

Sean nodded and edged down the bar. Clare came in for company, but he knew how to read her mood and when she wanted to be alone. He watched her take the laptop from her bag and open it up, blue light reflecting on her face and making her skin look almost transparent.

Clement's cheap owners nonetheless supplied free Wi-Fi, so when Sean had served Clare, he went to the computer behind the bar, mainly used for setting up playlists, managing the night's music — Bon Iver's "For Emma, Forever Ago", right now — clicked favorites, and came upon Clare's blog.

Many nights she came here, either alone or to meet a friend, and wrote about her day spent in nature — Strawberry Fields, the Ramble, Evodia Field, the Lake, Swindler Cove Park, Ebbets Field, Rockaway Beach, and Saw Mill Creek on Staten Island — the only borough, as she wrote, where Chuck-will's-widows still nest in the salt marsh and call through the summer nights.

She seemed to love raptors, nocturnal birds, and herons more than any others. Her posts were beautiful, spare impressions of what she saw and felt, more poem than essay. He drank in her photos, still and mysterious, as if taken by a wild creature instead of a human woman.

"You could just ask me about my day," she called, smiling from down the bar.

"I'd rather read it and look at the pictures," he said.

"Why don't you come out with me sometime?" she asked. "I'll show you where the owls roost."

"Sure, just tell me when," he said, but he knew the game they played, with her always inviting him and Sean always saying sure. There was nothing between them, not like that. She was older than his oldest sister; in fact, maybe that was the charm because in spite of their age difference, he and Eileen had been the closest in their family of seven.

Clare had to be closing on fifty, if you added it all up, the details of her life and all she'd been through, but she looked thirty-five. Most people would never guess she'd done time, but Sean could tell. Prison usually bled the life out of a woman, burned off her beauty and intelligence, left her looking bitter. His cousin Darlene, who'd gone in and out for kiting checks over a period of fifteen years, was forty-five but looked like a wizened winter apple.

Not Clare; she had a mysterious inner

49

glow. Soft smooth skin, eyes that saw every-thing — but sometimes, right in the middle of a conversation, she'd lose her train of thought, seem to forget what they'd been talking about, and when she raised her eyes again they'd be blank. That was prison.

He'd watched her with Paul, lately, seeing how she still held herself back. They met here sometimes, leaned in close over the candle while they talked about — what? Birds, no doubt. Sean knew the signs of romance — every bartender did — and he saw them between Clare and Paul. She guarded herself, though.

Sean made a couple vodka and tonics, poured a round of Pinot Grigios, spiked an Irish coffee. Two guys, art handlers from the look of them, ordered beers and while Sean pursued the art of the pour, he waited for the first half to settle and stared at the photo Clare had just put up, yellow owl eyes peering out from thick pine boughs, no other part of the bird visible.

Clare never gave away the locations of owls. The birds slept all day and were too vulnerable to idiots, but she'd written that the tree was on a well-trod path in Central Park, which meant to Sean that the owl was hidden in plain sight, just like the blog author herself. Serving the leather jacket art-handler guys, he glanced over at Clare. Sarah had come in, and they were hugging.

Sarah Hughes had come straight from Prada, where she sold clothes, and where one dress could cost more than all Clare's optics put together. Right now she was dressed in her work uniform: a finely tailored white cotton shirt, straight pants, and cropped jacket in black tech fabric, a Prada creation that reminded Clare of shark's skin: *real* shark's skin, not the material.

"Perfect timing — you caught me coming out of the subway," Sarah said, hugging Clare. "Long day, sore feet. What's up?"

"Sarah, look what came," Clare said, placing the letter on the table.

Sarah checked the return address and ran her thumb over the raised sealing wax. "Holy shit, *Anne?*"

"No, it's from Grit."

"You're kidding."

"Read the letter."

While Sarah smoothed out the sheet of stationery, Clare leaned in. The two friends were so absorbed in the letter they failed to see the young woman, hair tucked under a black wool cap, sitting at the end of the bar. Sean offered to refill her club soda, but she shook her head, impatient for him to get out of the way. He was blocking her view of Clare.

CHAPTER TWO

Clare arrived home to find her note to Grit still wedged into the buzzer panel. She tucked it into her pocket and entered the apartment. Wind whistled through the old window glass; the trees in the vest-pocket park, illuminated by streetlight, were leaning sideways, branches raking the sky. From inside the living room, she opened the French doors and grabbed a few logs from the half-cord of hardwood stacked on the narrow balcony.

Kneeling by the marble fireplace, she crumpled newspaper between cast-iron andirons that had been here since her childhood.

A deep, oblong copper kettle — a find from the old Sixth Avenue flea market, back when she and Paul had lived here — held twigs and broken branches picked up from the street outside. She built the fire with kindling and three logs arranged in a pyramid, allowing lots of air, just the way her father had taught.

She and Anne had grown up here. This part of far-west Chelsea had been neglected back then, not a fashionable place to live. Crime was high, and although there were many vacant buildings, the side streets were lined with architectural treasures, brownstone and brick town houses dating back to the 1840s, with the gothic General Theological Seminary at the neighborhood's center.

Their father, a real estate agent, had had the foresight to buy the house from an estate. Shabby, filled with the previous owner's old furniture, the house had become their parents' passion. Over the years — before the girls were born, then as they were growing up — they had restored the house on a shoestring, keeping the old fixtures, replacing only things that were beyond repair.

For Clare and Anne, it was like growing up in a secret pocket of New York history. They found yellowed newspaper clippings in bureau drawers, photos of the Chelsea waterfront when schooners and frigates had lined its docks, an original map of the Moore farm, on which Chelsea had eventually been built. Sometimes they felt *A Visit from St. Nicholas,* by Clement Clarke Moore, had been written just for them.

At night, when their father came home, if he did, the girls escaped their parents' constant fighting by exploring the house. They covered every inch, finding a trapdoor in the attic, a boarded-up dumbwaiter in the dining room, warrens of hiding places in the basement. When they discovered a fork and tin cup in the corner of one tiny room, Anne began to investigate.

"Someone was kept prisoner down here!" she said.

"I don't believe it," Clare said. "We would feel it if something bad happened here."

Anne nodded. They had their own troubles in this house, leaving them sensitive to other people's pain, even echoes from the past. The cellar hiding places had no chains, locks, bars, or keyholes. The spaces, although small and hidden between a second wall, seemed cozy and safe. Using flashlights, Anne and Clare found initials scratched into the exterior wall — the stone foundation — and a poem written, using the tip of a nail or a knife, in a roughhewn vertical beam support:

Take thee far from me, and me from thee,
No matter because our hearts hold fast

Like birds overhead in the sky so free
We shall someday fly together at last.

"A slave wrote this!" Anne said.

The sisters huddled together, examining the lines. Clare felt a tipping-over thrill of compassion, sadness, and discovery. The lines expressed grief, loss, and a soaring spirit. The girls had studied Phillis Wheatley in history class: born in West Africa, she had been ripped from her family, sold into slavery at age seven, sent to Boston. She'd learned the English alphabet and written a book of poems, the first by an African American to be published.

"Could it be Phillis?"

"No — she lived during the Revolution, way before this house was built. But another slave poet, it has to be. Clare, our house was part of the Underground Railroad!"

The sisters started spending hours at the New York Public Library, searching books about New York's network of safe houses where slaves hid on their escape routes north, looking for any mention of their house. Although they'd never found any proof, Anne had focused on the word "free," and Clare had held on to the word "birds."

Their old house, the poem, birds, history, and their own imaginations delivered them from family unhappiness. Born city girls, they learned early to escape into nature. Central Park was a haven, thirty-seven blocks and a world away from home. Exploring the park and the dusty corners of their own house taught the girls to look for meaning, magic, and comfort in places they least expected it.

Money had had a way of trickling through their father's fingers, and after his death, taxes took much of what was left. Their mother acknowledged the great investment her husband had made, buying the old house when Chelsea had been a wasteland. Now people recognized the neighborhood's beauty; it had been designated a historic district, and people were eager to move in. She divided their family home into five apartments and sold the top three stories, keeping the first two floors, basement, and back garden.

Clare and Paul had the parlor floor, with her mother living one flight up in the bedroom and sitting room she had always used. After she died, Clare became the co-op manager, collecting a small fee to keep the building running smoothly. Along with her work at the Institute for Avian Studies, it paid her bills.

Tonight Clare performed the tasks she did

every night, rituals of making herself feel cozy and not so alone. The folder of menus, tucked into the bookcase, came out, and she looked through them, trying to decide whether to order from Don Giovanni or Chelsea Cottage. Or maybe she should call Blossom, the vegan restaurant on Ninth Avenue. But she wasn't hungry.

Sitting in her armchair, she set aside the menus and felt the fire's warmth on her face. She looked around the room. Her cherished 1917 umber-toned owl lithographs by Louis Agassiz Fuertes — each one a gift from Paul their first four Christmases together — hung above the drop-leaf maple table. Agassiz's studies of barn, barred, long-eared, and great gray owls calmed her, made her think of Paul and the forest.

Volumes on nature filled a wall of bookcases — all the Peterson guides: *Birds of North America; Murphy's Ocean Birds; Bird Studies at Old Cape May;* John Muir's essays; Rockwell Kent's illustrated accounts of his Arctic expeditions; *The Compleat Naturalist* by Linnaeus; Robert Ball's 1909 *In Starry Realms* and John Herschel's 1833 *Treatise on Astronomy* — and many more, collected by Clare and Paul at tag sales and bookshops long ago.

She opened her laptop and scrolled through the bird lists — daily e-mail notifications of interest to local birders: New York State Birds, NYC Cyber Birds, and Rare-Birds-No-Exceptions. The lists had their own personalities: serious, anecdotal, strict rules. If a birder dared to post a commonly seen bird on Rare-Birds-No-Exceptions, or used a colloquial tone mentioning the weather or foliage, he would receive a strict reprimand from Seth Grunwald, the list manager.

The big issue stirring everyone lately regarded potential recreational improvement at Floyd Bennett Field in Brooklyn. New York's first municipal airport, now abandoned, Floyd Bennett's meadows and runways were a haven for grassland birds: American kestrels, northern harriers, peregrine falcons, upland sandpipers, meadowlarks, and grasshopper sparrows. An endangered red knot had been sighted last summer.

Clare had long known that New York birders were among the most passionate and activist people on earth; they split into factions, and even if they were on the same side, they rarely agreed on how to accomplish their goals. She enjoyed the online drama and bickering, and Seth's intractability. But right now she was monitoring the lists for clues.

The details were too amazing to release yet. She'd told only Paul, and knew the sighting would cause excitement to rival 2004, when an ivory-billed woodpecker, critically endangered and assumed extinct, had been spotted in an Arkansas swamp.

Two days ago she had received a blurry photo, e-mailed through her blog from a nonbirding tourist. People often sent images with requests for identification, or just out of enthusiasm, a desire to contribute to Clare's work of cataloguing every single bird in New York City.

She pulled up the photo now. Taken on Literary Walk just before dark on October 28, the grainy picture depicted a medium-sized owl perched on the back of an empty bench, a dead rat in its talons.

The owl was unusual, unlike any Clare had seen, not an obvious member of either *Strigidae,* the family of typical owls, or *Tytonidae,* the barn owl family. But what had made her skin tingle was the woman's description of its call: ". . . like a madwoman laughing. Just shrieking, as if hysterical, as if she found the scene unbearably funny."

Nature didn't lie. It presented itself to the imagination, but with limitations. A creature, or a plant, or a cloud was what it was. Dreaming or wishing didn't make it something else, and that's what Clare hung on to.

The photo showed a laughing owl. Alistair Fastnet had traveled to New Zealand in 1900 and brought a breeding pair back to New York, to the American Museum of Natural History. There had been much written about it, and one text showed a photo of Fastnet setting the raptors free in Central Park, across the street from the museum. He lost sight of them immediately.

Periodically the owls' eerie calls were heard, and eggshells and feathers were found through the park, but the original pair was rarely seen again. The bird's last recorded sighting on earth had been at Blue Cliffs in New Zealand, July 1914. The species was considered extinct.

The owl's call was key — it would be a shock to anyone who heard it, and she pored through the bird lists watching for any clue. One birder wrote he'd heard wild cackling in the North Woods of the park, and another said she'd heard what sounded like an owl imitating the high notes being played on an accordion at Bethesda Fountain.

Clare flagged both comments, especially

61

since Walter Lawry Buller, noted nineteenth-century naturalist, reported that laughing owls were attracted to accordion music because of the similarity to their call.

She checked the time: 9:15 P.M., and still no Grit. The fire crackled. Blackburn was curled up on the desk, her tiger face buried in her paws; the other cats slept in their secret places. Clare had created a cozy life for herself, but she felt a pang, wishing Paul were here.

The day she was released from Bedford Hills, he drove her home to Chelsea. Everything felt unfamiliar and raw: sun, sky, air, and his physical closeness. Her sentence had passed like a nightmare, with its own sense of unreality. Paul stayed around her life, though not precisely in it.

She had not only felt his distance, but demanded it. His visits had become too painful: the look in his eyes as he saw her in her green shirt and pants, growing fifteen pounds heavier on prison food, the way he'd tell her about birds, the sky, last night's planets, a Barrow's goldeneye sighted in Stuyvesant Cove, and her own silence, because she didn't want to tell him about the mean guard, the kind guard, the monthly lectures on "don't be gay for the stay."

The set of Paul's jaw got to her: pure determination, as if he was forcing himself to show up every week. She began to hate his reluctant devotion. It didn't feel real; it reminded her of the holy days of obligation of her Catholic childhood — being dragged to church only because it was the rule.

Six months into her sentence, she waited for him in the visitors' room. She couldn't stand the way she felt or looked — her skin was ashen from lack of fresh air, she felt she'd never get out of there — and she knew she had to get this over with.

Paul walked in, forcing a smile. She tried to fake one back, but couldn't summon the will.

"Hi," he said, sitting down. He picked up on her mood, the way he always could. "Are you okay?"

"No," Clare said. "How about you? Are you okay?"

He hesitated, then shook his head.

"This is hard," she said, steeling herself. She had rehearsed the words in her cell, and swore she wouldn't cry.

"I know," he said. "I miss you all day, every day. Seeing you here, I just want to break through the fucking walls and take you home. I hate your sister so much, you can't imagine what goes on in my mind."

"Paul," she said. "That's not what I mean by it being hard. I have something to tell you."

"What?"

She swallowed, forced herself to look into his eyes, so he'd know this was real. "I don't want you to come anymore."

"Don't be ridiculous. What am I going to do, stay home on Saturdays, forget you're here?"

"Yeah."

"Come on, Clare."

Now tears boiled up. She'd struggled with this, sleepless nights, sick over what she knew had to happen. There was so little she had control over, but this was her choice, and she knew it was right.

"We're not the same with me in here," she said. "I'm different. You don't know what I go through, and there's no way I can tell you. This has changed me; I'm not the same person anymore."

"Yes you are — come on! I love you, we'll get through this."

"You're not listening to me!" she said.

"It's one day, one week at a time," he said. "We're already a quarter of the way there — six months out of the way."

She looked down. He'd said "we," and she knew he meant it. She was locked inside, but this was Paul's sentence, too. Their life was not just on hold — it had been destroyed. Any trust, faith, sense of goodness in the world, was gone.

"I can't take it," she said, not looking up. "Having you come every week, pretending we'll be okay. I don't think we will. This is too much to survive."

"We love each other," he said. "We're dealing the best we can. Right?"

"Tell me you don't hate coming here."

"Of course I hate it! Seeing you here —"

"Me too," she said. "I can't stand it. I want this to be over."

"It will be. We have to stick together, and think about eighteen months from now."

"No," she said. "You don't get it. I want *us* to be over."

"You want to leave me?"

The question hit her — what a strange construction, as if she had the power to leave. But she grabbed on, because she was crawling out of her skin, and she knew he'd just handed her the words she needed to stop the pain.

"Yes."

She stood up, knowing this was it, if she didn't hold her ground now, she'd cave back in.

"I'm sorry, Paul." Those were the words

that came out instead of *I love you, I'm dying, I'm so sad.*

"Clare!" he called as she walked away.

She took him off her visitor list. He wrote constantly at first, then less frequently, then hardly at all; she got what she had asked for. One day, about five months after his last visit, he dropped the news in a letter: he finally got it, they had broken up, and he'd begun seeing someone. Maybe that was the moment she realized she hadn't meant what she'd said — she hadn't wanted him to leave her alone at all — she'd wanted him to fight her.

Life occurred, terrible things happened, people changed, drove loved ones away, carried torches, buried dreams, rolled a boulder in front of the door. Still, and oddly after all that had gone between them, Paul had continued living in their apartment while she was in prison, taking care of their three cats — predecessors of Blackburn, Olive, and Chat — and the day she was released, he picked her up at Bedford Hills.

She remembered odd details of that homecoming: sunlight splashing through trees lining the Henry Hudson Parkway; shadows spilling through the car's dusty windows; Paul taking her hand, making her want to die for reasons she refused to allow into her conscious mind.

"Are you still seeing her?" Clare asked as they drove under the George Washington Bridge.

"Yes," he said, but he didn't stop holding her hand.

The radio played so they wouldn't have to talk much.

When they reached the brownstone, her knees went weak. Except for the last two years, it had been her home forever. Paul was still here. He hadn't moved out. They had broken into pieces, but maybe now they could glue themselves together.

"I wasn't sure I'd ever get back," she said, staring at the wide steps and arched front door, the small front garden enclosed by a boxwood hedge and wrought-iron fence.

"Welcome home," he said.

Inside, she walked through the house. The familiar smell and the sight of objects — framed photos, a braided rug, a red wool blanket, the mantel clock, the Fuertes prints, her books — embraced her. She felt herself smiling.

"I got some champagne," he said.

They stood inches apart. She wanted him to hold her, but he didn't move, and his eyes looked hard. He'd said he was still see-ing the woman, and somehow Clare — feeling heavy, dull, marked by two years in prison — knew she was beautiful.

Paul went into the kitchen, and she heard the pop of a cork. She sat down on the sofa, and when he returned, he settled at the other end and seemed uncomfortable, as if he'd suddenly grown too big for the furniture.

The balcony doors opened to let the September breeze blow through the room. Clare shivered with freedom. So why was her heart racing, the top of her head about to blow off? She feared saying too much, too little. Fingers trembling, she raised her glass.

"To you," she said.

"Here's to you being home," he said, and they touched glasses.

"Our home."

They both drank, and he didn't reply.

"Paul," she said, rushing with the first alcohol she'd had in two years. "You've done so much for me. The whole time I was in there —"

"I wasn't even part of your life," he said. "That's what you wanted."

"Not what I *wanted* — it's what had to be."

"Look, you're free, it's over, right? Now we have to put it behind us and move on!"

He spoke sharply, stared straight at the black TV screen, and downed half his glass.

Talking about feelings had never been their strong suit. Clare knew that was one reason he loved the outdoors: it was physical, pure, took him out of himself. She'd loved that about him from when they were kids. When she wasn't in Central Park with Anne, she'd be there with Paul.

"Remember the first time we drank champagne?" she asked.

"North Woods," he said after a long pause.

The northwest corner of Central Park, its wildest part, had been home only to muggers and wildlife back then. Even the most stalwart birders avoided the area. One May night their senior year of high school, Clare and Paul took a bottle of Korbel into the woods, dared each other to climb a red oak all the way up to its canopy.

They did it because they could, and they were in love, and the park was theirs. Taxi horns and police sirens wailed along West 110th Street, but Clare and Paul were up in the branches, drinking from the bottle, listening to tree frogs and nighthawks.

"That's who we are," she said. "The people who went to the North Woods."

"Long time ago."

"Why did you get a TV?" she asked. "It

doesn't seem like you."

"It was quiet here, okay? With you gone? I just wanted to hear voices. I watched baseball. I was alone." He stopped talking.

Maybe this wasn't going to be bad, maybe the woman didn't mean anything to him, he wasn't going to leave Clare. She listened to the silence. It seemed peaceful, what she'd craved the entire time in jail, when every minute she'd heard screaming, crying, clanging, yelling, and pounding.

He gave her a half smile. Again she could see him at seventeen, trying to reassure her when there was no hope at all. Last semester of high school, college acceptances coming in, Clare had gotten into Columbia. That had been Paul's first choice too, but it was also his long shot. She'd kept pumping him up, saying he'd make it, Columbia would be idiotic not to accept him. Half smile, sad wisdom in those deep-set hazel eyes.

He wound up attending the University of Maine, majoring in land management. They'd broken up over Christmas vacation their freshman year. He'd given her the same wise-beyond-his-years half smile over beers at Chumley's as they made the grown-up and heartbreaking decision to see other people. Their schools were just too far apart.

He'd lived in a dorm on the Orono campus and wound up dating his roommate's sister, a big blond girl from Bowdoin. The news had pierced Clare. She'd been living with her parents in this house and felt so worn down by their fights and silent, seething drama, she took Anne up on her offer to move into her apartment.

Anne, a sophomore in NYU's biology department, had a large studio apartment on Perry Street. Separated by an apricot silk curtain, Anne's double bed nestled by the bookcases and Clare's couch faced the windows. The bathroom had just a toilet and tiny bathtub; the only sink stood in the broom-closet-sized kitchen.

Two walls were brick. Anne had painted plaster arches midnight blue with gold stars on them, and tall windows gave onto a block-long secret garden belonging to St. John's Episcopal Church, hidden behind the town houses on Perry and West Eleventh streets. The garden was magical, full of green leaves and shade, and Clare often went down there alone, sat on a stone bench, read her assignments, and tried not to think about Paul.

She commuted on the 1 train to Morningside Heights, immersing herself in the core curriculum so she could start studying

71

ecology and environmental biology as soon as possible. She tried to like the boys she met at school but was still too in love with Paul to do anything but meet them to study, eat Greek food at the Symposium, have coffee at the Hungarian Pastry Shop.

The Hungarian Pastry Shop was filled with beautiful paintings of bright crazy angels. It was cozy and dark, the perfect place to huddle over cappuccino and linzer torte. They served house-made seltzer shot from dark blue glass bottles. Clare would sit there talking to friends, wishing Paul were there.

He stood now, stared into her eyes, and her stomach fell. He looked so resolute; she felt anything but.

"You're going to be okay," he said.

"I am?"

"Yeah."

"Are you going to live with her? What's her name?"

"Elena, but I'm not. I'm sharing a place with a friend, another ranger, on West Ninety-fourth Street," he said. He wrote down the address, left it on her desk.

"Elena what?"

"Who cares? She has nothing to do with us."

"Do you love her?"

"Clare, stop, okay?"

He put his arms around her. She laid her head on his chest and heard his heart beating loudly, and they held on to each other for a long time.

He had already gathered his stuff together, taken it before she got home: his camping and climbing gear, the telescope she'd given him one Christmas, and the TV. He left everything they'd found together — books, prints, paintings — and he said good-bye to their three cats — Mavis, Borealis, and Cleo back then.

He paused at the door, looking at her. She saw worry in his eyes.

"What?" she asked.

"I'm just thinking of you and Anne," he said.

"That's over, too," she said. "I haven't heard a word from her and I know I won't."

"I don't believe it," Paul said. "The kids are going to grow up and be curious about you. They'll want to seek you out. And you can't tell me Anne doesn't think about you a hundred times a day. She should, anyway."

"Well," Clare said.

"I love you, Clare," he said, and then he left.

Now, waiting for Grit, she remembered how she'd hung on to those words. She

73

didn't hear from him the first month. After a while he started to call to say he'd read her blog that morning, to ask where she'd seen the magnolia warbler or white-throated sparrow, or to give her a heads-up about a snowy owl out on Rockaway Beach.

They would run into each other in Central Park, and eventually began having coffee at the Boathouse. They started planning walks along the Hudson, to catalogue water birds around the piers, and they'd wind up having dinner at Clement's. Nature continued to bring them together, a way to stay in each other's lives without really being together.

She stared at the photo on her screen: the owl had brown feathers speckled with bold white spots, gray facial disc with ferocious eyes, and that distinctive hawklike tail. This was an avowed absurdity, a *this can't be.* Clare intuitively felt a connection with that extinct species because, in so many ways, her own relationships had disappeared from the earth.

If she was a laughing owl, she would roost in the deepest part of the North Woods, and she began to write:

There is a place to go when you need to leave the paths of the standard, the "normal," the habitual, to lose yourself, or maybe find yourself, and I'm not at all sure about that distinction.

Then the door buzzer sounded and she jumped.

Paul Traynor stood in his small kitchen on West Ninety-fourth Street, heating up a can of soup. It smelled good, but only because he was starving. He'd fed the menagerie first, hoping Clare would ask if he felt like having dinner.

He could have called her, but he kept score, and knew that if he did it too often, she'd back away a little more. He had never stopped feeling that this apartment was a temporary solution, more like a dorm than a home, a way station until Clare came to her senses and asked him back home.

When the soup boiled, he filled a bowl and sat at the kitchen table. He wore a T-shirt, his uniform pants, and work boots. Maybe, if he didn't hear from Clare, he'd go back to the park later, look for the apparition. What did it say about him that he was playing along with a fantasy, just to make her happy? He'd gone to the American Museum of Natural History, borrowed a copy of James "Swamp Fox" McCrae's book, *The Question of Extinction.*

He turned to the section on the laughing owl. Also known as Whekau and the white-faced owl, it was native to New Zealand, and the last of its kind was found dead at Blue Cliffs Station in 1914. But uncon-firmed sightings throughout the twentieth century had been reported, mainly in the eastern hemisphere.

McCrae wrote about the failed experi-ment of his colleague Alistair Fastnet to introduce a pair of *Sceloglaux albifacies* — laughing owls — into Central Park.

People claimed to hear its cries, variously described as "sick laughter," "a rabid dog barking," "discordant accordion music," or "a tomcat yowling." In 1955, an unbroken laughing owl egg was discovered near the Ravine in the park's northern reaches, and in 2000, egg fragments were recovered from the forest floor in the North Woods. These were verified by ornithologists at the Ameri-can Museum of Natural History and Cor-nell University.

Paul finished his soup and stopped read-ing. One thing that came through in the literature of extinction was how difficult it was for people to admit a creature was gone. He stared at his phone, willing it to ring. He had wishes and delusions of his own, and one was that he and Clare would be together again.

He'd moved in here eighteen years ago, left their apartment in Chelsea because he was feeling his way, wanting to give her space after prison. He'd tried being with someone else. Even at the beginning with Elena he knew he was filling time. It wasn't fair to her, which was how he'd wound up in this revolving bachelor apartment anyway.

"Welcome to the club," Mark Riley, another Urban Park Ranger, had said when Paul had told him he was moving out of his and Clare's place. Mark and Tina had gotten separated that winter. The apartment had two bedrooms, and Mark was glad for the extra rent.

Paul and Mark had different shifts, so they hardly saw each other. Paul worked nights, mainly so he could keep track of the city's owl population. He'd roam the park recording great horned, barred, and barn owls, anything to keep himself from walking down to Chelsea and making sure Clare was okay. She didn't want him, but that didn't stop him from passing her door at the end of the night, on the pretext of wanting breakfast at the Empire Diner.

Mark and Tina got back together, and suddenly Paul was by himself. He got a roommate for a while, a professor in the

Stanford biology department, but that lasted only as long as his sabbatical. After that, Paul lived alone.

He checked his watch, wondered whether maybe Clare might have decided to head to the park. Ever since she'd gotten that photo, she'd been spending more time there after dark. Even though the shot had been taken on the heavily trafficked Literary Walk, she was convinced they'd find the bird in the North Woods.

Pulling on his jacket, Paul walked half a block to Central Park West. It was freezing out, so he jammed his hands into his pockets and headed north, watching for Clare and staying alert for anything that might sound like a howling tomcat.

CHAPTER THREE

Opening the door, Clare found a young woman standing in the hallway: glowing brown eyes, pink cheeks, hair tucked under a black wool hat, petite frame beneath a puffy maroon ski jacket. At her feet were two huge duffel bags.

"Grit?" Clare asked.

The young woman nodded, beaming. She held back as if unsure what to do next.

"It's really you," Clare said.

"Yeah," Grit said.

They hesitated, then embraced in a quick, awkward hug.

"I can't believe you're here," Clare said, breaking away first, pushing back to look at her. She felt nervous, unsure of what to say, how to act.

"I can't either. You look exactly the same as you did when you came to our house."

"You can't possibly remember me."

"I do," Grit said.

Clare's stomach clenched. Why was this girl here, and how could she possibly recall anything but the trauma of that day?

"Can you tell it's me? I know I'm grown up, but do I look like my mother?"

Clare studied her, nodded cautiously. "You have your mother's dark brown eyes. Those gold flecks around your irises, just like hers." She felt uncomfortable, talking about Anne, and silently reached for Grit's two nylon duffel bags.

"Whoa, that's okay," Grit said, grabbing them out of her hands, but not before Clare felt how heavy they were. She wondered uneasily what was inside.

She showed Grit the guest room, so she could drop her bags by the bed. Then she led her into the living room, aware of Grit taking in the apartment, checking out all the pictures and details.

"It's beautiful," Grit said, looking around.

"Thank you," Clare said, wondering whether Anne had told her anything about the house, about growing up here. "What can I get you?"

"Nothing, really," Grit said. They sat on the sofa, by the fire.

Olive jumped up between them, and Grit lowered her face to look her in the eyes. "Hello, beautiful, you darling," Grit said, petting her. "I love that you still have cats! These can't be the ones you had when I first met you, are they?"

"No, Olive and her sisters are their descendants," Clare said, surprised by the fact that Grit could remember the cats she had drawn that day.

The mantel clock chimed ten o'clock. Grit left Olive and went to the fireplace. She touched the square brass clock and read the engraving.

" 'Francis M. Burke, in honor of thirty years of service to O'Gorman, Driscoll,' " Grit said, her back to Clare.

"Your grandfather," Clare said. "His company gave it to him when he retired."

"I wish I could have met him."

"Well, he died before you were born."

"My mother never talked about him much . . ." She trailed off. "What is O'Gorman, Driscoll? What did he do?"

"He sold real estate here in the city."

"He must have been good at it."

Clare smiled. "My mother used to say he could sell someone his own car."

"We both have salesmen for fathers."

"Well, your father's mainly an artist," Clare said. It felt dishonest saying anything kind about Frederik, but she wanted to smooth the way for Grit to be comfortable

81

around her.

Grit didn't reply. She stayed facing the fire as if soaking up the warmth. Her hair was still covered by the black cap, and Clare saw her watching her in the mirror above the mantel. When she turned around, Clare looked for the crest ring on her finger. It wasn't there.

"Your letter came today," Clare said.

"I'm sorry for just showing up like this — I should have given you more warning."

"It's not that," Clare said. "Just, I was surprised to hear from you."

"I've thought about writing you for a long time."

"Does your mother know you did?"

Grit shook her head.

"Tell me, how is she?"

"Do you mind if we don't talk about her tonight? I just . . . I'm really happy to be here," Grit said, walking back to the sofa.

"We don't have to talk about her," Clare said slowly, "but I need to know — is she okay?"

Grit flushed, her face turning red.

"Grit, is she alive?" Clare asked.

"Yes. She is, and she's okay." Grit took a breath. "Can I tell you the rest later? I'm just so worn out from everything."

Clare's eyes burned. The first real word

she'd had about Anne in years. She impulsively reached for Grit's hand.

"What's wrong? Did something happen to her?"

"Just family stuff," Grit said. "You know how things go . . . all families."

"But she's really all right?"

"Yes."

"And where's Gilly? Did he go to college in the States, too?"

"No, he stayed in Denmark," Grit said, effectively changing the subject by turning to stir the fire, exploding the embers into low flames.

"You must be hungry," Clare said, shaken by the emotion of seeing Grit and by how much she wanted to hear about Anne. "We could have dinner."

"Haven't you eaten already?" Grit asked. "It's pretty late. I thought you would have eaten by now."

"I couldn't eat — I got your note and felt too excited about your coming. Are you starving? Let's order in."

"You know what?" Grit asked. "I'll cook for you, if you'd let me."

"That's very un-Burke-like. We're not known for our cuisine."

"Well, I am," Grit said.

"That's impressive. But my cupboards are

pretty bare."

"Let me see," Grit said. Clare led her into the small kitchen and watched her niece check every shelf, pulling out pots and random ingredients: half a box of spaghetti, frozen peas, a small jar of Salsa di Noci, Italian walnut sauce with garlic and olive oil, a gift Sarah had brought from Eataly last Christmas.

"Is that still good?" Clare asked.

"Yep," Grit said, reading the expiration date. "And it looks delicious, seriously. I can't believe you haven't used it yet." She rinsed out a pot, filled it with water, threw in some salt, and set it on the back burner. "Do you have any lettuce for a salad?"

In the refrigerator they found a Bosc pear, three green apples, and a few yogurts. "How embarrassing," Clare said. "It's worse than I thought. Come on, let's order in. It's your first night here, and my fridge is pathetic."

"Let me do this," Grit said. "I really want to."

Clare hesitated, then smiled. She left Grit in the kitchen, needing a minute herself, to stop her pulse from racing. Everything felt curious and strangely dreamlike. Her niece was here, a fact that in itself Clare wouldn't have believed possible twelve hours ago. She heard the quick and sharp sound of a knife against the cutting board, and felt the unexpected comfort of knowing another person was in the house. Taking down two wineglasses, she found a bottle of Pinot Noir in the sideboard, and had just lit the candles when Grit carried in the plates.

"What have you made?" Clare asked.

"Oh, just a little first course."

"Wow. It looks wonderful," Clare said, gazing at the thin-sliced fruit over yogurt, drizzled with balsamic vinegar and honey.

They sat opposite each other at the polished wood table, and Clare opened the wine. She started to pour, but Grit put her hand over the glass.

"That's okay," she said. "I'll get some water."

When they'd finished their fruit, Grit served the pasta. Clare took a bite. Perfectly cooked, it was coated with the garlic-walnut-pesto sauce, mixed with green peas.

"It's delicious," Clare said.

"Thank you," Grit said. "I'm really glad you like it. Maybe I could go to the market tomorrow and stock up a bit."

"Mmm," Clare said, eating slowly.

"I'm serious, I'd like to help out while I'm here."

"You don't have to," Clare said. Grit didn't reply, and Clare's heart pounded as she wondered again what this visit was really about. She ate silently, her mind working. How long did Grit plan to stay? Clare wanted to trust her, to believe that Grit really did have a project to work on. But considering their family history, how could she possibly not have a deeper agenda?

"I liked seeing the sealing wax on your envelope," Clare said. "Your mother and I used our rings to seal all our letters."

"I wasn't sure how you'd react, hearing from me out of the blue. I figured the family crest would prove my identity."

"Good thinking. Did your mother give you her ring?"

"Yeah."

"Our parents gave them to us when we each turned twenty. Is that when you got yours?"

"Around that time," Grit said. "It wasn't a big deal. Are you finished? Could I get you some more?"

"I'm full," Clare said. "It was great." Then, "Why aren't you wearing the ring?"

"It doesn't fit," Grit said.

They cleared the table and moved to the living room couch. The wind had picked up, and the trees outside were shaking. Clare threw another log on the fire. She felt nervous. The conversation had turned stilted the minute she'd brought up the crest ring — or had it been the mention of Anne?

"So," she said. "Your letter said you're studying documentaries — and you're a senior, right? Tell me how you're combining nature, sculpture, and film."

"I'm inspired by you," Grit said, tugging her cap tighter.

"Me? I've never made a film."

"But you make nature come alive on your blog. When I read it, I feel I'm on the trail with you."

"Really?"

"Totally! I've gotten to know Central Park almost by heart, just from what you post."

"Well, I'll have to take you there."

"Cool," Grit said.

"Is your work about birds?"

"No. It's about the earth."

"The planet?"

"The ground," Grit said. "But in a specific way, a certain habitat." She shook her head, blushing. "I can never talk about my work. I'm the worst at trying to explain it."

"But that's why you came to New York?"

Grit nodded. "Yeah."

"Well, I hope you'll tell me more about it," Clare said.

"If you're interested," Grit said, giving Clare a long look, as if testing her.

"I am," Clare said.

Grit nodded, pulled her wool cap over her ears.

"Don't you want to take that off?" Clare asked. She smiled, feeling more relaxed.

"You might not like what you see," Grit said.

"I think I can handle it," Clare said.

Grit pulled off the wool cap. Her once dark, curly hair was now white-blond, cropped short. Grit tilted her head one way, then the other, as if to give Clare a better look at the tattoos just behind and below her ears. Charmingly inked and colored, one depicted a seal, the other an owl, a phrase on the owl's body: *jeg hader dig.*

"Is that Danish?" Clare asked, leaning forward for a better look.

Grit nodded.

"What does it say?"

" 'I love you,' " Grit said.

Olive walked along the back of the sofa, casting a shadow on Grit's neck. Clare wasn't surprised by the tattoos, but seeing Grit with blond hair when she'd been expecting, actually hoping for, a jolt of Anne-ness, that dark brown tumble of loose curls was a shock.

"You look upset," Grit said.

"No," Clare said. "I just wasn't expecting

you to be blond. Last time I saw you, you were three, and your hair was dark, like your mom's. You actually look very striking."

"Do you hate the tattoos?" Grit asked.

Clare laughed. "This is New York. Who doesn't have at least one?"

"Do you?"

"Maybe," Clare said.

Grit smiled slowly. "Will you show me?"

Clare rolled up her pants leg to show Grit the snowy owl just above her ankle.

"Very much alike," Clare said. "Your mother loves owls, too. I'm sure you know that."

"Oh, yes," Grit said. "She adores them."

"You take after her," Clare said.

It was like throwing a switch. Grit's smile disappeared. She leaned back hard, scaring Olive off the sofa.

"Why do you think I love to cook?" Grit asked coldly. "Why do I not drink red wine, why is my hair blond? I'm nothing like my mother. Nothing at all."

Early next morning, Grit unpacked her bags. She had already made mistakes, big ones, and she felt as if she were hanging by a thread. It had been a mistake to let her aunt lift her duffel — she had to have noticed the weight and wondered what was in there.

Then there was Grit's reaction every time Clare mentioned her mother. It had felt like having sandpaper dragged across sunburned skin. Grit cringed, thinking of it now, how obvious her emotions must have been to Clare. It shocked her that after this whole year, she still felt as raw as she had that day. She moved silently, tucking her clothes into the bureau, hanging jackets in the closet, trying not to wake her aunt, hoping she hadn't seemed like a basket case last night.

Dawn light filtered through bare branches in the park across the street. The light looked cold and clear, as in Denmark, but the trees changed the landscape enough that Grit wasn't transported back home.

Leaving her car yesterday, she'd seen a sign for ALTERNATE SIDE PARKING. It sounded like something you'd get a ticket for, and Grit didn't need to owe more money than she already did. Her car was on its way to being sold; two possible buyers had found her ad on Craigslist, and she'd arranged to show it that afternoon. She just had to keep the car from being towed till then.

No jacket, she'd be that fast. Slipping out the entryway door, she muffled the sound and left it unlocked. The outer door was trickier — if it slammed behind her, she'd be sunk. She jammed a *New York Times* from the pile under the mailboxes into the doorway to hold it open a crack, and tore ass down the street.

She studied the street signs, much easier to read in daylight. Right in front of her Subaru, a white sign with red letters: ALTERNATE SIDE PARKING. STREET CLEANING. NO PARKING 9–10:30 TUES & FRI.

Today was Friday. Grit unlocked the car, turned the key. The old thing rattled, then started. It hadn't been serviced in more than a year. Her ex-roommate had let her stay in her family's Maine summer house, and if Grit hadn't gone through coat pockets in the closets and found a few dollars, she would have starved. She'd gone on eBay, sold two of her father's glass pieces for gas money. How appropriate.

She drove east across West Twenty-second, took a right on Ninth Avenue, then zigzagged west and east, scanning. Nothing so far, c'mon people, don't some of you drive to work? Around the block again, then bingo, a rather dashing middle-aged man unlocking an SUV with New Jersey plates. He glanced around as if afraid of being caught.

Grit glared at him, waiting for his spot.

91

He saw her watching him, and she pretended to write down his license number. *You're a cheater,* she mouthed. He looked scared and guilty, jumped into the driver's seat, and sped away. He was totally being unfaithful. Grit had learned to see the worst in people.

Funny, she had expected to see guilt in Clare. Grit had studied her carefully last night, waiting for some sign of it, but she'd seen none whatsoever. Only sorrow when she'd tried to talk about Grit's mother. Grit's stomach flipped, just thinking of that, of how she'd promised they could talk about her today.

First she texted the car's location to the Craigslist people, said she'd meet them at noon. She opened her trunk, grabbed two overflowing shopping bags. It would take her a few more trips to carry everything inside.

Rushing back to Clare's brownstone she spotted Clement's. Last night she had hung around until Clare returned home, then followed her to the pub. Grit hadn't wanted to rush in without getting a feel for how her aunt seemed. If she had seemed angry or volatile, Grit would have been out of there fast. But instead Clare had seemed quiet, gentle, talking with the bartender, meeting her friend.

Grit should have known. She had begged for Clare stories when she was young, and when they were alone and her mother could bring herself to talk about it, the tales were tender and sweet.

Her mother had used her detective skills to learn that Paul had deserted Clare while she was in jail. She would harp on that story, as if blaming Paul somehow mitigated the fact that she and Grit's father had sent Clare to prison.

Back at the brownstone, Grit found the outer door still wedged open. She let it close softly behind her, and then edged into the apartment. Listening carefully, she knew Clare was still asleep. She'd always been a vigilant child, alert as a cat.

Now Grit went into her bedroom, closed the door behind her, set the shopping bags by the bed. From one she removed her Cuisinart and all its attachments, her video camera, tripod, extra SIM cards, lights, and maps. The other bag contained her notebooks and cookbooks; she slid them under the bed.

Hearing noises in the kitchen, she left her room and found Clare making coffee. Her aunt wore a gray T-shirt, blue silk pajama bottoms, and bare feet. Grit hung back, watching for a second. Clare was used to living alone; what if she didn't want to be disturbed before coffee? Or what if she already had regrets about having a house-guest?

"Good morning," Grit said.

"Good morning," Clare said. She smiled, giving Grit a hug. Grit trembled and focused on not holding on too long or tight. She couldn't let herself seem needy. "You're dressed already!"

"I was so excited to be here," Grit said, the truth, "I woke up early."

"Did you sleep okay?" Clare said.

"Great," Grit lied. She sat at the small kitchen table, feeling tension unwind as her aunt brought out cups, milk, sugar, butter, and jam, and popped an English muffin into the toaster.

Picking up the jam jar, she read the label: *"Our June strawberry-picking trip to Saratoga,"* and recognized writing that made her stomach lurch. "Did someone make this for you?"

"Sarah, an old friend."

"I've heard of Sarah."

Clare gave her such an expectant look, wanting to hear something, anything about her mother; Grit tried to smile.

"She's an old friend, right?" Grit asked.

"Yes, we grew up on the same block, and stayed friends through college."

Somehow Grit knew Sarah had been the woman sitting with Clare at Clement's last night. They hadn't even glanced at her, alone at the end of the bar.

Sipping her coffee, Grit felt that the comfortable silence had turned awkward again. She steeled herself, knowing she had to give a little.

"My mother told me a little about her," Grit said.

"What did she say?"

"Not much. All I know is that the three of you were close until she married my father." Grit stared across the coffee cup, watching for Clare's reaction. "Right?"

"It's hard to know what happened," Clare said.

Grit saw her squirm, knew how reluctant she was to talk about it. Her heartbeat rocketed; last night she'd held back, but suddenly she was ripping to get into it.

"I can tell you don't want to badmouth my father. You want to be nice and not come right out and say my mother stopped speaking to you and your mother and Sarah right after my parents' wedding, right?"

"There are so many reasons we shouldn't go there," Clare said.

"Clare," Grit began. "Please?"

Clare stared, seeming to get her words together. Grit thought of her mother's secret trove, the countless hours she had spent reading every letter, even ones her mother had written and never sent. Those piles of letters and notebooks, hidden from Grit's father, provided an archaeological dig of her mother's life — a civilization long dead and extinct.

"I don't want to say anything against him," Clare said.

"What if I do?" Grit asked.

The English muffin burned in the toaster, sharp smoke filling the kitchen. Clare opened the window above the sink, cold air knifing in as the smoke wafted out toward a tiny back garden. Grit didn't stop staring, so when Clare turned to look at her, the question was still buzzing between them.

"It's an old toaster," Clare said. "I should have been watching. It doesn't pop up automatically."

"That's okay," Grit said. "I'm not that hungry. I just want to talk."

"It puts me in a difficult place," Clare said. "I hurt your father. I'm sure you know that. I'm not the person you should be talking to about him."

"You're exactly the right and only person

to tell the things I have to say," Grit said, and Clare looked down. "You mean you could get in trouble?" Grit asked. "Because you're on probation or something?"

Clare's expression turned to severe discomfort, verging on anger. "I'm not on probation anymore."

"I know you weren't allowed to be in touch with us," Grit said. "But I'm twenty-one now, we don't have that restriction anymore. I know what happened that day, even if I was only little. If there's a problem, I'll just swear we never talked about anything." She'd choked on the word "allowed." Why had she said *that?* Evil old don't-talk-about-the-family conditioning.

"Last night you didn't want to talk at all, when I asked about your mother."

"I will, though," Grit said. "I'll tell you everything."

Clare checked her watch. "I have to meet some birders in the park at seven-thirty; I should get moving."

"Then when you come home tonight?" Grit asked.

"We'll see. But yes — I do want to hear all about your mother." Clare rinsed her coffee cup. "Would you like to come with me now?"

Grit hesitated, wanting to be polite, reaching for the words to get out of it.

"Then again, you probably want to get started on your research," Clare said.

Grit nodded, shrugged. "Yeah," she said. "I probably should."

Clare's expression seemed to soften. Was she relieved to be off the hook, not having to hang out with her niece today? Clare opened her junk drawer, one that Grit had looked through earlier, and pulled out a small laminated subway map and a set of keys.

"This one's for the outside door, these unlock my apartment — bottom lock and the deadbolt. You'll need to double-lock when you leave, okay?"

"Thanks," Grit said, closing her hand around them.

"Do you know how to get around?" Clare asked. "How to get to the library, or the park, if you decide to go later —"

"I'm mainly checking out locations, wetlands in the New York area. That's the specific ground I was talking about."

"There are so many marshes in the city; if you have an idea of what you need, I can tell you the best train to take."

"I have a guidebook," Grit said. "And I'm pretty good in subways."

"Hard-core change from Maine, right?"

Grit laughed. "Slightly, yeah."

"I haven't even asked you what you were doing up there."

"Oh, I was filming," Grit said. "Part of the same project."

"Making your way down the east coast," Clare said. Their eyes met, and Grit looked away quickly, afraid Clare would read her emotions.

Clare headed down the hall to get dressed for work. Grit went into her room to pretend to get ready for a day exploring natural habitats in New York City. She tried to take deep breaths, to keep from feeling light-headed. She was really here, in her mother's childhood home. She couldn't wait to be alone so she could settle in, go searching for her aunt's secret drawer.

Somehow Grit knew she had one.

Chapter Four

Clare's birding group convened in the parking lot behind Central Park's Boathouse Café and headed straight into the Ramble, one of the least tamed parts of the park. Frost sparkled on trees and paths, and fallen leaves were an inch thick underfoot as Clare led the birders into the woods above the Lake. Rowboats were stacked and stowed for the season, and most of the migratory birds had already gone.

There were eight people, seven of them people Clare knew, serious birders who came on most of her walks and subscribed to her blog; two of those were rabble-rousers on the topic of Floyd Bennett Field and any other controversial birding topic. The eighth was a banker from London who followed her blog. Worldwide, Central Park was known as one of the great places to see birds.

"Have you signed the petition?" asked

Harry Leland, a corporate lawyer and member of the New York Conservation Trust and board, the governing body that oversaw funding for the Insitute for Avian Studies and Clare's blog.

"Which one?"

"Rockaway Birds. We're getting together a package to send to the National Park Service about Floyd Bennett Field. Prettying that place up would be a nightmare for conservation. Why aren't you blogging about it?"

"I write about the birds out there, and leave it to the readers to realize they need protection. My blog has never been political," she said, thinking what a corporate asshole he was.

"I'd like to see you take more of a stand," Harry said.

Clare gave him a Buddha smile. The board sometimes tried to influence the grant recipients' content, but Ariel, her boss at the institute, always pushed back. She'd heard rumors Harry wanted to replace her with someone who was more of an activist, less a nonpartisan observer.

Harry shook his head, then peeled away from the group. Passing Azalea Pond, they crossed the Gill, skirted Mugger's Woods and Tupelo Field on their way to Humming

Tombstone, where a yellow-breasted chat had been sighted yesterday. Once a common bird, its numbers had sharply declined; November was late for one of this species to remain so far north. The chat, along with a varied thrush, another rare bird lingering in the park, would be the big "get" for this morning.

As she walked, Clare scanned the bare branches, looking for owls. Most were nocturnal birds. They hunted by night and would be sleeping now, and if visible would appear as a lump — similar to a knot of mistletoe — in a tree. She stayed vigilant for the laughing owl. She knew from her research that they had been forest dwellers, ground feeders, had thrived on small mammals, which was why Fastnet had thought them suitable for release in Central Park. He hadn't seemed concerned about introducing a nonnative species.

Perhaps Fastnet had modeled his experiment on that of the European starling. Until 1860, no starlings existed in the United States. That year sixty were brought over from England and set loose in Central Park to kill insects. The following year another forty were imported. Now the birds were one of the most common in the United States, and in parts of Canada and Mexico, all descendants of those first English transplants.

For so long Clare had birded to escape hard facts of her life. She'd turned these forays into walking meditations, a type of waking dream. Searching for a bird long extinct twisted her heart. If a laughing owl — perhaps a descendant of that first bird set loose by Alistair Fastnet — existed in Central Park, then anything was possible. Her sister could come back.

But Grit was actually here. Clare felt the thrill of it, the shock of unexpected connection. Throughout the Ramble she pointed out a white-breasted nuthatch, a red-bellied woodpecker, several tufted titmice and downy woodpeckers, a yellow-bellied sapsucker, and a Cooper's hawk perched on a low branch, tearing apart a mouse. The birders held binoculars to their eyes while Clare watched for the owl and looked forward to getting home to her niece.

Clear November light filtered through thick branches, glinting on frost-coated boulders. The Londoner commented on the romantic wooden bridges and gazebo-like shelters. Men strolled the paths, eyes flicking toward men in the group. The Ramble was a gay cruising ground, and the two groups, gays and birders, coexisted peacefully. "The other wildlife," Paul always said.

"There she is," Clare said, locating the chat in a thicket behind the Humming Tombstone. The birders stopped, focused their binoculars and cameras. Clare took out her Canon and through the tangled branches and vines caught the chat's thin white spectacles, yellow breast, and olive cap, back, and wings, while the bird whistled and chattered.

The shutter clicked speedily, the camera compact and weighty, and Clare's nose and fingers stung in the cold air as she photographed the plucky little bird, namesake of her middle cat. Now she wished that Grit had come along. She wanted to introduce her niece to the park her mother had also loved.

"Ready to find the varied thrush?" she asked when people had had their fill and started to lower their cameras.

"You look happy this morning," Lorene, one of her regulars, said.

"I do?"

It was the warmth of having family again, even though she didn't know how long Grit would be staying. Clare watched Lorene fall into step with the tall, fair-haired Londoner, his oil-coated Barbour jacket swishing audibly as he strode along.

Clusters of other birders stood in the field and around the stone Ramble Shed, watching the varied thrush — a West Coast cousin of the robin, masked, with a rust-orange breast. This was Clare's third sighting since the large thrush had arrived over the weekend.

She took photos, answered questions about why the bird had flown so far from its regular habitat. In fact, the species was known to wander, leaving thick pine forests in the Pacific Northwest seeking food, sometimes wintering in the Midwest or Northeast, aggressively staking out bird feeders or foraging the ground for arthropods.

When she'd finished her talk, she said she'd see everyone next week and turned away. Four people who'd read her blog and wanted to see the long-eared owls tagged along. Lorene and the Englishman stayed behind.

Clare and the others walked toward the East Side, stopping by the tall, dense trees on Cedar Hill. Clare felt goose bumps whenever she got near owls.

Jonathan, Ted, Arthur, and Georgia fanned around the tallest cedar. Veteran owl watchers, they had seen long-eared owls here before, and remembered the year a family

105

of three had wintered in the Pinetum, the largest concentration of evergreens in Central Park, just steps from the West Eighty-sixth Street entrance.

The watchers stood in silence, and Clare's heart flooded with complicated love. Blinking into the sun, she found the black ovals in the thick cedar branches: sleeping owls, their hunger at rest. Owls were territorial, and because these were here, it meant no others would roost nearby.

They slept high in the tree, dark lumps nearly invisible to passersby. Clare thought of her nights with Anne, searching for raptors in the park. She felt an unexpected flash of hope: love for Anne, the wide-open possibility that Grit's being here would somehow bring Anne back into her life. If a young woman could forgive her for attacking her father, couldn't Anne, who knew the truth of why Clare had done it?

Love and hope. For Clare they hadn't gone together in years. Her skin rippled. Paul was somewhere in the park. She knew the way an owl, gliding low over hills, senses her mate without hearing his call. He'd be doing his Urban Park Ranger duties, and along the way keeping watch for the Whekau. Although he didn't believe in the bird the way she did, he had his own reasons for wishing a vanished species could some-day come back.

Grit had radar for hiding places, and she found Clare's right away: behind the winter coats in the rear of her bedroom closet, at the back of the bottom drawer of a file cabinet, there was a large maroon leather box.

Easily transportable, the box contained the secrets in her aunt's universe. Grit carried it into her bedroom. She knew she should have scruples, feel terrible and guilty for snooping, but this had always been her survival instinct. Information was how you stayed sane — people's mouths lied, but the things they kept hidden didn't. The cats gathered around her, right on her bed, as if giving her permission to go through Clare's things.

Clare and her mother had grown up in this house. Clare had to have some old letters, pictures, and diaries: magic carpets to take Grit into the realm of her mother. Behind her father's back, right up till winter break last year, her mother used to whisper to Grit, "Keep your passport close, we're getting on the next plane out of here."

"Where are we going, Mom?" Grit asked.

"ABWHI." Anyplace But Where He Is.

"What's wrong with him?" Grit would ask.

"Pick a card, any card. Oh, look!" her mother would say, taking a card from an imaginary deck. "He's an asshole!"

What did it say about Grit and her family that some of her favorite memories were of her mother calling her father names behind his back? She already had her mother's journal, but she needed more. There had to be some explanation buried in this childhood home for why a once-strong woman would subjugate every part of herself to her awful, controlling husband.

Grit had once believed they would really fly away. During their secret talks, her mother said they would go to Corfu or another Ionian island. Or possibly Paris, where they would cruise down the Seine and find an apartment on the Île Saint-Louis. Or, and this had always been Grit's favorite dream, they would move to New York City. They'd take an apartment in the old family brownstone, a flight up from Clare.

Remembering those hopeful times gave Grit a headache. It had taken her a long time to grow up enough to realize there was a huge gap between what her mother wanted — or said she did — and what she was actually capable of doing. Her brother had realized it even earlier. Deep and serious, always her protector, Gillis had understood their parents in ways it took Grit another decade to accept. She felt a sharp pang, missing him now, and she added this visit to Clare to the list of things she had to tell him.

Abuse turned people into witches — not just the abuser, but the one being controlled, too. It made them believe in a form of black magic, dangerous and destructive and evil. Grit's mother had lost her integrity, had done terrible things, just trying to survive her father's treatment. At least when Grit was home, her mother had an outlet. They could talk and joke about what was actually profoundly terrifying.

After Grit went to college, her mother withdrew; Grit felt so guilty for leaving her alone with him, she would pull out her own hair in her sleep, wake up with a pile of it on her pillow. More than once her roommate had woken her up, crying. Her mother's letters, long and warm at first, turned into postcards, one or two lines about her father's latest work — as if either of them cared.

Summer vacations were okay because after the first week or two, her mother would start joking about him again.

"Stay away from your father," she'd warn. "He forgot to take his Midol today." Or, "Darling, while you're out, could you pick up a little hemlock? I'm making your father a special soup. . . ."

Grit and her mother would get back to normal fast, using humor and their closeness to survive. Whenever Grit flew back to Boston, they'd both cry and promise to call and write constantly. Her mother had fought hard to get her father to agree to Emerson. She'd done it with flattery, saying Emerson was such an artistic school, just right for the daughter of the great Frederik Rasmussen.

Her mother's journal writings let Grit view Anne Burke's younger self: talking tough, sexy, and sometimes dreamy, almost always about boys. Grit had seen pictures — she'd been stunning, cool, and stylish. From what she wrote, boys seemed to fall at her feet, and she basically stepped over one to the next. She'd allude to moods around the house, and Grit could tell she had been afraid of her father. What a sitting duck she had been for the Master of All He Surveys.

This particular trove of Clare's — perhaps there were others — contained no letters, no sweet notes or cards, no journals. Here were court and prison documents, chilling and ugly. Grit set them aside. There was a pile of papers about an old airfield: Floyd Bennett Field and Gateway National Recreation Area. Beneath them were pages copied from books about *Sceloglaux albifacies* — the extinct laughing owl.

More bird stuff: lists of species, labeled photographs of a bobolink clinging to a tall grass stalk, a northern harrier flying low over a cracked asphalt landing strip, a short-eared owl eating a mouse. Grit turned back to the thick sheaf of documents from Clare's trial, health forms from Bedford Hills, and her prison release documents. Her mug shot shocked Grit: head tilted back, eyes wild, mouth half open as if to speak. Grit saw the camera had caught her in that moment when she still thought it had to be a mistake, if she could only make them understand.

Grit's hands shook, reading a deposition of her father's. She could hear him yelling when the trial was over. "Two years, they call that punishment for trying to kill a man?" he would rant, slamming around the house in his violent way, terrifying Grit and Gilly.

But as fascinated as Grit was with her aunt, as deeply as she longed to know her and understand everything, her real mission here had to do with her mother.

She found one thing. A segment of Clare's trial transcript: the day Grit's mother had testified. Clare had made notes all through the margins. Grit's stomach ached as she read.

District Attorney: Tell us what happened next.

Anne Rasmussen: The minute Frederik walked through the door, Clare went crazy.

DA: What do you mean by "crazy"? What did she do?

AR: She reached right into the fire and hit him with the burning log.

DA: Where did she hit him?

AR: In the face.

DA: What provoked her?

AR: Jealousy.

DA: Jealousy of what?

AR: Of . . . well, that is, I mean, I assume. Of my relationship with Frederik.

DA: Because your sister had feelings for your husband?

AR: Well, yes.

DA: Mrs. Rasmussen, did your sister believe you were in danger from your husband at that moment?

AR: I wasn't!

DA: What about your children? Did your sister believe your husband was about to hurt them?

AR: Frederik would never hurt us.

"Liar!" Grit wailed, reading the transcript, and the cats scattered like buckshot. She stared at the page till the words blurred, rocking like a zombie. Her mother had been under oath, sworn to tell the truth. And the worst part was, in some way, her mother might have convinced herself that that was what she was doing.

Grit needed a break. It was nearly noon, so she changed into warm clothes and headed down Tenth Avenue. Turning the corner onto Twentieth Street, she felt her heart quicken. Two people, a burly middle-aged man and slim young woman, were circling her 2002 Subaru.

Please let one of them buy it, she prayed. The collection agency had been on her case: repay the loan or get repo'd. Coming to New York made her a moving target, but how long before the cosmic tow truck found her?

"Hello, I'm Grit Rasmussen," she said.

"Hi," the young woman said. "I'm Alicia Antonia." She was fair skinned with blond

113

hair, green eyes behind geeky black-framed glasses, and an athletic-looking body. She wore a green army-type jacket and stylish tall black boots.

"Wait a minute!" the man said. "I thought I was the only buyer. I told you I'd take it sight unseen."

No fucking kidding, Grit thought. She still owed thirty-five hundred but had set the price at thirty-eight, way below the Blue Book value of forty-five hundred dollars. He knew he'd be getting the car for a steal.

"Well, I don't know you," Grit said, "so how could I be sure you'd really show?"

"I consider we have a deal," he said. "So start it up, open the hood, and I'll make sure it's all you say it is."

"I'd like the chance to bid," Alicia said.

"Bid?" the man said, puffing up and sounding intimidating. "No way."

"Let's start her up," Grit said, ignoring him and unlocking the Subaru's door.

The engine rumbled but turned over right away. She sat in the driver's seat, door open, one foot in the street, and popped the hood. The man shook his head. "Look at the corrosion on the battery. And is that oil? Do you have an oil leak?"

"Not as far as I know," she said. "It hasn't had a tune-up in a while, but I check the fluids, and oil is never a problem."

"When was the last oil change?" he asked.

"I did it myself on Wednesday."

"You changed your own oil?" Alicia asked, her voice full of admiration.

"Yeah," Grit said, smiling back.

"Well, the car isn't in great shape," the man said, touching rust in the left front wheel well.

"That's why I set the price so low."

"Fine," he said. "I'll write out a check."

"A personal check?"

"Yes, but I assure you I have more than enough to cover it."

"I brought cash," Alicia said. "But only thirty-five."

The heavy man snorted. "I'll give you the full thirty-eight. What's the problem?"

"I'm selling it to Alicia," Grit said.

"Are you joking?" he asked, stepping forward into Grit's space. That sealed it — he was an entitled, controlling jerk, a Frederik type, full of his own fucking importance.

"No joke, and get out of my face," Grit said.

They had an angry standoff, him trying to stare her down, Grit gazing back as placidly as possible. She was mentally figuring that three thousand, cash in hand, would give her leverage to work a deal with the credit agency.

Finally the guy walked away, and Grit and Alicia shook hands.

"There's one little thing," Grit said. "I don't have title to the car."

"You owe on your loan?"

"Yeah. But if I pay it off with your money, they'll give me the title, and you'll be all set."

"Shit," Alicia said. "I don't know. What if it doesn't work out?"

"You give me the money, and I'll pay the loan off right now," Grit said.

Alicia squinted, trying to decide. Grit struggled to smile, make herself seem more trustworthy than desperate.

"Well," Alicia said. "There's a check-cash place up on Twenty-fourth Street. You might be able to wire the money from there. We could give it a try, but if it doesn't work out, the deal's off."

"Fine. Let's go," Grit said.

"Can I drive?" Alicia asked.

Grit looked Alicia over as she handed her the keys.

"What do you do?" Grit asked.

"I'm a caterer. That's why I need a car — to get to my gigs. Otherwise, trust me, I wouldn't want to own one in New York.

Why are you selling, by the way?"

"Like you said — there's no point owning one in the city," Grit said.

"You have Massachusetts plates," Alicia said, glancing at Grit as she turned onto Tenth Avenue.

"Yeah, well, I live here now," Grit said. "Turn here."

"The check place is a few blocks up."

"I have to clean a few things out of the trunk," Grit said, gesturing for Alicia to pull up at the curb in front of Clare's.

"Amazing house!" Alicia said.

"Thanks," Grit said.

Alicia kept the car running while Grit lugged the rest of her belongings up to Clare's apartment. When she ran back to the Subaru, she had a slight lump in her throat. This car had been everything to her, including, at times, a home. It had taken good care of her.

"What kind of catering do you do?" Grit asked.

"I'm just starting out. Right now I have mainly birthday party clients, and a few holiday parties lining up. I'm definitely aiming for events and big parties." She handed Grit a business card: *Antonia's Picnic,* it said, with a tiny picture of a basket on a checked cloth.

"Cute name," Grit said.

"Thanks," Alicia said. "Now all I have to do is hire some staff and I'm ready for the holidays."

Grit instinctively liked Alicia and she needed a job; should she say something? No; staying with Clare would save money, and would give her time to work on her project.

Alicia pulled up in front of the check-cashing place, and Grit went inside the sleazy-looking storefront. Bulletproof glass covered the clerks' windows and cigarette burns marked the floor. Posters for food stamps, ways to quit smoking, and the U.S. Army covered fake-wood paneled walls. Signs for WESTERN UNION, PAY PHONE BILL HERE, and DISCUSS BOND POSTING WITH OUR BAIL SPECIALIST adorned another.

Grit had a pay-as-you-go cell phone; standing in line, she pulled a scrap of paper from her pocket and called the AAAA-1 Collection Service. A grim voice answered.

"Hello, this is Margarita Rasmussen, account number BA901442242230LSNB," Grit said.

"We've been trying to contact you," the voice said.

"I'm sorry for being out of touch," Grit

said. "But I would like to make full payment today."

"The entire amount of three thousand, eight hundred, forty-two dollars and ninety-two cents?"

"Here's the thing," Grit said. "I can wire you three thousand dollars cash this minute. Otherwise I'll have to keep making sporadic payments."

"Your last payment was six months ago. You are in violation of the law and we could put out a warrant for your arrest and repossess the vehicle. I hope you're aware this conversation is being recorded."

"Yes," Grit said, her heart pounding. She felt as seedy as this place, a fugitive who had run out on her debt. Not only that, she was cheating both Alicia and the collection agency, keeping the extra five hundred. "I feel terrible about not paying, and I would really like to cancel this out today. Please?"

"Let me speak to my supervisor."

Grit stayed on hold, listening to country music, her veins full of adrenaline. Moments later the voice returned.

"Okay. If you send three thousand dollars cash today, the loan will be forgiven."

"Will you send me the title?"

"Legally we have thirty days, but yes, we'll send it as soon as we process the payment," the person said, and gave Grit the wiring instructions.

"Thank you," Grit said, providing Alicia's address from the card.

At the window, she handed over the cash, pocketing five hundred to hold her for a while. She read the clerk the bank routing number and waited for her receipt. Once everything was set she stood in the doorway for a moment, looking out at her road-dusted white car. Saying good-bye to a good friend was never easy.

This was particularly hard, because she wasn't sure she could navigate the road ahead alone.

Walking through Chelsea from the subway Clare felt anticipation bordering on elation, and she made herself go slow, calm down. She wanted to take Grit at her word, but she couldn't help waiting for the other shoe to drop.

Climbing the front steps, she spotted lights inside her windows, warm and glowing behind the curtains. She picked up her mail and unlocked the door. The apartment smelled delicious.

Grit hovered at the stove, peering into a copper pot Clare had never seen, then she dropped her wooden spoon and turned to smile. Grit uncorked the red wine, poured a glass, and carried it over.

"Welcome home!" Grit said, handing Clare the wine.

"How wonderful," Clare said. She hesitated, then hugged Grit, dropped her bag on the floor. Still in her coat, she sipped the wine. "This smells so great. What are you making?"

"Boeuf bourguignon," Grit said. "You have great places in your neighborhood. Chelsea Market is amazing."

Clare noticed the counter piled with spices, herbs, olives, hazelnuts, raw cashews, heads of red leaf and Boston lettuce, baby spinach, lemons, oranges, a pineapple, sea salt, green peppercorns, bags of sugar and flour, and a bottle of greenish olive oil.

"You have to let me pay you for all this," Clare said.

"No, I wanted to do it," Grit said.

"You're a college student, and therefore not allowed. Isn't this what aunts are for?" Clare asked, digging into her purse. Grit pushed the cash back at her, smiling as they turned it into a little wrestling match. In the end, Grit won and refused to take the money back.

While the stew simmered, they built a fire and sat with the cats on the sofa. Clare removed some of her favorite New York guidebooks from the bookcase and placed them on the coffee table.

"There's a lot to show you in the city," Clare said. "Maybe I could take you around some."

"That'd be great."

"What are you interested in?"

"Your favorite places would be cool," Grit said.

Clare nodded. "Some of them were your mom's, too."

Grit looked down, didn't react to that.

"Central Park," Clare said, watching her. "The Met, MoMA. We could go to *The Nutcracker,* if you're still here when City Ballet starts performances, the day after Thanksgiving . . ."

Grit's gaze hardened, so slightly Clare almost missed it. Had she said something wrong?

"Maybe you're not planning to stay that long," Clare said. "I'm sure you'll have to get back to college for midterms. Do you take them in December?"

"That's when they're held, yes," Grit said.

"So there's some time pressure," Clare said. "When is your project due? How's it going?"

"Oh, fine."

"Will you show me some of what you've shot so far?"

"Yeah," Grit said. "I have some more editing to do first."

Clare felt Grit shut down, and she stopped asking questions. The fire crackled, filling the uncomfortable silence. After a while Olive curled up between them. Grit grabbed a stick from the copper bin, and they laughed as Olive batted it with her paws.

When dinner was ready, they carried their plates into the dining alcove. Beef, carrots, small white onions, sage, thyme had simmered for hours. Clare ate slowly, tasting the earthy flavors. Glancing up, she saw Grit watching her.

"It's delicious," Clare said.

"Thank you."

"Where did you learn to cook?"

"I taught myself. I found this amazing series of books — *France: The Beautiful Cookbook, Italy: The Beautiful,* everywhere the beautiful. They have gorgeous photos of food, amazing recipes. Plus, Denmark is a very gourmet place; I did the grocery shopping and pretty much cooked for the family."

"Really?" Clare asked.

"Someone had to do it."

"Well, I know your mom doesn't like the

kitchen, but she must have fed you."

"You might think so," Grit said.

They ate in silence for a while. The heart-warming feeling dimmed. Clare's pulse raced, and she took a deep breath and laid down her fork.

"What did she do?" Clare asked. "She didn't feed you?"

Grit shrugged and didn't meet her gaze.

"We said we'd talk about things tonight." The statement hung in the air, and Clare was afraid Grit would evade the subject of her family again.

"Where should I start?" Grit asked.

"Tell me about your mother. Grit, I miss her so much."

"She misses you, too," Grit said, looking straight into Clare's eyes.

Clare's heart seized. "Did she say that, in those words?"

"My mother speaks her own language; did she always? Never quite saying what she means?"

"Sometimes," Clare said.

"Well, she did mention you, but mostly in secret. My father's the one who constantly talks about you, and you can imagine . . . But I know for sure she misses you."

"How can you tell?"

"She used to say we'd run away from him

and come here — live upstairs from you."

"When?" Clare asked, shocked.

"I don't know. A lot, when I was younger."

"Really?"

"Yes," Grit said. "But what she said and what she did were always different. You must know that."

"But why do you say she misses me?"

"Because she keeps things," Grit said. "In a place where he'd never look. Stuff he would forbid. You should hear him: 'I *demand* you stop doing that! I *insist* that you cease doing this! I *forbid* you!' "

"Poor Anne!"

"Yeah, I know. Every letter you ever wrote her, pictures of you — alone, but especially of the two of you together. She kept an entire album."

"Those are all from long ago," Clare said. "They don't really prove anything about how she feels now."

"They do," Grit said. "Because he made her destroy every single object, picture, word, memento of you — and he believes she did. It happened when we first moved to Ebeltoft. He built a bonfire in our yard, and he made us throw in everything having to do with you. He said you'd used fire to kill all chance of being part of our family — so we would use it to kill any remembrance of you."

"And your mother did it?"

"She had to. He made Gilly and me burn the Valentines you'd brought us that day. Mom tossed in some brass candlesticks you'd given them for their wedding, and a few cards you'd sent when they were first married. I remember the candlesticks survived, but they were all black. I buried them to keep them safe."

"Why did you do that? You were very young. And you must have heard only terrible things about me."

"That's true. But I told you — I remember that day in Montauk; how nice you were to me and Gilly," Grit said. "I sometimes dreamed you'd save me."

"Save you?"

Grit squeezed her eyes tight.

As if she'd lost her voice, Grit stood up and glanced at Clare. They walked through the apartment to the guest room. Grit opened the door, and Clare stared in disbelief.

The room had been transformed. Grit had stacked books and CDs in piles along the wall. A full-sized computer and an iPod deck covered the oak desk. Three framed watercolors leaned against the desk, and photographs had been stuck in the mirror's gilt frame. A pink fleece blanket had been folded at the end of the bed, its chenille spread covered with a mauve satin quilt.

Cooking supplies — a Cuisinart, several copper pans, two enamel casseroles, and a stack of cookbooks, including *France: The Beautiful* — were piled beside a sleeping bag, tent, and ski boots. Cross-country skis leaned in the corner.

"What is this?" Clare asked.

"Everything I have," Grit said.

"You're moving in here."

"I have nowhere else. And no *one* else."

"What about Gilly?" Clare asked.

Grit turned away as if she hadn't heard. Burrowing in her bag, she pulled out a black leather notebook and handed it to Clare.

Clare opened to a random page and her heart seized. There, after all these years, was her sister's handwriting.

Tonight we went to the Jensens'. Before we left he said I looked pretty. He hugged me; we were getting along. I thought it was going to be okay. On the way he swerved to miss hitting a stray dog, and I grabbed the car seat. That changed everything. He snarled, hit the gas, drove so fast I was sure we'd die. I should drive us into a tree, he said. You're afraid of me, you know how that makes me feel? Why don't I fucking end it for you? I wanted to cry, I wanted it over, I wanted it over. Yet when we got to Diane and Eric's I smoothed my skirt. I held my head up. When he took my arm, I leaned into his shoulder. The Jensens saw a married couple, normal and happy, who loved each other. This is how we live.

The doorbell buzzed: two short, one long. Sarah was here. Clare stood still, stunned. Grit made no move to take the book back, so Clare put it in her room. Together she and Grit went to answer the door.

CHAPTER FIVE

Sarah Cole Hughes. Family but not. Watching them together, standing close, Sarah finishing Clare's sentences, laughing at easy jokes, Grit had a vision of what it might be like to see her aunt and mother together. She tested out niece-aunt feelings on Sarah and didn't have them. Nothing close to what she was starting to feel for Clare. Clare looked pale, and Grit knew she had to be thinking of the diary.

"Is this not the most amazing, wonderful thing?" Sarah asked, arm around Clare's shoulder. She reached out to pull Grit into the circle. "Grit, do you have any idea how much this means to your aunt?"

Grit looked at Clare, who nodded. Grit could tell she meant it.

"Well, I'm really glad to be here," Grit said.

"You should have been here for dinner," Clare said. "Grit's a great cook."

"How very un-Burke-like, and I say that with love!" Sarah said.

Grit's stomach clenched; she didn't want Clare to tell about how Grit had cooked for her family, or collected cookbooks, or anything, especially not about her mother's journal. She wanted to keep everything private, just between them. Some things had to stay in the family.

"The talent skipped a generation," Clare said.

"Oh, Anne must be so proud of you," Sarah said, a sudden rush of emotion as her voice caught, and Clare looked down so no one could see her eyes.

The room's energy buzzed as if charged with space rays. Grit saw a blue shape in the corner, and she could almost believe it was her mother, or maybe even Gilly, summoned by all the love and confusion. He probably needed this connection with Clare as much as Grit did.

"I hope so," Grit said.

"Clare told me you're a senior at Emerson," Sarah said.

"Yes, I liked their performing arts program, and my parents let me enroll, even though it's not in Denmark," Grit said. The blue shadow shimmered and dissolved.

"I'm sure they're proud of you."

"I work hard," Grit said.

"Smart and beautiful, just like your mom," Sarah said.

"My mom," Grit said.

"Yes," Sarah said. "Valedictorian in her high school class, and accepted into an advanced science program at NYU. I'm sure you already know."

Grit said nothing. Instead of rushing to fill the silence, she waited for Sarah to say more.

"Be right back," Clare said, disappearing into the kitchen. Grit watched her go. The sound of running water and scraping plates made Grit start to head in to help, but Sarah held her wrist.

"Sit with me," Sarah said, pulling her onto the sofa.

"Okay."

"I'm serious," Sarah said, lowering her voice. "I want you to know how much it means to Clare that you've come."

"Did she tell you?"

"Yes, but . . . she didn't have to. I just know."

"She's my family," Grit said.

Sarah nodded, staring at Grit as if surprised she would say that. "You've been at college in the States for a while now," Sarah said. "It must have taken real courage to

131

seek her out. I know what your father thinks of her. I'm sure he wouldn't approve."

"No," Grit said. "And he doesn't need to know."

Sarah laughed. "You sound feisty, just like Anne."

"She was feisty?"

"Oh, yeah. That's putting it mildly. Your mother could hold her own against absolutely anyone. We all grew up together; your mom and aunt were the closest I had to sisters. They called us 'the Chelsea girls' — we felt as if we owned the city."

Grit nodded, wanting more.

"Did you ever read *From the Mixed-up Files of Mrs. Basil E. Frankweiler?* About the kids who move into the Metropolitan Museum of Art and live there for a while?"

"I love that book."

"One night when Clare and I were twelve, I told my mom I was staying with the Burkes, and she and Anne told your grandmother they were staying with me. We went to the Jefferson Market Library in the Village — it has a narrow winding staircase leading up the tower to a big clock face. We waited for the library to close, and then we spent the night up there."

"Did you get caught?" Grit asked.

"Not by the guard, but by our mothers.

They were onto us before we'd left the block. But they had no idea where we'd gone, so they were pretty much tormented until we got home the next morning."

"Did they punish you?"

Sarah raised one eyebrow, a good trick. "They grounded us for a month — and kept us apart, which was the worst punishment. My mother made me wash all the woodwork around the windows. In New York, that's a pretty gross job. Buckets of black water."

"How about Clare and my mom?"

"Well, your grandmother loved books, so I think she was secretly amused. But your grandfather gave them the belt. He was strict."

"He hit them?"

"Well, yes. They were so strong, and tried to protect each other. Sometimes they could; I remember your mother throwing all his belts down the sewer one day. He had no idea where they went, and got so distracted he went to Brooks Brothers for new ones and forgot about whipping the girls."

"He sounds awful."

"He was really strict. But your mom loved him, sometimes more than Clare and I thought he deserved."

Real information, Grit thought, feeling

chills. She had grown up in the cycle of violence, understood to her bones how being abused once made it more likely you would feel so bad about yourself you'd let it happen again. You'd get used to accepting terrible treatment. Almost worse, if you didn't get help, you could turn into a batterer yourself.

"Do you have kids?" Grit asked.

"Two girls in college, and little Mikeyboy. He's five. I want you to meet everyone. Will you be here for Thanksgiving, or back to Boston?"

"I don't know yet," Grit said.

"Well, if you're like my daughters, you'll have tons of work over break. But Clare always comes to our apartment, and we'd love to have you, too. Hey, head back to Emerson for classes, then take the train back down for Thanksgiving! Now that you're here, we're not letting you go so easily."

"Thank you, that's so nice," Grit said, her mind racing, wondering when the time would be right to tell Clare the truth.

The phone rang, and they heard Clare answer in the kitchen. Sarah let Blackburn circle and curl up beside her. Grit noticed her perfect skin, chin-length auburn hair, wide-spaced green eyes sparkling with life.

Her clothes were great — black suit, white shirt, obviously superexpensive, probably Italian. Grit knew models in Copenhagen who walked the runway wearing clothes like that.

It made her sad to compare Clare with Sarah. Clare was beautiful — lean, strong, pale skin, long straight black hair with that crazy white streak in front — she was lovely and mysterious. But she had ancient gray-blue eyes. Not in a lined way, but in a suffering way.

After a few minutes, Clare came back in. She was smiling.

"Was that Paul?" Sarah asked.

"Yeah," Clare said. "He's in the park, tracking an owl."

"He called to tell you that?"

Clare nodded, her smile growing. "Grit, I think you've brought us luck."

"I doubt that," Grit said, before she could stop herself.

"So, Grit," Sarah said. "How's your mom?"

"She's fine."

"I guess she must love Denmark," Sarah said. "What's her life like, now that you and Gillis are grown up? Did he come to the States for college, too?"

"No," Grit said. "He stayed in Denmark."

"Twenty-one and twenty-three, incredible," Sarah said. "What does your mom do now, with you two grown up?"

"She photographs flowers and presses them," Grit said. "Between pages of a book. Or she'll iron them between two sheets of wax paper. She'd frame them and for a while she sold them through a gift shop in Ebeltoft."

Grit paused, remembering the smell of melting wax, scorching petals. She saw the wildflowers growing out of the bog, bees flying in lazy circles, helping her mother fill the basket with daisies, veronica, aniseed, and wild orchids. Grit had searched hardest for pink fairy orchids, treasures of the Grauballe bog.

"She loved nature and wild things, but she wasn't exactly a flowery person." Clare said. "Except for violet flower water."

"She still wears it!" Grit said.

"We used to collect and distill the violets ourselves," Clare said.

Grit felt the two women leaning in, arms touching hers. She closed her eyes to memorize the feeling — one she hadn't had in so long — of being loved.

And even though Clare was her aunt, being with her reminded Grit of something lost, long gone: how it felt to be a daughter.

Those times at the bog, picking flowers, seemed so far away now.

Grit sat still, squeezing her fists tight, fingernails digging into her palms. She was afraid to move or speak; if she did, everything would fly away. She pictured her mother's photograph, the last one she'd seen, of the pink flower in silver fog. When she opened her eyes, Clare's living room's blue shadows wavered as branches waved in the streetlight.

Yes, Gilly had stayed in Denmark — she hadn't been lying. She wished he were here right now. Closing her eyes again, she remembered one day after school, when she was thirteen and he was fifteen. He ignored her most of the time, in typical big brother style, but that day he'd spread his schoolwork all over the kitchen table, and she was trying to make a pie.

"Do you really want me to get butter all over your papers?" she'd asked.

"Yeah, try it, and you'll see what happens."

"Like what?"

"I'll steal your passport so you can't go with me," he'd said with a teasing smile. She grinned, because he was picking up on her latest thing — echoing their mother, saying that she and Gilly should grab their

137

passports and take off.

"Where are you going to go?" she'd asked.

"Rio de Janeiro," he'd said. "To meet a hot girl. You'd just get in the way."

"No, you'd need me. You're too shy to talk to anyone — I'd help you."

"Yeah, well, if you get pie crust on my report, I'm hiding your passport, so you won't be going anywhere."

"I'll find it," she'd said. "No one in this house hides anything from me for long. And besides, you're not leaving without me."

"We'll see," he'd said, laughing again. He brushed long dark hair back from his big brown eyes, still smiling. Grit loved her brother so much; she wanted him to look this happy all the time. They'd stared for another minute, and then he'd gone back to writing his report, drawing all kinds of graphs about the earth's temperature.

Sitting between Clare and Sarah now, she imagined Gilly taking his passport, leaving their house, and disappearing from their family. She didn't want to open her eyes, see the room's gray-blue shadows. She'd rather picture him in the sun on a white beach by the edge of the sea, arms around the most beautiful girl in Rio de Janeiro, Sugarloaf Mountain rising behind them.

■ ■ ■ ■

Paul was off-duty, but he patrolled the park as if it were still his shift. Temperatures kept dropping, and the path that led north from West 103rd Street felt frozen beneath his feet. He held a receiver with a green light that blinked rapidly, the closer he got to his quarry. The program was controversial, but a few years back, several eastern screech owls, rehabbed from injuries, had been introduced into Central Park. Some argued that this wasn't their natural habitat.

But the owls had bred, a sign that something was working, and Paul and other rangers had tagged and attached transmitters to as many as they could find. The owls eventually found a way to ditch the equipment, but for now, Paul was following one into the North Woods.

The park lights illuminated the path, but he left it at the top of the hill, taking an unmarked trail into the trees. He kept his eyes on the receiver, but he was listening for that cry again.

"I heard it," he'd said ten minutes ago, when he called Clare from his cell phone.

"Really? Where are you?"

"North Woods. Right where you said it

139

would be."

"Did it sound like crazy laughing?"

"Maniacal," he said.

"Nothing like any other owl, right?"

"Right."

"I want to meet you," she said. "So we can find it together."

His heart kicked over — seeing her was the point. It was also, given this circumstance, dicey. He wanted to support her theory, and if she actually showed up, she'd find out the shrieks he'd heard probably belonged to kids fooling around in the park at night. He waited for her to say she was heading up, but instead she cleared her throat.

"Um," she said. "But I can't leave right now."

He didn't speak right away, covering his disappointment. Then, "Are you working?"

"No, something else," she said.

"Like what?"

"I want to tell you in person."

"Okay, that's got me worried," he said.

"No, don't worry. It's really good."

"Should I come over later?"

"How about if we meet at the ferry tomorrow?" she asked. "Noon?"

"Yeah," he said. He'd rather see her

140

tonight, but a ferry ride was the next best thing.

"Let me know what you find," she said.

"Of course I will."

"What if we're right? Could it be a descendant of Fastnet's bird, after a century?"

He stayed silent because he couldn't flat out lie to her and say what she wanted to hear.

"A dormant egg, a *really* long gestation — or maybe laughing owls have been in the park all this time. They're just so shy, we've never seen one."

"Yeah," he said. "That's probably it." He listened, heard her laugh, as if she knew how crazy it was. "Okay, see you on the boat tomorrow."

They'd hung up, and he knew he could have headed home right then. But he kept moving, deeper into the dark. He really had heard insane laughter, and just because it made sense to think it had come from humans didn't mean he couldn't have Clare's wish at heart, her unreasonable desire that something so long gone from the park could return. Or, even better, that it might never have been gone at all.

When Sarah left, Clare and Grit went to the guest room. Clare stood in the doorway, staring at the transformation. From the spare landscape of single bed, bureau, writing desk, and chair, Grit had created another world.

"Everything you own?" Clare asked, picking up on what Grit had said before Sarah's arrival.

"I should have said, 'Everything I could carry.' The most important things, anyway."

"It looks like a dorm room, or a studio apartment. What about Emerson?"

"I should have asked you before putting all my stuff in here, right?"

"Well," Clare said. She wasn't sure. She felt the family connection, and a growing sense of herself as an aunt. But she'd lived alone so long, deliberately kept everyone out, and she couldn't help feeling a bit invaded. Still, there was something so warm about this: Grit's presence, her belongings, and the fact that she'd come to Clare. "It's amazing you could create such . . . coziness in one day, while I was out."

"Do you know about *Himmel?*"

"I remember the banner in the Montauk house. Your father used to say he and your mother were made in heaven. That's what it means, right?"

"Yeah, and he still says that. But it's all talk, just for show. I prefer another word —

Hyglig." She pronounced it *hoog*-lee. "It's a Danish concept of heaven, different than anywhere else in the Western world; it means comfortable, or cozy, and it's a feeling Danes try to create at home."

"I love that," Clare asked.

"It's so far north. The weather is stormy in winter, and it stays dark for so long. Most families do the best they can. My closest friend, Karin, had the coziest house ever. That's what I wanted."

"Your mother must have tried. She grew up with it here."

"I can tell," Grit said, looking around. "But it's more than colors and pretty things. It's the feeling that matters."

Clare understood. She walked to the desk, picked up a large snow globe, and shook it. Tiny flakes fell on a small village and a setting crimson sun.

"That's Ebeltoft," Grit said.

"I'm sure you'll be going back for the holidays, or after graduation, won't you?"

Grit took the snow globe from Clare's hand, and wound the key to play music.

"A Danish lullaby; 'The Sun Is So Red, Mother,' " Grit said.

"Did your mother sing it to you?"

"Yes, in English. That used to make my father mad — he wanted us to speak Danish only. So we'd hide from him, and she'd sing it to me." Grit waited for a place in the music, then sang, " 'The sun is so red, Mother / And the woods will get so black / Now the sun is dead, Mother / And the day has gone away / The fox is out there, Mother / Now we're locking our hall / Come sit by my pillow, Mother / And sing a little song.' "

"It sounds dark," Clare said.

"Maybe that's why we liked it so much," Grit said.

"What did your father do when he caught her singing in English? Did he ever hit her, Grit? Or you?"

"Just think of Montauk. I think you know the answer to that, and you'll realize more when you read her diary. Mostly he just seethed in silence, which was scary and, in a way, worse. Or he'd tell her she was mentally ill, unable to be a good wife, a real woman, a decent mother."

Clare didn't speak at first. "What did she do?"

"At first she'd cry. When we were little, she did that all the time. She'd say this weird thing, 'I'm dying of death.' It scared me so much, and she'd hold me and say she was going to get Gilly and me out of there, we'd leave him and never have to take it again. But she never could. After . . . well, just later on, when my father said cruel things, she'd just look blank. Nothing could touch her — not even me."

"I'm sure you helped her," Clare said.

"No," Grit said. "I didn't. He won."

"I feel that way sometimes," Clare said. "But he's your father. What could he win from you? What would he even want to?"

"You really have no idea," Grit said, sitting on her bed. She held the snow globe, then looked up at Clare.

"Where's Gillis? Please tell me about him."

"He couldn't do anything to help, any more than I could."

Clare stared at her niece, feeling a sudden ugly ripple under her skin.

"Sarah said you and my mother protected each other," Grit said. "I wanted that with Gillis, but he had a loneliness inside, wouldn't let anyone, even me, get close."

"Do you think it could have been because he's a boy? Maybe not as expressive as you were?"

"That's Gilly exactly — but I doubt it had much to do with being a boy. He just learned how to go inside, never come out, never let us in. He figured out a way to turn to stone."

Clare listened, thinking of how the trial

and prison had done that to her. She'd discovered a cave she'd never wanted to find; but she'd crawled all the way to the back, where no one could find her, because she'd stopped trusting everyone.

"Poor Gillis," Clare said. "It must have killed your mother to see him that way."

Grit put the snow globe on the desk, opened the top drawer, and stared inside as if looking into Pandora's box. "This is going to sound insulting," Grit said, "and I don't mean it that way at all. But you don't know anything about her."

"It's been years, that's true, but I know her, Grit. I watched her getting beaten down, and even in court — she lied because that's what he wanted. She's in an awful place, but she's a good person."

"Good, really? Would a good woman throw her own daughter away?"

"Of course not," Clare said, shocked by the violence in Grit's tone.

"Well, that's what my mother did." Grit reached into the drawer, handed Clare an envelope.

On Emerson College letterhead, the dean of students wrote that because of tuition nonpayment, Margarita Rasmussen would be unable to register for classes. Financial aid was an option the dean would be more than happy to help her explore. The letter was dated the previous August 11.

"What happened?" Clare asked. "You haven't been enrolled at all this semester?"

"No," Grit said.

" 'Nonpayment of tuition'?" Clare tried to understand.

"They stopped paying in the middle of last year, right after first semester."

"Were you having problems at school?"

"No. I was dean's list. I loved Emerson. Even though they didn't send payment for spring semester, I went anyway. I kept getting e-mails from the bursar's office, telling me I would be locked out of my dorm and kept from attending class if they didn't receive payment."

"Did you tell your parents?"

Grit seemed not to hear the question. "Somehow I talked Emerson into believing there had been a glitch with automatic transfer from Danske Bank — that went over for a while. Finally I told the dean, and she helped me get a student loan. Now I owe all last spring's tuition and board."

"Why would your parents cut you off?" Clare asked.

"Because I'm no longer part of the family."

"Grit!"

"They already kicked you out."

"But you're their child!"

"I stepped out of line," Grit said. "You know what that's like. If you don't see it their way, it's over. No second chance."

"Your father, maybe, but not Anne. She wouldn't do that to you."

"Oh yeah, she would. Just like she did to you. You should have heard her scream. It was last Christmas, you know, the supposedly most *hyglig* time of year — me home from college, Mom decorating the house. And my father in his chair with his feet up, so happy to have us waiting on him."

"What went wrong?"

"My father said you didn't exist. I'd always asked about you, and Mom would talk about you when we were alone. I knew you were real, we all did — but my father literally wanted us to believe that you had disappeared — that you were like some evil creature from a Norse myth. You went to prison, and that was the end of your story. If one of us talked about you, he'd break something of ours. I had other snow globes, but not anymore."

"You said my name?"

"Many times. I wanted to know about you. He hated it."

"Did that cause the problem last Christmas?"

"Oh, I did something much worse than ask about you. I told him I wanted to meet you. My mother would have understood once. But she didn't then. Especially because I wrote you a letter."

"But I never received it!"

"It never got mailed. My father went through all my things and found it in my backpack. He made me read it out loud — my mother lost it, I can't even stand remembering the sound of her voice."

"Because you wrote to me?"

"Yeah. She started the minute I read 'Dear Aunt Clare.' "

"Oh, Anne," Clare said.

"My father made me burn the letter, and also the notebook I'd written it in. The same fire pit in our backyard where we'd burned everything about you years ago. Mom stood there watching, just as angry as he was. When the notebook was all ash and just the charred metal spiral was left, my father fished it from the coals with tongs. He made my mother take it in her hand."

"Just out of the fire?" Clare asked.

Grit nodded. "Yeah."

"What happened then?" Clare asked, feeling sick.

149

"He told her to tell me I wasn't her daughter anymore," Grit said. "And she did. And she meant it."

"Grit, I'm sure it was just that terrible moment — he's crazy, and she must have felt afraid he would hurt you the way he had her."

"Actually *she* hurt me," Grit said. "My mother smacked me across the neck with that glowing hot spiral. That's how I got this."

Grit tilted her head to one side, so Clare could see the owl tattoo just below her ear. Leaning close, Clare saw that the ink covered narrow scars: hatch marks left by a notebook's red-hot metal spine.

Grit said nothing, but touched Clare's scarred hand.

"She did that to you? I can't believe it," Clare said, barely hearing Grit. "Did he tell her to?"

"No. She just lost it, went out of her mind. The burn hurt about a thousand times less than hearing her say, 'You're not my daughter anymore.' "

"She didn't mean it," Clare said. "She couldn't have, Grit."

When Grit didn't answer, Clare gently touched the tattoo, the tiny Danish words inscribed in the owl's body.

"You wouldn't have gotten 'I love you' tattooed on your neck if you didn't know that about her. The owl is for your mother, right?"

Grit raised her eyes to meet Clare's. Clare felt sorrow at the expression on her niece's face.

"I didn't want to lie to you," Grit said. "I couldn't tell you the truth until you knew the story, but *jeg hader dig* means 'I hate you.' "

Clare tried to speak, but the words caught in her throat. They hugged, and she left Grit to go to her own room. The black journal lay on her bed, where she'd left it. Closing the door behind her, Clare opened to the first page. In the top right corner, it was dated two years earlier. She began to read.

From Anne's diary:

Here I go, a brand new notebook. How many have I written over the years, and more to the point, why do I bother? When I think back to being young, starting a journal at 15, 16, into college, how everything would be about boys, and how earnest and innocent and full of hope all that writing was. As if putting dreams on the page could somehow make them come true. I wish I still believed that.

So why do I do it? The blank page of a

brand new diary seems a good place to ask. I keep doing it, no matter how life goes, and trust me I've no dreams left. Maybe I'm just putting everything down for the record. So after I die, Grit can find this and know what her mother was really thinking.

But honestly, do I want her or anyone reading this garbage? No. Part of me holds on to the last bit of illusion and imagines that people — even Grit — don't know what's really going on. Frederik trained me well, right from the beginning, to show the world how perfect we are. Do you know, I think he truly thinks that? He has no sense of nightmare. I didn't used to, either. For so many years! If I could look back through all my journals, I'm sure I'd see a different self at each stage, like a woman in a horror movie who thinks everything is wonderful until it methodically begins to dawn on her that she's living with a demon.

Well, that's something! Congratulations to me. This is the first notebook where I've dared to write that down. Not because I'm afraid he will find this — I've got too fantastic a hiding place, he'd never look, that's been proven out over the years — but because I never let myself say it before. Awareness always shocks me. It's a rock between tides. Sometimes the wave rolls out, and the rock is exposed, and I see. Then the sea rushes in, covers the surface, and I wonder, was it really there, did I only imagine it? That's what life with Frederik is like. It's always a push-pull between what I feel and what I'm told I feel.

Here's one thing I wonder: Did I bring this on? Why did I marry him? I can't help thinking of Jamey. How different everything would have been. I hate myself for what I'm showing Grit, but how do I stop it? I couldn't do it for Gilly, can't I do it for her?

Clare stopped reading and thought back to Jamey Leland. Anne and he had fallen in love, right after college, surprising everyone. Kind and steady, Jamey was a postdoc fellow in the NYU English department, a departure from Anne's usual bad-boy taste.

He had grown up on the Upper West Side and gone to Dalton. Although he and Anne had never dated in school, he said he'd never forget dancing with her at the Plaza, at the coming-out party of a Miss Porter's girl who wound up marrying an Austrian prince. Anne remembered leaving the ball to drink in the Oak Bar, and she said she *did* recall dancing with Jamey. He had been so handsome, danced so well, stood out from all the other boys.

Clare knew Anne's recollection was a total lie, one invented to pump up Jamey's ego — a job, no matter who the man was, Anne always seemed to feel responsible for. Yet Clare felt relieved to see her sister settling down, seeming so happy with a nice guy, someone like Paul, the opposite of their father. But peace and stability didn't sit well with Anne. She needed rockiness to test her loves and make sure they could take the worst of her, prove that they'd stick by her.

Or perhaps she knew Jamey was too staid for her. Even though she worked in the biology lab, she wasn't an academic the same way he was. She loved science and nature, and her work brought her into contact with both. But she made fun of staff meetings and faculty parties, and outside the lab she did her best to forget university life.

She'd been faithful to Jamey all along, for over a year. One April night she went to the bar at Raoul's, and ran into an old St. David's boyfriend — Tru Hayden, who during freshman year of high school had taken her to the Gold and Silvers, the formal ball that announced the start of New York private schools' Christmas vacations. Clare knew that Anne remembered *him* clearly — that night he'd given her the best weed she'd ever smoked, slid his hands under her red silk gown in an alcove behind the Waldorf-Astoria's coat-check room, and taken her to a banquette in Peacock Alley to get drunk and make out.

Tru became an investment banker and, as he put it, "a vulture capitalist." Married but separated, he took Anne to Paris for a long weekend of shopping and staying in bed at the Hotel George V. Anne returned to New York with a vintage Hermès alligator bag, Dior scarves for her mother and Clare, and tons of guilt over Jamey.

Anne's powers of seduction were great. She had adopted the motto "Deny, deny, deny" from their father and an old movie — and believed if she shined her light on any man, she could convince him to believe whatever she said.

But not Jamey; he was too smart and, saddest of all, too emotionally tied into Anne to believe her. The minute she told him she was going to Paris alone to think about him he knew she was having an affair. He confronted her simply, with no drama. She laughed before leaving, told him, "Don't be silly!" After her return she denied his accusation in her customary injured, outraged way. But Jamey wasn't up for listening.

He had been weighing offers, leaning toward accepting a teaching position in the English department at Barnard to stay near Anne. Instead he took one at the University of Chicago.

Clare had tried to comfort her sister, but Anne was inconsolable. She drank every night, crying until she blacked out. She'd weep that no one had ever known or loved her in the way Jamey did. Even the way he'd seen right through her story — that was because he knew and loved her so well.

Then she'd say she despised Jamey, they'd never been right for each other, why hadn't she realized sooner, how could she have loved and trusted such an unforgiving jerk?

Not only that, why couldn't Jamey understand that he'd *driven* Anne to Paris with Tru? She'd been bored stiff lately, all that academia; could she really expect to live that way her whole life? Still, in *spite* of her boredom and doubts, she'd returned to him, hadn't she? She should have stayed in Paris with Tru.

In fact she would go to Tru now, but it turned out he wasn't quite as separated as he'd led her to believe. He didn't love his wife: she was angry all the time and never wanted to sleep with him. They were staying together only for the sake of their two children. He sometimes called Anne and she'd wind up meeting him at the Gramercy Park Hotel. But he had no definite plans to leave his wife, and Anne was ready to settle down *now*.

Her work in the biology lab let her make a living studying bird molt — the color and age of plumage, molt patterns of shorebirds, and birds that molted during flight. But the job failed to soothe her heart; she was stuck inside while others did field research, and she envied Clare's freedom and ability to wander through New York's parks, observing birds in the wild.

One night, sitting in their family's back garden, Anne slit the tip of her left index finger. A heavy drop of blood formed, and she let it drip onto a page of *Perdido* by Jill Robinson, a favorite novel she'd picked up at a stoop sale when she was fifteen.

"By all that's holy," she said, "I swear I will be married within three months."

"Who's the lucky guy?" Clare asked.

"I don't know yet. He'll be handsome, mysterious, and not from New York City. This place is killing me."

"How can you plan to get married when you're not even seeing someone?"

"Easy. I'm going to arrange my own marriage."

"You're crazy. You have to fall in love first," Clare said.

"That's the easy part. Don't you know me by now?"

Anne scoured entertainment listings in *The New York Times* and *The New Yorker* magazine, and went to evening talks given by various experts at the American Museum of Natural History, the Ornithological League, New York City Audubon, and Clare's own Institute for Avian Studies — a lecture for every night of the week.

She went to Friday-night chamber music at the Metropolitan Museum of Art, openings at the Whitney and MoMA, and receptions at art galleries on Madison Avenue and close to home, at those just starting to emerge in Chelsea. She figured a brilliant artist or scientist, or a not-too-stodgy museum patron, would make a good prospect.

That June Frederik Rasmussen, already celebrated in Europe, had his first solo show in New York, at the Van Hanken Gallery on West Twenty-second Street, between Tenth and Eleventh avenues. The space was one block from their parents' house. Anne asked Clare to meet her there.

Clare hurried down from the park in her work clothes — jeans, T-shirt, and a navy windbreaker. Anne looked amazing, glamorous, in a tight Azzedine Alaïa dress and four-inch sling-back heels, each a season old, from Barney's last warehouse sale. When Clare hugged her, she smelled the violet water they'd both worn forever.

The gallery presented Frederik's glasswork as avant-garde art, not decorative objects, even though that's what they seemed to Clare. She and Anne looked around, eventually made their way over to the artist. Slight, bald, wearing heavy black-rimmed glasses and a slim black suit, he fixed his eyes on Anne the whole time.

"I love your work," Anne said.

"Thank you," he said. "Are you familiar with it?"

"Not before tonight," she said.

"Well, then it's good of you to come. I enjoy people discovering me. I'm Frederik."

"I'm Anne," she said. "This is my sister, Clare."

Frederik nodded, and they all shook hands.

"Are you enjoying New York?" Clare asked.

"Enjoying it?" he asked, as if he didn't understand.

"Yes," she said. "You're visiting from Denmark, right?"

"Visiting?"

"Yes," she said, wondering if he had a hard time with English.

"I hate Manhattan," he said, giving her a brilliant smile.

"It's the greatest city in the world," Clare said. She wanted to glance at Anne, share a private laugh at his arrogance, but she figured she'd save it for when they were alone.

"You said 'visiting,' as if you're not," Anne said. "Do you live here?"

"Thank God, no. I'm Danish, but your art world is my latest conquest. I have a studio in Montauk. I'm sustained by sky, sea, nature — not tall buildings and soot."

"Maybe you should go to Central Park," Clare began, but he cut her off. He turned his attention to Anne, asking if she'd ever been to Montauk, if she'd like to visit his studio.

"Oh, I'd love to," Anne said, touching his arm.

"The Van Hankens are taking me and a few collectors to dinner tonight. Come with us. And maybe I can tempt you to drive out east with me when I go back tomorrow."

"I'd love to," Anne said.

And so it had begun, with Clare as a witness.

CHAPTER SIX

The next morning Grit awoke from the valley of stormy dreams. Clare was up and out of the apartment so early, Grit didn't have the chance to see her, read her mood, or gauge her feelings for the troublesome niece who'd just taken over her guest room.

Gathering up her Cuisinart, copper pots, gratin dishes, and favorite whisks, Grit headed into the kitchen and managed to wedge everything into all the spare cabinet space she could find.

Clare had left the coffee on; Grit poured herself a cup. She looked for a note but didn't find one. Walking into her aunt's bedroom, she found all three cats sleeping on the bed, and her mother's journal on the bedside table. Cold clear light from the south-facing windows streamed in. Grit went to the mirror, used the good light to check out her neck.

She stared first at the owl, then at the seal.

She'd had them done at a tattoo parlor in Copenhagen this past summer, to cover the burn scar. The inspiration had been a talk with friends; the owl and seal images came from a Buddhist fable, a reminder of respect and boundaries.

After being kicked out, Grit had had to find places to stay. She'd spent June in Copenhagen with Lisa, an old friend from Ebeltoft, in the apartment she shared with her boyfriend, Eric. They lived in the Christianshavn district, once working class, now trendy and hipster-ridden.

Coffeehouses were everywhere; one morning they headed out for a late breakfast at Café Anika. The weather felt surprisingly hot for June, steamy, with a thunderstorm brewing. Eric had just returned from trekking in the high Himalayas. He'd spent time at a Buddhist monastery and was telling them what he'd learned from the monks.

He said even monks had negative feelings; they called them "unwanted emotions" and devoted their practice to dealing with them. The lessons were practical — real-life ways of living. People came into conflict with one another — that was natural, the human condition. But the point was to live with equanimity.

Grit listened, thinking of her family. She

163

felt tormented by fear, anger, doubt, and despair, and she knew her mother did, too. Eric talked about Milarepa, an eleventh-century Tibetan poet and sorcerer who'd lamented his sins and moved into a mountain cave to purge his evil deeds. Through years of study and meditation, Milarepa reversed his karma and found peace.

"Maybe I should move to Tibet and find a cave," Grit said.

"Why? You didn't do anything!" Lisa said. "Your parents are the ones who hurt you, not the other way around."

"Still, I have horrible karma," Grit said. "Obviously."

"Why, because you dared to be curious about your aunt? You're twenty, old enough to contact whomever you want," Lisa said.

"Yeah," Grit said. "But not in my family. We have to keep my father happy. I should have just kept the whole thing secret, written to my aunt when I went back to school."

"Keeping your father happy," Eric said. "According to the monks, that's pure *lenchak.*"

"Excuse me?"

"A Buddhist phrase. It's the basis of every fucked-up relationship you've ever had," Eric said. "Getting tangled in another person's emotional chains."

The concept of *lenchak,* Eric explained, was illustrated by a Tibetan Buddhist story. At the full moon, seals gather fish and feed them to hungry owls. Their only motivation is that the owls expect it. The seals got nothing for their efforts, and the owls were never satisfied.

"Wow," Lisa said. "I think we know Grit and her mother are seals and her father's the demanding owl."

But was that true? Sometimes her mother was the owl.

"My mother's a seal to him, but an owl to me," Grit said.

Lisa nodded knowingly. She and Grit had gone to grade school together; her father had been one of Grit's father's assistants.

Frederik fired people constantly — with the glass museum nearby, there were plenty of knowledgeable replacements. Lisa's father had lasted two years, a record, and gotten sacked one week before Christmas the year Grit and Lisa were ten, so Lisa knew Grit's father's ways firsthand.

After breakfast, Grit and her friends strolled around the area. Knippelsbro separated Christianshavners from the heart of Copenhagen; the quarter had its own hippie-bohemian identity. King Christian IV had founded the section in 1617 and

Grit loved the old architecture, old work-shops and factories with gabled windows lining the quay.

Now the area had an Amsterdam vibe: craftsmen, art galleries, cafés, bars, a sense you could find whatever you wanted right there. Grit would miss Lisa and this place, and wanted to take a memento with her to the States. Walking along the canal, Grit stopped in front of Half Moon Tattoo and looked inside. The place glowed, a tiny jewel, its walls lined with beautiful art.

"You should get one," Lisa said, arm around her shoulder.

"I'm thinking two," Grit said.

It turned out all the work was done by and for women. Eric said he'd meet them later, back at the apartment. Although Grit didn't have an appointment, Tonya Knudsen took an instant shine to Grit's smooth, pale skin, and set about creating a double mas-terpiece: the owl and the seal.

"Little pain or no pain?" Tonya asked.

"None," Lisa said quickly as Grit pon-dered, then agreed.

Tonya swabbed alcohol then numbing cream behind Grit's ears, and very slowly worked it into the rippled burn scar. She smelled of lemons and cinnamon, and Grit liked her pink hair. While the work progressed she got lost in Tonya's mysterious tattoo sleeves, extending from the backs of her small hands up to her bare shoulders.

Lisa was patient for a long while, but finally left to go home and meet Eric. Grit imagined them having sex in the afternoon. Being with a couple made her lonely for love, showed her how alone she was in this world. She'd be leaving soon, but flying *away,* not *toward* anyone or anything.

Tonya worked for hours, and Grit felt she was in a cocoon of hurt and lost love. The needle stung, and her neck ached, but she felt Tonya's tenderness; it made her think of her mother, pre-notebook, and tears ran down her cheeks.

"What is it?" Tonya asked, wiping Grit's eyes with a cotton ball.

"I hate someone," Grit said.

"The owl or the seal?" Tonya asked.

"Owl."

"Then we shall tell the owl so," Tonya said. She wrote the words in tiny perfect script for Grit to see, and when Grit nodded, Tonya inked them onto the owl's butter-colored breast.

Now, regarding Tonya's work, Grit knew the tattoos had kept her brave, been her badge of suffering, and reminded her of where she'd come from.

Drinking coffee in the kitchen, Grit logged on to her laptop and read last night's blog post. She had discovered that her aunt's posts revealed clues to her next day's adventures. Clare must have written it very late, after she and Grit had said good night.

November can be harsh for the migrants left behind. Frost hardens the ground, makes foraging difficult. But how paradoxically heartening it has been, walking through the Ramble, to come across the Yellow-Breasted Chat. Good luck if you go looking for her. Tomorrow I'll visit an old friend, Zelda, down in Battery Park.

Grit pulled out her map and found the spot: the southernmost tip of Manhattan, where the island juts into the harbor, the Atlantic Ocean beyond. Who was Zelda? Grit told herself she needed some salt air. But she knew the real truth: she wanted to spy on her aunt. See how she acted when she didn't know someone was watching. Her heart flipped a little. Her talents as a spy had been honed early in life.

The acts of following, hiding, watching gave her a sense of being with someone in the truest way. In her family, conversation and direct communication were so often lies. Grit liked seeing the essence of a person — their real selves, not the manufactured personas most people show to the world. *The truth of a person is in her secrets.* Grit had almost always known that.

She closed her laptop and hurried to get dressed.

Battery Park was blustery and cold, wind blowing straight off New York Harbor. Bare November branches tossed in the wind. Tourists huddled, waiting for the next Statue of Liberty boat. Clare roamed the south end of the park, waiting to board the Staten Island Ferry and meet Paul.

Pulling her scarf tighter around her neck, she smelled the sharp sea air blowing across New York Harbor from the ocean. Whitecaps chopped the surface. She shivered from the wind, or from knowing she was about to see him.

Love was a labyrinth, a single path leading in mysterious twists and circles to the center. Sometimes she felt she'd been walking toward Paul forever, catching sight of him, thinking she was getting close, then finding herself back where she'd started. Sometimes she'd wonder what would have happened if she hadn't gone to prison. Maybe they'd have had children; in fact, she was sure they would have.

Locked up, knowing she'd pushed him away, she had felt tortured by her thoughts. Writers, artists, therapists, nuns, and ministers would visit the inmates, talk to them about their choices, consequences, forgiveness.

The message, continually, was that the women were more than their crimes. At the beginning, Clare resisted everything she heard. After attacking Frederik, especially in front of her sister's kids, she'd been filled with shame. Her mind split in two — the part that knew she'd been saving Anne's life, and the part that hated Frederik, that wanted to kill him. Her act, and the guilt, had stopped her from feeling lovable. And had made her go inward, shut herself off.

She'd been assigned to work as assistant to the librarian, and being in the library among the books began to soothe her. She grew to love the teachers, people who would leave their freedom outside beyond the walls and rows of razor wire to spend a few hours helping murderers, robbers, violent first-timers, and recidivists. These people, along with inmate friends, helped Clare stay sane and work on finding the way to her own center. Loving Paul was impossible without it.

Now Clare paused by a London plane tree, just beside the ferry terminal, and gazed up at a juvenile black-crowned night heron, an unusual spotting for this time and place. Full white breast, sleek gray back, bright black eyes, and sharp black bill, the bird perched on a low branch with sturdy yellow legs.

Clare took notes, snapped a series of photographs, capturing the wader at odd angles. Zelda rustled through the bushes, searching for food in the frost-hard ground. Waiting for the ferry to come in, Clare left the heron and crouched down to watch Zelda.

The wild turkey had first arrived here nearly ten years ago, having made her way down the greensward from Westchester, through the Bronx into northern Manhattan, and through a string of green space to get to Battery Park.

Birders had named her after Zelda Fitzgerald, the beautiful, crazy poet-wife of F. Scott Fitzgerald, who, during one of her breakdowns, had been found wandering right here in Battery Park. Clare stopped to gaze at the wild turkey's glossy dark neck and tail, her powerful legs and white-and-gray-tipped wing feathers.

Zelda was eccentric, a loner, and would

sometimes stray through city traffic into Tribeca, Soho, and the Village. She had been spotted strolling down busy, crowded Houston Street, feeding in Washington Square Park, even visiting backyards in the West Village, but she always returned to the Battery. The park workers kept her well fed.

"Zelda Fitzgerald," Clare said.

Eye-to-eye through low branches, she smiled and Zelda gabbled. Pale sunlight shimmered on her iridescent neck feathers. Clare reached into her pocket and pulled out a handful of cracked corn, spread it close to Zelda's feet. Zelda pecked and chortled while Clare took her picture.

The ferry horn blew, and Clare headed through the Whitehall ferry terminal to board the boat. Paul was nowhere in sight. She hoped he hadn't gotten tied up with work, and realized how much she needed to see him. As the ferry began to move, she stood on deck facing Red Hook, at the far tip of Brooklyn. Biting wind blew her hair back from her face.

Large rafts of water birds — brants, buffle-heads, scoters — bobbed in the bottle-green waves; Clare raised her camera and zoomed in. New York Harbor was rough, and the birds kept disappearing in wave troughs. Salt spray filmed her lens; she cleared it off,

172

then gave up shooting and just watched. Buffleheads, with their black and white markings, dove and stayed under much longer than seemed possible for winged creatures.

"Hey," Paul said, and she turned around. He stood there in his ranger gear, olive green from head to toe. He pulled Clare into his arms, and kissing him, she tasted salt water on his lips. Wind howled and their thick jackets rustled, pressed together, as she tilted her head back.

"You made it," she said.

"Of course I did," Paul asked.

"So, you really heard the owl?"

"Maybe. I heard a call, an insane shriek. Tracked it into the North Woods. This is impossible, you realize this?"

"I do, but you saw the picture. Did you see anything?"

"Something flew overhead," he said. "It could have been a screech owl, but I don't know. The shape seemed different."

"Long hawklike tail, right?" she asked, getting excited.

"It happened fast, I only had an impression. But maybe." Then, seeing her expression, "Come on, don't get your hopes up."

"I'm not."

"We'll have to go back together. Okay,

your turn. What couldn't you tell me on the phone?" he asked.

"My niece is here," she said.

"What?" he asked, as if he'd misheard.

"Grit. Anne's daughter. She showed up two nights ago."

"You're kidding — that's a shock. What does she want?"

"At first she said it had to do with a film project, but that's not really it. Paul, they kicked her out of the house. She's completely alone."

Silent, he stared across the harbor. After a few seconds, he looked into Clare's eyes. "Abandoned their daughter? Why am I not surprised? She cut you off, now she's throwing her kid away."

"Frederik's the problem," Clare said, thinking of Anne's diary.

"You always say that. But your sister's just as bad, even worse." He took a deep breath. "Never mind. What's Grit like?"

"Beautiful, odd, incredibly strong. She seems to have moved in."

"Yeah?" he asked. "You said she could live with you?"

"She didn't ask."

"Maybe that's what I've been doing wrong — I should quit waiting for you to say the word, and just bring my stuff over."

"Right," she said.

Paul put his arm around her as they leaned against the rail and felt the engines slow. She pressed into his body, the ferry buffeting against barnacled pilings, docking at St. George.

He slid his hand under her jacket, down the back of her jeans. His cold fingers made her arch toward him. She stared into his gray eyes. They were as beautiful, pale-green-tinged, as sea ice, but so loving. Which made her love him back, but that was nothing new. She refused to smile.

"Come on," he said.

"Maybe I'd rather stay on deck and see the Statue of Liberty on the way back," she said, her heart starting to pick up pace.

"We'll see it next time," he said.

She followed him into the cabin, briefly empty while the Staten Island–bound passengers filed off the ferry and the Manhattan-bound travelers had not yet boarded. They avoided the gaze of one man sitting alone, stuck between islands.

Pulling a key ring from his pocket, Paul unlocked a steel door and preceded Clare down the steep companionway into the warm hold, the light orange with an odd night-vision quality.

There were four bunkrooms in a row, each

locked; the ferry crew used them to rest between shifts. Paul and other park rangers who spent lots of time in Battery Park or on Staten Island had made friends with the ferry guys and finagled sleep privileges. Paul had a key and opened one door, locking it behind them, not turning on the light.

They kissed, undressing each other in the dark. His body still felt straight and hard, all angles. Under their clothes their skin was hot. He knew every place to touch, and she knew where he liked her mouth. The engines drummed and the boat pitched in the windblown harbor.

She felt like lightning, her body dissolving into electric current, voltage crackling down the backs of her legs. He was so hard and scalding hot, moving inside, filling her up. His head was back, eyes closed, and she gripped his shoulders.

Now he lowered himself, his chest against her breasts, and their eyes locked. She loved when they watched each other. Her back curved, his hands on her bottom, pressing as close to him as she could.

"Paul."

"I've got you."

He held her so tightly, and she felt herself shatter, losing herself as they rocked together. They kissed for a long time, and she closed her eyes, waiting for her heart to calm down.

They'd broken up eighteen years ago, gone ten years without being together, and had started up again the best they could. Giving and taking love had become difficult for Clare, and also for Paul. The trial and prison, guilt and loss, had gutted her, and when she'd come back to some vestige of life, the part that had loved so easily was gone.

"You're my —" she began.

"I know."

"You do?"

"Yeah, you nut."

He stroked her hair. This was her favorite meeting place: warm, safe, completely removed from the real world. They dressed and headed back to the deck. They filed off the ship with all the other Manhattan-bound passengers. The dockhands waved to them.

Walking through the cold park, they saw Zelda, stood watching her for a minute.

"She's getting old," Paul said.

"I know," Clare said. How did creatures survive, exist in this world, and make their way back to safe, or at least familiar, territory? Zelda, with her crazy, suffering namesake, made Clare think of Anne, and of herself.

"When do we go looking for the owl?" she asked.

"When do I meet Grit?"

"Soon. Right away."

"When's 'right away'?"

Clare squinted, looking up into his gray eyes. "As soon as possible," she said.

"You always complicate things, you know that?"

He gave her a rough hug. Her face pressed against his jacket, eyes stinging from the wind, she glanced across the park and saw a thin young woman with bright-white hair.

"That's her! She's here!"

"You're kidding."

"Hey, Grit!" she called.

But the girl rushed into the crowd, losing herself behind a stream of people lined up to catch the Statue of Liberty boat, and by the time Clare and Paul ran over, she had disappeared.

How hard was she trying to fuck up the goodness between her and Clare? Grit was sure that her aunt and the guy she'd been hugging, obviously Paul, had seen her, and what would they think? She ducked behind a parade of sightseers, then across a busy street, traffic whizzing by, trying to get to the subway without being spotted.

Scooting down the steps into the South Ferry station, she jumped onto the 1 train and took a seat at the end of the car. Her heart raced from the stupidity and carelessness of getting caught. And it had all been going so well.

She'd arrived at Battery Park not long after Clare had, and spent such sweet time watching her aunt take pictures of a heron-like bird in a tree and then this wild turkey, the craziest thing Grit could imagine, a gawky yet regal game bird in the middle of the city. If her father had been there, he'd have bagged the turkey with his shotgun and the family would have eaten it for dinner.

But Clare had knelt on the ground, so close to the bird she could have touched her. Grit had inched closer, trying to see what was going on. Clare seemed to want to make eye contact with the turkey, and the two of them had simply communed in nature's silence.

Grit had observed, transfixed. It was just like watching her mother. Starting when she and Gillis were young, her mother would drive them along the coast road of Ebeltoft Vig, encircling the wide bay, then turn inland toward the bogs of Grauballe.

Bog bodies had been found there, especially Grauballe Man — known throughout Denmark for having lived during the Iron Age, in the late third century B.C. He had had his throat slit and been thrown into the bog, his body preserved by iron and acids in the peat. His murder had been human sacrifice, a Germanic pagan rite.

Grit's father seemed obsessed with the area, and used to mine the peat bog for iron ore, which he would use to color his glass rusty-red. When Grit was eight, his exhibit at the Glasmuseet had contained those pieces.

She remembered that as a confusing time. Her father's moods still scared her, but she had loved him for taking them to the bog, and for his reverence for nature and unusual places. She had felt proud of how he'd honored ancient, local tragedies: Grauballe Man, Silkeborg's Tollund Man, and Elling Woman. He told Grit and Gilly that the blood of those poor people had stained the peat and kept the bog both haunted and alive.

The critics had loved the exhibition; Queen Margrethe and Prince Henrik had visited the museum, and the newspaper published a photo of Grit's father with the royal couple. But after that show, he abandoned the bog and moved on to the beach, using sand to make a gritty texture, seaweed to color the glass pale green and brown.

"Daddy, can we go back to the bog?" Grit had asked. They lived by the beach, and she and Gilly could walk there themselves. But the bog had been special: hidden, mysterious, holy, a habitat for rare flowers.

"I am done with the bog," he said. "Right now my work is at the seashore."

"But can't we have both?" Grit asked. "You loved the bog, and made all that wonderful red glass —"

"That red glass has been sold," he said. "It is over. Now we collect seaweed. Do you understand?"

"Yes, but I love both places," Grit said.

"Your thinking is sentimental," her father said. "And that is inferior. If you ever want to be an artist, you need not to 'love' places in that way. You go where you can do your best work. The bog is finished for me now, okay? It no longer exists in my mind. Now all my attention is on this beach. Nowhere else."

Grit had felt stung, and had wished more than anything, though she couldn't put it into words back then, for her father's tenderness. While at the bog, he had seemed protective of her and Gilly, calling them

181

back when they inched too close to the swampy edge. He and their mother had walked with them, explaining how the mire's lack of oxygen caused everything to grow in miniature.

The family's time there had been magical, and it hurt Grit to know her father could so easily brush it aside, could say the bog was "finished." Perhaps that was why her mother had first started taking them back there. She was more "sentimental" than their father.

Grit had loved the ride to the bog, the way they'd sometimes sing in the car. Her mother would park under the same small pine tree every time, and lead them carefully along the trail. Kicking off their sandals, they'd walk barefoot around the bog's soft and squishy perimeter.

Other people might have minded the mud, but not them. The wide openness, the bog's warmth — "the earth's oven," Gilly wrote in a report for school — drew them back again and again. Grit loved the small flowers, especially pink fairy orchids; their mother would photograph them, and Grit and Gilly would gather them for her to press.

Once they came upon a marsh hen and her brood, bustling and clucking along the soggy path. Grit's mother crouched down,

holding Grit and Gilly close, keeping perfectly still to watch. They watched the hen
herd her chicks into a nearly invisible burrow woven from tall grass.

"It's their nest," Grit's mother whispered.

"I want a nest like that," Gilly said.

"We have our house," their mother said.

"It's not the same," Gilly said. "Dad's
there."

He picked up a stick and threw it into the
bog. Grit watched it sail from his hand,
landing in the brown peat. The dark and
glistening mud consumed it within a few
seconds. Overhead seagulls circled and
cried. Their mother didn't scold him for
what he'd said. She seemed not even to have
heard him.

Grit saw her mother gazing into the burrow. From the darkness, the mother hen's
glistening dark eyes stared back and seemed
to meet hers. The hair on the back of Grit's
neck stood up, and she knew she was seeing
something amazing.

And again today: Clare gazing into the
eyes of that wild turkey, communicating
something beyond human words. Grit had
had that memory of her mother, and just
for that moment felt close to her.

The subway sped north, screeching
through the tunnel. Grit traced the scars

below her ear. She cupped them with her palm, as if the warmth of her hand could make them go away.

Getting off at Twenty-third Street, she walked up the subway steps to Seventh Avenue, then headed west. She dreaded arriving at the apartment, having to explain herself to Clare. Yes, I'm a spy: you've discovered my secret.

The Chelsea Hotel loomed ahead, a red brick Gothic edifice with ornate wrought-iron balconies. Bronze plaques affixed to white Corinthian columns beside the door announced the famous who had lived, written, and created art in the hotel — including Brendan Behan, Thomas Wolfe, Arthur Miller, and Dylan Thomas, whose memorial read: DEDICATED TO THE MEMORY OF DYLAN THOMAS, WHO LIVED AND LABORED LAST HERE AT THE CHELSEA HOTEL AND FROM HERE SAILED OUT TO DIE.

Grit moved a few steps along and found a shop, within the hotel building, but with an entrance from the street: Green Dragon Tattoos. Her neck itched.

Walking in, she stood at the counter, looking at artwork displayed on the walls and in thick binders. A man emerged from a back room, tall, with a leather vest and bare arms.

"Can I help you?" he asked.

Grit touched her scar. The entire subway ride she had thought of her mother. Coming upon this parlor she'd had the impulse to remove, or at least ink out, the words *jeg hader dig.* But now, confronted with a snap decision, she felt her knees go wobbly.

"Whoa," the man said, coming around the counter to hold her elbow. "You okay?"

"I should have had more than coffee today," she said.

"Want a cookie?" he asked.

She nodded. He indicated for her to sit down, and he came back with a plate of chocolate chip cookies.

"My mom made them."

She nodded, eating half of one in a single bite. "Delicious," she said. "Nothing like home-baked. Does she send them to the shop every day?"

"No," he said. "Today's my birthday."

"Happy birthday!" she said, trying to figure out his age. He had big tattooed biceps and a quasi-biker look with that leather vest. He wore his dark brown hair in a ponytail, but his hazel eyes were gentle, unhurt, and innocent. She guessed he was about twenty-five — with a mom who sent cookies to work with him, for the love of God. He must have seen something in her expression.

"What's the problem?" he asked.

"Uh, nothing. Just, you're a little old for your mom to be baking you cookies."

"Your mom wouldn't?"

Grit exhaled. "My mother wouldn't give me water if I was dying of thirst."

"Whoa, that's intense," he said, seeming to perk up in a slightly creepy way. Grit was used to people getting fascinated by the dirt in her life, so she pulled back. "Let's talk about tattoos."

"Okay." He gestured at the owl behind her ear. "Nice art. Did you have it done in New York?"

"Copenhagen."

"Cool," he said. "What do the words mean?"

"Oh, just something in Danish. No big deal. I was thinking I wanted something new done."

"Sure. Did you see anything in the books or on the wall? Any artist you particularly like?"

"I have an idea in mind."

"Go ahead."

"I'm thinking of a wing," she said.

"Wow, you really like birds. The owl, now this."

She nodded.

"Where do you want it?"

"On my back. Right here," she said, reaching around to touch her right shoulder blade.

"The placement's interesting — do you want to fly?"

"Maybe."

"How big?" She calculated how much of the five hundred she dared to spend; the money needed to tide her over for a while. "About two inches across. Tiny."

They went back into an unoccupied booth. Grit took off her jacket and sweater, slipped off her shirt. She felt bold, sitting there in her pink bra. Maybe she should wait for a female artist to be free.

"You have to sign this form," he said, passing her a clipboard. She glanced at the disclaimer, wrote her name more clearly than normal.

"Grit?" he asked. "I like that. I'm Dennis."

He sketched out a wing, and it was gorgeous, just what she wanted. She thought of her mother gazing into that mother hen's burrow, oblivious to the gulls crying overhead. Clare had brought that memory back, and sitting beside Dennis, Grit closed her eyes to retain it.

"A white wing," she said, touching his drawing. "Of a seagull. Extended, in flight."

"You got it," he said, and she felt the needle's first sting.

CHAPTER SEVEN

Clare waited up for Grit, reading in bed. Having Anne's journal was such an invasion of privacy, but Clare couldn't help herself. Her sister wrote the way she'd always talked.

Today the sun came out. It was so welcome after days of rain. Frederik asked if I wanted to go out for lunch after he finished working. That surprised me, and I said yes. I gardened for a while, then took a long shower and wondered what I should wear. Decided why not put on a dress, it seemed like such a special occasion. I chose the yellow one.

He told me I looked pretty, and kissed my hair. We got into the car, and as he started it, he asked, "Where do you want to go?" I felt so happy, excited to be going out with him. He'd been sweet to ask me, so I said, "Wherever you want to go."

Wrong answer. He slammed on the brake, stared straight ahead. His hands gripped the steering wheel so tightly, I could feel him wanting to strangle me. I SAID WHERE DO YOU WANT TO GO? he asked again.

"Frederik, anyplace. How about Genever?" I spoke as fast as I could, wanting to undo my mistake, go back one minute and start over.

"You've ruined it."

"No, I just want us to have a good time, let's go to Genever."

He slammed his fist on the seat between us, and I must have jumped.

"You make me feel like an animal when you act like that," he said. "As if you're so afraid of me!"

Do you know what would have happened if I'd said yes, I'm afraid of you? Nothing. It would have gone in one ear and out the other. Being direct with him means nothing. We communicate only through intimidation and fear. Right now I feel as if I've been turned inside out. The air hurts my skin.

I miss Gilly. I want to go to him now. But I miss her so much. Far away at college is the safest place to be. She's supposed to come home for vacation, but I'm sure she's wishing she didn't have to. If she'd been here today, seen me get dressed to go out, then watched us sit in the car till her father decided it was time to storm back to his studio . . .

I'm just glad she wasn't here for that.

Does she know I spy on her when she visits? How can I tell my own daughter I feel closer to her when she doesn't know I'm there? I stand by her bed and watch her sleep. Her eyelids twitch when she dreams, just like when she was a baby. She goes out, and if I can guess where she is, I walk past. She and Lisa will meet for coffee, and I'll sit on a bench across the square, pretending to read.

It's terrible. I would have hated my mother for doing it. But Grit and I can't talk. We can hardly even look at each other. She's still my daughter, and I want to share her life — have little moments the way mothers and daughters are supposed to. Instead I rely on skills I developed a long time ago.

When Clare and I learned to make ourselves invisible . . .

Clare closed the book, her stomach in a knot. The cats slept in their places: foot of the bed, windowsill, and sweater drawer. The apartment was so silent she could hear the mantel clock ticking all the way from the other room. Or was that rain? She pushed back the covers, slipped on her robe, and looked out the window. Fog drifted past the glass, billowing off the river.

At one minute before midnight her cell phone vibrated — a text message from Paul. I want more days like today.

She wrote back: So do I.

Grit hadn't called to say she would be late, and she wasn't answering her cell phone. Clare paced the hallway. She opened the door to Grit's room, thought of Anne spying on her sleeping daughter. But Grit wasn't there.

The cookware had disappeared; Grit must have stowed it in the kitchen. Stacks of books seemed like fair territory, so Clare looked through the titles: *Mastering the Art of French Cooking,* volumes one and two, by Julia Child; *French Provincial Cooking,* by Elizabeth David; *North* by Seamus Heaney; and *Bogs and the Imagination,* by Maja Svensen.

Grit's bed was covered with a quilt patterned with pink clouds and the Danish words *drøm sødt.* She had brought her own pillow, soft and thin, as if it had lost many of its feathers. Clare trailed her fingers across the pillow, wondered if Grit had brought it from home.

A car drove down the street, tires making a swishing sound. The rain had started, and with the temperature dropping, it would soon turn to sleet. Clare fought panic rising in her chest. Waiting to hear a key in the lock gave her a knot in her stomach, reminded her of childhood, her father coming home whenever he felt like it.

She sat on the living room sofa and picked up *The New Yorker.* She and Anne had been raised on the magazine. Their mother subscribed, and the girls had pored through every issue.

They had loved the poems and cartoons, torn out favorites to tape inside their bedroom closets. Clare tried to read an article about fruit trees and couldn't concentrate. The mantel clock chimed one in the morning.

She was just an aunt, not a mother, but what did mothers do? Was it normal for a kid to stay out this late without calling? Why hadn't Grit replied to Clare's voice mails? Clare walked into the dark living room. She was sure Grit had seen her with Paul; had that somehow upset her, driven her away?

The idea made her angry. Forehead against cold window glass, she tried to breathe steadily. She suddenly felt furious with Grit for invading her life, and it snowballed into rage at Anne for abandoning her daughter.

She went online, searched for "Danish telephone numbers," "Danish people directory," finally "Frederik Rasmussen." His Web site came up, new pictures of recent glasswork, the same pretentious text she'd read before. She spotted the phone number listed under "contact." She had called it years ago, when she'd first found the page, and reached an assistant at his studio.

Clare wanted to call him right now, scream at him for what he'd done to his family. But that wouldn't help at all. It was 1:15, and Grit was missing. Should she go out and look for her? Call the police? She rang Sarah.

"Hello?" Max said, sounding wide-awake, television on in the background.

"It's me," she said. "I'm sorry to call so late."

"Never too late when it's you. I'll get her, hang on," he said.

Sarah picked up the extension. "Hey," she said, sounding half asleep.

"Grit's not home," Clare said.

"Okay," Sarah said. Clare heard the bed-clothes rustle as she sat up. "What time is it?"

"One-fifteen."

"Um, honey, that's not late."

"But she didn't call, and she's not answering."

"Does she have friends in the city?"

"Not that she's told me. Then again, she seems to let me know things at her own pace."

Clare pressed her cheek to the window, looked up and down the empty street, pavement black and rain-slick.

"Are you there?" Sarah asked.

"It took her a day to tell me her parents had kicked her out, and she's not in college anymore. And she brought all her stuff — obviously, she was planning to live here, before she even asked me. Today she saw me with Paul, and I'm wondering if maybe that's driving her away. I don't get it."

"You saw him today?" Sarah asked.

"Yes, it was no big deal," Clare said, slowing Sarah down on the topic of Paul. "The strange thing is, she must have followed me. There was no other way she could have known where I was going. I'm upset with her about that, plus worried out of my mind."

"I'll come over."

"Just tell me. Should I call 911?"

Sarah paused.

Clare was back at the desk, staring down

at the computer screen where garish images of Frederik's blown glass folded into one another, a continuous loop. "I thought I wanted to call Frederik and yell at him, but it's really Anne," she said. "Tell her how terrible she's being to Grit."

"Yeah, I can imagine," Sarah said. "But for now, why don't you give Grit another half hour, and if she's not home by then call me."

"Okay, thanks, pal . . . oops, I hear the lock."

"Bon courage," Sarah said.

Clare pulled her robe tight, took some deep breaths, waiting for the door to open, then for the sound of the locks being secured. Grit hadn't turned on any lights. Clare walked down the hall, and they met in the dark.

"You scared me," Grit said.

"Where were you? Why didn't you call?"

Grit stood shivering, white hair plastered to her head, water dripping on the wood floor. Without speaking Clare led her into the bathroom, took two towels from the linen cabinet. She helped Grit out of her soaked jacket, left her to dry off.

The shower went on. Clare hung the faded blue canvas jacket in the small laundry room off the kitchen. The pockets felt heavy; Clare reached in, pulled out Grit's cell phone, then replaced it again.

Finally the water stopped, and Clare went into the living room to wait. The fire had gone out, but she stirred the coals and threw on another log. She heard Grit pad down the hall, close her bedroom door behind her. Was it possible she wasn't going to have this conversation? Clare started to feel riled, but then Grit's door opened again and she walked in wearing flannel pajamas.

They sat on opposite ends of the couch, Grit staring at her hands folded in her lap. Clare's thoughts slowed to nothing. She felt completely blocked, no idea what to say. Should she be angry, understanding, stern, cool, upset, or just happy Grit was home safe?

"I was worried," she said.

"I'm really sorry for not calling," Grit said.

"Can you tell me why you didn't?"

"I lost my cell phone."

Clare stared at her niece. It had been so long since she'd been confronted with a bald-faced lie. Anne had been the master at it, and had clearly passed the talent along.

"I know you didn't," Clare said.

Grit still hadn't looked up from her hands. Chat wandered into the room, stretched, and yawned. Grit leaned over to burrow her face in her fur and avoid meeting Clare's gaze. Clare reached down, picked up Chat, and held her away from Grit.

"Look at me," Clare said.

Grit did, and Clare was shocked to see her eyes full of shame.

"I didn't lose my phone," Grit said. "I just . . . I'm not used to checking in. To calling anyone. I knew I should have, but I was at the movies. We sat through three in a row."

" 'We'?"

"I made a friend today," Grit said. "We went to Chelsea Cinemas after he got off work and just went to whatever movie was playing. I know I have no excuse for not calling. I just didn't, that's all. It won't happen again."

"Were you upset with me for some reason?" Clare asked.

"Why would I be?"

"I don't know. I'm not used to this. You saw me with Paul — did that throw you somehow?"

"Who?"

"Grit, we saw you in the park."

Grit seemed wired, not sure whether to admit it or not, her shoulders tense and eyes strained. Her mouth opened and closed, as if testing out what to say. Chat squirmed free from Clare's arms, and Grit took the opportunity to bury her face in the cat's fur, avoiding any reply.

"Okay," Clare said. "You're home, that's what's important for now. We can talk about the rest when I get home from work tomorrow."

Grit nodded, not lifting her head.

"Tell me one thing. What does *drøm sødt* mean?"

"Sweet dreams," Grit said, her voice muffled.

Clare pictured pink clouds drifting across the warm, worn quilt. She imagined Anne saying those words to her kids every night.

"Drøm sødt," Clare said. She hesitated before leaning down to kiss the top of her niece's head. Grit grabbed for her hand, squeezed, not saying a word.

Alone with Blackburn, Grit stared at the fire. She heard her aunt's bedroom door close, listened to the silence echo. She touched the top of her head where Clare had kissed it. She felt an aura there, a halo she didn't deserve. Kissed good night twice, once by Dennis, once by Clare.

She couldn't get control of her breath. Dennis had walked her home. She had come home late, gotten caught in a lie, been confronted about spying. Only it hadn't felt like confrontation — not the way it would have with her parents.

Every step out of line had brought some kind of punishment. Both her mother and father lied through their teeth about everything, but if Grit even exaggerated, her father would yell and tell her how terrible she was, and her mother would never stand up to him. Whenever Grit missed her mother, she had only to remember vivid little realities like that.

Clare deserved to be mad, but she hadn't seemed it. Was that why Grit had let herself be seen in the park, come home late, told a dumb lie? Testing to see if Clare actually cared? If so, Clare had passed.

She *had* been upset about seeing Clare with him, and she felt jealous and guilty without knowing why. She dug her fingernails into her palm, made deep marks in the skin. Then she bit her fingernails off, down to the quick. Two bled, and she burrowed her fingertips into Blackburn's fur. Blood in the bog, she thought.

She stood and in the dim light unbuttoned her pajama top and stood by the gilded mirror. Looking over her shoulder she saw her new tattoos. Dennis had bandaged them, told her to leave them covered overnight.

But she hadn't been able to wait and lifted the gauze to take a peek. They were completely beautiful: the gull's wing and a red sun.

"What's the significance?" he had asked her midway through inking in the sun's scarlet rays.

"They're both to remind me of my mother," she'd said. "The gull's wing because of our time at a peat bog."

"Okay . . ." he said, amusement in his voice.

"You don't believe me."

"Of course I do! I work in a tattoo parlor. And what's the red sun?"

"A lullaby she sang me." Unexpectedly her voice had caught and her eyes stung. The needle hurt, but not as much as missing her mother. Dennis touched her shoulder so tenderly, a million tears boiled up.

He stopped working, held her hand. This was the moment for her to tell him her mother was dead — as she'd told other new acquaintances during the last year. It was much simpler and far less awful than the truth. But the way he had spoken about his own parents, the spirit of gentle innocence in his hazel eyes, made her know she couldn't lie to him.

"She doesn't speak to me anymore," she said.

"That's impossible."

"You don't know her." Grit looked down. He was trying to be kind, but that put her on edge. Most people around her age had such different ideas about parents. They lumped everyone together. Mothers might be annoying, or fathers might be clueless, but that was about it. This guy was too sweet for his own good.

"Hey," he said. "Did I say something wrong?"

Only everything, she thought, tears scalding her eyes. She slashed them away.

"I mean, maybe if you talked to her."

I don't need a counselor, she was about to say, when he leaned down, put his arms around her with ridiculous tenderness, shielding the wounds of her new tattoos, and kissed her. She clung to his biceps and felt the venom melting out of her.

"I don't kiss customers," he said when they stopped.

"You just did."

"Yeah," he said. "But I think you're more than a customer, okay?"

"I know. You want to adopt me."

"Uh, that's not quite it." He kissed her again, and she liked it even more this time.

She could almost forget his greeting card approach to family.

Then he began to work again. "This is a good sun," he said. "What does the lullaby say?"

" 'Say'?"

"The lyrics. I mean, your inspiration for this."

"The sun is so red, Mother, and the forest is becoming so dark . . ."

He worked in silence for a while, and she tensed up, she could almost feel it coming.

"She'd sing that to you? See, she must love you," Dennis said. "My mom sang us to sleep, too."

Grit didn't reply. She forced herself to breathe steadily, getting through the pain of the needle and the irritation of happy family bullshit. He took the hint and shut up. Grit knew she brought it on herself, telling people bits of her story, then being pissed off when they wanted to hear more.

Now, back at Clare's, she gazed in the mirror at her bare back, imagined him tattooing the whole forest, illustrating the rest of the song. She could see right where the night trees would go and wondered whether he could capture moonlight, somehow paint her skin with silver.

His touch had felt good. "We really did sit

through three movies," she said out loud to Blackburn. They'd eaten popcorn, held hands, and dodged the ushers as they slipped from one movie into another. She liked his renegade side — more tattoo artist, less mama's boy.

Buttoning up her top, she walked over to Clare's desk. She'd been in New York a few days now, time to get moving. She probably had enough money, barely, to finish her project. But she would need much more to pay off last year's school loan, support herself, and go back to college.

Reading Clare's blog would help clear her head. Expecting to see it there on the computer, she saw instead her father's Web site: photos of blown glass slipping by, one after another.

Grit sat in the oak library chair, her palms damp. She started to shake, sitting in her aunt's place. She stared at the screen, seeing it through Clare's eyes. Clare had been on her father's site for a reason. Was she thinking of getting in touch? Had the diary hit a nerve? Or — considering how worried she'd seemed about Grit staying out and not calling — had Clare panicked and called Denmark?

She quivered, thinking of the night Clare had had. No one had worried about Grit for a long time. It was almost too much to take. After the year of long emptiness, all this love felt overwhelming.

Hurt followed love. Didn't it? She touched the scar beneath her ear, rubbing it with sore fingers, just to remind herself of what was possible, and cruel, and real. But then she thought of Clare's eyes, wide and frightened of what might have happened to Grit. A person couldn't fake that.

Grit closed her father's Web site and typed a familiar Web address into the browser. An image of the bog, wildflowers silhouetted by a crimson sun, filled the screen. This would be Grit's gift to Clare, to thank her for tonight.

CHAPTER EIGHT

Clare made coffee, fed the cats, and went into the living room. The sun wasn't up yet, so the room was as dark as it had been the night before. She turned on lamps, opened curtains to catch the dawn. Freezing rain ticked against the windowpanes. Streetlights and headlights revealed the sheen of black ice. Traffic crept slowly north on Tenth Avenue; even the yellow cabs were inching along.

Most days, weather didn't affect her desire to get outside, but today she felt like staying home. She had gone to bed feeling worried about Grit, woken up feeling even more so. Her niece had a problem with lying, an obvious sign of trouble, reminiscent of Anne.

She'd avoided letting anyone get too close for so long. She and Paul went warily around the idea of living together again, but Clare felt sure she would never be ready for that. She had come to need a lot of solitude. Yet having Grit in the apartment, fast asleep in the guest room, as worried as she was, gave her a feeling of love and family that she'd sorely missed.

Her blog waited to be written. Yesterday's turmoil had kept her from concentrating. She wanted to write about Zelda; the water birds surfing the harbor waves; and the day's prize, the juvenile black-crowned night heron. She sat in the kitchen, drinking coffee, taking her time before heading to her desk.

She and the Institute for Avian Studies went back such a long way. There had been a rocky period — they had let her go immediately after her conviction. Being fired by letter, while in prison, had devastated her. But one day, fourteen months into her sentence, she had a visitor.

Ariel Blake, the institute's director, sat across the desk when Clare entered the room. Ariel in her stylish black suit and Clare in her prison greens had faced each other shakily; to this day Clare wasn't sure which of them had been more nervous.

"Hi, Clare."

"Hi, Ariel."

"How are you?"

"Well," Clare said, a light shrug as she smiled.

"We know you don't belong here," Ariel said. "I just wanted to be sure you knew that."

"Thank you," Clare said.

"Letting you go was very hard. Your work was integral in forming the alliance with Cornell."

Clare had connected with a former Columbia classmate, by then a researcher at the Cornell Lab of Ornithology, the premier center for bird studies. Clare had proposed an information sharing relationship, with the institute reporting on counts and behavior of New York City birds and the lab sharing its vast library and resources in fields such as bioacoustics, bird population studies, and ornithological diversity.

The excitement of that time and success seemed very far away. Clare wrapped her arms tightly around herself, as if she could keep Ariel from noticing her prison clothes.

"It was the board," Ariel said. "They felt it would be bad for fund-raising to keep you on."

"I understand," Clare said. "How could you have kept me? Honestly, I'm surprised you came to see me."

"I've been wanting to," Ariel said. "All

along I've been thinking we'll hire you back when you're released."

Clare's skin tingled. She had eight months of her sentence left to serve. Was it possible she could leave here and reenter her life? She and Ariel had never been close friends, but respectful colleagues. It startled and touched Clare to learn she'd been thinking of future collaboration.

"I would love that," Clare said. She remembered her desk in the corner of a treetop-height office overlooking Central Park from Fifth Avenue. Had they kept her bulletin board, all the bird photos, postcards from birders around the world, articles, and poems about nature? Were her research and field notes still in the black binders, shelved along with reports from Cornell?

"Here's my idea," Ariel said. "I've always loved your writing. Scientific and specific, yet never dry. Your love of New York nature shines through."

"Thank you," Clare said.

"We received a grant — from Cornell, in fact — to put out a newsletter about urban birds, notes from the field. I thought of you."

"Wow. Thank you."

"Here's the thing. There's been so much publicity about you, and the trial. The board of directors has some concerns. I thought, maybe at the beginning, till the newsletter finds its way, you could use a pen name — the way Janet Flanner wrote about Paris as 'Genet.' . . . Would you be willing? There's no one I'd want more than you."

Clare's eyes filled, and she clenched her fists to keep from losing it entirely. This was beyond anything she had dared to hope. "Ariel, you're saving my life. You have no idea what this means to me."

"You must miss mornings in the Ramble."

Clare nodded. "So much. I hear birds calling in the yard, and I close my eyes, pretend I'm walking toward Azalea Pond."

"Well, our goal is to get you back in the park."

"Eight months," Clare said. "I'll live through it, thanks to knowing you want me back."

And she did survive. Under the pen name of Snowy Owl, she'd put out four newsletters a year. People had loved the mystery, tried to guess her real identity. In the digital age the institute decided to save on paper, and the newsletter became a blog. Clare wrote entries at least five days a week, sometimes seven. And for that Ariel paid her with the grant money.

Clare continued writing as Snowy Owl,

but along the way she'd started giving bird walks and workshops. Word had leaked out, and most loyal readers discovered her identity. As time went by, the board of directors dropped its objection to her using her own name. To them, her conviction had been sixteen years and a lifetime ago. To Clare, being found guilty and the effects of prison would never leave her.

She refilled her coffee, returned to her desk. The Battery Park essay formed in her mind. She knew her readers would rush down to see the heron and Zelda. Having left her laptop open, she saw the screen was dark, in sleep mode. She clicked a key to wake it up, remembering she'd been looking at Frederik's Web site last night.

Expecting to see his glasswork, she was surprised instead to find an image of flowers, tiny orchids, backlit by a blazing sun. Clare leaned closer; the plant seemed to be rooted in mud.

The URL was GillisKnutRasmussen.dk. Clare moved her cursor, searching for a way to enter the site. When she clicked on an orchid, she felt a shiver go down her spine. Below the flower a search window and padlock appeared. The page was password-protected.

Grit had left the Web site open for Clare

to find, along with a Post-it note: *My mother's Web site. Can you figure out the password?* Clare stared with shock, and when she touched the picture, she felt a sudden, electric connection to Anne. She tried to guess the password, typed in "Grit," "Gillis," "Frederik," their birth dates, "Ebeltoft," "Glasmuseet." She tried the old beloveds: "Central Park," "Owl," "Chelsea." Sitting hunched at the desk, Clare realized she was trying to think like an Anne she no longer knew.

She wanted to wake up Grit, ask her about the site, when she'd discovered it, her ideas about what the password might be; it killed her to think she really had lost all access to her sister's thinking. Did the photo's composition mean something?

When they'd been young, their worlds had overlapped. Their frames of reference had been identical. Although Anne was older, she hung out with Clare instead of her own classmates. Perhaps it was always that way with sisters who lived in a troubled house. They stuck together, kept each other's and the family's secrets.

The Burkes went to church every Sunday. Dressing right, attending Mass, sitting in a front pew, and watching their father go up to the altar to give the first reading. There he would stand, in his perfect Paul Stuart suit, rep tie in a Windsor knot, with an easy smile yet holy tone of voice, standing with a casual, attractive slouch as he gripped the lectern, almost as if standing at a bar, about to make everyone his best friend.

Their mother had trained herself to seem oblivious to, even amused by, the women who would approach him after Mass, telling him what a beautiful speaking voice he had, had he ever considered doing television ads? Or even acting? This was New York, after all, and shocking to think he'd never been discovered.

"Aren't you a doll? But I'm a real estate man," he'd say and laugh self-effacingly. "This is a skyscraper city, and I want the skyline to soar so when I drive down the West Side Highway I can point into the sky and tell my girls, 'That's one of mine.' "

Such a loving family man!

He'd never missed a parent-teacher conference, always took off from work no matter how crazed his day was. He'd drive down to the Village, park in the garage of a building his company managed, and take careful notes about how the girls could improve.

And when he was home, he would work on that with them. Business was so demanding, he never knew when he'd have to meet the councilmen, or the police chiefs, or even the mayor. Yet when Clare's teacher said Clare was very shy and had a tough time with presentations and oral reports, her father would make her practice in front of him, offering suggestions about the timbre of her voice, her choice of clothes, even encouraging a little blush on her cheeks.

Clare's mother's lips would tighten, and Clare knew she didn't approve of the way her father's solutions came from the outside — looks, hair, a smile — as opposed to from within, the depths of a person's heart and brain.

One day, when she was thirteen and Anne fourteen, they went to the Jefferson Market Library after school, as they often did. It was late October, and Greenwich Village was spooky with Halloween decorations, including a witch and a spider web on the library's pointed tower.

Walking up Seventh Avenue toward home, they plotted out their costumes. Anne would be a witch who lived on the Brooklyn Bridge, and Clare would be a wood sprite who haunted Belvedere Castle.

They would buy leotards and a bolt of black chiffon, go to Central Park to collect ivy and berries for Clare's garlands and crown, tree bark for Anne's witch's hat. Anne would wear her black velvet cape. Every year they liked to top themselves.

Night was falling, streetlights were on. The restaurants and bars were flickering to life. As they walked they played a game: if we were grown up, where would we hang out tonight? Their taste was the same: they liked small, warmly lit cafés and trattorias that looked as if they could have been in Paris or Rome.

When they got to Riley's, a very old New York dive bar, they paused. The sisters were sure no one they knew ever went there, but drawing near, they hung back and stared, fascinated.

That late afternoon, they watched a cab pull up. Shockingly, their father climbed out, lighting a cigarette as he checked his watch. Seeing him outside Riley's cut Clare to the quick. Even worse, they spotted a woman hurrying down the street. Small, brunette, wearing a bright pink wool jacket they had seen in school that day: Miss Langtry, Anne's favorite teacher.

Could it be some kind of confused, horrible parent-teacher meeting? Those questions were erased instantly when they saw their father put his arms around Miss Langtry, kiss her the way they did it in the movies, and whisk her through the dark oak door with frosted-glass panels.

"Did you see?" Anne said.

"It wasn't, it couldn't have been him."

But they both knew it was.

They hurried home, and in the few blocks to their town house, they both became ill. Anne immediately developed a stomachache so terrible they had to call the doctor. Clare's anxiety overcame her with violent shivers and such a bad chill, her mother thought she must have the flu.

When their father got home later that night, telling their mother about his meeting with an investor who wanted to take over several posh hotels on Central Park South, Clare suddenly saw — her mother didn't believe him. She was only pretending to. Anne hid her head under her pillow so she wouldn't have to speak to him.

Their mother kept both girls home from school the next day. Clare felt better after breakfast, and even though Anne seemed subdued, she said she was fine. Their mother let them go to Central Park for air and sunshine. Going to the most overgrown sections, especially the Ramble, they gathered bayberry, bittersweet, laurel, and holly for their Halloween costumes.

"Do you think Mom knows?" Clare asked.

"Yes, but she'll never do anything. Hail Mary, full of grace, keep me deaf, blind, and numb so we don't split up our family."

"He was with your favorite teacher."

"Not anymore."

Their school had a lab program with Teachers College at Columbia. Junior and senior education majors would spend a semester shadowing real teachers. No matter what Anne said, Clare knew she loved Miss Langtry — she was smart, funny, not too strict. Anne glowed whenever Miss Langtry praised her math, science, and art, told her she could be a doctor or researcher someday.

"She doesn't care about me," Anne said, picking English ivy. "And guess what? Dad doesn't care about us. I swear I'm going to stab him with a butter knife tonight. Don't think I won't!"

The old butter knife; Clare was used to hearing Anne talk that way. She was always going to stab someone with the bluntest object possible.

The next day the sisters returned to school, and Clare saw Anne in the lunchroom. Miss Langtry called, inviting Anne to join her and a few other students, but Anne just strode past with her tray, eyes hard and jaw set. When Clare looked back now, she saw the incident as a line in the sand. Her father's betrayal broke Anne in a way that changed her forever.

Walking home from school that day, the sisters avoided Riley's. Instead of going straight home, Anne steered them into Guardian Angel, their family's small, beautiful Romanesque church on Tenth Avenue. They knelt by the altar to the Virgin Mary, and Anne lit a candle. Clare glanced at her sister — usually the family lit candles when someone was sick or dying.

"Who is it?" Clare whispered.

"Dad," Anne said, choking back a sob.

"What about him?"

"Why did he do that? He has Mom and us. Aren't we enough, Clare?"

"I thought we were," Clare said.

"So did I . . ."

One morning in December Anne told Clare to dress warmly and wear comfortable shoes. Anne informed their mother they wanted to try out studying at the New York Public Library's main branch instead of Jefferson Market.

Their mission involved no library at all. Anne stationed them behind a large potted shrub outside a coffee shop at the corner of Park Avenue and East Fifty-seventh Street, right across from their father's office building. Anne told Clare to watch the street-level revolving door.

It was late afternoon, and their father could be anywhere — showing property, closing a big deal at a lawyer's office, meeting with city officials about a shopping mall on Staten Island. The girls tried to convince themselves he was working hard, that Miss Langtry had been only an aberration — but with Christmas coming fast, his staying out late at night had gotten worse.

Clare tried to assure Anne that nothing bad could happen at his office. Marianne Doyle, a girl from church, had dropped out of Hunter College and was working as an assistant. Their father wouldn't dare misbehave in front of her. But Anne had a feeling, and wouldn't call off the stakeout.

Two days in a row, from their spy position, they saw him enter his office building in his Chesterfield topcoat, carrying his briefcase. Clare felt a shock of pride in their important, handsome father. She glanced at Anne, wanting to go home. Couldn't they just assume everything was fine?

But the next day her father climbed out of a taxi, smoked a cigarette on the street, pacing up and down the block while craning his neck to look up, as if he could see straight into his office. The distant longing in his eyes made Clare feel she was going over the rim of a roller coaster.

Clare was cold, her stomach hurt, and she wanted to go home. She felt electricity pouring off Anne, and it scared her. But before she could speak, the revolving door spit a familiar person onto the sidewalk: the oldest Doyle daughter, dressed the way she did at church every Sunday, beaming in the presence of the girls' father.

"No!" Clare said, stunned.

"Of all the people," Anne said. "I can't stand it! Jesus, Clare."

They followed them down Park Avenue, passed St. Bart's Episcopal Church, the round gold dome glinting like a Byzantine citadel in the last light, and crossed the street toward a stocky yet soaring building. It was the Waldorf-Astoria, where many Christmas dances were held.

"Let's leave," Clare said, feeling sick.

"Come on," Anne said, closing the distance between them and their father so fast, Clare thought she was going to confront him. But she didn't. They watched him go to the long receptionist's counter, pay money, and get a key. Then he put his hand on the Doyle girl's back, steering her toward the elevator.

The lobby thronged with business travelers. Anne pulled Clare behind a column and bellowed, "Marianne Doyle!"

The girl glanced around nervously, his arm around her waist. "Repent, Marianne!" Anne yelled, then she and Clare hid behind a waiter rolling a cart into the Peacock Lounge. When they looked again, their father and Marianne had gone up in the elevator.

Anne rushed through the lobby, around the corner from the reception desk, to a long bank of pay phones. While Clare listened, she called information and asked for Doyle on West Nineteenth Street.

"What are you doing?" Clare asked.

"Telling on her. She deserves to be punished for this."

"It's not her fault, it's Dad's!"

"It's both of theirs," Anne said.

"Mrs. Doyle?" Anne said, muffling her voice. "I know you want to do what's right, and I thought you should know that Marianne is screwing a married man right now at the Waldorf-Astoria." Anne listened intently, then held the phone out so Clare could hear the mother crying.

A week later, sitting at the dinner table, their mother asked their father why Marianne Doyle had quit her job.

"Who said she did?" he asked, slicing into the roast beef.

"Her mother told me. She said there was a 'sinful atmosphere' at the company. Those were her exact words. What do you think she meant?" she asked, glaring at him.

"Oh, I don't know," he said. "Those Doyles are sheltered. Midtown's a different world from Chelsea. Maybe she just wasn't cut out for it."

"I have the feeling it's more than that. She sounded very cold and practically hung up on me," she said, frowning as she took a small bite of her own meat — the heel, overcooked and gristly. Clare glared at her mother, angry because she gave him the best pieces while taking the worst for herself.

"What is it, Clare?" her father asked, catching her gaze.

"Things should be better," she said, arms folded across her chest.

"We're having a nice dinner. Eat your roast beef."

"We saw you with Marianne," Clare said.

Her mother grabbed her wrist and shook it hard. Clare jerked back, more from the shock than the pain. "I'm sorry, sweetheart," her mother said. "It's just, we don't talk that way in this house. Your father is right — we have a lovely roast beef dinner."

Her father's face started turning red.

"Dad," Anne said, "if Marianne quit, maybe I could help out. I'm sure you do need help, right? And I'd like to —"

"My girls do not have to work," he said. "Your only job is excelling at school, getting into a good college, making your mother and me proud. Office workers come and go. I hardly even notice."

Clare hated him for that. She thought of all the lies: her mother's, her father's, the way she and Anne had been lulled into going along with them.

"Can we please have a peaceful dinner?" he asked.

She excused herself and walked into the bathroom. She felt as if she were going to be sick, but nothing happened. She just stayed there for a long time, hoping everyone would have left the table by the time she came out.

When she opened the door, she found her mother standing there. Her father's and Anne's voices drifted in from the dining room; they were talking as if everything was fine. Clare didn't want to meet her mother's eyes, but she felt arms around her.

"It's going to be okay," her mother said.

"How?" Clare asked.

"Because it has to be," her mother said.

No wonder Anne had learned how to lie to herself.

Now, after too many wrong guesses, the password window disappeared from Anne's site, leaving just the image of orchids growing in the mud. Clare stared for a minute, then gave up and went to waken Grit.

CHAPTER NINE

"Good morning."

Grit dragged herself out of deep sleep. She looked up at Clare, standing beside her bed with a mug of coffee. Grit struggled to sit up, shake dreams from her mind, and wonder if she was in trouble, her default mode of greeting the day.

"Morning," Grit said.

"Did you sleep well?"

"I did, thank you," Grit said as Clare handed her the coffee. She remembered that she'd left her mother's Web site open on Clare's computer. Sipping coffee, she waited for her to mention it. Her stomach flipped as she tensed up, ready for what was coming.

"Do you have plans today?" Clare asked, sitting at the end of the bed.

"Not really," Grit said.

"I thought I'd take the day off so we could spend it together."

"You're not mad at me?"

Clare hesitated, seeming to choose her words carefully. "I'm worried," she said. "But not mad."

"I'm sorry for everything," Grit said. The words spilled out, as natural to her as breathing. She meant "everything" — in her family she'd learned to apologize for her existence.

"Grit, everything's okay. I just want to understand."

Drinking coffee, Grit prepared herself to be grilled — about last night's lies, and the Web site, and what she was really doing here. But Clare stood, gave her a kind of devilish smile.

"Get ready. We're heading out."

"Where?"

"I'm not exactly sure. I thought we'd have an adventure day."

"What's that?" Grit asked.

"A day out in the city, with no particular destination, when anything can happen."

"Did you make it up?"

"My mother did," Clare said. "When your mom and I were little, and school was out, she'd take us exploring. We'd all get to choose things to do, not planned in advance, but as they come up. I'm cheating a tiny bit. I have the first destination in mind."

The minute she left the room Grit climbed out of bed. Standing in the shower, she felt her stomach calming down; Clare wasn't mad after all, but Grit still felt uneasy. She was used to the adults in her life saying one thing but meaning another. Drying off, she checked her tattoos. They were healing nicely.

"What a familiar scent," Clare said when Grit entered the kitchen, dressed and ready.

"Violet shampoo."

"And you said you don't take after your mother."

"It's one thing of hers I loved."

"Someday I'll tell you about Anne and violets."

"Are we going to talk about the Web site?"

"Oh, yeah," she said. Grit waited, but that was all.

It was pouring out, so they pulled on jackets and left the house with black umbrellas. An hour later they hurried from the 6 train's Eighty-sixth Street stop to the Metropolitan Museum of Art. The vast Beaux Arts building rose up from Fifth Avenue, gray in the rain.

Climbing the broad stone stairs, Grit looked up at colorful exhibition banners hanging between Greek columns and remembered coming to this museum long ago, with her mother and Gilly. Had that day in New York been an adventure day and her mother just forgotten to mention it?

Grit and Clare checked their coats and umbrellas and walked through the Great Hall, where four alcoves contained enormous vases towering with brilliant orange, rust, and yellow flowers. Clare showed her membership card at the desk and was given two green metal disks marked with the Met's Renaissance "M" logo.

Climbing the wide center staircase, they passed the large paintings by Tiepolo. They spoke to Grit: intense blue sky, angels, and violence. She walked alongside Clare, into the European painting galleries.

Grit felt a secret love for the prettiness painted by French Impressionists; their too-lovely-to-be-believed worldview, and their happy family–perfect garden subject matter. Renoir painted mothers and children in scenes she wished had come from her life.

Rounding the corner they stopped beside Rousseau's *The Repast of the Lion.* Grit gazed at the flowering jungle, blood dripping down the mouth of a male lion as it devoured its prey.

"You know what I see in Rousseau?" Clare asked.

"Nature, obviously."

"Yeah. The beauty of it. But always with brutality."

Now Clare turned a half-step to face Rousseau's *Soleil Rouge* (*Red Sun*). Grit moved beside her for a better look.

The canvas was twelve by sixteen inches. Rousseau had painted a red sun glowing over mud flats. From a mound of loam grew one single plant: delicate green leaves and curved stem, three purple bell-shaped blossoms. In spite of the flower's beauty, the painting made Grit feel sick.

"Why did you want me to see this?" she asked.

"Why did you want me to see that Web page?"

"You could have just asked me. You didn't have to bring me here."

"I had to show you, so you'd understand. When we were young and would come to the museum, your mother always wanted to see this painting. Doesn't it remind you of the photograph?"

"They all go together," Grit said, stunned.

"What do?"

"This painting, her photo, the flower, the red sun, the bog," Grit said.

"What bog?"

"The one in the picture on her Web site. My father used the peat's iron ore to color his glass, and my mother would look for wildflowers. Gilly . . . he was obsessed with the bog people."

"Who are they?"

"People murdered hundreds of years ago. Their bodies were thrown in the bogs, and they'd be perfectly preserved. Mummies. That's where we'd go to hang out. Gilly wrote about them for a school report. He . . ." She wanted to tell Clare, but couldn't make herself say the words.

"Where is he, Grit?" Clare asked. "You never talk about Gilly at all. Did your parents kick him out too?"

She shook her head. "No."

"Tell me about him."

Grit glanced around. Could she find her way? She wanted to tell Clare everything, but even thinking about saying the words filled her with panic. She stared at Rousseau's painting of the red sun. She inched closer, and a guard stepped forward, his body language warning her not to touch it.

"You know how I found my mother's Web site?" she asked, still gazing at the sun.

"How?"

"Googling my brother's name. My mother had tagged the Web site 'Gillis Knut Rasmussen.' "

"What are you telling me, Grit? Why were

you looking for him online? Don't you know where he is?"

"I just felt like looking for his name; it made me feel close to him. There's a painting I want to show you, okay?"

Clare nodded.

Grit led them away from Rousseau's works. She headed through the rooms, steered more by instinct and a childhood impression than actual memory.

When they entered the gallery where the J.M.W. Turner paintings soared, Grit's heart sped up. She walked straight past the great oils of seascapes and Royal Navy battle scenes to a wall of less dramatic works. There it was: an 8 3/8 × 11-inch watercolor and gouache over graphite.

Fog and Steam," Clare said, reading the legend. Mist hovered above a marsh. Will-o-the-wisps, greenish orbs caused by swamp gas, lit the fog from within.

"You know what makes those lights glow?" Grit asked. "Decaying biological matter. Could be vegetation, could be bog people. Like the ones I told you about."

"Spooky, but beautiful," Clare said.

"Similar theme to my mother's photograph. Just different weather conditions," Grit said.

"Is this the painting that reminds you of

Gilly?" Clare asked.

Grit nodded. "Did you know peat is very fragile? A footprint can last a year. His did. I know, because my mother and I would go back."

"What happened?"

"One day he just walked into the fog. He was fifteen."

"The fog?"

"Mist, thick over the bog. I watched him go." She paused, gathering her breath. "And he didn't come out," she said.

"Oh, Grit," Clare said, and they clutched each other. Grit could feel her aunt shaking, and that allowed the tears to flow, knowing she felt the loss, too. Standing there in Clare's arms, Grit was thirteen again.

The drive to Grauballe had taken a long time because of the thick fog. Their mother had spent the ride praising Gilly's schoolwork, maybe overly so. She was trying to make up for their father's outburst; earlier that day he had ripped up Gillis's entire science report on bog ecology, geothermal vents, and how they helped preserve the bog people.

Their father had read the report and been furious: Gillis's discussion of temperature at the earth's core had been faulty. Did Gillis know what would happen if the fire in his studio was off by a single degree — even half a degree?

Such an error would cause disaster — potentially a fatal one. Glass artists had been critically injured by such carelessness. Didn't Gillis respect his father's work enough to be precise in matters of temperature? After he destroyed Gillis's report, he shouted at their mother.

"You cow! Raising such a stupid, disrespectful son!"

"It's not Mom's fault," Gilly had said, stepping between them.

"Stay out of it," their father said, smacking his head.

"Frederik!" their mother said, grabbing his arm. He shook her loose and backhanded her across the mouth.

"Don't you know how to do anything? You spoil the children, you take their side, you've raised an idiot for a son. I'm done with all of you." He stalked out of the house toward his studio.

Their mother wiped the blood off her mouth, checked Gilly's head. A lump was starting to form behind his ear; she took an ice pack from the freezer, pressed it to the spot. She told them they were going for a ride, and they got into the car. Driving through Ebeltoft, Grit felt everyone's desperation. The fog outside seemed to mirror the heaviness in the car.

"Don't let him get to you," Grit whispered. "You know how he is."

Gillis didn't reply. He hardly ever talked — not just to Grit, but to anyone. He'd been turning inward, ignoring his friends, refusing to speak.

"You're the smartest boy in school," she continued. "*He's* the idiot for putting down your report."

Gillis stared straight ahead. The blankness of his expression made him seem calm, at such odds with the passion Grit felt. When they got to the bog, their mother gathered her things and strode ahead. Why didn't she say something, hug Gilly, say that what their father had done was unforgivable?

"He's wrong about the earth's temperature," he said to Grit.

"All he cares about is how many degrees it takes to melt glass," Grit said. "He's an asshole."

"This bog would be a good place to study," Gillis said. "If someone could measure deep into the core, the temperature would surprise everyone. He should try that sometime. Learn more about something that supposedly inspired him so much."

"He's 'finished' with bogs forever, remember?" Grit asked, trying to get him to smile.

"Maybe not," he said. "Maybe he'll never forget it."

Their mother was a dark shadow in the fog; if she took a few steps farther, they'd lose sight of her, so Grit hurried Gilly along. They stopped in a familiar spot, where their mother found some of her best flowers for pressing. She had brought a basket for them to fill.

"Are you going to help?" she asked.

"Yeah," Grit said.

Picking flowers seemed insane after what they'd just been through. Their mother had been cool enough to get them out of the house, but now she was numbing herself out again instead of dealing with the nightmare. She made little money selling her pressed flowers at the gift shop, and all their father ever did was ridicule her for doing it.

"Gilly, you're so quiet," their mother said while she and Grit filled the basket. He didn't reply, and when they turned to look, he wasn't there.

The fog had been thick but it seemed to thin in that moment, sun starting to shine through: just enough to silhouette the body of a tall boy walking into the middle of the bog.

"Gilly!" Grit screamed.

"Sweetheart, stop, don't take another step," their mother called. "Oh God, Gilly, don't move, you'll sink."

But they heard the slurping sounds of his feet walking, each step a little deeper. Now the sun went away and the fog thickened again, and all they could hear was the terrible sucking, hating it but wanting it to continue because once it stopped he was gone.

"I'm coming out to get you," their mother cried. She began to tear off her jacket, boots, socks, trying to make herself as light as possible. Grit tried to hold her back, but her mother tore away, flew over the hard path into the soggy ground, practically swimming through the thigh-deep mud. Grit plunged after her, clinging to her waist.

"Go back," her mother said, pushing her hard, barely seeing Grit — her entire focus was on her son and the mist-obscured bog.

"Mom, Gilly!" Grit wept. She felt the mud, cool on top, pulling her down into warmth. Small and thin, the more she struggled, the more Grit went down.

"Gilly!" her mother yelled, plodding out, away from Grit. "Sweetheart, come back!"

"Mommy," Grit said as the mud rose to her waist, chest. Her arms flailed as she tried to move toward her mother and she swallowed her first mouthful. She gagged, choked, panicked.

Her mother was ten yards away from her, also chest high. Grit's eyes met hers, and she saw the terrible decision she'd forced her to make. Turning her back on Gillis, her mother made it to Grit in three long steps. She wrapped her arms around her, hauled her free of the bog, and together they crawled up the bank.

Grit froze, listening. She heard only silence, and that made her scream.

"Gillis!" she cried.

Her mother held her, wiping mud from her eyes, nose, and ears. The fog swaddled them in peace, and Grit saw terror and grief in her mother's eyes as they sat together beside the basket of beautiful mud flowers.

Clare and Grit left the Met, bundled up against the stiff November wind. The rain had stopped, so they headed west across Central Park. As they walked past Cleopatra's Needle, Clare reached for Grit's hand.

"Are you okay?" she asked.

"Yes," Grit said.

"I know you can't be," Clare said.

"I'm glad I told you," Grit said. "It was strange being with you, knowing you had no idea about Gillis."

"Was it hard to tell me?"

Grit nodded.

They headed through the park, hearing wind in the trees above. Clare held Grit's hand tighter. When they reached the cedar trees, she directed Grit's gaze into the thick branches. It took a moment, but Grit spotted the sleeping owls. Clare felt her niece's arm tense as she focused her attention into the heart of the tree.

"They're long-eared owls," Clare said. "I like to think they're descendants of the ones your mother and I used to see."

Cold light trickled through the branches and fine green needles, and the longer they stared, the more obvious the owl shapes became.

"Do you think it's possible?" Grit asked. "That he's still alive?"

"Gilly?" Clare asked, surprised.

"Why couldn't he be?" Grit asked. "What if he walked in and just kept going? He might have climbed out the other side."

"I don't know," Clare said gently.

"It's an adventure day, that's what you said," Grit said. "I want the adventure to take me back in time, to make Gillis be alive. If my mother hadn't grabbed me, she could have gone after him. Saved him."

"Oh, Grit —"

"The police looked for Gilly and didn't find him. My father let them stop searching. I *never* would have; they'd *still* be looking if it were up to me."

"And your mother?"

"She went along with whatever he said."

"Oh God, Anne," Clare said, filled with sorrow and frustration for her sister.

They continued their walk. Heading past the Boathouse Café and around the lake, they entered the dark and mysterious Ramble. Navigating twisting paths, they walked in silence except for a downy woodpecker working the bark of a maple tree near Azalea Pond.

Birders walked the paths, nodding to Clare. After a while she and Grit were alone on the trail, lost in the sound of bare branches clicking and brushing overhead. A white-crowned sparrow flew ahead of them, leading them into adventure. It felt like a fairy-tale forest, and Clare could easily imagine an almost-extinct owl seeking refuge here.

"Tell me about Gilly," Clare said.

"He would love this walk."

"Did you and he walk together?"

"Yes. On the beach a lot. We'd look for shells and fossils. And in the fields. We hung out with each other's friends, never at our house, though. Our father hated everyone we liked."

"I think your father hates everyone."

Grit glanced up, looking relieved to hear Clare finally speaking about Frederik.

They crossed the Lake's upper lobe and emerged on Central Park West. The sun looked white through thin clouds and cast pale shadows on the sidewalks. "When you mentioned an adventure day," Grit said, "I'm sure you didn't know I was going to lay something so heavy on you."

"I'm glad you talked to me," Clare said.

"You would have loved Gilly."

"I know," Clare said.

"I have more to tell you," Grit said, her gaze lightening.

"What is it?"

Grit smiled. "Not yet."

"Whatever you say. Let's get something to eat, are you hungry?"

"Starving."

The Upper West Side had cozy restaurants on Columbus and Amsterdam avenues and tucked away on the side streets. Clare took Grit to Caruso's, a favorite of hers and Paul's — a tiny, dark Italian place that specialized in thin-crust pizza cooked in a wood-fired brick oven.

Stepping inside, they instantly warmed up. Autographed photos of great opera stars adorned the red brick walls. Maria Callas singing "Una Macchia" from *Macbeth* played from speakers in the ceiling. The handsome young waiter identified it for them while taking their order.

"It's the sleepwalking scene," he said, dropping off glasses of water. "I'd have given anything to see Callas sing."

"Guess he really loves opera," Grit said.

"Maybe he sings himself," Clare said. "Lincoln Center is just around the corner."

Clare's phone vibrated: a text from Paul. Can you meet now?

She hesitated, remembering their earlier texts about meeting in the park's northern section and she texted back: At caruso's, in the midst with g. Will you go and let me know what you see?

Yep, he replied. The problem with texts was that they made it really hard to pick up someone's tone. But in this case, Clare felt the chill there. She sensed him wanting to be invited to join them, but this wasn't the moment.

She looked up, saw Grit watching her. "Everything okay?" Grit asked.

"Fine," Clare said, just as the waiter brought their pizza margherita. They helped

241

themselves and ate in silence for a while. Clare kept her phone close, in case Paul texted back. "So, tell me about Maine. Why were you there?"

"Oh," Grit said. "I needed somewhere to go. My old college roommate let me use her family cabin, near Mount Katahdin."

"You must have been so lonely up there. I wish you had come here right away."

"I was afraid to at first. I didn't know how you'd feel about me." Grit stared at her plate, then looked up. "Besides, there are bogs in Maine. I shot up there."

"Filming wetlands, you said," Clare said.

Grit's eyes were luminous, meeting Clare's gaze. "My project has to do with resurrection," she said. "Restoration and resurgence. Everything I believe about nature."

"I feel that, too," Clare said. "The earth is wild, and it goes on no matter what. I thought about that when I was . . ."

Grit waited for Clare to finish her sentence.

"When I was in prison," Clare said. "It gave me hope to think of the seasons changing, life going on."

Grit smiled.

"I can't wait to see what you've done. What does it, well, look like?"

"I set up my camera, and I build things

from whatever is there — fallen branches, stones, dry grass." She gave Clare a sidelong glance. "I never know what's going to be there, so it's always a surprise. It's just . . . when I get to the bog, and let my thoughts settle, I feel something. Clare, it's the most wonderful thing. I feel Gilly. As if he's laying these things at my feet. As if he's sending me gifts, from wherever he is."

"It sounds incredible."

"It is," Grit said.

"How do you 'feel' Gilly? Is he with you?"

"Of course, but not in a spooky way, not like a ghost. More like . . . air. Clear, bright air. Earlier, when I said I wish he would come back to life — I do, more than anything. But going to bogs, finding what he's left for me — it's even better, in a way. I can't explain it. I wish you could feel it too. Maybe you will —"

"I can't wait to see your film, and to go to a bog with you. There's one in the city — on Staten Island; excellent bird habitat."

"I know. I researched before I came."

"Is that your main reason for being here?" Clare asked.

Grit tilted her head. "What do you think?"

"I . . . guess I hope not."

"You're the reason. Bogs are everywhere. I'm just happy there's one near you. Know

243

how I found out about it?"

"No."

"From your blog," Grit said. "See, I've been stalking you forever. I thought I dreamed you into existence, all those bad years. Then I came here and made you real. You're real, Aunt Clare."

"So are you, Grit," Clare said.

Paul approached the Blockhouse, where they'd received the report of an unknown raptor, and knew this was a combination labor of love and fool's errand. Here he was, playing along with the fallacy that a pair of owls dropped in Central Park in 1900 had somehow produced a descendant that had decided to wait more than a hundred years to prove that the entire species was not extinct.

"Shit," he said, tripping over a fallen branch. He lugged it out of the way, doing some other ranger's job for him. Everything ticked him off right now. He was hungry, had been waiting to hear from Clare, assumed they'd have dinner after meeting up. He could practically taste Caruso's pizza right now.

That was another thing. As patient as he tried to be, he couldn't understand how Grit could be here this long without Clare introducing them. They didn't live together, they didn't see each other every day — sometimes he felt lucky to see her once a week. She always dangled the hope that things would change.

Yet here he was, at the edge of the North Woods, chasing her phantom owl while she went to their place with a niece he wondered if he'd ever meet. All that talk on the ferry had probably meant nothing. He was so sick of being the prototypical sensitive man, waiting for her to heal from her years in prison and the loss of the sister who'd put her there.

"Hey, no dogs off the leash!" he yelled at a couple letting their bulldog run free.

They continued on, ignoring him.

"Want a citation?" he called, and they just kept going.

He walked uphill toward the Blockhouse, the oldest building in Central Park. The ruin was an old fort, built in 1814 to stave off a possible British invasion, on a foundation dating back to the Revolutionary War. He shined his flashlight on the rocky path to see where he was going. If an owl was around — and it wouldn't be a fucking Whekau, that was for sure — he'd spook it, and he barely cared.

He unlocked the fort's metal gate, let

himself in. The stone building was stuffy and damp; shafts of city light came through narrow gun ports. Pigeons roosted in here; the place smelled like two hundred years' worth of guano. Listening, he expected to hear cooing, and feathers rustling.

When he didn't, he began to swing his flashlight beam into the rafters. No birds. He shined the light down, walked across the floor. Urban Park Rangers kept the place decent; they gave occasional tours, so most of the bird shit was cleaned out.

The beam picked up two small oval shapes, about a yard apart. He crouched to examine them. Owls ate mice and birds, coughed up the bones, skulls, fur, and feathers they couldn't digest. One of the pellets looked slick and recent, the other as if it had been there for a while. An owl had moved in, chased the pigeons away. He shined the beam around the fort again, looking for yellow eyes. But it was nighttime, and the owl would be hunting.

Now he pulled out his phone. He stared at the last text, wondered if Clare and Grit were still at Caruso's.

Hey, you still at dinner?

He could head down there now. Or maybe they could come to the fort, meet him here, wait for the owl to return. It would be an eastern screech owl, or maybe a great horned owl — not the phantom Clare wished for, but still exciting. Waiting for Clare to reply, he used a pen to break apart the dry pellet. It contained gray fur and the tiny skull, femurs, and rib cage of a mouse.

No, we're heading home.

Come up to the blockhouse

What did you find?

Owl pellets

Holy s!

Yeah. come up. bring grit.

Can't now. tomorrow instead?

No, i'll be at fbf.

Floyd Bennett Field.

Ok, i'll go too. See you there.

Whatever, he would have written, but didn't bother. Hey, he wrote. It's not a whekau pellet.

No? How do you know?

Her question was valid — papers written by Alistair Fastnet and Walter Buller said the laughing owl's diet had been the same as any other owl: small mammals, birds, amphibians.

Because the fucking bird's extinct, he wrote.

She didn't respond. Leaving the Blockhouse and locking up behind him, he felt slightly sick. Probably from being shut up for so long, he told himself.

247

CHAPTER TEN

Early in the morning Clare took the 2 train to Flatbush Avenue, then the Q35 bus to the far reaches of Queens, and felt ready for a fight. The long ride from Brooklyn College to Rockaway Beach took her through neighborhoods she wouldn't see otherwise, gave her a long time to think. She held her notebook, but didn't write anything. After an amazing day with Grit, Paul's text had felt like a slap.

She walked from the bus stop into a sharp wind straight off the ocean. Approaching Floyd Bennett Field, she took a deep breath. This was one of New York's sacred places. Named for the man who'd been first to fly over the North Pole, the airport had originally been built on Barren Island in Jamaica Bay. Robert Moses, the urban planner and impresario, had brought in landfill to connect it with the mainland.

Taking off from this field, Amelia Earhart

had set her many records: first woman to fly transatlantic solo; first woman to fly transatlantic twice; first woman to fly transcontinental without stopping. Then, after serving as New York's first municipal airport, the field was converted into a naval air station in 1941, and became the United States' busiest airport during World War II.

But to Clare, Paul, and most urban nature lovers, it was a haven for birds. The North Forty Woods and grasslands, even the old runways overgrown with weeds and bushes, were alive with late migratory birds and winter residents. Walking faster, she glanced around, trying to imagine what this place would be like if private development was allowed.

She hurried toward the far end of the parking lot, closest to the beach. Paul's Jeep was parked there; he sat inside, staying warm, obviously waiting for her. She slowed down as he turned off the engine, climbed out. He wore a big down parka over his ranger uniform. They stood a foot apart, neither one of them making the first move.

"I would have given you a ride," he said.

"I wasn't sure you really wanted me to come."

"Yeah, that's it," he said.

"Well, after that text."

"How was Caruso's with Grit?"

"Is that what you're upset about? Me having dinner with my niece?"

He glared at her, and she felt embarrassed. She knew that wasn't the problem. He held a clipboard. A blue page flapped in the wind, and he smacked it down. She saw the checklist of concerns sent in by birders worried about development. Clare saw that he'd added his own notes.

"What have you got?" she asked, moving to relatively neutral territory.

"Dave Brill's worried about light pollution if they beef up the parking lot. Roberta Sokolowski thinks more bathrooms will cause runoff. Any kind of building will destroy habitat and screw up Jamaica Bay."

"They're right," Clare said.

"I was about to head over to Dead Horse Bay and check out shorebirds. Make a count."

"Let's go," Clare said.

They hiked onto a dirt road and found an abandoned, burned-out yellow school bus behind a row of scrub pines. A joyride had ended in a bonfire. Paul called park headquarters, told them about it.

They walked onto a narrow, rocky beach, surprising a flock of a hundred snow buntings, flying and wheeling away in a white

250

cloud. An oldsquaw — long-tailed duck — bobbed in the bay's small waves. A male common merganser dove for fish. Thirteen black skimmers and nine scoters mixed with small flocks of common and laughing gulls resting on the beach. Seven purple sandpipers darted along the tide line. Paul made note of them all.

The rough beach was littered with old bottles. Before the airfield's creation in 1931, Barren Island had been home to rendering plants, a fertilizer factory, incinerators, and a dump. Generations later the beach gave up long-buried refuse, mainly glass bottles and horse bones from the rendering station.

"So, I'm serious," he said. "How was dinner with Grit? She like Caruso's?"

"She loved it. We had a long talk."

"I can imagine there's a lot to cover."

"Yeah. That's why I couldn't run uptown to meet you."

"You could have brought her."

"I know, Paul. But it wasn't the right time."

"No?" he asked, eyes narrowed as if he wasn't sure there'd ever be a right time. She felt like shoving him.

"No," she said. "Can't you trust me to know?"

"I think you've just found another way to keep me out."

"She didn't come here to 'keep you out.' "

"I'm not blaming her."

"Good. Because this is big for both of us."

"Why did she come?"

"She needs me," Clare said, and let out a long exhale. "Paul, her brother killed himself in a bog in Denmark."

Paul stopped. "Oh, God."

"He was only fifteen. Grit saw him do it. Anne, too."

"That poor kid."

"I know, and Anne."

"Fuck Anne," Paul said. "I hope she blames herself."

"Don't say that! It's all Frederik. You should hear what he did to Gilly the day he died."

"Look, we know Frederik's a monster. But Anne . . . this isn't new to you, Clare. She's dropped the ball with everyone she loves. You! Do you need me to remind you? And us too, you know?"

Clare walked ahead, trying to breathe.

"She puts Frederik first," Paul said. "And it destroys everyone around her. Maybe he controls her, but she lets him."

"No!" Clare said. "She's abused — she doesn't have a choice anymore. I'm reading her diary. You have no idea what it's like for her."

"And I don't care," Paul said. "Forget being a sister — she's a mother. And her own kid killed himself. Doesn't that tell you everything?"

"It tells me she's going through hell."

"Anne doesn't deserve any loyalty from you," Paul said. He'd been holding an old beach-worn bottle, but now threw it, smashing the glass on the rocks. "Jesus Christ, how can you stand to say one good thing about her? After Gillis killing himself? And after what she did to you?"

"She's still my sister."

"She hasn't acted like one in decades, Clare. Got that? Decades. She sent you to prison and didn't bat an eye. I saw her on that witness stand, lying through her teeth, so calm. She threw you into a snake pit for the sake of her selfish, selfish husband."

Clare trembled with rage — the experience of prison still lived in her body.

"Why are you doing this?" she asked. "She hurt me, okay? I've faced it. Now I'm trying to talk to you, and I want you to understand —"

"She hurt me too!" Paul bellowed, scaring every bird into swift flight. "We were going to be married. I watched you shrink and withdraw, turn into a woman I didn't know. I still wanted you, Clare. I would have waited forever — two years was nothing. But you couldn't handle that. You fucking broke up with me."

"That was years ago," Clare said, her voice cracking. "I'm here with you now, aren't I?"

"What a joke that is," Paul said. "You're too proud even to let me drive you out here. You had to take an hour-and-a-half-goddamn-long bus ride. And now we're having our special time squeezed into my workday, and it will end really soon because you'll have to get going home to write your blog, or meet your niece, or whatever."

"If you feel that way, why do you even want me? You're the one who moved on with someone else, by the way."

"Only because you fucking forced me."

The sea wind blew his hair into his eyes, and he roughly pushed it away.

"It didn't take much," Clare said. "You were with her while I was still in prison."

"No," he said. "And don't twist it. Even after I gave in and stopped visiting, I'd write you. If I got one letter back for every ten I sent, that was a lot. All I could think was how you wanted me gone."

"You couldn't read my mind. You don't know what I was thinking."

"Why didn't you try to tell me?"

"I was locked in," she said. "Not just behind walls, but in my mind. Do you have any idea? Everything I loved in life was over." Her chest ached, as if she'd just climbed a mountain into thin air. "Our life together was finished. No matter how or why, it just was."

"What are we doing?" he asked. "Why do we even meet?"

She made herself breathe. They stood there for a minute, not looking at each other. Clare turned toward him, reached for his hands. His fingers felt cold, and she pulled his arms around her body, slid his hands up under her jacket, where it was warm. Her heart raced.

"We meet because —" She stopped. "I love you."

They stood so still, looking into each other's eyes.

"And I love you," he said.

Clare smiled. They didn't move for a long time, and he began to smile, too.

"Did you mean what you said in your text?" she asked. "Or were you just mad?"

"I was mad," he said, still holding her hand. "But I meant what I wrote."

"Then what's in those photographs?"

"I don't know. But that owl hasn't lived in

the park since 1900."

Clare took his words in. She knew she should try to persuade him to keep searching and believing, but she'd started to feel a shift inside. It was as if she were looking at the tourist's photo for the first time, only this time seeing something completely different: a Cooper's hawk, not uncommon to the park. Which was it? The return of a rare bird or a visit from an old friend? Clare closed her eyes for a minute, hoping for the impossible.

The police had arrived and were boarding the torched school bus. A City of New York tow truck idled, waiting to haul it away. Clare and Paul sat atop a small dune between the bus and the water, listening to police radio chatter. Beneath that they heard the constant roar of Atlantic waves, breaking on Rockaway Beach across the bay.

Clare turned her head, stared out at the ocean and blue sky. Her love for Paul had never died, but it had changed. Maybe she wasn't quite so desperate to prove the existence of an extinct owl because she was right here with Paul, they were still in each other's lives, and they weren't going anywhere.

"People get addicted," Dennis said. "I've

seen it."

"This isn't an addiction. I just want one more," Grit said, trying to keep her voice from shaking.

He gave her a cockeyed smile as if he'd heard that before. They sat in his booth at the Green Dragon, Dennis's laptop between them. Grit pulled up her mother's Web page, then found an image of Rousseau's *Soleil Rouge.*

Today Dennis wore his hair down and a brown Coney Island T-shirt under his leather vest. She felt the warmth of his arm against hers as he studied the pictures.

"So you're saying you want an amalgamation of the two — the flower in the photo and the one in the painting?"

"Yes," Grit said, impressed that he knew so quickly what she wanted. "You have an artist's eye."

"I wanted to be. I got into Cooper Union, wanted to study painting, but went off course. I wound up down on East Second Street, hanging out with Tsao, this guy who's been tattooing the Hells Angels for thirty years."

"It's still art," she said.

"Thanks," he said. "But this will be your third tattoo in less than a week. For some people, that's normal. But you have such pure skin, only four tattoos on your whole body. This is a big step."

"An artist and a psychologist," Grit said.

"My mother's a psychologist," he said. "Growing up around it does affect the way you see people."

"How do you see me?" Grit asked.

"I don't know yet," he said. "I want to find out."

"Do the flower, and I'll tell you everything."

Dennis studied the images, sketched out a stencil. "Obviously the painting inspired the photographer. Who took the picture?"

"My mother." Her voice started to break, but she swallowed hard, got herself under control. "She searched the bog, found the exact flower from her favorite painting."

"Huh," he said. She felt him watching her.

"What?" she asked. "You want to know why I'm getting this tattoo if I hate her so much?"

"Kind of," he said.

"Let's just say it's complicated," she said. "Okay?"

"Yeah, fine." Concentrating hard, he transferred the stencil to her inner forearm. He began to remove the needles from their sterile pouches, then loaded the machine.

Grit's stomach clenched, anticipating

pain. The needle hovered, making the moment exquisite and intense. She stared at her arm, the purple stencil a replica of the image she'd been holding in her mind since visiting the Met. Her eyes filled, and her breath caught with a little gasp.

"I can't do it," Dennis said, turning off the machine.

"Why?" she asked, instantly hurt and offended. He hadn't even kissed her this time.

"I want to say because your skin is too beautiful, and that's true. But also because you seem upset."

"I am sad, it's true. But I still want the flower," she said, holding back tears.

He gave her a tilting smile, full of compassion. She shook as she grabbed her jacket. If she didn't get out of here in five seconds, she'd lose it. When she turned to run, he put his arms around her from behind.

"Why are you doing this?" she asked as he rocked her.

"Because I care about you, and I can't work on you while you're like this. I have my own ethics."

"I might be a little emotional," she said. "But that's why I need the flower. I'll explain if it will make you understand."

"Okay," he said, sounding eager, as she'd known he would.

"I lost my brother," she said. "When I was thirteen. And I lost my mother last year, when I was twenty. I want this flower because it will remind me of the best things about her."

He held her tight, kissed the side of her neck, as if she'd just said the sexiest thing in the world.

"A tattoo won't do anything," he said. "It might make you feel worse. You already have the owl and the red sun, right? And they're not helping, are they? You have to talk to her."

Grit felt warning signs, as if her family trauma was part of the seduction. She could only blame herself for spilling so many personal details. But she needed physical connection, and his words melted her knees. She leaned into his body, arching as he pressed his hand into the small of her back.

"Why don't you call her?" he asked.

"She refuses to speak to me," Grit said, wishing he'd drop it, wanting just to make out and forget.

"I can't believe that."

"No one does."

"Want to talk to my mom?"

"I have my aunt," Grit said. "Thank you, but I have Clare."

"Okay. Whatever you say. But it really does

seem as if you could use a shrink."

"I don't want to think about it anymore," Grit said, standing on her tiptoes, slinging her bare arm around his neck, kissing him, spilling a little cup of ink as they stumbled into the table.

CHAPTER ELEVEN

Clare usually had Thanksgiving at Sarah and Max's. Whenever possible they banded together on holidays, forming a sort of a cobbled-together family, to keep Clare from being alone. Paul was always invited, and often came.

Deep down, in spite of loving Sarah and feeling grateful to have her, Clare had always felt the emptiness of not being with her own blood family; the season had seemed like something to be endured, gotten through. But this year Grit was here, and Clare found herself really looking forward to celebrating.

The Saturday before Thanksgiving Clare and Grit walked cross-town to the Union Square Greenmarket. Sarah had assigned Clare a few dishes, and Grit had volunteered to make the pies. Farms and vendors from around the state occupied stands all around the park's perimeter, the south end devoted to a Christmas village of quirky, colorful, often handmade gifts.

Union Square's north end, along East Seventeenth Street, and the west side, edging Broadway, overflowed with pumpkins, squash, gourds, apples, pears, chrysanthemums, fresh-baked pies, bread, muffins, organic vegetables, fresh-caught fish, grass-fed beef, free-range eggs, farm-raised chickens and turkeys. Clare and Grit looked into every stand, tasting free samples and buying what they needed to cook.

"It's just like a market street in Europe," Grit said.

"I love coming with a real cook."

Grit beamed. "At least I'm doing something to pay you back for letting me stay."

"You don't have to pay me back," Clare said.

They filled their bags with acorn squash, tiny white onions, fresh sage, whole nutmegs, cranberries, oranges, heavy cream from an upstate dairy farm, Concord grapes, walnuts, Bosc pears, Granny Smith and McIntosh apples until their arms ached with the weight.

The scent of hot cider drew them to a booth covered with a yellow-and-white-striped tent. They put down their bags and sipped cardboard cups of cider. Clare glanced at Grit, noticed her platinum hair was growing out, half an inch of dark roots showing. Was that just style, or had she decided to go back to her natural color?

"I was thinking," Grit said, warming her hands on the cup. "I might like to invite Dennis over for dinner some night."

"That would be great," Clare said. "I'd like to meet him."

Grit finished her cider, threw the cup in the trash, unzipped her down jacket, and pulled her left arm free. Pushing up her sleeve, she showed Clare a faded-purple drawing of, unmistakably, the flower on Anne's Web site.

"What's that?"

"Dennis stenciled my arm, but wouldn't do the tattoo."

"Why not?"

"I don't know. He vetoed me, said I was too emotional."

The word "veto" grated on Clare, reminded her of Frederik telling Anne what she could and couldn't do. "It's up to you, not him," she said.

Grit stared at the ghost of the flower on her arm.

"I want it."

"Then get it."

"I will," Grit said.

They left the bustling market, started to head home. The side streets were shadowed, dark after the bright park.

"I want the flower because it reminds me of Mom," Grit said. "Do you think that's weird?"

"No, why would I?"

"I don't know. Some people would wonder why I want to think of her at all. But I do. The good parts of her."

"Same for me," Clare said.

"That's kind of what my film's about," Grit said. "Missing someone so much, knowing they're gone from your life, but finding ways to bring them back."

"And the film helps do that?"

"Not enough," Grit said. "Sometimes I want to see them so much I think I'll vaporize. But I find things around the bog and build little towers, or arrange them in patterns or whatever, and now I'm having this tattoo. That's how I feel them with me."

"And putting it on video gives you a record?"

"Exactly," Grit said.

"Maybe we should visit that bog in Staten Island," Clare said.

"Really?"

"Yeah," Clare said. "I know someone who'd be very happy to take us there."

■ ■ ■ ■

That night after Grit fell asleep, Clare stood in the doorway of her room. She thought of Anne doing this, feeling close to Grit only when she didn't know her mother was there. Clare ached, wishing everything was different, and that Anne showed Grit the love she had to feel.

The diary, and the aftershocks of reading about Anne's life, kept Clare awake. At first she had felt uneasy, guilty for invading her sister's privacy. But now these moments late at night gave her the feeling of being together, whispering to each other, things sisters could say only to each other, secrets they didn't want anyone else to hear.

We picked Grit up at the airport yesterday. God, it was so good to see her — coming off the plane, looking so happy and confident. She hugged me so hard, as if she'd missed me as much as I missed her. Frederik joined in, arms around both of us. My heart caught, because in that moment I knew how we looked from the outside — a tight family reuniting. Our college girl home for the holidays.

We stopped for late breakfast on the way

home, and Frederik made sure Grit ordered all her favorite things. She was obviously jet-lagged, trying not to yawn. One hour back, and she was already holding herself in check so as not to displease him. I saw him watching her — I swear he looked proud. And she didn't say anything to upset him, and I barely opened my mouth. Great, right? With all the questions I have, so much curiosity about her school year, and friends, and classes, and her film, I kept it all inside. The wrong word would have ruined everything.

Grit knew exactly what I was doing, too. But instead of feeling we were in cahoots against him, I saw her judging me. That look in her eyes was not warm. Later, walking back to the car, I tried to hug her again, and this time she was stiff. God, it threw a switch in me.

As soon as he disappeared into the studio, I made tea. Served it to her as if she were a guest. I felt her scorn, and it made me angry. We made a little small talk — truly, that's all it was. After dreaming of this day, when she'd come home for her vacation and we'd get to have mother-daughter talks, our usual pattern asserted itself. Grit acting disappointed in me, me feeling defensive about every single thing

I've ever done.

Grit went into her room for a nap. I hovered by her bed, and all the bad feelings went away. She was my baby again, innocent and trusting, and I was her mother. I covered her with a blanket, moving lightly and carefully so she wouldn't wake up. But she was deeply asleep, totally unaware of my presence.

Later she woke up and said she wanted to go into town. I offered to drive, but she said no. That feeling of love stayed with me — mine for her, and hers for me — and I wanted to hold on to it. She walked down the street, and I gave her a head start. After twenty minutes I went the long way around, parked on a side street. I know her favorite places. It's cold, and the café tables are inside, but I spotted her through the front window. She sat alone. I wanted to walk in, join her, make everything right between us. But it hurt me so much to think she'd rather sit in the café by herself than stay home with me, or invite me to come along, I just stayed where I was.

I found myself thinking of Clare. It hurts to even write her name. Realizing how Grit feels about me, knowing I let her down every minute, makes me wonder what my sister must think. The hate she must have for me.

All the poison Frederik pours into me, constantly reliving his version of what Clare did — as if it were yesterday, not almost twenty years ago — isn't he tired of it? He's kept us apart this long — or I have — doesn't he trust that there's no hope of ever seeing her again? He's done his work there.

But right now, writing this, I want to talk to her more than anything. Things I'd say: I love you. I'm sorry. Can you ever forgive me?

And I'd ask her: What should I do?

Clare's hands tingled. She closed the diary, just to hold on to Anne's words in her head. The entries had been written a year ago — before the attack on Grit. But they felt so immediate, Clare heard her sister's voice, as if she were sitting right there.

"I love you," Clare said out loud. "You're already forgiven. It's Thanksgiving. Leave him, and come be with us. We'll take care of you."

But all she heard back was silence, except for the mantel clock ticking in the other room, and Blackburn's tail whisking back and forth as she lay at the end of the bed.

They set off for Staten Island on Sunday afternoon, after Clare finished guiding her regular bird walk through the Ramble in Central Park. Grit had gone with her, and Clare had shown her the varied thrush, still present in Maintenance Meadow.

They had watched a major drama between a peregrine falcon and a black vulture — the falcon chasing the vulture away from Azalea Pond, and Clare telling the group a black vulture sighting was a personal first for Central Park. Grit felt proud of her aunt, obviously beloved by the birders; she glowed, being introduced as her niece.

At three o'clock, Paul picked them up at the town house. He jumped out of the Jeep; Grit recognized him from seeing him in Battery Park. Pretty hot for an older guy, he was tall and strong, with craggy outdoorsman looks and bright blue eyes. He kissed Clare and shook Grit's hand.

"Hi, Grit," Paul said. "Your aunt has told me so much about you."

"Uh-oh," Grit said.

"All good," he said.

"Well, I'm the niece who came in from

the cold," she said. "And took over the guest room."

"I didn't know what I was missing," Clare said.

"See?" Paul said.

Clare's affirmation made Grit feel backed up, as if she really had family behind her now. She stowed her tripod, took her camcorder from the camera bag. While Paul drove them out of Chelsea, Grit removed the Maine memory card and inserted a new one for New York.

Grit filmed a few minutes of the long drive, brief clips of the West Side Highway, entering the Brooklyn Battery Tunnel, merging onto the parkway and crossing the Verrazano-Narrows Bridge: light glinted through clouds, sparking the gunmetal gray harbor.

For this film, she wasn't recording sound. This would be the most silent film ever. Paul glanced into the rearview mirror just in time to see Grit checking the shots she'd just taken.

"I'm very sorry about your brother," he said.

"Thank you," Grit said. She stared at the back of Clare's head. What did it mean that she'd discussed her with Paul, told him something so dark and intimate? Grit

271

watched for signals between them, to see how close they were, but couldn't tell yet.

"Do you have a title?" Clare asked, half turning around.

"I'm thinking of 'Invisible Family,' " Grit said.

"Beautiful," Clare said.

"Creative and mysterious," Paul said.

Grit flooded with love for Gilly. She knew how much he would love these people, kind and gentle, inclined to see the best, not the worst, in everyone. Paul drove them through neighborhoods, then past a seemingly endless mound of dirt, seagulls wheeling and screeching overhead. Grit's heart quickened, and she filmed a few seconds through the window.

"What is this place?" she asked.

"Staten Island Landfill," Paul said. "After September eleven, all through the recovery process, debris from the towers was brought here."

Grit stared out at the birds, and the refuse, and felt a shiver of grief.

"They sifted through every piece of rubble," Clare said, following Grit's gaze. "They found letters and photographs, buttons, rings, cell phones with saved messages from family members."

When Paul braked, turned down a dirt

road, climbed out of the Jeep to unlock a metal gate across the road, Grit knew they'd reached the bog.

"Why do they keep the road blocked off?" Grit asked as they bumped along the unpaved road.

"Because for a long time it was used as a dumping ground."

"For what?"

"Just about everything you can think of," Paul said. "The EPA marked it as a toxic site. The levels have improved, but it's off-limits to the public."

"Thanks for bringing me," Grit said.

"Glad to do it." Paul glanced in the rearview mirror. "You're going to be careful, right?"

"Yes, please don't worry."

The bog came into view: a long, barren expanse of mud and swamp vegetation. Although it was too cold for flowers to bloom, scrawny scrub oaks and gnarled pines grew throughout the wetland. Grit hadn't been bogging in more than a month, since her trip to Sunkhaze Meadows near Katahdin Lake in Maine.

"Familiar landscape?" Clare asked.

Grit nodded, mesmerized.

All bogs began with a glacier, raking the land nine thousand years ago, removing bedrock, leaving a basin filled with glacial and marine sediment. Rain and snow melt-off created a freshwater pond where algae, aquatic plants, and scrub trees grew, the water becoming choked with organic matter, fallen trees and broken branches.

With drainage blocked, the peat retained water that prevented total decay — just as the Grauballe Man and other bog bodies proved. All peat was 90 percent water, 10 percent vegetation, and some people used it to make healing poultices. Animals and birds nested in the moss. Rare orchids grew from the rich soil.

"Can we help?" Clare asked as Grit started gathering her gear.

"Nope, I'm fine."

"Okay, we'll just watch."

"Awesome. Just stay back, no matter what. Trust me, I've done it before."

Clare pointed at the sky. "Redtail." She and Paul stayed in the front seat, watching the hawk fly by.

Climbing out of the Jeep, Grit tested the ground: good and hard. Carrying her camera and tripod she walked toward the bog, gently sloping from sand-filled dirt into a wide expanse of deep-brown loam.

A ten-foot-long oak limb lay in tall grass; she tested to make sure it wasn't rotted, then pulled it to the bog's edge. She found an abandoned fire pit and gathered smooth gray stones, pieces of gravel, and charred bits of wood. Amazing that she barely had to go looking for things to build the sculpture. Every object had meaning: the branch was the family tree, the stones were the weight of her heart, and the fire represented Gilly's school paper about heat at the earth's core.

Memories flooded in, making her breathe faster. Why had Gilly chosen that topic? Sometimes Grit drove herself crazy, going back in time and trying to put the pieces together differently. If Gilly hadn't written that report, if their father hadn't torn it up, would he still be alive? If the day hadn't been foggy, if their mother hadn't taken them to Grauballe bog?

No matter what, their father could find a reason to rage. There was no undoing that.

Grit checked the camera. She wondered what her father would think if he ever saw this film. She would tell him it was about Gilly, her beautiful brother. Her father had killed his spirit.

She set the tripod on the slope's soggy edge. She slipped, nearly went down, caught herself just before sliding into the bog, camera and all. Glancing over, she saw

Clare and Paul talking, not noticing. She hesitated, then unlaced her boots. Stepping barefoot onto partly frozen ground, she dug in and screwed the camera to the tripod base. Taking a deep breath, she checked to make sure the record button was on.

Red light, ready to go.

Twenty yards out, in the middle of the bog, was a small island covered with tall, brown grass. She zoomed in for a close-up of wildflower skeletons: Queen Anne's lace, thistles, and daisies. Their seeds would fall into the bog, and new flowers would grow next spring. She held the shot for a long moment.

She heard Paul and Clare get out of the Jeep. The mic picked up the sound of their doors closing, but she blocked it out. She was in the zone now. The sky was pearl-white, shafts of sunlight breaking through the clouds. It glinted on the stones and pieces of charcoal.

"Come on, Gilly," she said from behind the camera.

Saying his name out loud made her tingle, as if he were right there with her. Her feet stung from the cold, but she didn't care. She anchored the long, twisted branch into the bank and pointed the long, skinny part out toward the tiny island. Light streamed through the clouds and bounced off every surface, the amazing radiance of shallow water.

Now she crouched by the limb. She placed a gray stone on the bark. Beside it she balanced a piece of charcoal from the fire. The thin sunlight made them look silver. She continued in that pattern, forming a line all along the branch.

The cold went down her spine. Balancing on the log, she walked slowly backward, hunched over, making a row of charred wood and stones. It was like leaving a trail of breadcrumbs for her brother and her mother, a secret path so they could safely get away from her father.

Being at a bog brought them back to her, and the shock they'd all felt that day. Her father's rage had finally scraped Gilly so raw he couldn't stay in his own skin. She stood still now, teetering near the end of the branch. If she closed her eyes tightly enough, she could bring him back. They would be together right now, they could undo that other day — her mother taking pictures while she and Gilly explored the banks.

"Mom," she heard herself say.

A hawk swooped out of the cedar, flying overhead; Grit looked up, half-turning, and started to slide. She hovered on the brink, and had a split second to react: run back to shore, or fall in. The frail, pointy tip of the branch snapped, scattering all the stones and charcoal, and she crashed into the bog.

Clare called, but Grit barely heard. She felt something slice her foot as the bog tugged her down. The mud felt warm compared with the air. She gulped a breath, grabbed for the branch. The bark scratched her hands, and she sobbed because she realized she was sinking, and was surprised to feel so suddenly glad about it — as if it were meant, she belonged with Gilly.

She heard footsteps coming for her and there was Paul, nearly chest-high in mud. Time sped backward, and she felt her mother's arms around her, dragging her out of Grauballe bog, letting Gilly die. Paul was pulling her onto shore, but she fought him as hard as she could, and she heard Clare crying, just the way she'd heard her mother so long ago.

Clare knelt beside Grit, hugging her for warmth, shocked at the blood streaming from her big toe, sliced to the bone. Paul ran to the Jeep, got his first aid kit. He cleaned the open wound with bottled water, then hydrogen peroxide. Grit howled.

"Grit," Clare said, holding her tighter. "It's going to be okay."

"Gilly." Grit wept.

"Hold tight now," Paul said. He pressed the edges of skin together, wrapped the toe in gauze and tape. Blood instantly soaked the bandage. Lifting her, he hurried toward the Jeep. Clare grabbed the camera, held the door open. She buckled Grit into the backseat and climbed in beside her as Paul sped out of the parking lot.

"He died, and it was my fault," Grit cried.

"How can you say that?"

"My mother couldn't save him because she had to pull me out instead."

"You were trying to stop him," Clare said.

"But I didn't! He died, and now she hates me, and none of us are together."

"She doesn't hate you, Grit. I promise, I know that about her. No matter how she's been acting, she loves you."

Grit shook her head, sobbing quietly.

The sun dipped down behind the woods, bare branches stark against pale twilight. On the main road, all the cars had their headlights on. Clare held Grit's hand.

"You're freezing," Clare said, but Grit didn't reply. Paul turned up the heat, and Clare tucked her down jacket around her. She sat, stunned by what she'd seen, and by a feeling in her gut about what had happened. Maybe Grit hadn't intended to die, but once she slipped in, she certainly hadn't fought against it.

Paul drove fast, across the Verrazano, heading through Brooklyn for Manhattan. Once they hit the FDR Drive, it was a straight shot to Stuyvesant Cove Hospital. Paul let them out at the ER entrance, then went to park the car.

The ER was just behind a sliding steel door, and Clare helped Grit limp inside. A nurse told Grit to get out of her wet clothes, handed her a hospital gown. Once Clare had helped Grit change, the nurse came back. She eased Grit onto an exam table, took her vital signs.

"Now why are you all wet?" the nurse asked.

"She fell into a bog," Clare said.

"Wow," the nurse asked. "I hear everything, but that's a new one on me."

Grit held the electronic thermometer in her mouth, didn't reply.

"She's ice-cold, and I'm worried about infections in her toe, her eyes, her whole system."

"She's going to get a tetanus shot," the nurse said. "And we'll wrap her in a hypothermia blanket while she waits for the doctor."

"How long will that be?" Clare asked.

"Depends," the nurse said. "I'm sure you can see how busy it is tonight."

"She needs to be seen now," Clare said.

"Let me take a look."

"No, don't touch me," Grit said in a small voice.

"Come on now, sweetie," the nurse said. "I'm sure it hurts, and we'll give you something as soon as the doctor sees you."

She unwound the bloody gauze, peered at the cut.

"Okay, it's a bad one. Someone did a good job with first aid, but I think you're going to need more than stitches. We'll get a surgeon to check on those tendons and bone."

"Surgeon," Grit said, looking to Clare. "No, I want to go home. Just stitches . . ."

Clare held her shoulders, staring into the dark red wound, the white bone shocking in contrast. The nurse bandaged Grit's toe, wrapping her entire foot. She helped Grit into a wheelchair.

"Hey, Grit, how are you doing?" Paul asked, standing when Clare pushed Grit into the waiting room.

"Not so great," Grit mumbled.

"I bet," Paul said. "Would you like something from the machine?"

"My stomach's upset," Grit said.

"Maybe some ginger ale," Clare said. Paul went to get it, and she felt relieved to see Grit take a sip.

"What did the doctor say?" Paul asked.

"The nurse saw her," Clare said. "They're going to get her in as soon as possible."

"I want to go home," Grit said; she sounded young, frail, as if she were a child. "I don't want you to leave me alone here."

"I'll be right here," Clare said.

Grit cried helplessly, frustrated and in pain. Clare knew she needed her mother. She thought of Anne, an ocean away, not knowing her daughter was hurt.

"Tell me," Clare said. "How can I get hold of your mother?"

"No," Grit said, sobbing. "I told you, she doesn't love me, I'm not her daughter anymore! Now you know why. You saw what happened in the bog. I didn't want it to, I didn't know it would, I just wanted to bring us all together —"

"She loves you," Clare said.

"You do," Grit said. "Not her . . ."

An hour passed. Clare and Paul sat there in mud-caked clothes. At nine P.M., an orderly gave Clare another cotton blanket

282

to wrap around Grit, but it wasn't enough. Grit shivered harder, her lips tinged with blue.

"C'mon," Paul said. "Let's get her seen."

"I'll do it," Clare said, and walked over to the admitting desk.

"My niece needs help," Clare said. "Right now."

"Ma'am, we are doing our best."

"You want her to go into shock right here?" Clare asked, raising her voice.

She stood there shaking. She'd never had to advocate at a hospital for anyone before; she disliked making scenes, never wanting to call attention to herself. A bone-deep desire to stay out of trouble, out of Bedford Hills, had taught her to blend in, keep herself from being noticed.

But within five minutes a nurse called Grit's name, and when Clare pushed her over to the door, the nurse said a doctor was waiting and Clare could have a seat until they needed her.

"Good job," Paul said when she sat down.

"Thank you," she said.

A television blared in a corner of the waiting room, and people came and went with black eyes, bandaged wounds, and hacking coughs. The walls were mint green. The vinyl seats smelled like disinfectant. Time passed: an hour, then another.

"What's taking so long?" Clare asked.

"ERs take forever," he said. "Try to relax, okay?"

Clare stood, made a circuit around the waiting room. She stepped outside to get some air. Although city lights bleached the night sky, she managed to locate Orion. She found Rigel and Betelgeuse, using the two bright stars to calm herself. By the time she headed back inside, she saw Paul talking to a young woman in light-blue scrubs.

"This is Grit's aunt," Paul said as Clare walked over.

"I'm Dr. Jenkins," she said, shaking Clare's hand. "I'm the attending."

"How is she? It's been taking so long."

"She was down in X-ray, I'm sorry no one let you know. She's got a very deep cut," Dr. Jenkins said. "I'm sure I don't have to tell you. We're just waiting for the surgeon."

"I thought she *was* seeing the surgeon."

"A bad accident came in, and he's been in the OR. He'll be by very soon."

"It's past midnight," Clare said. "She hasn't had anything to eat, and she must be exhausted."

"She'll need to stay the night and probably longer."

"Really, longer?" Clare asked.

"Most likely tonight and tomorrow."

"If she has to, of course," Clare said.

"Now," Dr. Jenkins said, "she told me she's making a film, and that she fell into the pond accidentally. Were you there? Is that how you saw it?"

"Well," Paul began.

"It is," Clare said sharply, not daring to look at Paul.

"Any chance she wanted to harm herself?"

"I thought yes," Paul said.

"I am concerned and want to get a psych evaluation."

"Please, just let me see her," Clare said.

Clare followed Dr. Jenkins down the hall, into a cubicle. Grit lay back on an exam table, wearing a hospital gown. A white-coated technician finished taking blood, taped a piece of gauze to the crook of Grit's arm. He smiled, left the room.

"Oh, Grit," Clare said, hugging her. "How do you feel?"

"A lot better," Grit said, as if trying to convince her. "Really. I want to get out of here. I've had a chance to think about everything and I'm really embarrassed. I'm sorry for being such an idiot and falling in. Poor Paul. I didn't even apologize to him."

"I'm sure he knows how you feel," Clare said.

"Can I ask you something? I don't have insurance," Grit said.

"I know."

"So, who — ?"

"Don't worry about it, okay?" Clare had already signed the financial form. "Just let them take care of you. Did Dr. Jenkins tell you she wants you to stay?"

"Yes, but I don't want to," Grit said.

"I know, but you have to listen to her."

Grit stared down at her bandaged toe. "It nearly got cut off. I guess my foot was so numb in that cold water, I didn't realize how deep the glass, or whatever it was, went. Now I'm all shot up with Novocain and a really strong painkiller. They finally gave it to me. So I'm fine."

Clare barely heard. She focused on formulating the words.

"Grit," Clare said, holding her hands. "I want us to be straight with each other right now because we have to get this right."

"Get what right?" Grit said.

"Did you try to kill yourself? Like Gilly did?"

"No!" Grit said.

"Because I saw you swinging at Paul, and it didn't look like you wanted him to get you out."

"I'm really sorry for that," Grit said. "I

286

told you! And I'll tell him myself."

"This has nothing to do with apologizing."

Grit folded her arms across her chest, stubborn and defensive.

"Then what?"

"It looked to me as if you didn't want to be rescued. In fact, it looked as if you went in on purpose."

"That is a total lie!"

"Grit, I saw what I saw. Paul did, too. Dr. Jenkins is going to have you talk to a psychiatrist," Clare said.

"I don't need that. I'm not going to."

"I'd feel a lot better if you did."

"Is that why they're keeping me here? Because they think I'm crazy? I'm not!"

"I know that."

"A strange thing happens," Grit said, arms folded tighter. "It's part of filming. I trance out and, yes — I do feel a connection with Gilly and Mom. But I *never* try to hurt myself. If I hit Paul, I'm sorry. But you're both wrong. I didn't want to die. It's the opposite — I feel life in the bog."

"You kept calling Gilly's name."

Grit looked down. "Okay. I did freak out when I fell in. But I told you — visiting bogs reminds me of him. That's the point. You must know what it's like, the way you find meaning in nature and birds, and write about it on your blog. Isn't this how we make sense of all the bad stuff?"

"Yes, it is," Clare said.

"Well, then, you get it. Honestly, please don't worry . . ."

Clare leaned down to hug her, felt her trembling.

"Are you still cold?" Clare asked. "I'll ask for more blankets."

Grit took a deep breath. "Could I have your sweater instead? If they're going to make me stay here, I'd like to sleep with it on."

Clare smiled. She peeled off her blue cardigan, helped her into it.

"My arms feel like lead. Must be the medication," Grit said. She lay back on the pillow and closed her eyes.

Clare stayed until Dr. Bodhi entered the cubicle about an hour later. Tall, lean, with sharp brown eyes, he stood at the end of Grit's bed with carefully folded hands. He smiled at Grit reassuringly.

"So, you don't like your right toe?" he asked.

"I was a little tired of it," Grit said, trying to chuckle.

"Well, fortunately it is quite resilient. The cut was very severe, but I shall fix it. Now, will you flex your foot for me? Now let me see you wiggle your toes." She did. "Lovely," he said.

"That's a good sign, right?" Clare asked.

"I will know more about nerve impingement when we get into the operating room. But her X-rays look very good, I was heartened by what I saw. The cut goes through to the bone, but did not deeply slice the bone itself. That is excellent news."

"Thank you," Clare said.

"You are her mother?" Dr. Bodhi asked.

"Her aunt," Clare said.

He nodded. "Now Dr. Jenkins will come back in. Grit, when you see your aunt again, your toe will be as good as new."

"Thank you," Grit said, but she was watching Clare, not Dr. Bodhi. She didn't take her eyes off her until Dr. Jenkins and the orderly arrived, to take Grit for surgery. Then Clare went to find Paul and wait.

Grit had made it through surgery well, and by four A.M. was in the recovery room. Dr. Bodhi gave Clare and Paul the details, told them to go home and rest and return in the morning when Grit would be awake and feeling better, in a room on the surgical floor.

Paul stretched out on the couch while

Clare went to her desk. She found Frederik's Web site, looked for his gallery information, and dialed the number listed. A woman's voice, not Anne's, answered in Danish.

"Do you speak English?" Clare asked.

"Yes," the woman said.

"I am trying to reach Anne Rasmussen."

"This is the gallery, not the home."

"I realize that, but this is an emergency, and I don't have her number," Clare said.

"I am sorry, but I cannot give that number out."

"I'm her sister."

"Regardless. If you would like to leave a message —"

"Tell Anne, not Frederik, that her daughter cut her foot straight to the bone. She had surgery tonight, and is in Stuyvesant Cove Hospital."

"But this is Mr. Rasmussen's line. I shall call him and he will doubtlessly pass the message to Mrs. —"

"Not Frederik," Clare repeated. "Please tell my sister directly. Tell Anne her daughter needs her right now. It's very urgent she calls me. Do you understand?"

"I shall give the message to the family," the assistant said, as if she hadn't heard Clare at all.

Clare heard Paul snoring softly. She felt exhausted but wanted to stay awake for Anne's call — there was no way she could get news like this and not check on Grit. Clicking on Anne's Web site, she saw the unchanging red sunset, the same pink orchid growing out of the dark and unfathomable bog.

The cats were fast asleep. Paul's arm was flung out; she sat on the sofa's edge, and he moved over, putting his arm around her as she lay down beside him. The moon cast squares of pale light on the floor. Branches scratched the glass, and Clare listened with her eyes open, waiting for the phone to ring.

CHAPTER TWELVE

After leaving the recovery room, Grit was taken to a double room. Her roommate was another college-age girl who liked to talk. Within twenty minutes Grit knew everything. Her name was Lacey, her parents were divorced, she had two brothers, and she was in the hospital to receive fluids because she had a bad eating disorder. Grit felt exhausted just listening to her.

The medications made Grit dizzy. Her toe was infected, and Dr. Bodhi had ordered heavy-duty IV antibiotics, dripping into her arm through a huge needle in the back of her hand. Now he was saying she might have to remain in the hospital for two more nights, until they were sure the infection was under control.

Clare arrived first thing in the morning and stayed all day. At first all Grit could do was doze, drifting in and out of weird, troubled sleep. When she woke up, her stomach was upset, and Clare held the little spit-up basin while Grit retched. Clare went for ice chips, feeding them to Grit a little at a time. Grit fell back to sleep, aware of Clare sitting quietly in the vinyl chair beside her.

Lacey's mother showed up in the late afternoon and bounced around the room, talking loudly about the damage Lacey had done to the enamel on her perfect teeth by all that vomiting, why had they even bothered paying for orthodontia if this was how Lacey wanted to treat her mouth?

Did all crazy girls have mental mothers? And was the inverse true? Grit assumed the answer had to be yes. Awake again, she stared at the ghost of Dennis's stencil on her pale inner arm. She had based it on her mother's photo, taken at the edge of the bog where Gillis had died, inspired by the hallucinatory painting by Henri Rousseau. Wasn't that at least slightly insane?

She traced the flower with her index finger, thinking of how small bog plants were. It was because the bog environment was so strange, with a lack of quality nutrients, that the plants living there turned into dwarf versions of themselves. It was how they adapted, maybe how people adapted, too. She stared at the flower, thinking of her invisible family.

When she looked up, Clare was watching her.

"Can I get you more ice?" Clare asked.

"No, I'm fine."

"Ginger ale?"

Grit shook her head.

But Clare got up anyway, walked out to the nurses' station, and returned with a cup of ginger ale, some crackers, and a bowl of crushed ice. Grit felt thankful; she had gotten so used to not asking anyone for anything. Grit stared at her aunt.

"What are you thinking?" Grit asked.

"Just how have I lived without you so long?"

"That's how I feel," Grit said.

It was late, time for visitors to leave. Lacey's mother was still talking loudly, making no move to put on her coat. Clare leaned down to kiss Grit, told her to have sweet dreams — she'd be back tomorrow.

When her aunt left the room, Grit burst into tears. Clare acted like a mother, the way a mother should act. Grit wept silently, so Lacey and her mother wouldn't see. She felt so much love for Clare, but she also missed her mother so much she thought her heart would explode.

Clare took the cross-town bus to Chelsea,

walked a block from the bus stop. Inside, the apartment was silent; she heard the clock ticking, and Chat purring in the dark. Clare walked around turning on lights, trying to see the apartment through a niece's eyes: cozy, welcoming, lived-in. She hadn't had a Christmas tree in years, but she and Grit would get one as soon as the tree sellers arrived from the north woods. They'd rummage through the basement, looking for the old family decorations.

She checked her answering machine. No messages. Her laptop glowed with blue light. Hitting the refresh button, she was back at Anne's screen and felt shocked to see a completely different image.

Was it a coincidence the photo had been changed, or was it the result of Anne's having received the message about Grit? Was this Anne's messed-up way of communicating? Now the screen showed the mere silver silhouette of violets growing out of the bog seen through sunlit mist — the feeling was melancholy, elegiac. The sight of the violets made Clare tingle.

She clicked on the flower and the password window opened up. She typed in song titles, favorite movies, sections of Central Park, old Bleecker Street and West Fourth Street cafés, owl names, including the Latin.

She tried the names of their schools and colleges, even their old phone numbers. Marianne Doyle, Miss Langtry. No luck.

"This isn't you," Clare said to the screen. "You're not this person who would leave her daughter, and not call to see if she's all right."

But the phone didn't ring, and the password didn't work, and Clare felt sick to think that Anne actually *was* that person.

Now she went to her room, climbed into bed, and opened Anne's journal. Her stomach was in a knot. Reading these entries had made her feel closer to Anne than she had in years. But it was like looking through a kaleidoscope: now you see her this way, but a quick shift, and now you see her in completely different light, colors, and shape. Clare read the entry dated exactly a year ago.

That little bitch. After everything Clare did to us, Grit has the fucking gall to want to "get to know her." That's what she said. Frederik found the letter she'd written, and I cannot blame him one bit for his reaction. He feels so betrayed, and do I. After what Clare did to us, how dare Grit devastate us this way?

Loyalty means more to us than anything. And honesty. The fact Grit has been

296

harboring this wish to know Clare, not saying one word to us or asking how we'd feel about it, is despicable. We have protected her from Clare her whole life. Frederik never considered not sending her to college, although he did warn me that she might get ideas. I defended her. Stupid me.

We've just lost our daughter — her choice. Reading those words, seeing her refer to Clare as her "aunt" really set Frederik off. Clare is not her aunt. She lost that privilege long ago, when she attacked my husband. Frederik made Grit throw the notebook with that vile letter straight into the fire. We watched it burn, and Grit just stood there, stoic as hell, refusing to back down or apologize.

Frederik told me what to do, but I swear I would have done it myself. I grabbed the metal spiral and hit her with it. It burned her — me, too — a reminder for both of us that loyalty matters in this family, and betrayal is not an option. Grit is dead to us now. Both of our children are gone.

Clare had to force herself to keep from bolting out of bed. She made herself still and turned the page to read the next entry, written later that day:

What have I done? Help me. Frederik won't let me take back what I said. He won't let her stay.

And the final entry:

I used to tell the children fairy tales. Sometimes I'd read ones written by Hans Christian Andersen, but more often I'd make them up. Oh, the moon was always coming through the trees, shining its silver light on the sleeping heads of the prince and princess. Fairy tales always have castles, and princes and princesses, and climbing roses, and hidden woods. Who ever decided they were for children? They're full of lies and jealousy, and there's always someone lurking just around the bend, with fangs or a knife or an evil spell.

We live in a fairy tale. Frederik has cast a spell over all of us. He is the king and makes the rules, and I am the foolish queen, and Grit is our sleeping beauty. She woke up, and that is the problem. Living in Boston, being away from us, let her see us from a distance, and she knew. She saw through the fairy tale.

I'm writing this knowing I'm about to lose my daughter. She is packing her things. I am in the bedroom writing this while Frederik stands in her doorway watching her. I can hear his voice from here, he won't shut up. I want to kill him. I want to go into the kitchen, get a knife, and stab him in the heart.

I hit Grit in the neck with that red-hot thing. She needs to go to the ER. I freaked out when I realized what I'd done — how fucking disgusting am I, that it took me nearly an hour to click out of Frederik-mode, that self-righteous sickness I get when I listen to him. I want to drive her to the hospital.

She wouldn't go with me, even if he'd let me take her. She heard what I said outside. She's on her way. And you know what? I swear, I'm glad for her. She should leave us. Maybe I broke her heart with those words and hitting her, but at least she's getting away. She doesn't have to pretend to want to come home anymore. Because she can't.

The entries stopped there, and Clare realized Grit must have grabbed the book before she left the house. Clare knew she had to go out. The apartment felt claustrophobic, the walls closing in as if she were back in prison. She pulled on her jacket, stuck the journal in her pocket.

She texted Paul, asked him to meet her at the fenced path that leads into the wildflower meadow, west of the big red oak near the 102nd Street transverse. He texted back:

Are you ok? is grit?

We're ok.

When she reached the spot forty-five minutes later, Paul was waiting. They struck off through the trees, rounding the Loch. Cold wind knifed across the park. It was late, and as they walked, they didn't see anyone.

"What's going on?" Paul asked. "Did something happen with Grit?"

"No. She's the same."

"Then what?"

"I thought Anne would call me back."

Paul walked in silence for a minute. "Why would she suddenly do the right thing, act like a mother or a sister?" he asked.

"I've been reading her journal," she said.

"I know."

"It's a nightmare. What she's done to Grit, to herself." Clare tugged the notebook from her pocket. They circled Lasker Rink and headed toward the Blockhouse.

Clare thought of how many times she and Anne had come to the park. All the nights they'd explored the paths, looking for owls. This had been their enchanted place, where they'd come to escape the awful realities of home. Clare listened now, still wishing deep down that she could hear the eerie call of an extinct bird. She wanted something wonderful, impossible to happen.

"I want to break his spell," she said, grabbing Paul's hand.

"Clare."

"How can I do it? How can I help my sister?"

Clare felt tears sting her eyes. They filled her eyes as Paul pulled her into his arms. He held her tightly while she cried. Anne had held her hand when they were little, when Clare was scared. She felt that way now, terrified for her sister and the life she'd made.

Paul took the journal from her hands, pressed it against her heart. He kissed her eyes, her tears, her lips. She leaned against him, the hard edges of the book there between them. Something cracked inside, a wall that had been there since she'd gone to prison. She'd built it strong and thick, to withstand anything. It had a locked door, and she opened it rarely, even for Paul.

"You texted me tonight," he said, his voice full of emotion. "Do you know what that means to me?"

Clare could have said she always called him, but she didn't bother, because she understood. Tonight was different, and everything was changing.

"I needed you," she said.

"I need you, Clare. I always have."

■ ■ ■ ■

The next morning, Clare dedicated her blog post to Grit — partly just because she wanted to, but mostly hoping that Anne would see:

My niece is in the hospital. She came to New York to visit me and see the house where her mother and I grew up. Like us, Grit loves and finds inspiration in nature. Before leaving college, she majored in documentary film production. She is making a film now, and that's how she was injured.

She was trying to tell the truth about her life, through metaphor and imagery. I was there when it happened — she fell into a bog, right here in New York City, and cut her foot badly. Maybe that's part of the story she's telling — it's a modern-day fairy tale about the people she loves most, and it's full of danger and injury, but most of all, redemption.

My niece has a story to tell, and I'm so proud of her. This post is more personal than most, but it seemed worth writing. She's helping me see beauty in shadow — love everywhere, places we're all afraid to look: into the fire, into the darkest forest, into a lonely bog on Staten Island.

Anne, come home to us.

"Maybe I shouldn't put this up," she said, showing Paul.

He read it, looked up into her eyes. "No, you should."

"It's not too personal?"

"It is, a little," he said. "That's why I like it."

They stared at each other. Something had happened last night, out in the North Woods. She'd stopped holding back.

"Even the last line?" she asked. "About Anne?"

He nodded. "Maybe she'll actually see it."

Clare started to look away. Emotion flooded her chest. Paul touched her cheek, brought her gaze back to him.

"It's okay, Clare. I know you want her here."

"For Grit," Clare said.

"Yeah. But for you, too." He gave a crooked smile. He didn't like Anne, but he understood. She remembered the moment last night when he'd taken the journal from her hands, held it to her breast. Anne had held that book, written in it, hidden it.

Every page was filled with her handwriting. He'd known the sisters when they were young, and seen their closeness, and knew that that journal was the closest Clare had been to Anne in twenty years.

She kissed him now, her heart expanding. He hadn't shaved since Sunday, and his dark beard shadow was scratchy and sexy. She wanted to tell him how much it meant to her, how enormous it felt to be able to open up a little more, but she had the sense he was feeling the same way.

Clare went to the kitchen, refilled their coffee. They both drank it black. Standing by the coffeepot, she remembered her parents. They had gotten married young, stayed together, learned to understand each other well but never managed to find a way to communicate their own thoughts and desires. She thought of Paul, of the patience he'd had, waiting for this to happen. He knew Clare so well, and he'd loved her till she was ready.

Her parents had played roles, as if they were imitating what they thought a married couple should be like. No matter what her father did, her mother pretended not to notice. His behavior must have torn her up inside, but she'd never give in to her feelings. Her job was to please him, and when he wanted coffee, she'd scramble.

He preferred to drink from bone china, and the cup had to be three-quarters full. He liked whole milk, never cream or half-and-half, and two heaping spoonfuls of sugar. If Clare's mother delivered the cup with one element off — too much or too little milk or sugar — he would set it down, rise without a word, and go alone to the diner. And her mother would just wash his cup. Clare went back to the living room, set the mugs down, and sat beside Paul. He had stoked the fire, and it crackled and sparked. He slid his arm around her waist.

"What are you thinking?" he asked.

"About my family."

"What about it?"

"Just that we grew up being told every-thing was wonderful. We learned how to act a certain way in front of the neighbors, we were told what was and wasn't okay to talk about. After a while we learned how to keep secrets, and secret keeping became our art."

"Don't keep secrets from me," he said.

"I don't," she said. And it was true, on one level. She didn't lie to him, or hide the observable details of her life. But for so long she had locked away her deepest, darkest thoughts and feelings. She glanced around the room, remembering when this had been his apartment, too.

"I want," she began, then stopped herself. She wasn't ready to say the words it would take to invite him back home. But he read her mind.

"Yeah," he said. "I want it, too."

They sat in silence, finishing their coffee as the fire settled down. The sun had risen over buildings to the east, shining on the bare branches of the trees in the small square across the street.

"What's your day like?" she asked.

"I'll be in the Bronx," he said. "Yesterday I roped off a section of Van Cortlandt Park around a pine struck by lightning last summer. All fall it's been fine, but now the trunk seems to be splitting in half. I have to cut it down."

"Be careful."

He smiled. "I will. You going to the hospital?"

"Yes," she said. "After I do a few things in the kitchen. I can't believe it's Tuesday, and Thanksgiving is two days away. Are you coming to Sarah and Max's?"

By way of answering, he held her. Of course he was, he wanted to be with her. She knew he worked at the Aquinas Food Bank every year. Depending on how things were between them, he'd often, but not always, show up at the Hugheses' house for dinner.

"Grit will be happy," Clare said. "She likes you."

"Here's another idea. Why don't I pick you two up, take you to Aquinas for an hour or so? We could use the help, and we'd have more time together. She can sit in a chair, stay off her feet."

"As long as she's out of the hospital in time. God, I hope she is."

"Me too," he said.

They kissed again, and he left. She watched him all the way down the street, until he disappeared from view. Returning to her computer, she stared at the last line of her new post: *Anne, come home to us.*

She felt Paul's support as she hit "publish," and the blog post went out into the world for everyone to see.

Grit lay in her hospital bed, wondering who was going to show up next. She had seen a parade of doctors. The psychiatrist had actually been okay. He seemed to be about Clare's age, with gray hair and a nice smile. He'd asked if Grit felt like talking, and to her surprise, she did. Lacey and her mother had actually fallen silent — obviously wanting to listen in.

Dr. Archer had helped her into the wheelchair. They went down the hall, to a small
room with two chairs and a desk. Grit
stretched her legs, glad to be out of bed. He
saw, and asked if she wanted to stand for a
minute.

"Am I allowed?" she asked. The only other
times she'd stood had been with Dr. Bodhi
or the nurses.

"As long as you don't put pressure on
your toe," he said.

"Okay," she said. He stood beside her, and
she leaned on him, walking a few steps to
the desk and back. She felt stupid for asking if she was allowed. Being in the hospital,
feeling so dependent, she felt as if she'd
regressed to being that scared little girl
afraid to do anything that might displease
the adults.

Sitting down again, she realized how
nervous she felt, afraid to meet his eyes. He
stayed quiet, maybe waiting for her to say
something. This was strange, being with a
psychiatrist. As a kid, she'd wished someone
would notice that something was wrong,
send her to someone to talk to. She'd
wanted an outward sign that she was disin-
tegrating: a broken bone, a black eye, a scar.
Now she had a big bandage on her foot,
and she'd finally attracted some attention,

but she was afraid of saying anything that might keep her here an extra day and prevent her from going home to Clare's.

"What would you like to talk about?" he asked.

"Um, I don't know," she said. "Nothing, I guess."

"Can you tell me what brought you to the hospital?"

She raised her foot and tried to laugh. He seemed to be waiting, and the silence drove her crazy, so she continued. "I nearly cut my toe off. It was an accident."

"How did it happen?"

"Oh, I'm making a film. I've been shooting it in bogs, so I got my aunt and her friend to take me to one on Staten Island, and I kind of fell off a log."

"Bogs," he said. "They're amazing places."

"They are," she said. "They're kind of like a furnace. All this alchemy goes on down deep. Most people think it's just rotting vegetation."

"But not you?"

She shook her head. "I love them." She glanced up, saw that he was watching, looked away again. "I have to be home for Thanksgiving."

"Where's home?"

"Chelsea," she said. Then, to fill in the

space, "My aunt's house."

"Have you lived with her long?"

"Nope. I showed up this month." She felt torn, wanting to spill the whole story, afraid he might think she was really crazy and lock her up.

"How is it to be there?"

"It's wonderful. She's made me feel completely welcome. I didn't dive into that bog on purpose."

"You said it was an accident."

"Exactly." She heard herself breathing so hard, she was practically panting. She dug her nails into her palm, so tense she couldn't relax. He was going to notice, and she wouldn't get home for Thanksgiving. "Look, I'll tell you one thing, but it's not what you think. The reason I'm filming in bogs has to do with my family. My parents and brother, back in Denmark."

"How old is your brother?"

"He'd be twenty-three."

Dr. Archer waited.

"I don't have insurance, you know," she said. "The hospital should just kick me out. My aunt would take care of me."

He still didn't say anything. Grit closed her eyes, wanting to just get it over with.

"The reason I'm with my aunt," she said, "is that my parents threw me out a year ago.

310

They stopped paying tuition and said I couldn't come back. I had nowhere to go, no money to tide me through. I finished the year at school, took on a ton of debt. Then I had to drop out. The last time I called home, my mother hung up on me."

Grit was on a roll, suddenly couldn't stop herself.

"I wouldn't care if my father did it, kicked me out or hung up on me, anything. It's my mother . . . we were so close. She used to say we were going to hide our passports, run away from him. I knew she never could, but at least she said it."

She wrapped her arms around herself, trying to catch her breath.

"She still wants to leave him, I know. But she's not brave enough. It takes a lot to stand up to him, more courage than she has." She stopped, gathering her own courage. "My brother died. In a bog, which is why I need to visit them. It makes me feel close to him. He couldn't take it anymore. My father was killing him — I mean that — so Gilly killed himself first. Now you know."

"I'm so sorry about your brother, Grit."

"Thank you," she said. His kind voice made her cry. But she held herself together so she didn't move at all; the only way he would know was from the tears on her cheeks. She felt better for letting it out, like a geyser that had needed to erupt, but now she had to take the consequences. "You're going to make me stay here, aren't you?"

"Do you think you need to stay?"

"No." Thinking back to the bog, she knew what had happened, what she'd done. It was true, she'd wanted to be with Gilly. She always would, but she didn't want to die. "I'm okay now."

"The way we put it here is to ask if you can be safe."

Safe. If that meant loved, cared for, a little clearer in the head, having Thanksgiving with Clare, the answer was yes. "I can," she said.

"Good," he said.

"You'll let me go?"

"Once Dr. Bodhi says you can."

"Thank you."

"I'm going to recommend you see someone, once you go home. I think it would help for you to talk about everything."

"That's what the film is for," she said. "My way of talking about it."

"That sounds good, too," he said, smiling. He pushed her back to her room.

"I'll come back to see you tomorrow," Dr. Archer said.

"As long as I'm home for Thanksgiving,"

Grit said. She lay back on her pillow. She felt like a sorcerer, conjuring lightning bolts and hurricane winds. Usually working on her project made her feel bright, as if lit from within. Tonight she just felt tired. Closing her eyes, she fell fast asleep.

CHAPTER THIRTEEN

When Dennis came off the elevator the next day, Grit watched all the patients sitting around the nurses' station check him out. She felt proud when he handed her a shopping bag — not only was he hot, he'd come bearing gifts. She peeked in to see a paperback edition of poems by E. E. Cummings and a catalogue of Francesco Clemente's *Bestiary* exhibition at the Guggenheim.

"Wow," she said. "I didn't expect you to bring anything."

"Of course I did," he said, gingerly encircling her with his arms as if afraid he might bruise her. His embrace felt so solicitous, it nearly annoyed her. But she felt too good to let it really get to her.

That morning she'd been taken off IV antibiotics, and they'd removed the Port-A-Cath from her vein. Physical therapy had sent someone up with an orthopedic shoe, and as long as she didn't put pressure on her toe, she could get around again.

"Thanks for the book," Grit said, limping as she led him down the hall toward the solarium.

"Clemente's pretty rad. The way he paints animals. And combines some of his art with Allen Ginsberg's poems."

"Cool."

"Yeah, whenever I tattoo animals I always check out his book. You'll see why."

"Poems and animals, awesome."

"My mom made you brownies," he said, taking an aluminum foil packet from the pocket of his black leather trench coat.

"Yum," she said.

They headed down to the common room, found an unoccupied couch in a dark corner. Lacey sat at a table with a few other people waiting for beds on the psych unit. Grit felt so glad she was on the mend, heading home soon. Dennis made her comfortable with a pillow propped against the sofa arm, so she could rest her foot on his lap.

"Your poor toe," he said, staring down at the thick bandage in the weird shoe.

"The bog monster nearly bit it off," she said. "I was being stupid."

"I'm sure you weren't."

Grit looked at her inner arm.

"Almost faded away," he said.

"Has enough time passed that you consider me competent to make a decision on the tattoo?"

"Yes, as soon as you get out," Dennis said.

"Cool," Grit said.

They sat in silence, people watching. Rachel, a woman with swollen hands and legs, stared at the TV, slumped into her seat like a grossly large, misshapen, state fair–winning pumpkin. Jamie, the girl with no hair, here for chemo treatments, sat with her parents. The sight of them tugged at Grit's heart.

The mental patients stuck together. Lacey talked with another girl who had eating issues. An old man, Gary, stared straight ahead with watery, emotional eyes. He had stringy gray hair, and he looked like he might be a street person. A young girl had her laptop open, listening to Taylor Swift, and a young man across the table stared at her with deep longing.

"He wants her but can never have her," Grit said.

"Why, if he loves her enough?"

"Because he thinks he's a piece of crap."

"I can't see that in him," Dennis said. "How can you tell?"

"I just can," Grit said. "He has family

316

pain. I can feel it. He's heading to the flight deck."

" 'The flight deck'?"

"The psych ward. I was a little afraid they'd send me there."

"Why would they put you on the psych unit? Did they think you hurt yourself on purpose?" He leaned in closer.

"I didn't," she said. She liked Dennis, found him so hot with his ponytail, torn T-shirt, and tattoos covering both arms from wrist to shoulder, but once again she felt the smallest cold gleam that he might be an emotional adventurer. There were such people.

She had discovered them in school, after Gilly's death. Certain people were drawn to suicide; it made Grit sick. They don't want to kill themselves — someone has already done that for them. But they're sensitive souls and they want you to know it. It was the same with troubled-family vampires. They feast on the pain and strangeness of your family while theirs is normal, watches TV together, and discusses problems in a reasonable way.

Dennis had a mother who baked brownies for a strange girl in the hospital: red flag? Now he switched positions, moved her legs and sat close beside her on the sofa.

"What's wrong?" he asked.

"I'm fine," she said.

"No, you're not. Did I just upset you?"

"No, there's just a lot of stuff going on," she said, wanting to trust him, but not sure if she could. It had been a relief to talk to Dr. Archer; it would be even better to have a friend.

"I thought the branch would hold my weight," she said. "I should have known it would break, but I wasn't paying attention."

"You were into your work?" he said, with a question mark at the end.

"Yeah," she said, not ready to say more. "But it's not real 'work.' I need a job."

"I'm sure you'll find something."

"I hope so." Something made her look at Gary again, the old man with the sad eyes. Who took care of him? Had he once had a family that had kicked him out? She could tell he was homeless, and she felt a shiver go down her spine. If not for Clare, she would be, too.

"Well," Dennis said, glancing up at the clock. "I should probably leave and let you get some rest."

"I'm glad you came," she said. "Sorry I acted weird before."

"Weird makes my day," he said, grinning.

After he left Grit hobbled back to her

room. She stripped all her clothes off, gathered her two tiny white towels, washcloth, and the violet shampoo Clare had brought from home, and stepped into the bathroom. Showering with this bandage was going to be a challenge.

She held her foot outside the shower curtain and stood in the hot water. Dennis's obvious interest in her threw her off balance. She'd gone out with boys before, but never let anyone get really close. It was as if her body rejected them.

She had gotten her period when she was fourteen, and her cycles had been regular until that December night at the second bonfire. Grit's body had shut down then, as if knowing that hormones and periods led to womanhood, and if her mother was her prime example, Grit didn't want any of it.

The water flowed over her body, and she closed her eyes, thinking of Dennis. She imagined what it would feel like to have his hands on her skin.

"Grit, do you need help with your foot?" Nina the nurse called from outside the bathroom door.

"I'm fine," Grit said, practically jumping.

"Need a towel?"

Grit turned off the water and stood shivering. A moment later, a white towel came waving through the curtain. She took it, wrapped it around her body, stepped out into the tiled bathroom. Nina, with brown hair and wise dark eyes, wearing a pink nurse's smock, stood there. "I was afraid you'd fall, standing in there on one foot!"

"Thank you," Grit said. "I'm fine."

"Okay, just making sure," Nina said.

Grit climbed into bed and turned off the light. The nurses were keeping close watch over her, as if they knew something she didn't. She flexed her toe, felt a shock of pain. She swallowed down tears. Curled on her side, she burrowed her head under the covers and let herself feel: even after everything, she wanted her mother.

She fell asleep. When she woke up, hours later, she wondered what had wakened her. She heard a small sound, someone stirring in the corner. Grit blinked trying to see. The door was partly shut, the room dark. She could just make out the wall clock: 2:00 A.M.

A nurse rose from the chair and stood in the dark beside her bed. Silhouetted by hall light, her hair fell in long waves. Grit's mother had hair like that, and she used to watch her sleep. Grit had always pretended not to see. She'd lie there perfectly still, just the way she was doing now. Her heart began to race.

"Mom," she whispered.

Suddenly the woman was gone, the room empty, the scent of violets dissolving in the air.

CHAPTER FOURTEEN

Grit's release on Wednesday was delayed by the fact that Dr. Bohdi had to see her, and he was tied up with an emergency. Clare had come to pick her up, and while they waited for the doctor, Paul sat in the car outside. Grit couldn't stop thinking about last night, the midnight visitor she'd dreamed up.

"Remember when you said there was a story about my mother and violets?" Grit asked.

"Yes," Clare said. "When we were young, we'd go to Central Park to look for signs of spring. Snowdrops and crocuses were the first, and then came daffodils and violets. Your mom and I found a whole carpet of white and purple violets, on the hillside just beyond the zoo."

"Which did you like better? Purple or white?"

"Both. We'd take them home, soak them

in water for days."

Grit listened, picturing the sisters concocting their flower water.

"I smelled violets last night," she said.

"Really, here at the hospital?"

"Yes. It was probably my shampoo, though." Grit leaned closer, so Clare could smell her hair.

"Just like that carpet of violets," Clare said. "Such a beautiful scent."

"But part of me doesn't think it was just the shampoo."

"Then what?"

"I think she came," Grit said. "I woke up, and she was standing there. My mother. You read her diary, you know."

"She used to watch you sleep."

"I was probably dreaming last night," Grit said. "But it didn't feel that way."

Dr. Bodhi came to check her toe, then let the nurses know Grit was ready to go home. Grit had been dying to leave but now she felt a pang. She wanted that smell of violets again; she wanted her mother to come back.

Christina, one of the nicest nurses, pushed her down to the lobby in a wheelchair. Grit said she could walk, but honestly she felt glad for the ride. Clare carried her overnight bag, and Grit held Dennis's books in her lap.

Paul's Jeep idled on the street outside the admissions entrance; as soon as Christina pushed Grit through the doors under the portico, he drove in, and Clare opened the front door.

"Seat of honor," Paul said, "and more room for your foot!"

"Did you get checked for sludge damage?" Grit asked. "I'm really sorry for making you jump in after me."

"Okay, you've officially apologized enough. Besides, I hear you're in charge of baking pies for tomorrow, so we'll be even."

"What's your favorite?" Grit asked.

"Apple," he said.

"You got it," Grit said.

When they got home, Paul helped her up the steps, and Clare carried her books. Grit hobbled into the living room, aching to continue the conversation with her aunt.

"I've got to go uptown and hang out in the park while the parade balloons are being blown up. You two sure you don't want to come?" Paul asked.

"It would be fun," Clare said, "but Grit needs to settle back in."

"I have baking to do," Grit said. "We'll watch the parade tomorrow and know you helped inflate Snoopy and Garfield."

"Okay, then," Paul said.

He left, and Clare helped Grit off with her coat. They dropped her things in her room. First thing, Grit pulled out her Sanyo camera and checked that it had caught the footage; she watched just a few seconds to make sure. Then she arranged Dennis's books on her bedside table. All three cats came out of their hiding places to welcome her home.

"I missed you," Grit said to them, petting Olive, Chat, and Blackburn in turn. They made her feel so good, as if they remembered her and really had noticed her absence, too. She looked up at Clare.

"You didn't say anything in front of Paul," Grit said. "Is that because you don't believe me?"

"I totally believe you," Clare said.

"That my mother was there?"

"That you at least believe she was there."

"That's like saying I'm crazy."

Clare sat beside her on the bed. "I don't think that at all. It's just that institutions, hospitals, I mean, are strange places. The air is stale, and the environment is unfamiliar, and voices echo from all over."

"How do you know? Why were you in the hospital?"

"I was in prison," Clare said.

"I know . . . are you saying you suddenly

saw my mother once?"

"No, I never did. I dreamed about her a lot. So many bizarre dreams, though, and with all the background noise, I wasn't sure of where being awake ended and being asleep began." Clare stared at Grit. "Listen, the thing is, I don't want you to be disappointed."

"How?"

"By believing your mother has come back. If she really had, why wouldn't she have stayed?"

Grit ducked her head and, like a little kid, put her hands over her ears. She didn't want to hear it, couldn't stand to follow Clare's logic through and answer that question.

Clare gave her a long hug, and when they broke apart, the look on Grit's face said she didn't want to talk about it anymore. Clare went into the kitchen, and Grit hobbled after her.

The kitchen smelled savory. Looking around, Grit discovered that Clare had already peeled the white onions and braised them in chicken broth, peeled most of the apples, and left them in a crockery bowl drizzled with sugar, cinnamon, and lemon juice.

"Wow, I am proud of you," Grit said. "And you told me you couldn't cook."

"You've gotten me interested in it. Who would ever guess that I'd start actually using my kitchen to cook?"

"That is what it's for, Aunty," Grit said.

She stationed herself on a tall stool, the right height for rolling out pastry. Clare measured the flour, lard, and butter in the right proportions — Grit preferred a French-style crust with more butter, just enough lard to stiffen it slightly while not impeding the flakiness factor. It felt warm and lovely; Grit didn't believe that Dennis's brownie-baking mom could create any more normal and cozy an atmosphere than this.

She used Clare's rolling pin — old-fashioned, with wobbly red handles, the wood darkened by time and many piecrusts — to roll out a large circle of crust.

"That was your grandmother's," Clare said, "and these are her pie plates."

They were Pyrex, crimped around the rim. Grit held one up, admiring it, before lifting the crust, unbroken, into it. The glass was yellow and aged, and Grit imagined her grandmother standing right here, in this kitchen, baking pies for long-ago Thanksgivings.

"Did you both help?" Grit asked.

"Your mom didn't like baking," Clare said. "But she loved to mash the potatoes;

she always added a ton of butter. And she was big on basting the turkey. Did she cook for your Thanksgivings?"

"We never had them."

"I mean before you moved to Demark. Back when you still lived in the States."

Grit shook her head. "My father didn't like American holidays. He said they made him feel left out."

Clare kept checking her cell phone, and Grit knew exactly who she hoped would call.

"You left my mother a message — right?"

"Yes," Clare said. "I called the gallery and spoke to your father's assistant. I'm worried she may have given the message to him, not her. She might not even know."

Grit knew. Clare was trying to protect her. She was right about the strange sounds and smells, the fine line between being awake and asleep. Plus Grit still felt traces of anesthesia, painkillers, and antibiotics, all of them affecting her mood and mind.

"It's okay," Grit said. "Let's just cook now."

They made one pumpkin and two apple pies and stuck them in the oven. Clare had sliced and precooked the acorn squash to the point where it was ready for the cranberry-orange–maple syrup mixture. The parboiled onions awaited tomorrow's heavy cream and fresh-grated nutmeg.

"What was your favorite holiday?" Grit asked.

"Christmas," Clare said. "There was always delicious food, and we'd make decorations, or pull out really old ones passed down from our grandmothers."

"Where are they now?" Grit asked.

"Somewhere in the basement," Clare said. "Do you want to put up a tree this year?"

"That would be great," Grit said. "Was your family always happy at Christmas?"

"Yes, mostly," Clare said. "But it's tricky, isn't it? Holidays are the time we want to feel closest to our family, so disappointments can hurt even more. My father had a way . . . he'd get drunk, or go off on a 'business trip' he forgot to tell us about. Did your mom ever tell you we used to follow him?"

"No," Grit said. "She almost never talked about him."

"Well, she was a really good detective. It was her way of figuring things out. He stayed out so often, and even though it was painful to learn the truth, it was better than staying in the dark."

"Well, yeah. That's why I stole her diary."

"You took it the day they kicked you out?"

Grit nodded. "She was in her room, crying. I went in to say good-bye and saw it sitting on the bed beside her. It's weird. I'd always known she had it, and she used to hide it right under my father's nose — in his study, in a bookcase full of art books. He had them just for show, never looked at them."

"Wasn't she afraid he'd read it?"

"Of course. But if she'd put it in their room, or her closet, or anywhere that was 'hers,' she knew he'd find it. He ransacked our stuff all the time." Grit's jaw clenched, remembering how he had acted as if he owned everything about them, including their thoughts.

"So you went into her room to say good-bye —"

"She was sitting on her bed. Her face was so red, and when she looked at me, I could tell she was my mom again — not the monster out in the yard, hitting me and screaming at me." Grit's eyes filled with tears. She could see her mother now, remorse in her eyes, but also that sweet, funny recognition they'd always had for each other, the glance that only they knew, the one thing her father couldn't ruin.

"What did she say?"

"Well, you read the last page of her journal, right? The switch had flipped back again, and she hated him. But he was standing right there, waiting for me to leave. Right up to the last minute, I hoped she'd say something, tell me to stay, but she didn't."

"Did you speak at all?"

"Nope. But I did save her ass. My father saw the pen and the diary sitting next to her on the bed, and he asked what it was. I told him it was mine, and grabbed it."

"He'd never seen her writing in it before?"

"No. She was just as secretive with him as you say she was with your dad. She could hide anything. But that day, she was too much of a wreck to care."

"So you took it to protect her?"

Grit had to think about that. Yes, she had protected her mother. But it had been more than that. By stealing the journal, she had taken something deep and important, the thoughts her mother had never been able to share with her.

"If he'd read what she wrote," Clare said, "I'm afraid he would have killed her. Why didn't he try to take the journal away from you?"

"It's hard to explain, but he saw me change that day. This burn on my neck," Grit said, touching the scar beneath the tattoo, "made me strong, right then. I saw him for exactly who he was. A pathetic bully."

"You're right," Clare said. "But your mother? She didn't try to stop you from taking it?"

Grit shook her head. "You know, I think she wanted me to have it. So I'd know the truth."

Clare checked the oven and the timer. "I want to show you something."

They went into the living room, and Grit followed Clare to her desk.

When she looked at the computer screen, she couldn't believe her eyes. There was her mother's Web site — with a brand-new photo of fog-silvered violets.

"When did she put this up?" Grit asked, shocked.

"I'm not sure," Clare said. "I saw it this morning before I went to the hospital."

"She's never changed the picture on her home page before. In all the time I've been looking, it's been that pink fairy orchid."

Grit and Clare stared for a long time. Grit moved the cursor to open the password window and typed in "violets." Nothing happened.

"I think the password has to do with you," Clare said. "Something only you would know."

"I've tried everything."

"It will come to you," Clare said. "Keep thinking."

Grit closed her eyes. The new picture had to mean something — her mother had changed it now, today, for a reason. The fog had to do with Gilly, and the violets were for Grit.

The apple pie bubbled over, and they heard the juice sizzle. Clare ran into the kitchen to rescue it, and Grit slowly followed. She felt a lump in her throat, but from almost unbearable happiness. Her mother had come. She'd worn her violet perfume and left that photo for Grit to find.

Invisible family. Clare bent over the oven to pull out the pie, and Grit stood back. She could almost see her grandmother, baking so long ago. It shimmered in her mind, like an old home movie. Her mother and aunt were right there, too — one sister helping with the pie, the other holding back, planning her next move.

CHAPTER FIFTEEN

The food pantry was located at St. Thomas Aquinas, a 150-year-old landmark church on Tenth Avenue and Twenty-fifth Street. Inside, tall pillars supported a vaulted ceiling above Florentine-style groin arches. Dappled light came through the stained-glass windows.

Clare, Paul, and Grit passed a long line of people waiting in the cold, wishing everyone happy Thanksgiving, receiving greetings back. Most of the people in line were homeless men and women; they would receive their meal tickets and at 10:30 A.M. go into the Aquinas mission house to fill their plates at the serving stations. According to Paul, the church served fifteen hundred hot meals every single day.

Grit limped along in her special shoe, and an old woman mumbled that a shoe like that would be good for her bone spurs. Grit's heart opened instantly to the homeless woman. Until finding Clare, she'd rarely been completely sure where she was going to sleep the next night. Seeing these people reminded her of that, and she bent down and gave the woman her shoe.

Paul had a pair of basketball sneakers in the Jeep; he helped Grit slide one onto her right foot, and let her lean on his arm as they walked in. Grit felt excited to be here with him and Clare. But what would make it absolutely perfect would be if her mother showed up to surprise everyone.

It was 9:45 A.M. now; in Denmark it would be 3:45 in the afternoon, pitch dark. She pictured her father watching the BBC news. It ran twenty-four hours a day and gave him many opportunities to complain and hate this leader being stupid, that leader a coward, this group being deluded, that group being brilliant, and why didn't the world see? There was so much to be against in this world, and he found all of it.

Once inside, Grit and Clare headed for the kitchen, and Paul joined up with a bunch of volunteers setting up round tables and folding chairs. The dinner smelled so great, Grit's stomach rumbled. A woman named Marie gave them white aprons and paper caps and showed them their jobs. There was a stack of plastic cafeteria trays and containers sectioned off for the meal. One tall man was rolling utensils inside paper napkins.

"Grit, would you like to be on utensil duty?" Marie asked. "You could take over from Daniel."

"Sure," Grit said.

"She's an awfully good cook," Clare said. "In case you need extra help with the food."

"Well, we have fifteen minutes before we ring the bell, and we do have more potatoes to be mashed."

"Cool," Grit said, beaming.

She took over from Daniel, who went outside to pass out tickets. Perched on a stool by the stainless steel sink, she saw a mountain of boiled potatoes steaming in metal colanders and knew this was a sign: here she was, doing her mother's favorite holiday dinner job.

Marie drained one large colander, turned it over so the potatoes tumbled back into the heavy pot, placed milk and butter within easy reach; Grit added double the butter, along with plenty of salt and pepper.

"Oh, they're going to love you," Marie said.

"Thanks," Grit said, watching the feast emerge: golden brown turkeys being carved, gravy being seasoned, cans of cranberry sauce opened, stuffing, yellow turnips and small green peas waiting to be served.

She attacked the potatoes with the enormous, institutional-sized masher to break up the potatoes and smooth them into creamy whiteness. She did it quickly, but with gentleness. There was never a reason to be rough with food. These were going to be the most delicious potatoes the soup kitchen patrons had ever tasted.

Now it was time to serve, and Grit joined the assembly line. She arranged the food in big metal pans, making it as attractive as possible. Daniel rang the bell, and the door opened.

People filed in. Some smiled and said thank you. Most looked down, focused on the main thing: loading up their trays. Grit stared at them, loving everyone. They had suffered. These people had scars, injuries, sadness in their eyes, holey clothing.

I love you, I love you, I love you, she said silently, trying to catch everyone's eyes.

She spotted a seventy-year-old man, wiry, with dirty gray hair falling in his face, head down and mumbling; it was Gary, from the hospital. Seeing him, Grit's heart skipped and she wondered why he'd been released so soon. Hadn't they found him a bed in the psych ward? He approached her station, and she waited for him to recognize her. She had her smile ready.

"Hi, Gary," she said.

He looked up, surprised. His eyes narrowed as he stared at her.

"Hi," he said.

"Do you remember me?" she asked.

"Yes," he said, his eyes starting to water. But she didn't see recognition in them, and knew he was still crying for someone else.

"Happy Thanksgiving," Grit said.

"Thank you," he said. "Same to you." He gave her a mournful glance, went back to staring down as he moved away. He didn't know who she was, but she had helped feed him. Grit was glad she'd said hello; sometimes paying attention, even in a small way, was the best a person could do.

Afterward, they stopped at Clare's to change clothes and grab the food. Clare recorded a new outgoing message, replacing the one about having breakfast at Clement's: "Happy Thanksgiving. If you want to find Grit or me, we'll be at Sarah's," and gave the number.

"She's going to show up," Grit said.

Clare paused, taking care with her reply. "I'm just hoping she'll call from Denmark."

"A call would be great, but I'd rather have

her show up," Grit said.

They fed the cats, then Paul drove them two blocks to the Hugheses' apartment on West Twentieth Street, lucking into a parking spot three doors down. They lived in a duplex, including the garden unit, in a town house toward the Tenth Avenue end of the Seminary Block.

"You *drove?*" Sarah asked, greeting them at the door in a russet wool dress.

"My fault," Grit said, lifting up her bandaged foot in Paul's big shoe.

"Oh, your poor broken toe! I'm an idiot! Come on in, meet everyone, sit down and put that foot up!"

Sarah led them toward animated voices in the other room. Grit gave off electricity — happiness mixed with anticipation. Clare had been sure Anne would have called by now; she hoped it would be soon, to keep Grit from being devastated. She'd pinned so much hope on that scent of violets.

"Everyone!" Sarah said. "Glenne, Dorothea, Mikey — meet Grit. Mikey, play your game over there, away from her toe."

"She has a broken foot!" Mikey said.

"That's right, honey. Don't go near it. Grit, that big guy talking to Paul is Max."

Max bounded across the room to hug

339

Clare and Grit, and to hold Grit at arm's length.

"You look exactly like your mother," he said. Tall, husky, with a full beard he swore he wouldn't shave until he found another job, he shined his warmth on Grit. "Sarah told me, but I can't believe the resemblance. Your eyes, cheekbones, your smile —"

"Bet she never had two-toned hair," Grit said, smiling.

"I love it," Glenne said. She and Dorothea came over to greet Grit. They led her to the sofa and had her sit between them. Clare was struck by how grown-up the girls seemed, slim and poised, Glenne with her mother's auburn hair and Dorothea with Max's dark brown.

The phone rang, and Sarah went into the kitchen to answer it. Clare followed, and found Sarah had already hung up.

"No one there," Sarah said.

Clare looked at the caller ID: Unknown.

"Glenne broke up with a boy from Yale, and he's been persistent. But he doesn't usually hang up — he wants to talk to her."

"Jesus, I think —" Clare began.

"Don't tell me, let me guess."

"I left her a message on Monday," Clare said. "With someone at Frederik's gallery. I said it was an emergency, Grit was in the hospital. Then I posted about it, on my blog."

"Then she has to call," Sarah asked, stirring the gravy.

"I know, and I gave both my numbers. Today I left yours on the answering machine so she'd know where we are."

"Goddamn, it was her," Sarah said. "I heard breathing, and she didn't hang up right away."

"She changed the picture on her home page," Clare said. "Right after I called the gallery. Grit said she did it on purpose, to send us a message."

"God, poor kid," Sarah said. "Looking for meaning in her mother's goddamn choice of Web site photos. How is she doing, anyway?"

"She's glowing," Clare said, lowering her voice. "She swears Anne showed up at the hospital. A woman stood by her bed — Anne used to do that, watch her sleeping. When she left, Grit smelled violets."

"It had to be part of a dream," Sarah said. "Right?"

"I think so."

Sarah put her arms around her. "You're doing great," she said. "You know what I think? She's finally starting to feel safe, so some of the deepest things can start to come up."

"Everything reminds her of her mother."

"You know I love Anne," Sarah said. "But right now I'd like to punch her. Staying with that fucking creep, doing this to Grit. I can't imagine turning my back on my daughters."

"Most of the time, I don't think Anne can imagine it either," Clare said, gazing down the narrow hallway at Grit talking to Glenne and Doro.

Eventually Max carved the turkey and everyone crowded into the dining room to help themselves. They squeezed around the long cherry table, and Paul and Clare served red and white wine and sparkling cider. Grit ladled out the creamed onions she'd made, grating another dash of fresh nutmeg on top.

When they were all seated, Sarah looked around the table.

"Wow," Sarah said. "We have so much to be thankful for this year. Starting with Grit — having you here is the best part of all. And Clare . . . and Paul . . . you know how much we love having you. You're family to us."

"To Grit, Clare, and Paul," Max said as they raised their glasses.

"And to all of you," Paul toasted back.

Everyone drank. Sarah spoke again. "Now, this isn't one of those toasts that will go on forever. I just want to remind you of our Thanksgiving tradition. Clare, would you tell it?"

"Every year, after dinner and before dessert, we go around the table and say or show something we're grateful for. It doesn't have to be long, even just a word will do."

"You'll be surprised how easily it comes to you after so much good food," Max said, bowing his head. "So, Lord bless our dinner, bless each other, bless the ones we're missing. Amen."

"Amen," they said.

The feast began; there were so many compliments on Grit's creamed onions and cranberry-stuffed squash, Clare was thrilled to see Grit beaming from the praise. Dorothea had noticed the flower inked on her arm, and they started talking about tattoos.

"I think she's having a good time," Paul said, squeezing Clare's hand under the table.

"So do I."

"What about you?"

"I love it." She smiled and meant it, but she couldn't escape the holiday layer of enforced warmth. This was a moment to dream of being together, giving up their prickly lives of solitude, banding into a family, Grit part of the glue. Clare tried to give herself over to it.

Bach played on the stereo, seconds were offered, and everyone took them. The room buzzed with conversation, everyone talking to and over one another. Clare watched the excited discussion between Grit and the Hughes sisters.

"Your film sounds really cool," Glenne said.

"Thanks," Grit said. "You might think it's strange."

"I doubt it."

"I'll have to edit out the part where I fall into the bog," Grit said. She laughed nervously.

"So when you're not falling in," Glenne said, "what do you do?"

"Well, I build these sculptures out of whatever I find around the bog," Grit said. "It's hard to explain; I feel as if I'm gathering the three of us together again — my mother, my brother, and me." Her gaze went to the door.

"Sounds freaking poetic and mystical," Doro said.

"I try," Grit said.

"We should have a screening when you finish shooting," Max said.

"It's not that good," Grit said. "Besides, I doubt most people would understand."

"We would," Sarah said.

"I think anyone who's ever lost someone would," Paul said.

"Hey, that black-box theater on Eleventh Avenue — just down the block from your house," Max said.

"The old Juno Acting Studio," Sarah said.

"It's just sitting there right now," Max said. "Juno got too old to keep giving classes, and his son can't find any theater companies to rent it out. It's small, and close by. I bet we could have a pretty great screening there."

"I'm sure that would cost a lot," Grit said.

"Behind every artist there are patrons. They keep the work afloat, and help the artist show her talent."

Clare watched Grit redden. Maybe she was thinking of Frederik, the way he courted patrons. Ready to step in and change the subject, she was relieved when Dorothea spoke up.

"You've got to see it," Doro said. "It's truly a black box — walls painted black, about five rows of folding chairs, but has a really awesome vibe. Plus, it's right across Twenty-third Street from the strip club and evil hotel."

"Evil hotel?" Grit asked.

"A by-the-hour place," Glenne said. "You have to read about it on Travelocity! Someone wrote in to say that he saw human blood on the wall, and a rat ate his sandwich while he went to the bathroom."

"Just like the old days, right, Sarah?" Clare asked.

Sarah laughed.

Clare remembered how, when they were young, they used to find secret entrances to the High Line, the then-abandoned elevated train bed that ran up Tenth Avenue. The wild weeds had been beautiful, even more magical, and definitely more remote, than it was now, having been turned into a public park.

"You look so far away," Grit said. "What are you thinking?"

"Oh, about this old rail line. It's a park now, but when we were young, we used to sneak up. It felt like our private place."

"My mom talked about that!" Grit said.

"We'd climb up all the time," Sarah said, leaning against Max. "Remember, Paul?"

"Oh, yeah," he said, staring at Clare.

The telephone rang, startling Clare so much she jumped. "Let Grit answer," she said.

The room fell silent except for the ringing

346

phone, and the sound of Grit pushing her chair back. Clare watched her face, the expression wavering between wild hope and trepidation. She limped over to the phone, lifted the receiver.

"Hello?" Grit said, smiling.

Clare couldn't stand to watch. After a few seconds the smile drained away. "Hello?" Grit said again. "Hello?" She turned her back to the room, lowered her voice. "Mom, are you there? I know you came to see me last night!"

Clare watched Grit hold the receiver to her ear for a long time, not saying anything more, just standing very still, long after the other person had hung up.

CHAPTER SIXTEEN

By the time they got around to giving thanks, Grit was so tired and blank all she could say was something dumb, sentimental, and crowd-pleasing: "For all the wonderful people at this table." That phone call, with no one there but the entire universe washing over the line, had been so bizarre, so painful, she couldn't wait to get home.

Clare got it. In Paul's Jeep on the way home, she'd reached back to touch Grit's knee.

"I'm sorry," she said. "I really had the feeling that was Anne calling, and I thought if she heard your voice —"

"It was her," Grit said. She knew it deep down, just as she believed in the night visitor, the trace of violets. But hearing that hang-up, if it really had been her mother, was worse than no call at all.

The weekend went by slowly. There were no mysterious phone calls. It seemed the more time passed, the stiffer Grit's toe felt.

She dreamed her mother had come to stand beside her bed again; Grit reached up to hug her, and they both dissolved into black vapor, horrible fog. Grit woke up crying, and Clare came to sit on her bed until she fell back to sleep.

By Sunday she felt restless. Clare had gone to Central Park to look for some rare owl. Grit wondered whether she'd meet Paul there. He hadn't been around since Thanksgiving, a fact that made Grit uneasy. She was surprised by how much she wanted them to be together.

She hadn't gone through Clare's things in a while, but suddenly she burned to know what was going on with Paul. Maybe there was evidence. She went into Clare's bedroom, opened the cupboard, and took out the document box. Nothing obvious about Paul; the first thing she saw was a batch of photos taken long ago — Grit was sure they hadn't been here before.

They were of her mother, Clare, and Sarah stretched out on blankets in tall grass with a low iron wall behind them. City buildings rose all around, and Grit realized she was looking at the High Line.

Grit's mother had always made it seem like the best adventure, a hidden garden up above the street, overgrown with wispy weeds, stray grasses, and wildflowers.

Grit and Gilly had begged to hear High Line stories — her mother would make up tales of phantom railroad cars, hoboes traveling from New York to California. She said every rare bird in the world visited it, feeding on wildflower seeds. And best of all, if a grown-up in your life was being mean, the High Line's magic would hide you from everyone. It was a garden in the sky, a place to stay safe.

Now, looking at the picture of her mother and the others, Grit felt despair. Sometimes she felt so comfortable here at Clare's. Life had seemed to be on the upswing, but right now she fell back into the grim reality of life with her family.

Grit shook, staring at the photo of her mother's happy face. The world rocked; so much had happened before Grit was even born. Why couldn't she have known her mother the way she'd been then? She had glimmers of those moments — the knowing look in her mother's eye, the way she'd tell Grit to keep her passport ready. She clutched her mother's photo, closed the box, and returned it to its hiding place.

By the time she got back to her room, she saw she had a text from Dennis on her cell phone. Can I come over?

Yes, she texted back. Maybe he would pull her out of this funk, keep her from going insane. She felt dread, as if life was about to end.

Ten minutes later, her phone rang.

"I'm standing outside your door," he said.

"I'll be right there."

When she let him in, he stood there shivering. He stepped closer, and they kissed. His black leather coat felt slick and cold — it was sleeting outside. Grit led him into the living room where he removed his coat and hung it over a door.

"How was your Thanksgiving?" she asked.

"Really good. Our cousins came from Pennsylvania. How was yours?"

Grit hesitated. This was the moment she could lie and say everything was great. Could he see her trembling, know she felt as if she were going down the drain? She controlled her voice.

"Well, my mother might have called. The phone rang, and they had me answer. I heard her breathing, but she wouldn't say anything. She just hung up."

"Could it have been a wrong number?" Dennis asked. "It's so hard to think of your mother hanging up on you."

"She wouldn't," Grit said. "Would she?"

The crazy thing was, she really didn't know. She wanted Dennis to tell her no, her mother would never do that.

He kissed her instead of answering. She lost herself a little, wrapped in his arms, her thoughts fading. But the minute they stopped kissing, her thoughts began to race again.

"I keep hearing her," she said, and made herself breathe. "Sometimes, when I think about my bog project, it seems I conjured her."

"Maybe you did."

"Well, if I did, she's gone again. And it seems harder now — makes me miss her even more."

"I'm sorry."

"Thanks. When I film, I start to pick up hidden threads. I'm sometimes incredibly happy because I feel these invisible ties to my mother and brother. Just because things are unseen doesn't mean they aren't there."

"Doesn't knowing that help you now?"

She thought about it. No, it didn't, and that made her afraid. She'd been collecting moments on film, returning to the environment where she'd lost the two people she loved most. She'd found a way to gather her missing family close, making their love for each other real, filming the bog again and again.

"Everything was coming together," Grit said. "But it's not anymore. I'm afraid if I don't grab it right now, I'll lose my connection with her . . . it will just dissolve, and I'll have nothing. I'll look at my film and not be able to make sense of any of it."

"But it won't be gone," Dennis said. "You know what you're doing, you've shot footage that's not about to disappear."

He didn't know all that she knew: life was one long disappearing. Her heart raced. What did her film show, after all? She had felt love, at times so pure she'd felt herself levitating.

"I have to finish it soon," she said quietly. "So I can see."

"What will it take?"

"I need to buy a new program so I can edit my film. Look at all the pieces, all the different places, and see if they add up to anything."

She went to her room, looked through her top drawer, found the wrinkled card; it had been in her jeans pocket and gone through the wash before she had fished it out.

Returning to the living room, she showed the card to Dennis.

" 'Antonia's Picnic,' " he read.

"Maybe she'll hire me."

"Go ahead — give her a try!"

Grit called, getting voice mail: "Hi, Alicia, it's Grit Rasmussen. When you bought my car you mentioned you were hiring. Do you still need someone? Call me if you do." She left her phone number.

"I want to help you," he said.

"You do help me," she said. "You're here. And you gave me this. . . ." She turned her arm over so they could see the gray ghost of his drawing.

"It's faded out," he said. "Are you ready for me to ink it in?"

She nodded.

He played lightly with her hair. She leaned her head on his shoulder, wanting him to hold her tight. They kissed, and life sped up all at once. Plans filled her head. Work with Alicia, buy Final Cut Pro, edit her film, tattoo her body, figure out love, fill the black box theater with love and beauty, show her mother, and show the entire world, before every bit of it disappeared.

Clare walked in with a pizza she'd picked up from Don Giovanni's and found Grit reclining on the sofa beside a tall, tattooed young man with a ponytail.

"Oops, hi," Clare said. "You must be Dennis. I'm Clare."

"Good to meet you," he said, standing up to shake her hand.

"Hi, Aunty," Grit said.

"Hi," Clare said and kissed the top of her head. "Any calls today?"

"No," Grit said.

"Dennis, would you like to stay for pizza?" she asked.

"I wish I could, but I'm working six to eleven tonight. Actually, I'd better get going."

"Nighttime tattoos must be the most interesting," Grit said.

"On Friday and Saturday nights, definitely. Sundays are a little more tame." He paused. "Do you know when you might come by?"

"I'll call you."

"Cool," he said.

He slipped on his coat, pressed Grit's shoulder so she wouldn't get up, kissed her on the lips. "Hope your toe feels better."

"Thanks," she said.

When he left, Grit made room on the sofa and Clare set up the pizza on the low table. She poured sparkling water and lit candles. The cats, who must have been hiding during Dennis's visit, came out to investigate the food. Grit fed Blackburn a tiny piece of cheese.

"He seems nice," Clare said.

"He's really great," Grit said, blushing.

"You let him know you want that tattoo?" Clare asked.

"Yeah." She turned her arm over, revealed the nearly invisible flower. "He's going to do this one, and another on my back. We're getting really close."

"I'm glad you're doing what you want."

"Clare, I feel bad about staying here without pulling my weight. I'm getting a job, and I'm going to start paying you rent really soon."

"You're not going to pay me rent!" Clare said.

"I want to. I want to be more solid. All that time I spent in bogs was my way of being with my mom and Gilly. I don't know why, but I don't want to do that anymore. I just want to edit the film and have it all be over."

"Because of how badly you got hurt on Staten Island?" Clare asked.

"It scared me," Grit said. "And I don't like to be scared."

"No one does."

"I'm just worried I'll put the film together, and all I'll see is how alone I am. They were never with me at all."

"I'll tell you what," Clare said. "Let's

watch and see."

"It's not ready, I haven't edited — or even uploaded the latest to my computer."

"That's okay. Let's just watch the Staten Island footage. We can plug the camera into the TV."

And they did. Grit was reluctant, didn't speak. Turning off lights, they sat in the dark watching a slice of that day fill the screen: the soft white November sky, the rich brown bog, a close-up of dry flowers. The camera wobbled as Grit secured the tripod, her palm casting a pink shadow over the lens.

Now the film showed her at the fire pit, collecting stones and bits of burned wood. She dragged the limb to the bog and slid it into position, pointing outward, perpendicular to the bank. Slipping on the icy mud, she took off her shoes and began arranging the things she'd gathered. She walked backward, balancing on the log, like a fairy-tale character dropping crumbs so she could find her way home.

Clare saw Grit's grace, the delicacy of movement, but most of all, her bearing, the way she opened to the world. She was slight, and Clare could almost imagine she was seeing her as a child, playing in the bog. But her stature was eloquent, and Clare could see the emotion in every movement.

Clare saw watery light glisten on the bog's surface, and could almost believe it reflected off Grit herself. Watching the screen, Clare put her arm around Grit's shoulders. She wanted her to see what she saw: a beautiful young woman.

Seagulls circled, and then the hawk flew overhead. Clare knew what would happen next, and she hit the pause button.

"Don't you want to see my big dramatic fall?" Grit said.

"Not now," Clare said.

"It wasn't part of the plan. And you don't have to worry about me."

"I know. I can tell. Did you see how strong you were, dragging that big log into place? And then how ethereal, when you started to walk? You balanced like a ballet dancer. It was almost as if your feet weren't even touching the log."

"Are you serious?" Grit asked, her eyes glistening. "That's how I always feel. As if I'm moving above the ground."

"I think you are," Clare said.

"Are you just saying that?"

"No. We can rewind and look again."

They did, and there were Grit's bare feet, tiptoeing along the ragged bark. Delicate feet, curved arches, gliding with grace. Water pooled beneath the branch, shimmering like a mirage. Clare knew it was an optical illusion, but that didn't matter.

"You're illuminated," Clare said. "With whatever you are feeling. It shows in your face and movement, and I don't know how you do it, but it shines out into the bog."

"That's where they are," Grit said.

"Your family."

"Can you see them?"

"No, but I know they're there. I love what you're doing here. I want you to keep it up, and believe in it. Your mother shook you up."

"In life?" Grit asked.

"Yes," Clare said. "And right here, in New York. She called, I have no doubt about that."

"And she visited?"

Clare smiled. "I can't go quite that far."

Grit peered at her. "Did you leave some pictures for me to find?"

"Thanksgiving night, after we got home from dinner. Yes — I dug out some of your mom, Sarah, and me on the High Line."

"You knew I'd look in that box?"

"I guessed," Clare said. "I'd noticed the papers looked out of order. Don't feel bad; I grew up with secrets, too. Everyone in our family has a hiding place."

"I like those pictures," Grit said. "Mom

looked happy. She's not like that anymore."

Clare stared at Grit; what would a real mother do right now? Should she trust her niece to find her own way? The stakes were high, and Clare felt so new at this.

The telephone rang. Clare jumped, gesturing for Grit to answer, and she did. But it wasn't Anne.

"Hi, Alicia," Grit said. "Did you get my message?"

Clare left the room so Grit could take the call.

CHAPTER SEVENTEEN

Two weeks passed, and the first real snow fell. It covered the streets and sidewalks, coating brownstone steps and iron railings. The small park across the street glistened, the bare branches outlined in white. During that first storm, children made forts and snowmen while their mothers stood beside them, bundled up for the cold.

There had been no more mysterious phone calls. Clare and Grit worked to unlock Anne's Web site with no luck; the photo of violets in the fog remained the same: elusive, haunting, and frustrating.

Late Saturday afternoon, dusk falling just behind the snow, Clare wandered Shakespeare Garden — Central Park's best birding spot, after the Ramble, not counting the North Woods. Four hilly acres climbed Vista Rock, the park's only rock garden planted with trees and flowers mentioned in the bard's plays and sonnets: primrose, columbine, rue, wormwood, quince, lark's heel, holly, and hemlocks. After watching a brown creeper climb an eastern hemlock, she gazed down at a bronze plaque bearing one of her favorite quotations:

> THERE'S ROSEMARY, THAT'S FOR REMEMBRANCE; PRAY, LOVE, REMEMBER: AND THERE IS PANSIES. THAT'S FOR THOUGHTS. ~HAMLET

Originally Central Park's planners had called this area "The Garden of the Heart." In 2006, a wild gale knocked over a mulberry tree grafted — legend had it — from one planted by Shakespeare at New Place, Stratford-on-Avon, in 1602. Back when they were young, she and Anne had come here, looking for birds, dreaming of love. Still in high school, Clare and Paul had walked the winding paths to the summit, sat on rustic bentwood benches, kissed and talked for hours.

A male eastern towhee foraged through the English ivy just behind another favorite quote. Clare photographed the bird, but also the plaque:

> THIS BUD OF LOVE, BY SUMMER'S RIPENING BREATH, MAY PROVE A BEAUTEOUS FLOW'R

The garden was quaint and archaic. Clare found herself listening for the laughing owl. The myth of the ancient mulberry tree seemed to welcome the ghost bird. When Alistair Fastnet had released the original pair into the park, had they roosted here?

Clare still hoping to see an obviously extinct raptor, Grit smelling her mother's perfume: wishful thinking ran in the family. She spotted and photographed black-capped chickadees and a white-throated sparrow. A redheaded woodpecker had been reported on one of the bird lists; hearing a rat-tat-tat she turned left, saw a woman whirl and head down the path toward the Delacorte Theater.

The woman glanced back, but not long enough for Clare to see her face. The sight of the woman in a long, black cloak made Clare's scalp tingle. It was that family wishful thinking again.

Clare finally left the park, heading to Lincoln Center to buy tickets to *The Nutcracker*. It would be so much easier to dismiss the sight of that woman if she hadn't been wearing a black cape. Anne had worn one on Halloween, but she'd liked it so much she'd started wearing it around the city whenever it was cold. She filed the thought in her mind along with violet water and an extinct owl.

Walking past the blue-white illuminated fountain, she ducked into the theater. Standing in line at the New York City Ballet box office, she studied the schedule. Would it be better to buy the first available *Nutcracker* tickets or pick a date closer to Christmas?

The line moved slowly, and Clare unzipped her jacket to cool off. She thought of her last time seeing the ballet — as a young girl, certainly, with Anne and their parents. The magic and beauty onstage had transfixed her.

She wanted that for Grit: to sit in the dark and watch the "Waltz of the Snowflakes." The ballet's mystical grace had always seemed like a promise to Clare, as if it could take her away from the harshness of real life. And it did — for the performance's duration. But her family's troubles returned the minute they left the theater.

When she got to the head of the line, she asked for three tickets for Christmas Eve. Walking into the cold wind, she paused at the bright fountain. She glanced around, and suddenly the sense of having seen Anne was gone. The Metropolitan Opera House reigned over the plaza, with Chagall's two great paintings *The Triumph of Music* and *The Sources of Music* filling the massive arched windows.

Back at Bedford Hills, she had started paying attention to her dreams. One night in her cell, she dreamed herself into Chagall's paintings: soft colors, nature, art, angels, lovers, and heavenly music. Paul had been with her, and they'd been entwined in each other's arms, rising above the world, lifted by their love. She had wakened in her bed, tears on her cheeks, locked in the same impenetrable space.

Now, at the corner of Broadway and West Sixty-fifth Street, she stood still in the whipping wind. Snow blew sideways from the west, off the Hudson. Home was forty blocks south; Paul's apartment was thirty blocks north. Grit had spent the day with Dennis. She would start working at Antonia's Picnic when her bandage came off on Wednesday, and tonight she and Alicia were having a drink at Clement's.

Clare turned north up Broadway, stopped at Zabar's to fill a basket with wine, cheese, bread, a steak, and a bunch of red-leaf lettuce.

She passed Christmas tree sellers along

the way, stands of fir and pine direct from Nova Scotia, Alaska, Minnesota, and New Hampshire. A thin Salvation Army Santa stood at Eighty-sixth Street, ringing his bell and blasting carols on a tinny CD player.

Paul's building was all the way east on West Ninety-fourth Street, almost to Central Park. She loved these old brownstones, more decorative than the ones in Chelsea, and the way snow covered gargoyles and wrought-iron railings, filling the hollows and curlicues. She climbed Paul's steps and rang his bell.

"Hello?" his voice crackled through the speaker.

"It's Clare," she said.

"Wow," he said, buzzing her in; she moved quickly through the outer and inner doors, then started up the stairs. She heard a door unlock up above her. He lived on the fifth floor, and she trekked up.

"Surprise," she said.

"Yeah, an awesome one," he said, taking the bags from her hand, leading her into the broom closet–sized kitchen. Mysteriously, birds called from another room. Stashing everything on the narrow counter, he kissed her. She leaned into him, feeling desire and the audacity of having shown up unannounced.

"This is good," he said, holding her face in his hands. "You're really catching on."

"I was in the park, thinking of you," she said. "I found that bench in Shakespeare Garden, where we sat that time, talked so long."

"I remember," he said. "I was too madly in love with you to care there was a pileated woodpecker in the tree behind us."

"That was a great bird," she said.

He laughed. "Speaking of birds, I'm sharing my space right now. Come on, I'll show you."

Clare hardly ever came here; it reminded her of his exile, how he'd moved out of Chelsea after her release. This place was his home, but also a symbol of their life apart. She couldn't help thinking of Elena, wondering how much time she had spent here.

Paul led her through the living room, filled with comfortable furniture, stacks of nature journals piled high. Books filled a wall of bookcases. His desk overflowed with documents and reports.

The mantel shelf was devoted to photos: his parents, siblings, nieces and nephews, and Clare. She saw two framed pictures of herself: one young, grinning over her shoulder as they hiked the North Woods, and another more recent, standing by the rail of the Staten Island ferry when she hadn't been aware. The place felt warm, lived-in, very much Paul.

They headed down the hall and the bird-calls grew louder. He opened a bedroom door, and Clare saw two cages, each containing one starling.

"As you can see, I have guests."

The starlings' iridescent blue-black feathers looked dull under electric light. Clare crouched down, watching them peck and pace, gazing at their bright onyx eyes.

"Are they injured? Are you rehabbing them?"

"No," he said. "Come on, I'll tell you."

Instead of going to the kitchen he pulled her into his bedroom. He turned on a small brass lamp; she saw his boots by the door, a pile of laundry by the bureau, a freshly cleaned uniform hanging from the doorjamb. Two dark, mystical oil paintings of Central Park, one of Poet's Walk, the other of Belvedere Castle, hung over his bed.

He held Clare, easing her down. She'd brought dinner, but this was what she'd really come for. He smoothed her hair back from her face. She touched his cheek. His face had character, another word for years. They had each earned their lines, but it made Clare sad to think of how many they'd gotten while apart.

"A lot of wasted time," she said.

"That's over," he said, stroking her face.

She raised her head to meet his lips, arm around his neck. Unzipping, unbuttoning, cold air, hot skin against skin. He ripped the covers away and they slid between cool sheets. She arched into him, needing more before they even started.

His body was all muscle, and she held him tight, digging her fingers in to make him go deeper. She held her breath, wild with emotion.

"That's it, I'm with you, I love you . . ."

Clare clutched him, chest pressed against his, and she felt it building: her blood racing with his, everything falling, the most delicate break, revealing everything, letting him see without trying to hide.

They slept, waking at nine P.M. Standing in his claw-foot bathtub, shower curtain drawn, they held each other, kissing in the blast of hot water. They leaned against the tiles, washed each other, taking a long time. Stepping out they dried off, stood naked hugging in the small, steamy bathroom.

"I came to cook you dinner," she said.

"I'm starving," he said. "But I have to head out at ten."

"Really?" she asked.

He nodded. "I got a call about a Cooper's hawk, trapped in the state supreme court rotunda. They're letting me in at ten-thirty."

"Really? Weren't you going to call me?" she asked.

"I did," he said, holding her tight. "Have you checked your messages? We'll eat right now, and then you're coming with me to save the bird."

"I guess that explains the starlings," she said.

"Yep," he said.

They dressed quickly, and she made a salad, seasoned the steak. The broiler heated up, and she slid the pan under the heat. Whisking vinaigrette, she drizzled it over the lettuce. Paul cleared a small table, his catchall space, covered with keys, his camera, binoculars, and a pile of well-used black Moleskine notebooks.

He carried over his desk chair for Clare, and took his coat off the back of a metal café chair for himself. Clare served the steak and salad and poured each of them a glass of wine.

"This is great," he said. "I can't remember the last time I used the stove. What put you in the mood to cook?"

Clare pictured Grit, the joy she got from shopping the market, slowly preparing a meal as if that was every bit as pleasurable as sitting down to dinner and eating the food.

A skillful enough cook, Clare had never let herself enjoy the sensual gifts of working with fresh, fragrant, sustaining food. Watching Grit, she saw how love was an active ingredient in each meal.

Walking through Shakespeare Garden had clinched it.

"You," Clare said.

"You wanted to feed me?"

"Yes."

"Thank you," he said. He raised his glass, and they clinked. "It really is different, isn't it?"

Clare nodded. She wanted to tell him how much, but she couldn't quite believe it herself. She felt the concrete around her heart smashing open. This last month had been a sledgehammer. The closeness she felt to him, and to Grit, scared her less each day.

They cleaned up the dishes, pulled on scarves and parkas. Paul disappeared into the back bedroom, returned with a large empty cage; next he got the starlings in their smaller cages and a wide roll of seine netting. Before leaving the apartment he covered the starlings' cages with a towel, not wanting to disorient the birds more than necessary. As they headed downtown in the Jeep, Clare held the birds on her lap.

"Where did you get them?" she asked.

"At the Alice in Wonderland statue. I threw down some millet, and they walked straight into the cages."

Clare felt deep love for starlings, maligned birds, an invasive species brought from another continent, just like the laughing owl. People didn't want them in their yards. When families put out suet or sunflower seeds in the snow, starlings were the birds they really wished would go away. They wanted cardinals, finches, orioles: birds that sang and look pretty, instead of starlings, who squawked.

Starlings fly in a cloud: a black umbrella turned inside out over fields, city parks. Black birds with feathers blazing, black opals, flying in formation, sticking together by instinct. Wing-to-wing they swooped, made figure eights a kite maker would envy. Yet still no one wanted them in their yards.

"You'll be free soon," she said, reaching under the towel, through the small cage bars, letting one of the birds peck her fingertip. She knew they'd be bait, but Paul would trap the raptor before it caught the starlings.

"Let's hope they work. The hawk has been flying in circles since sometime last night; he's dehydrated, and I'm worried he'll injure his wing on the ceiling or the light fixtures."

Clare nodded. She had often gone with him to rescue birds from indoor spaces. She loved his ability to coax species from hawks to passerines into a safety net, then release them back to the wild.

Wall Street and Centre Street, the financial and government districts, were deserted, the granite buildings old-fashioned under falling snow. A plow rattled by, sparks flying from pavement. Paul parked on a dark side street off Foley Square, and they carried the starlings and net up the hundred-foot-wide stone steps of the state supreme courthouse.

Corinthian columns formed a graceful colonnade topped with a triangle featuring statues representing law, truth, and equity. The wall was chiseled with words spoken by George Washington: THE TRUE ADMINISTRATION OF JUSTICE IS THE FIRMEST PILLAR OF GOOD GOVERNMENT. The words scathed, and, as always, Clare found it painful to enter any courthouse.

A guard let them in. Their footsteps echoed in the rotunda, vestibule walls adorned with WPA murals. The grand Italian decorative-style paintings rose to the rotunda dome, bright in the gleam of the enormous bronze chandelier. Clare read the plaque on the wall: LAW THROUGH THE AGES, PAINTED BY ATTILIO PUSTERLA (1862–1931).

Now she stood with Paul, each with binoculars pressed to their eyes, scanning the dome. Above the chandelier, arched clerestory windows rose to the oculus, a large circular glass "eye" gazing into the sky, allowing for natural light to fill the vestibule by day.

"There," she said when she had the hawk in sight.

"Got him," Paul said.

They watched the Cooper's, a medium-sized accipiter, fly in circles in a series of quick wing beats. By size and markings Clare knew he was a juvenile male with short, rounded wings, a very long black-banded tail, neck extended in flight.

The hawk soared up to the oculus; they heard his hooked bill smack against the glass, followed by a piercing *kick-kick-kick* alarm call.

"He's been doing that all night," the watchman said.

"Calling or banging into the glass?"

"Both," the watchman said. "Crazy,

haunted sound."

" 'Crazy, haunted sound,' " Clare repeated, and looked at Paul. She thought of the reports on the bird lists, how easy it was to see what you wanted to see, and hear what you wanted to hear. She was becoming more convinced that her laughing owl was really a Cooper's hawk. Paul smiled, as if he was thinking the same thing.

"How did he get in?" Paul asked.

"We think maybe through a broken window in Judge Tsao's chambers. Part of the day the bird rested on the chandelier, calm as can be with all the people coming and going. Then he'd fly around and make that *kick-kick* sound. But now it's like he's panicked. He knows he's done for."

"He's not," Paul said. "We're going to catch him. In ten minutes will you turn off that chandelier? And all the vestibule lights?"

"Sure. It'll be damned dark, though."

"That's good. When I give the signal, flip the lights back on and stand still, okay?"

Beneath the towel, the starlings were silent. Paul walked backward, holding the edge of the fishing net, and Clare stood still holding the spool. He attached his end to a granite pillar, tying it on with a long length of twine. Clare affixed her end to a second column. The six-foot-wide net passed directly over the two cages. Paul removed the towel, and the starlings began to squawk and caw.

"Now," Paul said.

The guard hit the switch and the rotunda went black. Clare stood with Paul behind a pillar, blind in the dark. Outside, snow clouds held city light, the loom of the Brooklyn Bridge, and cast it through the oculus, a ghostly beam falling toward the floor.

The hawk would be hungry, and it would hear the starlings. Raptors had vision like telescopes. Clare looked up; she imagined a laughing owl silhouetted by the oculus, wings spread, with a similar long tail. Now Clare kept her eye on the cages; she heard the dive-bombing whistle of speed, then the hawk's cry as his extended talons snagged the netting just above his would-be prey.

Paul rushed over, struggled with the hawk to keep him from escaping. He wore thick leather falconer's gloves, embracing the hawk to immobilize his wings. Clare threw the towel around the raptor's shoulders as Paul untangled his claws from the net. They placed him in the large cage, closed the door.

"Holy shit," the watchman said. "He

didn't even get the birds."

Paul nodded, checking on the starlings.

"Wait'll I tell everyone how you did it. Simple as anything. Takes a bird man, I guess."

"That's me," Paul said.

The guard laughed, crouching by the big cage. "Wow, he looks mean and mad. Put my finger in there I bet ya he'd bite it off."

"I wouldn't test him," Paul said.

They all shook hands. The guard turned on the lights, and Paul and Clare carried the cages back to the Jeep. They drove uptown. Clare knew they both wanted to release the Cooper's right away, but he might have injured himself and had to be checked. Paul phoned Annette, the only raptor rehabilitator in the city, and told her they'd be there in five minutes.

Clare watched Paul stand out front of the brick apartment house on East Eighty-third Street. These had been built as tenements to house workers, back when this part of the Upper East Side had been Germantown.

The front door opened, Paul handed Annette the cage, and Annette leaned out to wave to Clare. They were all part of the odd, passionate network of New York City birders. Annette would observe and hydrate the hawk and, if all was well, release him into Central Park tomorrow.

Snow fell harder. Paul drove to Fifth Avenue, found a parking spot around the corner on East Seventy-sixth Street. Heads down into the wind, they entered Central Park carrying the two small cages. Branches clicked and rustled overhead. A thick white blanket covered the paths, hills, benches, and the large bronze statue of Alice in Wonderland.

As children Clare and Anne had sailed boats on Conservatory Water, then run a few steps to climb on Alice, her friends the Mad Hatter and the March Hare, pet the Cheshire Cat, step from toadstool to toadstool.

"Right where you found them," Clare said.

"That's right," Paul said.

It was nighttime, and all the park's starlings were asleep. Crouching, Paul opened both cages. The birds seemed slow to realize they were free, then stepped out at once, up to their bellies in snow. They flapped their wings and flew into the white veil. Clare's chest ached.

Freedom always did that to her. Paul knew, and put his arm around her. He probably didn't realize how acutely Clare was thinking of her sister, the little girls they had been, holding hands to protect each other, but brave enough to climb into Wonderland.

She was thinking of that woman she'd seen across the park a few hours ago, leaving Shakespeare Garden in her black cloak, trailing a dreamy scent of imaginary violets, and of the extinct owl that Clare seemed not to need anymore.

CHAPTER EIGHTEEN

The tables turned: now Grit was waiting up for Clare. Her aunt was obviously a grown woman and had a life, although Grit honestly hadn't seen much of it, except for daytime birding excursions. Night was another story.

She paced through the apartment. Her toe felt better, but her shoulder blade burned from the panoramic tattoo Dennis had completed earlier. Stopping by the bathroom mirror, Grit checked out his art: the red sun, and the filigree branches, gentle moonlight glistening through the trees. Dennis had dressed her with her mother's lullaby.

Now she wandered back to the living room, peered out the window into the snow, golden in streetlight. Clare hadn't said anything about plans. Had she met up with Paul? Grit really hoped they were having a Saturday night date.

Curling up with Blackburn on the couch, she relived the meeting she'd had with Alicia at Clement's.

Sean Kilroy, the bartender, had welcomed them and served them drinks on the house in honor of the city's first real snowstorm.

"How's the Subaru treating you?" Grit asked.

"Great. She's amazing in this weather."

"Yeah, she's a Boston car," Grit said. "She took me through a blizzard and plenty of snowstorms."

They drank to the car. Then Alicia pulled a pale pink folder from her backpack. The Antonia's Picnic logo was embossed in dark rose; when Grit looked inside, she found menus, full-color photographs of event venues throughout the city, and testimonials from customers.

"They're my mother and aunts," Alicia said, laughing. "Is that cheating?"

"No way! Especially if you've actually cooked for them."

"I totally have, many times. I got my start catering my brothers' and cousins' birthdays."

"Then you're cool. Besides, what's family for?" Grit asked, feeling semiphony.

"I've booked a few things for Christmas," Alicia said. "My aunts' and uncles' office parties, that's four; a launch party in this amazing loft for a PR client my friend represents, that's five; and a cupcake and hot chocolate party for the kids my cousin nannies for, that's six!"

"You've done so much since I met you," Grit said. "Six bookings, and all these menus — you're on a huge roll."

"That's why I'm thinking yes, hiring you would be a good thing."

"Awesome," Grit said.

They studied the menus for a few minutes, Grit trying to calm down. She loved Alicia's food aesthetic, as hearty as chicken breasts stuffed with prosciutto and Saint André triple crème cheese, and as playful as chocolate-covered gummy bears. Not only that, she was already counting the money she'd make.

In anticipation and on faith, she'd gone to the Fourteenth Street Apple Store and used the last of her five hundred dollars to buy Final Cut Pro, the film editing software she'd learned to use at Emerson. Clare's words about the film had really inspired her to edit what she had, and now she'd have the income to accomplish that.

"If we work together, I'd like you to come up with some Christmas, Super Bowl, and Valentine's Day menus," Alicia said.

"I'd love to," Grit said.

"I'm still worried the name is misleading. 'Antonia's Picnic.' My mother's trying to get me to change it. She thinks it sounds like a seasonal business."

"I think 'Antonia's Picnic' is a magical name."

"Magical?" Alicia asked.

Grit paused, sipping her soda. She thought of how picnics brought everyone together. They were supposed to be joyful and carefree, but sometimes they were just moments of peace amid the tempest of life. Grit couldn't help thinking of one in particular.

"Yes," Grit said. "Picnics make people happy. Every day's a sunny day. Every night is full of magic. That's what picnics bring."

"Thank you. Wow. That's the whole spirit. That's what we want our customers to feel after we've catered their event. I'm only hiring servers with good personalities and big smiles."

"You want me for a server?" Grit asked, her heart falling.

"No," Alicia said. "I need someone who can cook and sees the big picture, which clearly you do."

"Thank you," Grit said with a big smile. "I'm excited, and I'll really try."

"This is going to be great," Alicia said,

and they shook hands.

Now, home and waiting for Clare, Grit couldn't wait to tell her aunt about the meeting. She parted the curtains to check on the snowstorm. Her gaze fell upon the small park across the street.

Snow fell so thickly, she could barely make out the wrought-iron fence, tall tree, benches arranged around the square. A statue stood in the center. Funny, Grit had noticed the snowman earlier, but this sculpture was much larger, the size of an adult. She didn't remember seeing it there before.

It was nearly midnight. The statue seemed to sway, as if in the wind, and Grit suddenly realized she was seeing a person. The shadowy figure inched deeper into the park, hidden by the snow's opaque curtain. Was it a homeless person, seeking refuge in the peaceful park? Grit pressed her forehead to the window.

The memory came out of nowhere: outside in the dark, a snow picnic. Every night is full of magic. . . .

Suddenly Grit was seven years old. Mesmerized by falling snow, she had stood in her nightgown, staring out. Their yard in Ebeltoft looked soft and white. Earlier that night Gillis had broken one of her father's swirled orange-and-red glass tubes, and she'd hidden the pieces to protect him. When her father found out, he spanked her so hard, he left welts on the backs of her legs.

She had refused to cry.

Her skin hurt like the worst sunburn. Her father went storming out of the house, shouting why did he have such stupid children, why was their mother so incompetent and unable to keep them from damaging everything?

Gillis was in bed, probably asleep. Grit couldn't hear her mother, but she smelled warm milk and chocolate. Touching the windowpane, she felt the ice crystals soothe her fingers. She wanted to go outside, lie in the snow, feel the soft coldness on the backs of her legs. Her yard looked serene, a place to feel better.

Her mother stood beside her. Grit could hear her breathing. Grit froze, unable to speak. Her mother leaned down to kiss her, and Grit felt the brush of fur on the hood of her mother's parka. Her mother held Grit's winter coat and helped her into it.

"Where are we going?" Grit asked.

"Outside," her mother said. "For a night-time picnic."

They put on boots, walked out the front door. Beneath the pine tree, they spread a plaid wool blanket. Sheltered from the snow they sat on the cold ground, and her mother produced a small silver thermos and poured hot chocolate into two tiny silver cups. She opened a brown paper bag filled with sugar cookies.

The scent of pine surrounded them as they drank chocolate and ate cookies. Ice glittered on the needles. The hint of a moon glowed behind the snow.

Grit let her mother rock her, the frozen earth numbing the backs of her legs, making her feel better. She felt her mother's warm breath in her hair, closed her eyes. Her mother patted snow on the welts, killing the pain.

"Everything's going to be okay, Little Night," her mother said.

"Why do you call me that?"

"Because of your beautiful dark hair and because you protect creatures from the hunter."

"*He's* the hunter," Grit said, eyes brimming.

"Yes, he is. And you stood between him and Gilly. That was very brave."

"I just wish it would stop," Grit said. "And that he'd be nice."

"Oh, Grit. I know. So do I. But people are who they are. Your father never changes. I tell you what; we'll get a sleigh and some reindeer, and I'll bundle you and Gilly up in Christmas blankets, and we'll go away."

"Forever?" Grit asked.

"Yes, sweetheart. I'll make the hurt stop, take you somewhere he can never hurt you again. We'll look back and remember this night, how we had a picnic and made our plans. I love you so much."

Grit had been young enough to still believe her mother's promise, to have her hopes raised enough to think that night picnics had power, and that the sleigh would come and save the three of them.

The clock struck twelve. Grit stared into the park and suddenly everything coalesced, and she realized what she was seeing through the snow.

She dressed quickly in her jacket and boots and ran outside, carrying a thick wool blanket. The sidewalks hadn't been shoveled. She slipped, righted herself, and half-ran, half-limped across the street. She grabbed for the iron fence and lifted the latch to open the massive gate and enter Clement Clarke Moore Park.

The park seemed deserted, the snow untrammeled by footprints. But Grit knew she was here.

"Mom!" she yelled.

No one answered. Grit stood in complete silence for a few moments. Listening closely she heard the clink of metal chain: the swing set. She started toward the playground when she picked up a single set of footprints. She glanced around, feeling panic. The swing set stood straight ahead, one unoccupied swing creaking back and forth.

Grit wished she'd brought a blanket, wanting to wrap it around her mother, make her warm, tell her they were safe now, they'd both gotten away from him. But no one was there. The park was empty, all but for Grit and footsteps in the fallen snow, so close together they formed letters, spelled out: GRIT

Clare sat in Paul's Jeep, parked in front of her building.

"Let me stay with you," he said.

She shook her head. "I want that, but Grit's here. I know she likes you, but I just want to move slowly with her. Tonight was incredible, though."

"Yeah," he said, kissing her hard. "It was pretty great. But someday —"

"You won't be living on Ninety-fourth Street anymore," she said.

"I can't wait," he said.

Clare climbed the front steps, waved to let

him know she was safe inside. He drove away, and she took a last glance down the street. She heard the incongruous sound of springtime, the rhythmic back-and-forth rasp of the park's swing set.

"Grit?" she called, recognizing her niece's small frame.

Her niece seemed not to hear. She swung vigorously, pumping her legs to fly higher. Clare walked to the Tenth Avenue entrance and hurried through blowing snow toward the playground area.

"Stop!" Grit said, putting on the brakes as Clare approached, the swing halting at once. Clare kept moving, and Grit howled, "NO!"

"What's the matter?" Clare asked, stopping short.

"Don't step there. The snow's already ruining it!"

"Ruining what? I don't see," Clare said.

"There!" Grit said, pointing.

Barely visible, Grit's name had been traced in the snow.

"My mother was here. We were in the park at the same time — she was in here waiting, all the time it snowed. Her footprints didn't lead in from the street; she was standing by that bench while the snow covered her! I saw her from the window, but I didn't see her leave."

"Oh, God."

"Do you have your camera?" Grit asked.

"I do," Clare said, still carrying everything she'd taken when she'd left the house that morning. Reaching into her backpack, she pulled out her Nikon, set the flash, and photographed the nearly obscured "Grit."

"Did you get it?"

"Yes," Clare said, showing Grit the snow-blurred image.

"We have to go home," Grit said. "I figured it out."

They hurried through the park, onto Tenth Avenue, around the corner, and entered the brownstone.

Anne had made her own pattern, cut from *The New York Times,* the newsprint pieces held together by straight pins. She had based her design on a swirling cape worn by Anouk Aimée, photographed for *Vogue* in Paris, on the Pont des Arts in winter.

"It drives men mad," Anne said, once the cape had been sewn, worn, proven its worth. Clare had to admit her sister did cut a dramatic figure, striding home from school clutching her books, black velvet billowing behind her. Most boys were intimidated, but the ones Anne liked, the growly, edgy, bad boys, couldn't get enough.

The cape marked the beginning of Anne's

promiscuous period. Still in high school, but long after they'd discovered the truth about their father, she dated college boys and men she met in hotel bars.

She had a particular fondness for the Plaza's Oak Bar, even though it was easier to get served at Trader Vic's, also in the hotel. Manhattan private school kids ordered a Buddha Bowl, clustered around the white ceramic Buddha, communally sipping a mixture of pineapple juice and four kinds of alcohol through surreally long straws.

Anne would leave everyone to drink that sweet cocktail and slink, black caped, into the Oak Bar. She'd sit in a chair, take out a cigarette, and wait for a man in a dark suit to light it. She preferred the businessmen who frequented the Plaza to artistic types downtown, found it easier to sleep with them without getting attached.

"They love me when I'm a virgin," she told Clare.

"Isn't that wishful thinking?" Clare asked.

"Of course not," Anne said. "It happens all the time."

"Tell me how."

"We go to his room, whatever hotel, whoever he may be," Anne said, a dreamy, drifty look in her eyes. "Maybe he's from London, maybe he's from Perth, maybe he's from Billings, Montana. He climbs into bed, and I tell him to wait for me while I go into the powder room to freshen up. I take off my clothes, everything but the cape. And I walk into the bedroom, and his eyes grow wide, and I let the cape drop from my shoulders, and he is the first man ever to see me naked."

Clare had both loved Anne and feared for her when she told that story. Anne was following their father's path and either didn't know or didn't care. The cape had been her costume, her entry into each night's adventure.

"Did your mother wear a cape in Denmark?" Clare asked Grit.

"A long time ago I think. Why?"

"I just wondered. She had one when we lived here."

Grit went to Clare's desk, turned on the computer. It took a few seconds to boot up. The cats slept in their corners. When Clare looked toward the tall window, she saw a face print from where Grit had leaned into the glass, watching her mother in the park.

Clare's screensaver opened up, and even without being asked, she knew what to do: she typed "gillygrit.dk" into the search window. Anne's Web site opened up, eerie white violets in the fog.

Grit's hands hovered over the keyboard. She hesitated, then typed the words LITTLE NIGHT. The pale flowers shattered into a million silver petals, the site opened up, and they were in.

■ ■ ■ ■

PART TWO

■ ■ ■ ■

CHAPTER NINETEEN

There is no excuse.

I get by on three hours of sleep at night.

I don't think that is penance, but I don't know for sure. I haven't had red wine in four days, and I think of "special intentions" back when I went to church, when we'd give up something we enjoyed as insurance on our prayers.

For instance, on nights when my father didn't come home, I'd deprive myself of the grapes and cherries, my favorites, in our nightly serving of Del Monte fruit cocktail, push them aside, and pray that my father would walk through the door *right now,* or at least soon, and that my parents wouldn't get a divorce.

My father not coming home kept me up many nights. That might explain my insomnia, although it's not exactly an inability to sleep, it's more that I need to be up at night, keep vigilant, watch out for monsters.

Although what can any monster do to us now? Not much, I maintain.

One thing I didn't know is that there are hard-and-fast rules for fruit cocktail. The USDA requires that any commercially canned product sold as "fruit cocktail" contain the following within the percentages stipulated:

30–50 percent diced peaches, must be yellow
25–45 percent diced pears, any variety
6–20 percent seedless whole green grapes
Little to no cherry halves, artificial variety is fine

Now, when I read the rules about fruit cocktail, I felt agitated. All those years I had hoped to have many grapes and cherries in my serving, I had not known that the percentages were not only against me, but in the case of cherries, the possibility existed that any given can might contain exactly *zero.*

So much in life involves trickery and false hopes. And this is the thing: once you start down the false hope road, it becomes very difficult to turn back. For this very reason: *false hope* is built into the journey!

You go one mile, then another, you hit a dust storm, travel up a mountain, get stung by a bee, fall over a cliff. Okay — BAD ROAD. But then, lying at the base of the cliff with a fractured skull and an agonizing bee sting, you realize you've landed on a secret beach with cerulean waters, and it's not a fractured skull at all but just a stress headache, and the bee was only a mosquito, and so you are led to believe there will be more beaches, more azure seas, fewer precipices, gentler insects.

Only wow. Look at me. I've been so inured to false hope and the bad road, I'm sticking up for mosquitoes when, frankly, they are disease carriers. Encephalitis, West Nile virus, malaria, and yellow fever among others. I need a new way of thinking and of categorizing what is "good" and what is "bad." I knew a Tibetan Buddhist who warned against absolute labels such as "good" and "bad." She encouraged the term "unwanted." If you think about it, the word "unwanted" allows for gray areas.

I am not a fan of the gray area.

The Tibetan Buddhist is a collector of my husband's glasswork. Because much of his glass is very colorful — shades of orange, blue, maroon, saffron — this woman enjoys displaying her large pieces amid her shrines at her ten-thousand-square-foot home in the Hollywood Hills. She enjoys my husband's philosophy of art, which changes to suit his collectors. For Tibetan Buddhists it is: *Glass is air, breath, a cloudless sky, compassion, the clarity of a pure mind. The peace of glass allows one to just be.*

Tibetan Buddhists believe in compassion for all sentient beings. They are devoted to His Holiness the Dalai Lama. He wears maroon and saffron robes. Are you getting the idea?

My husband is no fool, and he has learned to create glasswork to match his clients' shrine rooms. One reality by which I have come to feel jaded is the way the collectors shop for expensive art that seems somehow, vaguely, possibly Buddhist. As if they're not into meditation as much as home decor. They are akin to the people who choose a painting not because it moves them but because its colors match the sofa.

This woman is very rich and donates large sums of money to good causes, including environmental groups, international children's rights groups, and one of the major United States–based Save Tibet organizations.

She spares no amount on herself: she wears Helmut Lang, Prada, and Commes des Garçons, and her enormous house, designed by Sango-Chan, with views over the Los Angeles basin, all the way out to Catalina Island, has been featured in *Architectural Digest,* Italian *Vogue, Quest,* and other publications that make my husband very happy. His work always rates at least a quarter page.

Here is another story about a different Buddhist collector of my husband's glass. A New York–based rock musician, he also happens to be a Zen monk affiliated with a monastery in Copenhagen.

This musician visited the Glasmuseet in Ebeltoft after a long retreat of silent meditation and sought out my husband's studio. I happened to be there that day and recognized him immediately. He had been a very cute boy when his band first started up but had aged into a paunchy, florid, balding man with — I saw right away — anger issues. Although, like most angry people, he tried to hide his deep rage by seeming friendly, warm, humble, and funny, I have been well trained by life to read his true self.

It was May, and the rock-star monk wore a gray-and-black *koromo,* or meditation robe. With him was a younger woman. Blond, with big lips, small hips, and big breasts, she chewed gum, smoked cigarettes, and tried never to take her hands off him.

He would occasionally bow, easing her arm from around his waist, offering a beatific smile as he discussed how present, how in the moment, how unencumbered by negativity my husband's pieces were.

My husband considers himself to be quite erudite. When we lived in Montauk he submitted a fifty-page article to *The New Yorker* titled "My Advice to Odin." When they sent the manuscript back with a prim, cream-colored printed rejection slip, he told me that the editors had obviously recognized his genius and knew their readership was beneath him. By the way, Odin is the head god in Norse mythology, which gives you an idea of where my husband places himself.

He recognized that musician's vanity, summed him up in one glance, and brought forth his most colorless vases, tubes, bowls, and installations. "As a Zen practitioner," he threw in. And, "As a Rinzai Zen monk . . ." Then, sealing it, "As a man of great wisdom, perhaps you would enjoy my philosophy."

"Yes?" the musician asked.

My husband stood still, hands folded, with a matching humble smile.

"Well?" the musician pressed.

"I let the clear glass tube speak for me,"

he said. "Emptiness."

"That is your philosophy, how marvelous, how perfect," the musician said. "I must have that tube. Also that vase and that bowl. I must have several — for each of my homes, and to keep backstage when I perform."

"He's about to headline a huge benefit for world hunger in London," the blond woman said.

"Not for," the musician had said, laughing modestly. "Against. But nevertheless, we'll be shooting a concert film, and I'll need space and absolute privacy for meditation. I do a great deal of unconscious work to be fully present. I find Zen practice helps enormously."

"Wonderful," my husband said. "How honored I am to have a musician of your stature as one of my collectors."

"And I am so terribly humbled to stand in the presence of such a great artist and spiritual giant."

Those two fuckers believed every word — in that moment, at least. My husband has a pattern. Every new collector is his favorite and can do no wrong. He drops their names to the museum board, Googles them obsessively — if they are high-profile and in the news, he takes it personally, as if he had something to do with their success. He remembers their birthdays, writes them letters, and sometimes, if he feels they are intellectually deserving, sends them self-published copies of "My Advice to Odin."

But then he can't help himself — he tears his clients down. He'll relive their visits. Trash their appearances, expressions, diction, facial hair, nail polish, jewelry, height, size of their feet. He calls them poseurs, frauds, neophytes, know-nothings, with — if they are men — small penises or — if they are women — man-hating tendencies. He dismisses everyone.

The Zen musician did show his anger. I didn't witness it personally, but read about it in the paper. Holding that benefit in London, he had several meltdowns that got tweeted into the world.

He told one guitar tech, a twenty-two-year-old Berklee graduate, that he had dared meet his sightline while he was walking on-stage after a two-hour meditation, disrupting his privacy and serenity, and fired him on the spot.

When another guitar tech could not be found right away, he went ballistic in his trailer, breaking all the glass he'd bought from Frederik, along with his cell phone and makeup mirror.

I could tell he was that kind of person. I saw the black glint behind his brown eyes. And for this reason as well: because back in Ebeltoft, when I asked his girlfriend if she would like to see the garden and have a cup of tea, he grabbed her arm. After forty-five minutes of pushing her hands off him, disengaging from her in a way I found humiliating to watch, the minute she was invited to step away, he wouldn't allow it.

"Vangie is a talented decorator, among *many* other things," he said suggestively, finally embracing her the way she'd wanted all along. "I need her advice on everything I buy."

"Of course," my husband said appreciatively, eyeing Vangie's bosom because he knew that would please the actor. "So gifted *and* so lovely."

Poor Vangie got the worst of the rocker's London tantrum. A piece of flying glass cut her cheek. I can still picture her peaches-and-cream face, enhanced by makeup and plastic surgery, and I am sure she suffered terribly, both physically and psychologically, in that moment and its aftermath. The newspaper said she refused to press charges.

How well I understand that decision. She is a fellow traveler on the road of false hope. The actor no doubt took her to Bentley &

Skinner, jewelers by appointment to Her Majesty the Queen. He probably steered her into La Perla, letting her think the lingerie was for her pleasure. Everything was made right again. All of her doubts dissolved.

Recently I saw he'd broken up with her and started dating someone new. Vangie did a series of interviews for tabloid television.

"He's not a Buddhist at all — he just wears the robes. To be honest, he's a sex addict. I can't lie."

Good for Vangie. She told the truth.

I haven't been so successful at that. I'm trying now, can't you tell? I'll let my thoughts out and try not to censor them. There are a few things I can't discuss yet. Okay, two, and they're not "things," they are my children.

Just this single exception for now: I can't stop thinking about Grit's accident. She could have lost her toe. Almost cut it off, in a bog, on a piece of glass. Glass. Jagged shard of broken glass. How symbolic.

I was sometimes a good mother. I did the best I could under trying circumstances. I know she remembers the times I told her to get her passport, that we were leaving. Does she realize that I meant it at the time? I could have done things differently, but she has to know — she could have, too.

She abandoned me. We were so close, and she ran off and left me behind. I can't blame her one bit. At least I know I shouldn't. But deep down I do.

Clare and Grit hovered over the computer screen. The Web site contained a series of photographs showing GRIT spelled out in different elements of nature. Written on a beach, round stones on a riverbank, long icicles broken to form block letters.

Troublingly, knives set out on a white damask tablecloth. Then, sweet again, GRIT in white violets, green leaves, stalks of marsh grass, and obviously in Clement Clarke Moore Park, last night, deep footprints in the snow.

"Why would she come so close, but keep herself away from us?" Grit said.

"I don't know," Clare said. "But she must have come for you — hearing you were in the hospital got her here, nothing else."

"She saw me in the park last night — what if she thinks I'm completely fine and now she can go back to him?"

"Do you think she's here alone?" Clare asked. "Maybe your father came, too."

"I hadn't thought of that," Grit said. "It's true, he wouldn't let her travel without him.

But he would never come to see me."

She pushed back her hair so Clare could see the owl tattoo: the words *jeg hader dig* had been inked out, woven into a garland of ivy.

"You don't hate her anymore?" Clare asked.

"No," Grit said, then smiled. "Most of the time anyway."

She pulled down the neck of her faded blue Henley shirt, showing Clare the finished scene on her back. A red sun sank into a winter forest, moonlight spilling from the sky. Shadows hid a rabbit from a fox.

"It's beautiful," Clare said. "Night, but very alive."

"Why would she post a photo of knives? They're not 'funny,' like butter knives might be. They're sharp."

"I don't know," Clare said.

They shut down the computer and hugged good night. Clare walked around the apartment, turning off lights, filling the cats' water bowls. Sometimes she let herself forget that this was the house she had grown up in. Her parents and sisters had lived here. The walls were soaked with her family's secrets. She went to her bedroom, opened her closet door.

You wouldn't see the poems unless you

were looking for them. Torn from magazines, copied from books, the paper was yellowed and fragile and taped onto the old plaster — similar to what Buddy and Seymour Glass, two of the sisters' favorite J. D. Salinger characters, had done in their family's Manhattan apartment. Anne had taped "Dagger" to the door. Clare had always known her sister's fascination with the poem was a clue to who she was, the part she didn't want people to know.

The sisters had been so close. Yet, *"You know what's under my pillow,"* Anne would quote with a dangerous glint in her eyes whenever she wanted to put Clare on notice. Clare thought of the knife pictures, then stood in the closet and read the poem her sister had left there:

Dagger
BY *LUCINDA WEST*

It's night, but I don't sleep.
I listen for footsteps
that might be yours.
The light of a waning moon
strikes the creek bed
pebbles instead of water
Everything is dry.
The drought followed you here

You think it will kill me
but I'll get you first.
You know what's under my pillow
It could slit your throat
if I tell it to: not
that I don't love you,
but because I do.

A poem taped to the wall by a complicated
sister.

CHAPTER TWENTY

On Wednesday Grit suited up for work: black pants, white shirt, and, because Alicia had asked her to wear something celebratory, a pair of tiny shiny red Christmas tree-ball earrings. Clare had helped her pack all the food she had precooked into big, double-thick Whole Foods bags, and Grit unloaded them from a cab outside Alicia's uncle's office building on West Twenty-eighth Street.

Even in the snow, the street between Sixth and Seventh avenues was filled with trucks delivering azaleas, tulips, roses, lilies, white birch trees, and holly bushes, a secret garden in one of the busiest parts of the city.

Grit's mood was high; she was still reeling from the fact that her mother had created an online world for them. She felt charmed, twirling around, when a flower vendor handed her a sprig of holly. She scanned the street, wondering if her mother was hiding, watching her.

Alicia pulled up in the Subaru, unloaded a stack of plastic-covered trays and set them on the sidewalk, hugged Grit, then parked in the garage next door. She came back loaded down with bags of bread.

"Ready for your first gig?" Alicia asked.

"Definitely! Do I look festive enough?" Grit asked.

"Perfect!"

"This must be the strangest street in New York," Grit said, looking up and down the sidewalk: tall trees, thick bushes, flowering hibiscus, all in pots, waiting to be picked up or carted inside, husky men in barn jackets and overalls hefting cartons of delicate orchids, freesia, sweet peas.

"We'll be here a lot," Alicia said, "picking up centerpieces for parties. Uncle Vincent gives the Picnic a sweet discount."

They lugged everything into a freight elevator, and Alicia used a key to open the fourth floor. They stepped into an enormous floor-through loft, rough wood floors and Corinthian columns rising to a pressed-tin ceiling. Dirty windows overlooked the street. One end of the loft was an overgrown jungle, a tropical wonderland with palm trees, ficus trees, and sharp-edged orange and purple birds-of-paradise.

"He mainly supplies the entertainment industry," Alicia said. "Stage and film. He used to advertise in *Variety* and *Backstage,* but he doesn't have to anymore. They come to him."

"Cool," Grit said, eyeing the greenery. "Looks like this movie's about Tahiti."

The elevator buzzed, and Alicia let in Hugh Whitley, an actor between jobs. They said hello, and while he started setting up long tables and chairs, Grit joined Alicia in the small kitchen area. The servers and bartender arrived: Melissa, Patrick, and Kayla.

Grit had done her homework and provided some menus, and she felt proud that Alicia had incorporated several of her dishes into her uncle's Christmas party. Grit hadn't had far to go for inspiration; she'd just conjured up the food she'd prepared for her own family.

Roast duck with prunes and apples, tiny caramel potatoes, red cabbage, and pebernødder — "pepper nut" cookies. Alicia's family was Italian, so they mixed their specialties — Grit's roast duck, potatoes, and cookies, Alicia's lasagna, garlic bread, and chocolate-amaretto balls.

It felt exhilarating, working together,

crisscrossing the kitchen to put one dish into the oven while removing another, checking the potatoes on the back burner to make sure they were browning slowly, taking turns in the loft to set the long tables with plates, glasses, and cutlery that Hugh unloaded from the car.

Stirring the potatoes, adding more sugar, Grit savored the smell. She hadn't cooked these dishes since leaving Denmark.

"My mother's in New York," she heard herself say.

"What did you say?" Alicia asked, pulling her head and the lasagna from the oven.

"Just that my mom's in the city."

"Really? Were you expecting her?"

"No," Grit said. "She surprised me."

"Wow, all the way from Denmark. Right in time for Christmas," Alicia said.

"Exactly," Grit said. She didn't feel the need to elaborate. Somehow she was starting to accept that her mother was hiding, spying, showing love in her own way. When it was time to reveal herself she would. Instead of feeling rattled by her mother's behavior, Grit embraced it. Hadn't she done her share of spying on Clare herself?

So everything felt like a possible surprise — walking down the street, rounding every corner, even sitting at home — the phone could ring, a face might pop up in the window, the caped woman could appear in the park across the street. What might her mother use to spell her name next?

Guests arrived. The giddiness of having her mother in town, avoiding her while managing to get up in her grill at every turn, was exciting but fearsome, sort of like a perverse scavenger hunt.

"Grit, this is my uncle, Vincent Antonia," Alicia said.

"Wonderful to meet you, Grit," he said. Tall, trim, with white hair, he had movie-star eyes and an instant-friend smile.

"Great to meet you," she said. "I love your jungle!"

"Ha!" he said. "That's going to Silvercup Studios tomorrow for a film about a girl who lives in a greenhouse."

"That's a film I want to see," Grit said.

"Should we start passing hors d'oeuvres?" Alicia asked.

"Definitely, people await *il bello picnic!*" Vincent said, then went out to the loft where conversation had started to buzz.

"He's nice," Grit said as Alicia loaded trays with Gorgonzola straws and miniature prosciutto quiches.

"He's my mother's brother, my godfather. You'll meet my aunt and cousins in a minute. They all work here."

"Can't wait," Grit said. Her toe began to ache. She found she didn't want to go into the big room, meet more of Alicia's family. Her mother did love her, did have original ways of showing it. She had come to New York to see her, but Grit wished for once her mother could just be normal.

Later that afternoon, Clare wrote her blog about that morning's walk with Paul along the Hudson River, broken ice floating like chainmail on the blue-steel surface. She had seen Iceland gulls, black-backed gulls, laughing gulls, brants, buffleheads, and, swimming among the ghostly pier pilings off Canal Street, a single harbor seal.

In a maple tree growing from the snow-covered green swath — Hudson River Park, Paul's official reason for being there — between the river and the West Side High-way, she'd photographed a flock of crows mobbing a red-tailed hawk.

She went through her camera, posting photos. She paused at one of Paul, where he'd happened to glance over and she'd caught his smile. The wish to publish it was strong; she had a rare impulse to let people know they were together. She had the thought that he should be here now, cozy by the fire, waiting to hear about Grit's first day of catering.

While on the computer Clare checked Anne's site, saw that a new photo had been posted: GRIT traced in thick dust on what looked like a concrete floor. The sisters' way of communicating was clandestine, obscure — Clare wanting to reveal her feelings for Paul by posting his photo, Anne sending messages to Grit in the dust. Perhaps Grit's own way, searching for her family in bogs, was the most byzantine.

Hearing a car pull up, she went to the window. Grit climbed out of a van with the logo "Antonia's Picnic." She watched a man walk around back, open the door, and haul out a tall white spruce tree. Pulling on boots, she ran outside to greet them.

"You must be Grit's aunt Clare," the man said, balancing the tree in the crook of his arm. "I'm Alicia's uncle Vincent."

"So good to meet you," Clare said.

"Vincent is giving us a Christmas tree!" Grit said.

The spruce was alive, twelve feet tall, planted in a terra-cotta pot decorated with molded fruit and garlands.

"How wonderful," Clare said. "We can plant it in the back garden after Christmas. In fact, let me get the keys — we'll leave it outside until we dig out the ornaments."

She went back inside, grabbed the key ring, and returned to the street. Between her brownstone and the one next door was a nearly invisible gate, set back several feet and leading down an impossibly narrow tunnel to the overgrown backyard.

"So this is how you get in," Grit said. "I looked out the kitchen window and wondered."

"I'm sure you would have asked if it were more appealing," Clare said. "At this time of year it's so barren. It's lovely and shady in the summer — that's a willow tree, and that's a ginkgo, one of the tallest in Chelsea. Ivy and wisteria climb that back wall, and I clean off those stone benches, have coffee here some mornings."

"Does anyone else in the building use it?" Grit asked.

"No, it's ours," Clare said. "When your grandmother split the house into apartments, she kept this garden for us."

"Smart woman. These town house gardens are great," Vincent said, placing the Christmas tree in the corner. "You won't get much sun back here, so what's already planted is perfect. And this spruce will do well. Call me in the spring and I'll come plant it for you."

"Thank you," Clare said, although she knew she and Paul would do it.

After Vincent left, Clare took Grit through the rear door to enter the house through the basement. She clicked on the timer light and they walked past bicycles, skis, a storage bin, and the creaky old boiler.

"The decorations are in there," Clare said, pointing at the bin. "We'll come back down for them when we bring the tree in."

"Hiding places I didn't even know existed," Grit said.

Cellars can be scary places, and children often sense someone behind the furnace, or in the shadows, or hidden in the rafters. Old houses breathe, but in cellars the breath is audible: the boiler's hum, the pipes' quiet rattle, the creak of footsteps on floors above. Clare paused, listening.

She knew her house so well, could sense the smallest disturbance. Every surface was covered with dust. If Anne had been here, Clare would know; they'd been expert at sneaking into their own house after dark, coming in through the back basement door. More wishful thinking, Clare realized. Anne no longer had a key; she couldn't walk through walls.

Still, Clare couldn't deny the prickles on the back of her neck. She turned on the yellow overhead light for a minute, did a quick walk-through, scanning the shadows, looking for a name scrawled in dust. Grit stood by the stairs, not asking.

Back in the apartment, Grit handed Clare a bag of leftovers she'd snagged from the party and sprawled on the living room sofa. Clare heated up the duck and potatoes, served them on the table in front of the fireplace.

"Alicia's lasagna was the best, but there was none left. She uses five Italian cheeses. I've got to make it for you," Grit said.

"This is delicious too," Clare said. "So how did everything go?"

"The party was great, and everyone clapped for us. She has a good family — they're all like Vincent, incredibly nice and generous. I thought it was an office party, which it was, but the interesting part is that everyone who works there is a relative."

"A family business," Clare said.

"I kept thinking, how do they all get along? Work together all day, then go home to dinner at night? I asked Alicia if anyone was estranged, and she looked at me like I was nuts."

"I learned a long time ago," Clare said, "to not compare our family with anyone else's."

"It's so stupid, the way I can get tempted to think things can be different."

"Oh, Grit. It's not stupid. Even when I was in prison I hoped your mother would come see me, that we could talk and figure out everything had been a terrible mistake."

"Prison cured you from thinking that way?"

" 'Cured.' I guess that's one way to put it. It started driving me crazy, so I finally stopped."

"That's how I feel now — crazy. I mean, that picture of my name in the snow. I was at the party, caramelizing these potatoes, trying to feel all jolly about the fact that she's nearby somewhere, that hearing about my broken toe was too much for her, awakened her maternal instincts, made her fly over from Denmark. She cares about me! But then I just felt sad. I mean, seriously?"

"She sent you another message."

Clare went to her desk, got her laptop. She and Grit studied the picture of Grit's name in the dust.

"She loves you," Clare said.

"But why can't she show herself? This is insane."

"It is. I'm sure she's ashamed," Clare said. "Of how she's treated you."

"Then why come here at all?"

Anne had always shown love in mysterious ways. When the sisters were fifteen and sixteen, their mother bought new everyday china. She and the girls had set aside the old, chipped, faded tea rose set to send to the Salvation Army. Anne had retrieved the carton, hidden it behind the furnace in the basement until she was ready.

One chilly April school night, Anne told their mother she had to watch *Emma* at the Film Forum for English class, and was taking Clare because sisters should see Jane Austen films together.

Clare ran to her room to get her jacket and popcorn money, but Anne told her to empty her backpack, take out all her schoolbooks, and meet her in the back garden.

"What are we doing?" Clare asked as Anne unlocked the basement door.

"We're on a mission," Anne said, filling Clare's backpack and her own with the old china.

"But we told Mom we're going to the movies. You're not really studying Jane Austen?"

"I am," Anne said. "*Emma,* as a matter of fact. That's why I know 'Seldom, very seldom, does complete truth belong to any human disclosure; seldom can it happen that something is not a little disguised, or a little mistaken.' Jane wrote that, and it's true, so don't feel bad about Mom."

"Right," Clare said, long aware of her sister's relationship with the truth. With Callery pear trees in bloom up and down the streets of Chelsea and the Village, Clare and Anne carried their treasures beneath clouds of white blossoms, crockery clinking and rattling in their backpacks. They took the subway south to Houston Street, came out at the Varick Street exit.

"Why are we doing this?" Clare asked.

"Because sometimes you just can't say it with a Hallmark card," Anne said. They trudged east to Sixth Avenue, stopped in front of a brick apartment house. Moonlight came through the flowering pears, dappled the sidewalk. Anne removed a plate, whispered, "William Childers," and shattered it in the gutter. Heading up MacDougal Street, Anne whispered "Guy LeMay" and "Harry Roberts," and broke two teacups in front of a green building with an Italian restaurant on the ground floor.

Zigzagging around, they hit Greenwich Avenue, Charles Street, and Jane Street. Boys from their school, liked or loved at different times by Anne, lived at these addresses. Each time she broke a plate or cup, she murmured the name of the boy who lived there.

"Why are you doing this?" Clare asked.

"Because I loved them."

When they got to Riley's Bar, Anne threw down the large serving platter that had held many Thanksgiving turkeys and Christmas roast beefs. Then she said, "Dad."

"Why him?"

"Because he's our father and we loved him before any other guy, and he betrayed us," Anne said. "Come on, let's head to Ninth Avenue."

"Home?" Clare asked, relieved.

But they rounded the corner on West Nineteenth Street, stopping halfway down the block in front of the apartment house where Paul's family lived.

"Here," Anne said, handing Clare a plate. "Break it and say his name."

The plate felt cold in Clare's hands. The night smelled like white flowers. Looking up at the building, she picked out Paul's window. She pictured him studying inside. If she broke the dish, he would hear it. He might look out, see her hurrying away.

"Hurry up," Anne urged. "It feels so good, I promise."

Clare had followed her big sister all night, getting a wicked thrill out of Anne's peculiarity and the passion with which she destroyed the china. Holding the plate, Clare had a strong flash of knowing she and her sister were different. The idea of breakage seemed violent, anarchic; spring rain would wash the pieces of polluting, ceramic litter three short blocks into the Hudson River.

"I don't want to," Clare said.

"If you don't, your love for Paul means nothing."

"That's not true. I don't need to break a plate to prove something."

"It's a poetic gesture that speaks louder than words."

"It's waking up the neighborhood."

"Fine," Anne said. "Just know you're missing a very big chance. You're negating love."

Clare squinted at her sister. "Didn't you just break about twenty plates? You mean you love all those guys, every single one?"

"I do, or at least I did," Anne said. "I'm dying of love. Don't you get it? Sometimes you have to act a little crazy just to stay sane."

Clare had felt her sister's gaze, sharp and insistent, as if she was trying to tell her the most important thing. Staring at Anne, Clare entered her sister's world. Suddenly Clare *did* get it. She raised the plate above her head, whispered "Paul Traynor," and smashed it on the street.

Washing the dishes now, Clare still remembered the power she'd felt breaking that plate. An invisible thread zoomed from her hands straight up the building to Paul's window. She had stared up, head back, actually hoping he had heard the sound and would look out.

"They never hear," Anne had said, putting her arm around Clare's waist. "That's the secret part. They wake up in the morning and see the pieces and wonder how they got there. Somehow they know it has to do with them. But they're deaf to the breaking. All they hear is silence, yet they find themselves thinking of us."

Clare and Anne had walked home, Clare wondering all the way whether Paul *had* thought of her in that instant, whether he would see the bits of cracked tea rose china in front of his doorway and somehow know she had done it. A light wind began to blow, a few white petals showering down from the pear trees, catching in the sisters' dark hair.

CHAPTER TWENTY-ONE

Call me Ishmael. Just kidding.

I don't really feel like getting started today. Hanging out in the old neighborhood is giving me vertigo, as if I've climbed a really high wall and am about to fall off — which, in fact, I am.

Moby-Dick is nothing to me, nothing. If I had to allude to any one novel, well, actually two long short stories in the same volume, it should be *Franny and Zooey.* The part where Franny tells about Zooey sitting in the kitchen reading *Dombey and Son* when Jesus appears and asks him for a small glass of ginger ale. "A *small* glass, mind you," Franny says.

Clare and I adored that book. We could quote paragraphs verbatim. Why bother to analyze our feelings for something so obvious: a pair of stories about very close siblings, closer than anything but also likely to look askance at each other and say things like "A *small* glass, mind you."

When we became teenagers you'd think I wanted to leave her to her own friends, but mostly I didn't. She looked up to me, thought I was daring and cool, but also — odd, because she was younger — I felt her wanting to protect me. Not let me out of her sight because of the trouble I might get into.

I'm the one who led her and Sarah down the road of lying to our mothers the night we hid out and slept in the library tower. I took her to Central Park after dark, got high with her, took her owling even before she and Paul got into it.

Seeing her in Shakespeare Garden this week nearly killed me. I read her blog and know her weekly routine. I'd staked her out in the Ramble a few times, but she nearly caught me, and I ran away. But that day, somehow I knew she'd be wandering the winding trails up Vista Rock.

I sat on a bench near the top of Shakespeare Garden, just below the castle, in the snow. It fell so thickly I nearly gave up. Flakes dusted my velvet cape, which doesn't give much warmth, and blinded my eyes. I heard the downy woodpecker tapping, and it seemed like Morse code telling me to wait, she was coming. And she did, and for the first time since arriving in New York, I cried.

Too far up the hill for her to hear, I didn't even try to muffle the sound. I couldn't have held it back if I wanted to. I do have a heart. Seeing her back in the park, where we spent so much time, undid the spell cast a hundred years ago. In that moment I loved her and believed she still loves me.

A wicked stepmother cast that spell — me. She was my sister, but the troubles in our house so often left her in my care, for me to worry about, for me to hurt or make mistakes with, as I later did with my own children. Clare was different from me: more innocent, less jaded, charmed. She loved in an uncomplicated way, at least it seemed that way to me, while I always felt I was pushing a boulder up a steep hill to get anyone to love me. I spent most of my early years dying of death.

Clare had Paul, for one thing. They'd fallen in love young, and no matter what got in their way, it was obvious to everyone they were meant to be together. I know men wanted me, I had my choice, but none of them really mattered, not even Jamey, until Frederik, and we know how that's turned out.

Anyway, seeing Clare in Shakespeare

Garden. My little sister is middle-aged. She wears it well; she's thin, with those same high cheekbones, longer hair than last time I saw her, now with a white streak in front, but still, she's not a girl anymore, and more than anything that's what made me cry.

I took away her life. Two years in a maximum-security prison. She lost Paul, lost the job she loved. What I said on the witness stand could have sent her away for much longer.

Frederik had insisted they prosecute her for attempted murder. He told the police, district attorney, reporters, anyone who would listen that my sister hated him and had gone to Montauk that day intending to kill him.

He made me believe it. I took in his words, his being, his way of seeing the world, swallowed them whole. His perspective entered my bones, beat with my heart, overtook my bloodstream. Any book about abuse tells you abusers are controlling, that slowly the woman loses her will, alienates her family and friends, walks on eggshells to make sure he stays happy and appeased. But for me it didn't happen slowly. A lightning bolt struck me, days after meeting Frederik, and I realized I had a choice to make: continue life as I knew it, or take a leap and enter the Great Man's world.

"The husband and wife become a new family," he told me, cradling me in his arms in a suite at the St. Regis. We lay amid ivory percale sheets, leaning against the saffron satin headboard in a nest of down pillows.

" 'Husband and wife'?" I asked.

"That is our destiny," he said.

We had met two nights earlier, at his Chelsea opening, and although we had been inseparable ever since, he hadn't mentioned marriage.

"Do you mean . . . ?" I asked.

"We shall be married, Anne," he said.

"Oh, my God, Frederik!" I said, sitting straight up. I blushed, felt dizzy, waiting for his actual proposal. It didn't come then, and never would. By saying "We shall be married," he was stating a foregone fact.

I was young, twenty-five, and although I'd been engaged to Jamey, it hadn't worked out. I drove him away. Now I was with this older man, a great artist (I thought then) willing to take care of me. Why did that seem so appealing? I had always been über-independent. I suppose, as I think about it now, I felt Frederik was offering me a contract: I would be his, accept his pronouncements, and in return, never be alone, never be unloved.

"What is the worst thing that ever happened to you?" Frederik asked me that night in bed.

I had to think.

"My father dying," I said.

He nodded, held me tenderly. "I know what a terrible effect that has on a daughter. I am so sorry."

"Thank you."

"But at the same time, a bit relieved. I must confess something to you, Anne. I lived with a woman, until recently. Helen was English, and I must say, it worked well, living at my house in Montauk, so far from her family in London."

What did that mean? I wondered.

"I asked you what was the worst ever to happen to you. I'll tell you my most devastating thing: Helen's father died."

"Oh, Frederik," I said. "You cared that much for her father?"

"That is not what I said," he told me. "His death was a disaster to our marriage because it took her away from me. She returned to England once a month during his illness, and after his death, her grief was total."

"But it was just once a month?" I asked.

"Don't you understand? You should know what I mean — even while she was home, her thoughts were with her family, not on

432

ours. As I told you, it is my strongest belief that a husband and wife create their own family. They leave their pasts behind."

I nearly chuckled, imagining what Clare would think of being considered my past, being left on the dock as I sailed away forever.

"What is amusing?" he asked.

"Oh, just that could never happen with my family. We're very close, especially me and my sister."

"What is her name?" he asked.

"Clare," I said.

He didn't say another word, but kissed me so hard he bit my lip. I didn't realize it then, but he was claiming me. He asked my sister's name, not out of curiosity but so he would know the identity of his enemy.

I can write these things now, because of what I did in Ebeltoft. I woke up in a start, saw everything in a new light. But back then, my unsigned contract with Frederik included turning my thoughts over to him.

It was nothing like the insights and secret language between Clare and me. This was mind control, exactly as if Frederik had sat before me with a colored pinwheel, staring piercingly into my eyes, saying, "Count backward from one hundred, you are getting sleepy. . . ."

The day Clare came to Montauk bearing roses and Valentine cards, she broke Frederik's spell for approximately one hour. Seeing my sister at the door, her expression hopeful yet afraid, split my heart open. Years had gone by without Clare, and how could that have been? "What if one of us dies?" I would sometimes wonder.

We had gazed at each other over our mother's grave. Standing with Frederik and my perfect children, I thought only that Clare must envy me. Frederik had whispered those words in church. "Still unmarried, a career woman, with no family of her own."

But in Montauk, our broken hearts merged, mine and Clare's. We sat by the fire in that chilly house, and I felt so happy to see her playing with the children. Grit seemed especially fascinated. She touched her aunt's silky hair and patted her own curly mop. Gilly's shyness made him hold back at first. We never had visitors, and Frederik was training the children that anyone outside the family was not to be trusted.

Clare's warmth won Gilly over. I told her he liked to draw, and she asked if she could see his pictures. Soon he was sprawled on the floor beside her, drawing birds because she said she liked them. For that hour, life felt sweet. Clare asked about my bruises, and I told her. She said she would get me out of there, and I was ready to go.

Seeing my face through her eyes made me realize how horrible things had gotten, how ashamed I felt, and how worried I was to have the children see me taking it, taking it, and their father giving it, giving it.

When Frederik barged in, it was as if he'd caught me cheating. He shoved Clare and the kids aside and came straight at my throat. His hands felt massive; they were covered with glass dust from the studio, and I felt tiny shards digging into my skin as I kicked and tried to pry his fingers away, the kids screaming and Clare shouting. My eyes popped and saw pinpricks of light. I couldn't take a breath, and I felt myself start to pass out.

Then *bang* — I heard the blow strike Frederik's head, saw sparks fly everywhere. I gasped for air, clutching my throat, feeling my crushed larynx. Frederik touched his head, blood running down his hand as he batted at his sweater, flames licking his right shoulder. Clare tried pulling me to my feet; I smelled burning flesh and saw her blistered hands.

"Come on," she said. "Anne, hold on to me, I'm getting you out of here."

"Okay," I croaked, feeling her arms under mine. My legs wouldn't work; my mind spun, and I felt as if I might be dying — parts of me broken by my husband's hands.

"Children, did you see what she did?" Frederik asked. "Your aunt came here to murder me. Did you see? Look at your papa's head — do you see the blood?"

"Shut up, Frederik," Clare said, holding me up. "Come on, Grit and Gilly. We're taking your mother to the hospital."

"YOU ARE TAKING HER NO-WHERE!" Frederik yelled.

"I'm calling the police," Clare said, easing me down and lifting the kitchen phone. She dialed 911, and I heard a terrible crack. Frederik had thrown her against the wall, taken the phone from her hand.

"I would like to report an attack," Frederik said into the receiver. "An attempted murder. Hurry, the murderer is still here."

While Clare, slumped on the floor, tried to crawl toward me, Frederik lifted me into his arms. He held me against his chest, soothing me, kissing my neck. He reached into the freezer for an ice pack, held it to my larynx, making me cry — from what? A winter scarf hung on the coat hook, and he gently wrapped it around my neck.

"Anne," he said, staring into my eyes.

"You know how much I love you and the children. We belong to each other. Your sister will tear us apart, don't you see? She tried to kill me just to get to you. That's what we'll say, darling. Our family will stand strong and together, won't we?"

My voice wouldn't work. The sirens grew louder, and police officers with guns came into our kitchen. Clare, still on the floor, looked wild and dangerous.

"He beats my sister!" she said, sounding ferocious. "He was strangling her when I hit him!"

"I called you," Frederik said in a calm voice, showing the officers the cut and burns on his temple, the black burn marks on his sweater. "You can see for yourself what she did to me. She has always hated me, and today she came here to kill me."

A policewoman stared at me, with neither kindness nor judgment. I felt her assessing me, to determine the truth. The scarf around my neck should have seemed natural in our freezing house.

"Ma'am, can you tell us what happened?" she asked.

"My wife has a very sore throat," Frederik said. "She's lost her voice."

"Do your best," the officer said to me.

"Anne, take off your scarf, let her see the

bruises," Clare begged. She hauled herself up, came toward me. Frederik stepped in her way, and a male officer restrained her. My children sobbed. They clung to my legs.

"Please, Officer," Frederik said. "They are traumatized by seeing their aunt attack me. Children, tell the police. Did she attack me with that burning log or did she not?"

"She did," Gilly said, his voice tiny. "But she was only trying —"

"Grit?" Frederik asked.

Grit said nothing, just stared at her feet.

The family's wagons were circling. I felt pulled toward the center. Frederik's arm came around my shoulder. I thought of our life, of our children, of how we had created everything from scratch, without any of the pain of the past. It wasn't all perfect, but we were a unit, and no one else belonged. In Montauk we were at the end of the world, far from everyone, just us.

"Anne," Frederik said gently, with great patience. "Tell the police. Did your sister try to kill me?"

In that moment I went back to sleep. Clare had wakened me an hour ago with roses and a hug, her goodness and humor. But that belonged to another me, another time. I belonged to Frederik, to *our* small and complete family, and so I said, "Yes."

CHAPTER TWENTY-TWO

Clare kept looking out the window, wondering when Grit would get home from the party she was catering with Alicia. She'd sensed a new edginess in her niece, and she felt it herself, too. The holidays couldn't help bringing up more than some families could bear. Clare missed her mother and sister more than ever.

The white spruce waited out back. Paul would help them bring it inside tomorrow, and they'd dig out the ornaments and decorate it. Clare turned to the sofa; he was sleeping there now, a book folded on his chest and Blackburn sprawled across the book.

They had had dinner together, then hung out reading by the fire. They leaned into each other, dozing and reading and dozing again. Around nine, he sleepily reached for his coat, kissed her, and said he'd see her in the morning. They held each other for a long minute, and he left.

She was still dressed, just unbuttoning her shirt, when the doorbell rang. It seemed early for Grit to be home from the party, but she must have forgotten her key.

When she opened the door, she found two men standing on the top step. They wore coats and ties, and they introduced themselves as New York City police detectives.

"Is Anne Rasmussen here?" one asked.

"No," she said. "Why?"

"We'd like to ask her some questions. Is it okay if we come in and look around?"

She ignored the question. "Why do you want her?"

"We just want to talk to her."

"Why would you even look for her here?" Clare asked, her mouth dry.

"It's the address she provided on her immigration form," the detective said.

"Immigration form?" Clare asked.

"She's a Danish national. Can you tell us how you know her? Look, it's cold out here. Mind if we come in?"

"Yes, I do mind," Clare said, shocked by all of it, her mind racing. "You can't come in without a warrant."

"Miss, if we could just —" the detective said hurriedly.

But Clare had already slammed the door.

She walked into the kitchen, stared at the basement door. She suddenly realized what she should have known all alone. Hand on the brass knob, she turned it, gazed into the dark cellar, and started down.

The party, for a client of Alicia's PR friend Tace, was at an old printing warehouse downtown, tall windows giving onto the Hudson River and West Side Highway, ribbons of red and white lights streaming north and south. Grit wore sneakers, her toe still hurting without the big bandage. She caught Alicia's disapproving look: apparently sneakers had been okay for the family business party, but not this one.

The client was *UrBanX,* a new style magazine aimed at people under thirty. The offices occupied this and one other floor in the former printing plant, and the magazine seemed to employ no one who was not attractive, skinny, black-clad, and snobbish. The editorial people mingled with advertising people, and there were celebrities Grit figured she should know, but didn't. Two idiots wore tinted aviator glasses, even though the space was lit only by candles and dim, Gothic-looking chandeliers.

Grit had never cooked so well for people who cared so little. They could really put away the vodka, but pizza seemed out of the question — even four pizzas specially designed for undereaters: arugula, shaved Parmigiano-Reggiano, and trumpet mushrooms; Taleggio cheese and grilled asparagus; tomatoes, ricotta, and basil; and freshly shucked and chopped littlenecks, garlic, and hot pepper.

The DJ was pretty good. Grit and Alicia leaned against the kitchen door, watching everyone ignore the buffet table but cluster ten deep at the bar.

"Are we failing?" Grit asked.

"Not at all! This is fabulous," Alicia said. "I'm really getting my name out there. This is maximum exposure — I mean if the magazine takes an interest, they could do a piece on Antonia's Picnic. Tace is working on it."

But they're not eating our food, Grit thought but didn't say. All those little pizzas laden with fresh food straight from the Union Square Greenmarket, cooling and wilting on the table.

"Maybe they're too loaded to eat," Grit said. "Why is there only vodka?"

Alicia pointed at a neon blue banner. There were no words, only azure waves and a deserted island flying a pirate flag. The image looked vaguely familiar.

"Blackbeard Vodka is one of *UrBanX*'s sponsors," Alicia said. "That's their logo. They're supplying their premium vodka, in cups with their blue waves on it, in return for optimum ad space in the magazine. Tace paired them up. Also, she got the stars of *Gossip Girl* to come. So cool, right?"

"Uh," Grit said.

Grit gazed across the large open space, saw Tace sitting in with the DJ, headphones on as she bobbed her head and eyed the crowd. Petite with streaked-blond hair, toothpick arms, smoky eye makeup giving her a sort of heroin-overdose look, a skin-tight cleavagey black dress, and six-inch heels, she looked like a fallen rock star who'd never quite made it.

"Are you close to Tace?" Grit asked.

"In a business way. We met at a group for young businesspeople just starting out. She's in PR and booked me for this party, and if I get successful, I'll hire her. Hopefully she'll get us into the magazine. You should really come to the next group, start networking."

"Thanks," Grit said. She loved cooking and liked Alicia, but wondered why both of her gigs had left her feeling down, in different ways. Once again she felt as if she didn't belong. Networking seemed as alien to her tonight as Alicia's close family had at her uncle's loft.

"Look, I'd better go mingle and meet the editors," Alicia said. "We're not going to cook anymore, and Hugh can help me break it down later. Why don't you go?"

"Okay," Grit said. Alicia counted out two hundred dollars in cash, paid it to Grit. Was it Grit's imagination, or was Alicia hurrying her out of there? Maybe it was because of her uncool footwear, or maybe she could read Grit's opinion of Tace and the pretentious magazine people. The whole thing reminded her of any number of her father's ass-kissing exhibition openings. No one ate food; they just drank and air-kissed.

Leaving the warehouse, she stepped into the cold, crisp night. Wind off the river stung her cheeks and made her eyes water. Traffic rushed up and down the highway, and she caught a cab.

When she got home she paid the driver and started toward the front steps, but a set of footprints caught her eye: in the snow, leading through the locked gate and down the narrow path between Clare's house and the one next door. She felt an instant thrill, adrenaline spiking, and stared at the prints as if she were a tracker looking for clues.

Running up the steps, she let herself in

and looked around for Clare. Her aunt's door was partly closed; Grit glanced in, saw Clare asleep, quilt drawn up to her chin. Wanting to wake her, Grit hesitated. Maybe she should investigate on her own. Quietly shutting the bedroom door, Grit went to the kitchen, ransacked the junk drawer. She grabbed a flashlight and found three keys on a ring marked "Garden."

She stepped out the front door into the bitter cold. Her fingers felt numb trying the three keys on the gate's sturdy lock. The action felt frozen, but she worked it for a minute, was able to turn the key and let herself in. The path was dark, illuminated only by the narrow beam of Grit's flashlight.

The footprints looked fresh, delicate. There was just one set, leading into the garden, as if whoever had left them was back there now. The new snow had covered hers, Clare's, and Vincent's. These were brand new.

She tracked them into the back garden. They aimed toward the Christmas tree, and Grit followed. The person had stood here, admiring the tree; she had reached up, brushed a branch — Grit knew, because snow had been cleared, and she could see the imprint of small fingers.

A deep breath rattled her lungs, and sud-

445

denly, she knew — she was standing there with her mother. She looked around, found herself alone in the garden, but had the strongest feeling of standing by her mother's side. She reached for her hand.

"Mom," Grit said. "I'm here."

No tension or suspense, just a warm feeling in Grit's chest as she followed the footsteps from the tree to the cellar door. Most of the surrounding town houses facing these back gardens were dark, lights off in the rooms, a few white Christmas lights twinkling on balconies.

She turned the key in the old lock. Stepping out of the icy night, she entered the basement, toasty warm with the heat thrown off by the big boiler. Grit heard the hiss of steam and the rumble and click of fire in the furnace. The space smelled airless and musty. But floating above it all was the faintest hint of violets.

Grit pointed her flashlight downward, looking for prints on the concrete floor. There were none, but she moved through the space slowly, checking every corner, each cardboard box, the locked storage unit. She came upon some old furniture: a tall chest of drawers and an armoire.

"Mom," she said again. The feeling that she was not alone had only gotten stronger, but even in this spooky space she didn't feel afraid. The armoire was six feet tall and four feet wide; it looked French, and Grit could see cracks in the wood, one door loose on its hinge. Hands on the brass door pulls, she held her breath and whisked them open. A few old clothes hung on hangers, but her mother wasn't hiding inside.

Disappointed, wondering if her instincts had let her down, she stepped over to the tall chest and opened the top drawer. Empty, filled with cobwebs and dust. She opened the second and third, found the same nothing. Then the fourth, and she gasped and put her hand over her mouth.

GRIT

Her name written in the dust, just as it had appeared in her mother's photo. She stared into the drawer for a long time, feeling a trance of closeness here in the dark, in the middle of the night. Reaching inside, she drew a pine tree next to her name, and signed it LITTLE NIGHT.

The scent of violets seemed stronger. Grit returned to the armoire, trailed her fingers across the clothes hanging inside. She felt velvet, buried her face in the garment, lost in a blanket of springtime, white and purple violets growing everywhere. Slipping it off the hanger, she held her mother's black cape

— velvet lined with black satin, a voluminous hood.

Shining the flashlight down into the armoire's lower reaches, she saw boots. Oh, such familiar, beautiful boots. They had marked the snow outside, but Grit knew them from an earlier time.

Her mother had had them for ages. Black leather, cracked with age, lovingly cared for — conditioned, buffed, rubbed with cream to keep them supple and make them last. Grit had sat cross-legged in the kitchen, polishing one boot while Gilly did the other — they were that old.

Sitting on the floor in front of the armoire, Grit gathered the boots into her arms. She shrugged off her jacket and sweater, then took off her cotton T-shirt. Pulling her sweater back on, draping the cape over her shoulders, she spit on the left boot and began to rub circles with her T-shirt. The soles had been replaced so many times, she saw the leather strain and start to split at the boot's base. The black was dulled by salt and melted snow, but Grit knew she could get her mother's boots back in shape. She'd been doing this since she was a kid.

The furnace hummed. Footsteps sounded overhead; maybe Clare was still awake. But Grit barely noticed. She was hard at work, helping her mother, and overwhelmed that they were together again.

CHAPTER TWENTY-THREE

And I have nothing to say, nothing at all. Because now she is here. Sitting on the floor in a hunched-over posture that reminds me of the little girl she used to be, and still is. My daughter, my only living child, and she is polishing my boots.

I'm in my makeshift quarters, the narrow space between walls, where slaves once slept. I could have gone upstairs with Clare, let her help me figure out where to go and what to do now, but maybe, at least for the next few hours, this is the safest place. This spot once hid people more desperate than I.

The old poem is still here, carved into the beam:

Take thee far from me, and me from thee,
No matter because our hearts hold fast
Like birds overhead in the sky so free
We shall someday fly together at last.

And if I'd gone upstairs, left the house, I wouldn't be able to see Grit now. I can't take my gaze off her, peering as I am through a crack in the wood. We are separated by this wall, by 350-some starry nights, and by the knife I drove into her heart. Well, not a knife. But even from here, with her white-blond hair cut so short, I can see the ugly red scars. She tried to hide them with an owl tattoo, a fact that kills me.

Owls, to Grit, are *me.* I know because I've always talked to her about them, told her about times Clare and I stood for hours on Cedar Hill, waiting for twilight and darkness to watch them wake up, stretch their wings, preen a little, then fly out for the night. She would ask for that story over and over.

I'd tell her about old Alistair Fastnet, the Noah of New York City. He'd traveled the world, bringing back pairs of species he wanted to introduce into Central Park — the foolish egomaniac. Pairs of flying squirrels, lynx, California phoebes. And laughing owls. He'd gone to New Zealand, captured a pair from Blue Cliffs, and transported them by steamer halfway around the world to New York, just in time for them to become extinct.

So to see she used an owl to cover that scar I left, well. That is a kindness I don't deserve.

She's not searching. She's not tearing the place apart. I would deserve for her to turn her back on me, walk upstairs and never think of me again. Or for her to start screaming until I couldn't take it anymore and came out to face her. I have a lot to answer for.

Instead she sits there, gently cleaning my boots. I crane to see her foot, to check on her toe, but she's wearing sneakers. She's humming, and maybe she knows that her song is irresistible to me. I sang it to her and Gilly every night when they were children.

I dust myself off and try to stand tall in this cramped little space. In the odd mixture of darkness and light from Grit's flashlight beam, I see the poem, and again wonder who wrote it.

How long did the poet stay, where had she come from, where was she going? This house must have been new then. The owner must have been kind, and believed in the goodness of people and in the necessity of freedom. And the poet must have been so brave.

And so am I. How much time do I have

left? I had originally guessed I'd have forty-eight hours before it was over. The longer time went on, the more hope I had, and that was very dangerous. But then Clare came down, and we couldn't even have our moment, say what we need to say, because she had to warn me and plead with me to go. The police will be back, and they will want to send me back. I won't say called back "home," because Denmark is not home anymore.

If it ever was at all.

Oh, Grit. By staying hidden, I'm able to stay close to you. I know the minute I hug you, it will be the beginning of the end. I wish I could prolong this closeness forever — being near you, watching you, sending you messages the best I can.

But I can't wait a moment longer. You're right in front of me, and the pull is too much. Here I come . . .

Stepping out into the main cellar, Anne walked across the floor and stood directly above her daughter, and she put her hand on the top of her head.

"Mom," Grit said, not looking up.

"Sweetheart."

"You have the same boots," Grit said. "I'm worried, they're coming apart. Your feet must get cold and wet, snow must get in."

"Oh, Grit," Anne said, and she started to lean down, and Grit sprang up, and they held each other, rocking and rocking, kissing and hugging, and Grit crying with high, sharp agony.

Anne cradled her daughter the way she used to. "I love you," Anne said as Grit wept against her shoulder.

"Mom," Grit said, clutching her hard, nails digging in, as if making sure Anne was here and real.

"My little girl," Anne said.

Grit nodded, pulling back and looking into Anne's face.

"Why did you come?" Grit asked.

"I got Clare's message, that you were in the hospital. And I couldn't stay away," Anne said.

"You came as soon as you heard?"

"Yes," Anne said, and it was true, and it was also not the whole truth.

They stood beside the armoire, and Anne leaned over to look inside the open drawer. She saw the old, beloved nickname written in the dust.

And from that she could see the pine tree in their backyard, the welts on the backs of Grit's legs, their night picnic in the snow. Blue moonlight shining through branches while the two of them huddled together where Frederik wouldn't find them.

She touched the tattooed owl, felt the ridge of scars beneath it. Grit seemed lulled into leaning into her hand, then jerked away.

"Don't," she said.

"Grit, I have so much to say to you," Anne said.

"Don't apologize. Just, please, Mom — don't say you're sorry," Grit said, eyes narrowed. Anne felt afraid of whatever emotion was in Grit's eyes.

"What happened is beyond apology," Anne said. "I hate myself for it. I always will."

Grit backed off, wildness in her eyes. Anne realized the soft moment was gone, and her daughter was full of rage about to explode. Anne tensed, waiting for it to come.

"Don't look that way," Grit said. "That's how you look when he gets mad! Because you know he's going to belittle you or take something away or hit you! Smack you! But I'm not like that! I'm just angry, not about to hurt you. See the difference?"

Anne nodded, but she wasn't sure.

"Sometimes," Grit said, "I think of the worst things. There are so many, I don't always know where to start. His silence, the pit in my stomach every time I did something 'wrong.' The way you'd treat him so well no matter what."

Anne's shoulders clenched as she listened.

"Gilly," Grit said. "*The* worst thing. I miss him so much it hurts to breathe. It hurts to move my eyes, to look around. Because I know he won't be there. I'll never see him again!"

"Stop," Anne gasped. It had become impossible for her to hear about Gilly. For years she had gone to the bog the way other mothers might tend graves. To pick flowers, and take pictures, sit quietly on the cool earth gazing out at the spot where he had gone in, letting him know she was there.

"Mom, why did you hide?" Grit asked. "How long have you been here, just hiding in the basement? You know Clare would have wanted you to stay upstairs with us."

"I know," Anne said. This was the moment. Would Grit be able to handle it?

"Then why sleep down here?"

"I've done something," Anne said. "Once people find out, I won't be able to see you anymore."

"Does Dad know you're here?" Grit asked, and Anne could see the great intelligence in her eyes, wheels turning as she started to figure it out.

"He would never have let me come."

"He couldn't have stopped you! You're strong, look at you. You're here now. What did he say?"

"He did stop me," Anne said in a steady voice. "For so long, he kept me from leaving."

"You tried?"

"Yes. After Christmas last year, I wanted to fly to Boston to see you. He cut off my credit cards. I finally applied for one that he never found out about."

"How did you know I'd even be in Boston? As far as you were concerned, you'd cut me off from my college fund. I had to trick my way through spring semester."

"I know. I kept track of you till May, when the semester ended, and then you disappeared. I had no idea where you were till Clare called the gallery and left that message."

"Didn't you think I'd come here?"

"Of course. But I didn't know when. I wasn't sure how Clare would take it, considering what our family has put her through."

"Are you serious? Clare is wonderful. She loves me, no matter what happened between you. And she forgives you, too. If you talked to her, showed up at the door like a normal person, you'd know that."

"I do know that," Anne said. She glanced

up the stairs, at the closed door. She knew what Clare wanted, what her good advice had been, but Anne couldn't run. She wasn't made for it. "Let's go see her now," Anne said.

And together she and Grit began walking up the stairs.

Chapter Twenty-Four

"Anne," Clare said. She stared at her sister, the last two hours shimmering between them. Their eyes met, and again she flooded with love and emotion and dread. Her big sister was standing in the kitchen with her.

"I can't believe it," Anne whispered, looking around.

"Please, go back down," Clare pleaded. But Anne opened her arms, and Clare stepped forward, and they hugged. Clare's heart had been broken so long, and nothing, not even loving Paul, had been able to touch the pain. She sobbed quietly, having her sister right here in their old kitchen.

"How long, do you think?" Anne asked.

"I don't know," Clare said. "Not long. We have to get you out of here."

"What are you talking about?" Grit asked.

Now she and Anne broke apart, but stayed holding hands. Anne's expression was grave, and Clare's throat tightened as she read her sister's eyes. They both turned to Grit. Clare saw the play of emotion in her face, the hope she felt giving way to trepidation.

"What's wrong?" Grit asked. "Why do you have to get out of here?"

"I don't," Anne said, holding Grit's hand. "I'm not leaving you until I have to."

"You knew she was here?" Grit asked Clare.

"Not till tonight."

"Mom, you've been staying in the basement all this time? Since that night you came to the hospital?"

Anne frowned, looked puzzled. "I didn't go to the hospital," she said. "I wanted to, but . . . I couldn't be seen there."

"So I was dreaming," Grit said.

"You must have been," Anne said.

What was real and what was illusion, and did any of it matter as long as they were together right now? Clare's gaze fell on Anne's diary, left on the table where she'd been reading it before. She picked it up and handed it to her.

"Sorry," Grit said. "I took it when I left."

"I noticed," Anne said.

"I don't want to lie to you. We read it," Grit said. "Clare and I."

Anne cringed. Clare knew there wasn't time to apologize or talk about it now.

460

"I called Paul," Clare said, jostling Anne's arm. "He'll be here any minute, and he'll let us use his Jeep."

"Where are we going?" Grit asked.

"Where was that place you stayed in Maine?" Clare asked. It had sounded remote, hidden in the wilderness near Mount Katahdin. "Do you still have the key?"

"Why do you even want to help me?" Anne asked. "After what I did?"

"Because you're my sister," Clare said, but even as she spoke she knew the police would be chasing Anne, and if they caught Clare trying to help her, she'd go back to prison.

"Mom," Grit said, "Clare and I don't want to lose you again."

"I know. I feel it," Anne said, her eyes filling.

"That's all that matters," Grit said, stubbornly.

"No, it's not all," Anne said.

Anne glanced at Clare, as if for strength. Clare nodded back, just once, telling her she was doing the right thing, wanting her to talk fast so they could be ready to go as soon as Paul arrived.

"I did something," Anne said. "I was hiding in the basement because I didn't want anyone to find me. I'm in trouble."

"I don't care what you did. You're here," Grit said.

"Oh, Grit. You will care. Your father —"

"I don't want to hear about him!" Grit said.

Anne looked at the mantel clock, drifted toward the window. Clare watched her peek furtively through the curtain. Clare reached for her arm, eased her back from the glass.

"You have to tell her," Clare said. "Now."

Anne nodded. She reached into a small buttoned-vest pocket on her black dress, removed a business card. Clare and Grit read it together. Clare stared at her sister as Grit spoke out loud.

"William Harrison?" Grit asked.

"He was the banker in charge of our father's estate," Anne said. "There's not much left, but I want you to have it."

"For what?"

Anne's voice cracked. "Grit, listen to me carefully, and Clare, too. Clare will help you with this. It's all I have left to give you."

"I only want you, Mom, and you need it. So you can have a life."

"A life?" Anne asked.

"Yes," Grit said. "You've gotten away, haven't you? Why else would you be here? He wouldn't have let you leave. I read your diary, I know what he did to you. You must have snuck out somehow, right?"

"I didn't sneak away," Anne said, staring at Clare; they both knew Grit was spinning a story she didn't even believe herself.

"Well, you're here! And he's not, right?"

Anne's eyes flashed, and Clare saw the quick anger. Anne grabbed Grit's shoulders and shook them lightly.

"Yes, that's right," Anne said, straightening her back, arm around Grit in a more gentle way. "I'm here and he's not. He wouldn't let me come, even after we got Clare's message about you being in the hospital. See, I've been telling him I had to see you all along. From the very day you left, when we were so vicious to you."

"You said you hated me," Grit said.

"I love you more than anything."

"I know," Grit said.

The three women were silent. Anne and Clare stood by Grit, and as the mantel clock ticked, Clare stared at the fire and sensed her sister handing Grit over to her. Their arms overlapped, across Grit's shoulders, and without looking at each other, Anne and Clare grasped each other's arms.

"Those pictures on your Web site," Grit said.

"My feeble attempt to reach you."

"It worked, once I had the password."

"What other password could I have used?"
Anne asked.

Sometimes police don't use their sirens.
In Montauk they had arrived with lights and
sirens blaring, but this time they used only
lights. Silently the cars arrived, red and blue
strobes flashing. The detectives had gotten
their warrant.

Clare glanced between the curtains, saw
two unmarked cars stopping outside the
building.

"They're here?" Anne asked.

"Come on," Clare said, grabbing her arm.
"Back down into the cellar. Hide in the
slave room, and once they leave, we can go
away."

Anne resisted, standing tall. She turned to
Grit, hands on her shoulders.

"I had to stop him," she said.

"Mom, you couldn't let him hurt you
anymore," Grit said, tears streaming down
her cheeks.

"Anne." Clare put her hands on her
sister's cheeks, stared into her deep blue
eyes. Years flew away and they were the
sisters they'd always been: together, united,
able to sneak away and spy and make
themselves invisible when they had to.
"You've just come back. I can't lose you.
Not because of him."

"I know," Anne said, holding Clare tight.

"That hiding place is safe — you know it is. Now get down there!"

"I sent you to prison," Anne said, breaking down. "I deserve —"

"Shut up," Clare said. "Hurry now —" They heard policemen outside, talking on the street. She glanced outside, saw Paul coming up the stairs. She opened the door a crack, and Paul slipped in.

He slammed the door behind him, but almost immediately, a loud rap sounded. The strobe lights flashed, throwing harsh blue light through the windows. Paul's eyes met Anne's, then Grit's. He walked over to Clare and held her.

"They have a warrant," he said.

"I thought they would have come after me sooner," Anne said, standing still. "I killed him the day I left, because he wouldn't let me come to see Grit."

Grit held her mother, sobbing quietly.

"Take your mother downstairs," Clare said, trying to push them toward the cellar door, still believing they could hide her, keep her from being arrested, from spending even one night in jail. Anne shook herself free, stood her ground. The doorbell rang, and the knocking got louder.

"Let them in, Paul," Anne said. "My sister

won't. I want you to open the door. Will you do that, please?"

Paul glanced at Grit, hesitated, then unlocked the door. Clare stared at Anne, knew from her defiant gaze that it was over, that she wasn't going to hide anymore.

"We'll get you the best lawyer," Clare said, taking the diary from Anne's hand, the chronicles of domestic violence. "This is proof of what Frederik did. We'll show them."

"Just take care of Grit, promise me?"

"Of course," Clare said, tears flooding her eyes. "But I'll take care of you, too."

"I love you," Anne said.

"Don't say one word to the police," Clare said. "Okay? Are you hearing me?"

Anne nodded.

The two detectives who had been there earlier walked in, handed Clare the warrant. Then they turned to Anne.

"Anne Rasmussen, you're under arrest for the murder of your husband, Frederik Rasmussen. . . ."

They tried to handcuff her, but she yanked away just long enough to grab Grit, clutch her tight, kiss her face.

"I love you, Little Night," she said. "I always will."

"Mom, don't go!" Then to the detectives,

"You can't take her! You have no idea what it was like, what we went through! I'm her daughter, I know everything. He beat her, he —"

Clare grabbed her. "Shhh," she said. "Not now, not to them. We'll tell the lawyer everything."

"Mom!" Grit sobbed.

"I'm always with you," Anne said.

Then the detectives led her away; Clare, Paul, and Grit followed her outside. They had to hold Grit back, to keep her from tearing after her mother, into the idling police car.

They wrapped Grit in arms so tight, letting her know they'd be with her forever. And Clare met Anne's eyes, seeing every single thing she'd always loved about her; the sisters stared, not breaking their gaze until the car drove away, the promise to love Grit glimmering between them.

Even before the police car disappeared from sight, Clare was walking up the steps, Paul and Grit right behind her.

ABOUT THE AUTHOR

Luanne Rice is the author of thirty novels, twenty-two of which have been *New York Times* bestsellers. Five of her novels have become movies or miniseries, and two of her short pieces were featured in off-Broadway productions. There are more than twenty-two million copies of her books in print in twenty-four territories around the world. A bicoastal advocate of the environment, she divides her time between New York City and Southern California.